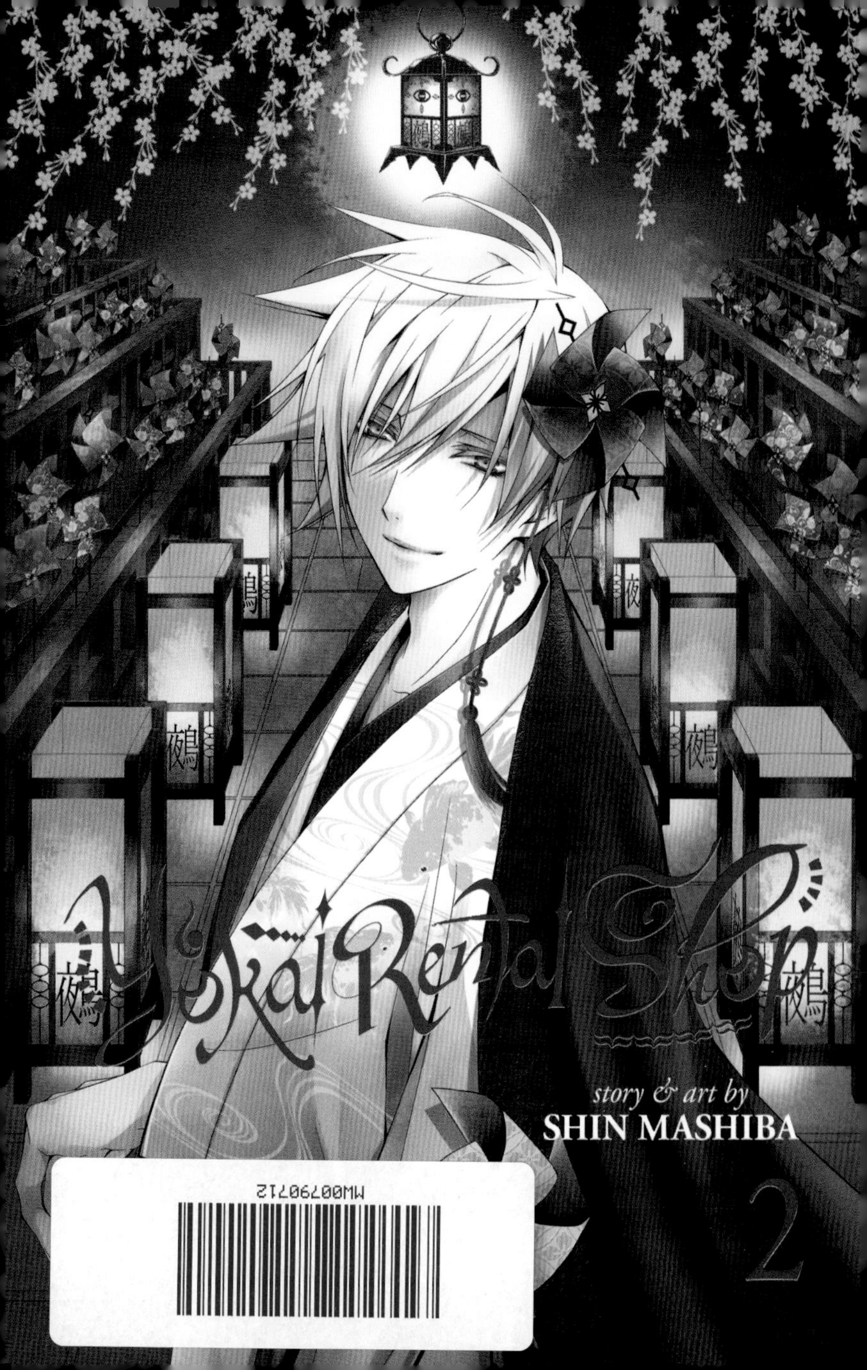
Yokai Rental Shop
story & art by
SHIN MASHIBA
2

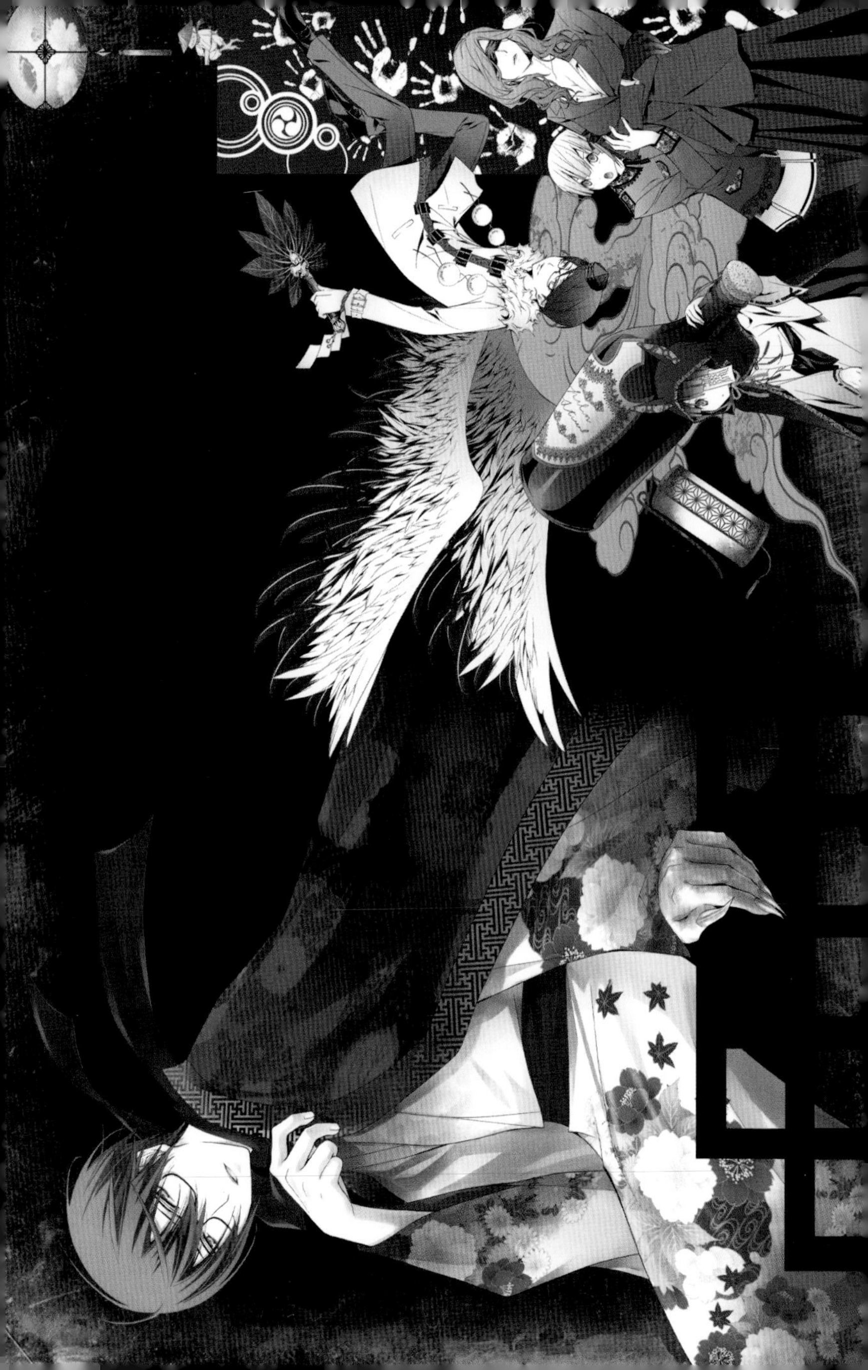

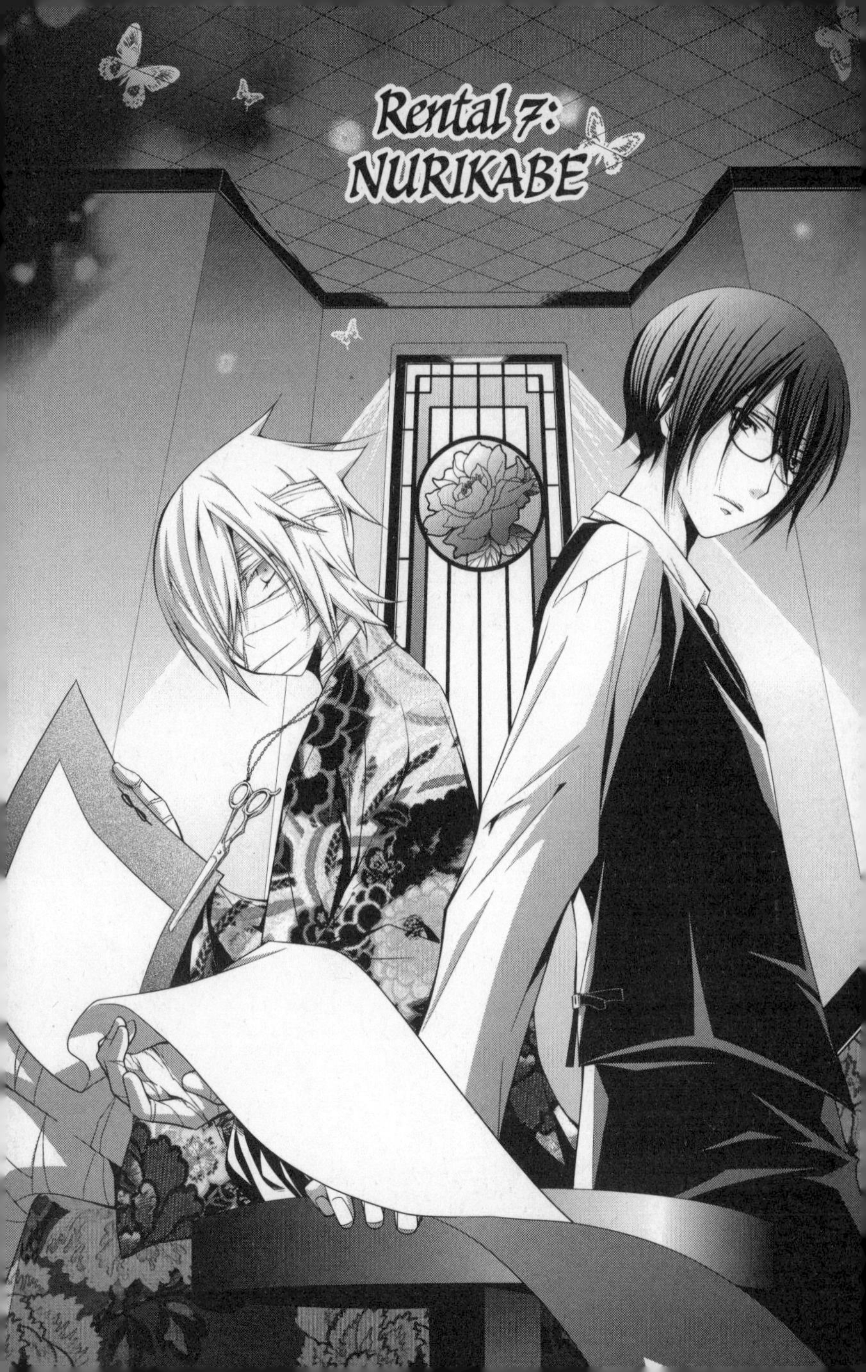
Rental 7:
NURIKABE

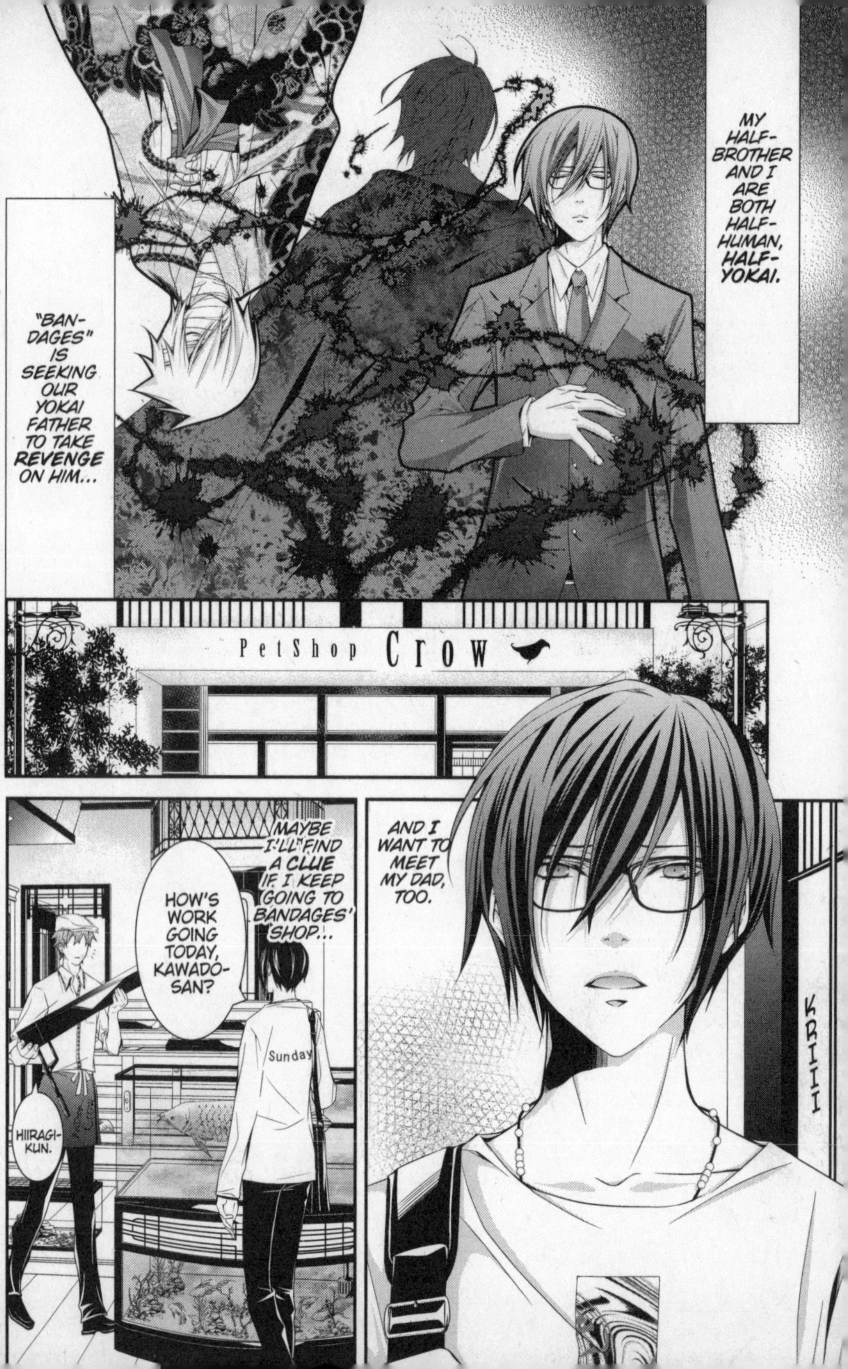
MY HALF-BROTHER AND I ARE BOTH HALF-HUMAN, HALF-YOKAI.
"BAN-DAGES" IS SEEKING OUR YOKAI FATHER TO TAKE REVENGE ON HIM...
PetShop Crow
MAYBE I'LL FIND A CLUE IF I KEEP GOING TO BANDAGES' SHOP...
AND I WANT TO MEET MY DAD, TOO.
KRIII
HOW'S WORK GOING TODAY, KAWADO-SAN?
Sunday
HIIRAGI-KUN.

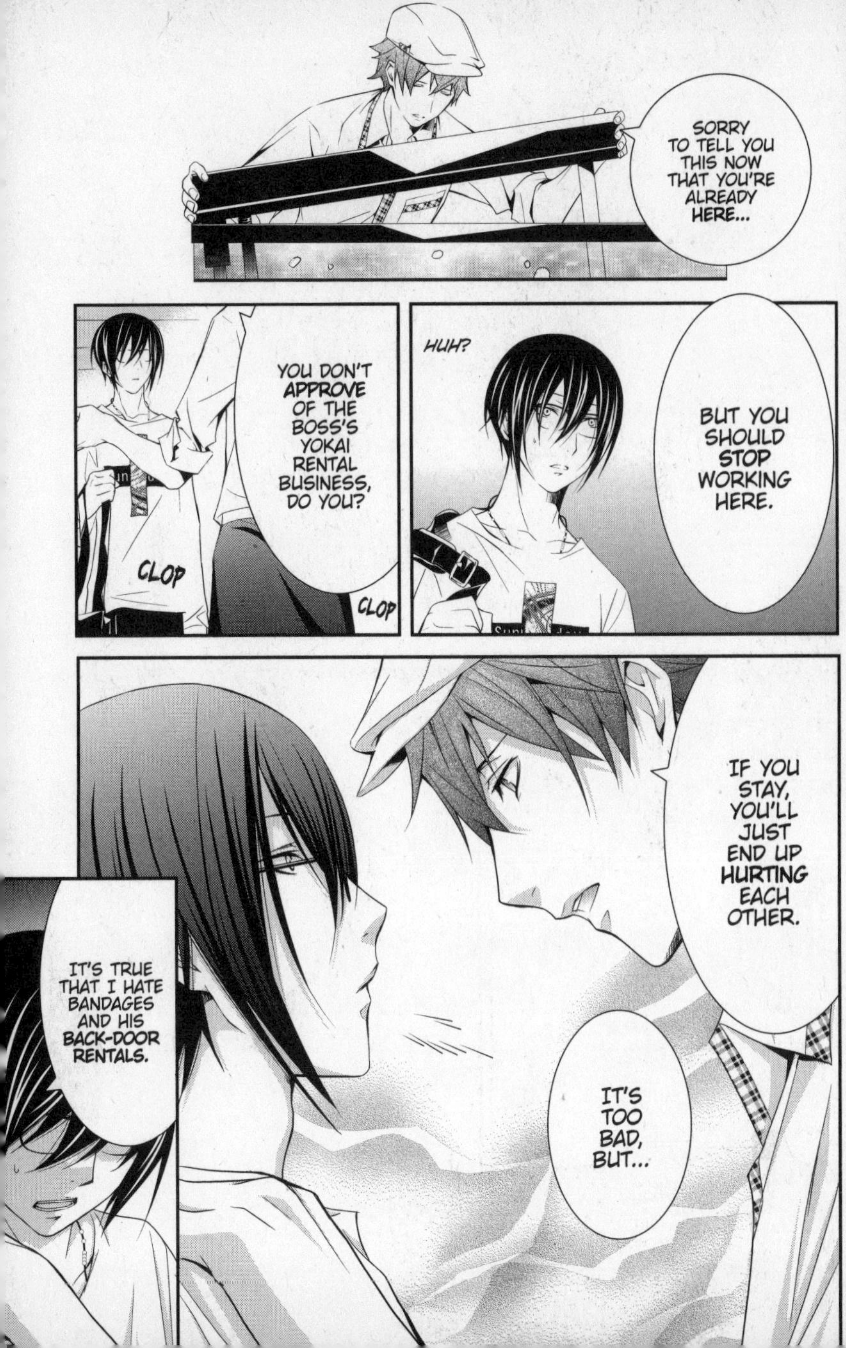
SORRY TO TELL YOU THIS NOW THAT YOU'RE ALREADY HERE...
BUT YOU SHOULD STOP WORKING HERE.
HUH?
YOU DON'T APPROVE OF THE BOSS'S YOKAI RENTAL BUSINESS, DO YOU?
CLOP
CLOP
IF YOU STAY, YOU'LL JUST END UP HURTING EACH OTHER.
IT'S TOO BAD, BUT...
IT'S TRUE THAT I HATE BANDAGES AND HIS BACK-DOOR RENTALS.

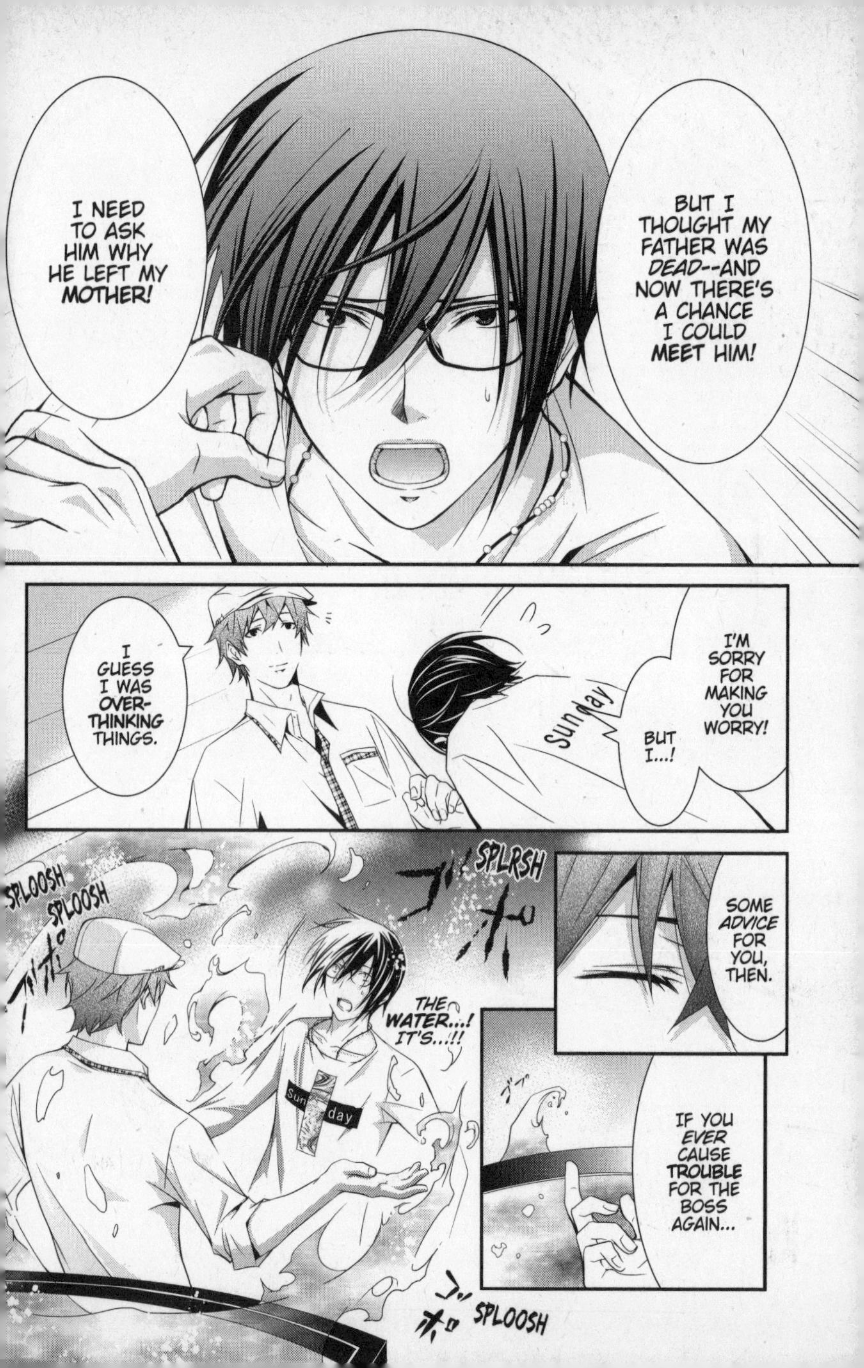
BUT I THOUGHT MY FATHER WAS *DEAD*--AND NOW THERE'S A CHANCE I COULD MEET HIM!
I NEED TO ASK HIM WHY HE LEFT MY MOTHER!
I'M SORRY FOR MAKING YOU WORRY!
BUT I...!
Sunday
I GUESS I WAS OVER-THINKING THINGS.
SOME *ADVICE* FOR YOU, THEN.
IF YOU *EVER* CAUSE TROUBLE FOR THE BOSS AGAIN...
SPLRSH
THE WATER...! IT'S...!!!
SPLOOSH
SPLOOSH
sun day
SPLOOSH

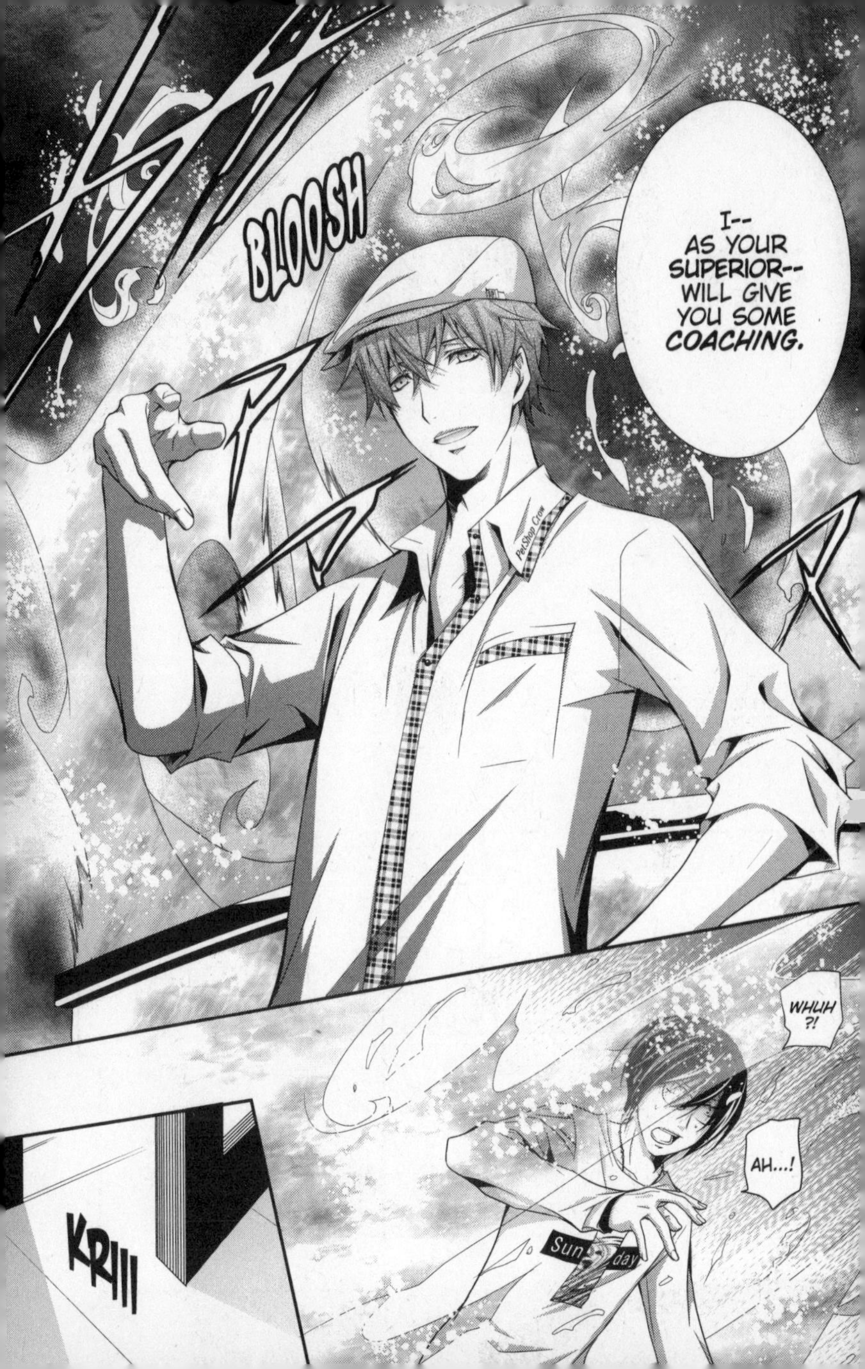
I-- AS YOUR SUPERIOR-- WILL GIVE YOU SOME *COACHING.*
BLOOSH
PetShop Crow
WHUH ?!
AH...!
KRIII
Sun day

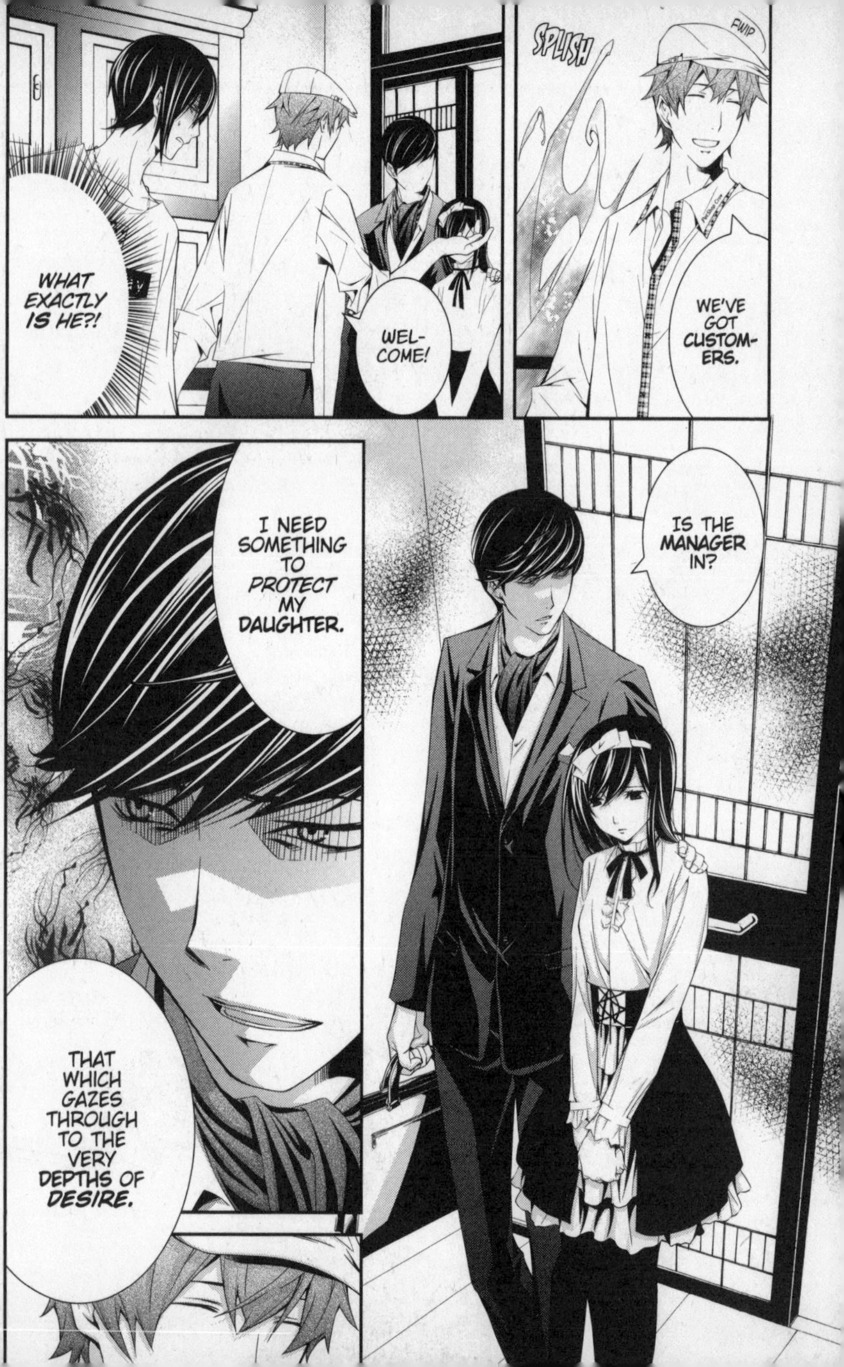
SPLISH
FWIP
WE'VE GOT CUSTOM-ERS.
WEL-COME!
WHAT EXACTLY IS HE?!
IS THE MANAGER IN?
I NEED SOMETHING TO PROTECT MY DAUGHTER.
THAT WHICH GAZES THROUGH TO THE VERY DEPTHS OF DESIRE.

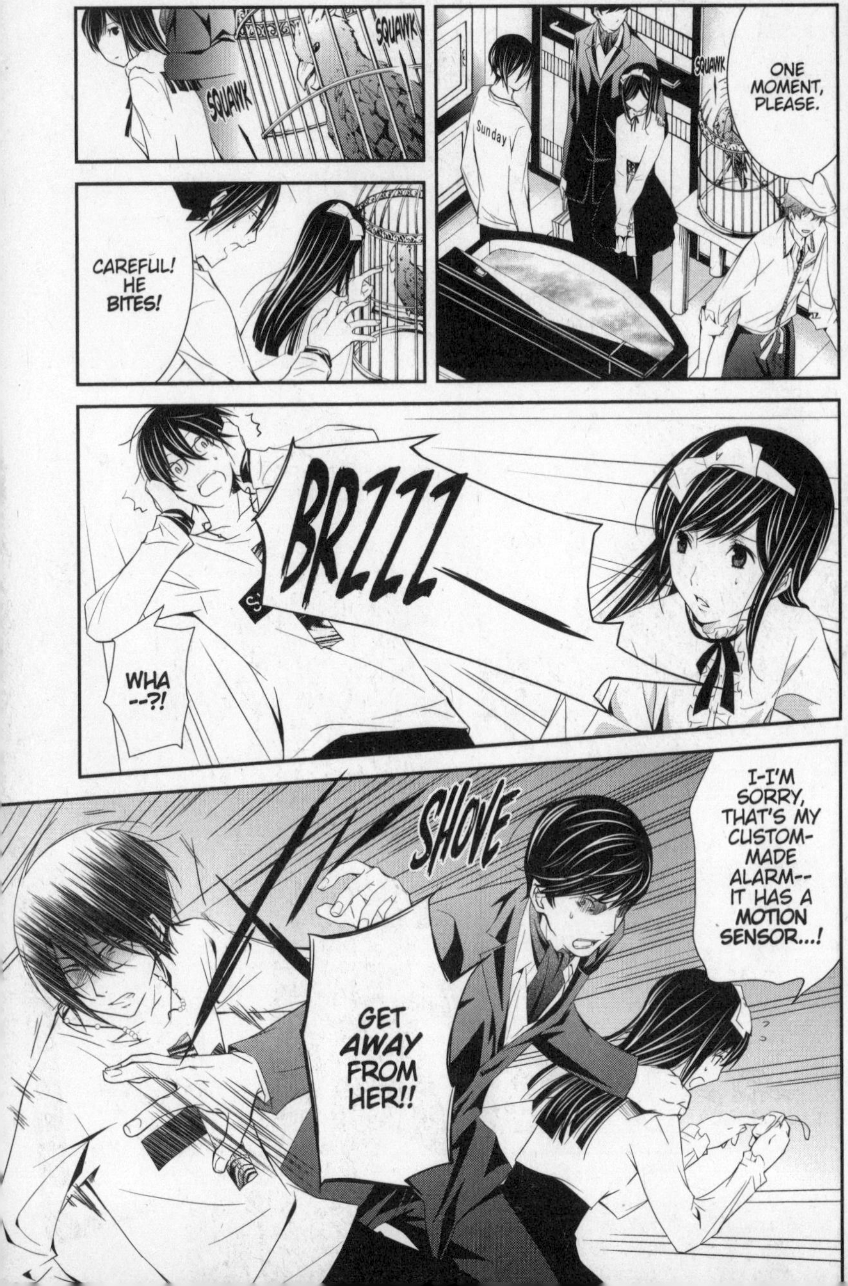
ONE MOMENT, PLEASE.
SQUAWK
Sunday
SQUAWK
SQUAWK
CAREFUL! HE BITES!
BRZZZ
WHA--?!
I-I'M SORRY, THAT'S MY CUSTOM-MADE ALARM-- IT HAS A MOTION SENSOR...!
SHOVE
GET AWAY FROM HER!!

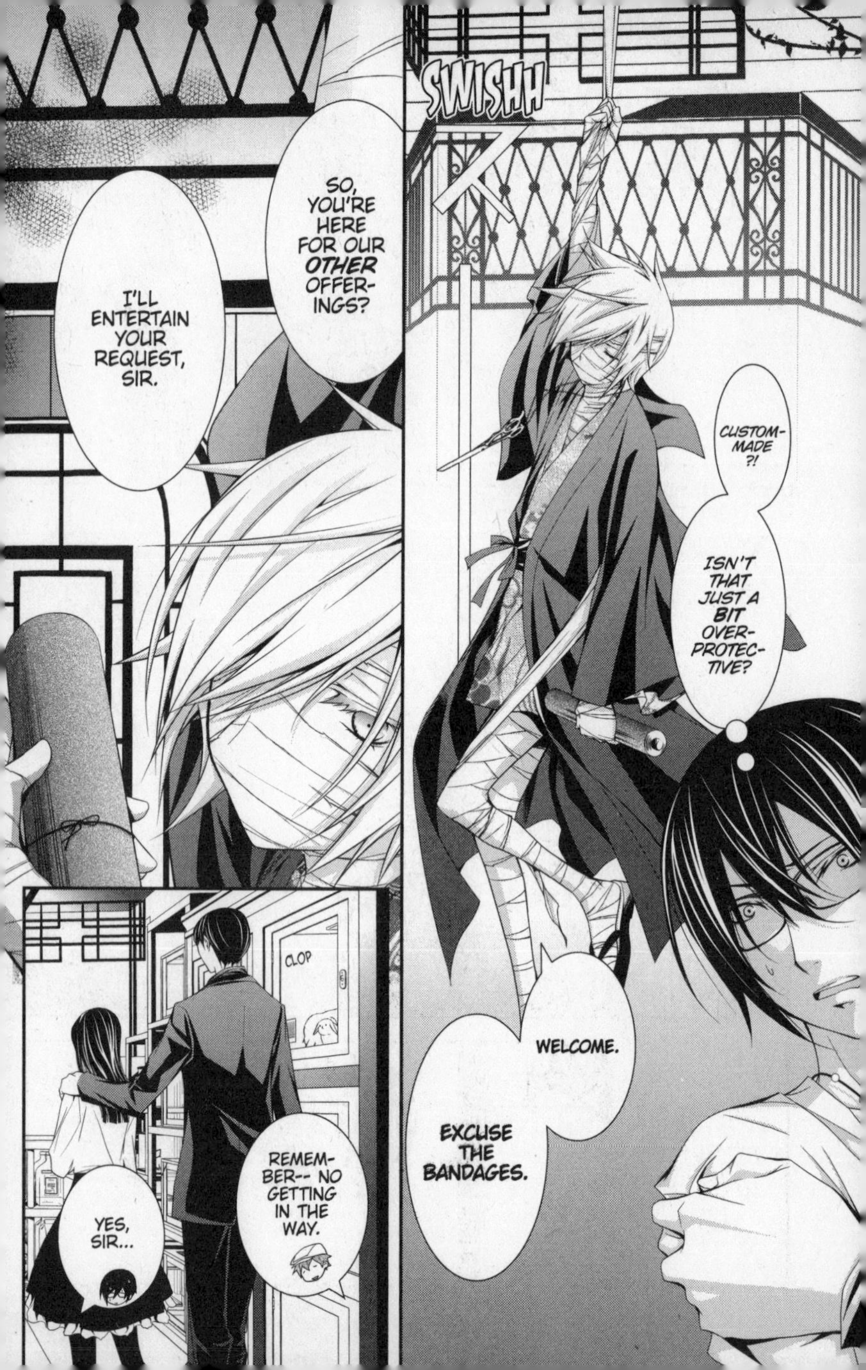
SWISHH
CUSTOM-MADE?!
ISN'T THAT JUST A BIT OVER-PROTECTIVE?
WELCOME.
EXCUSE THE BANDAGES.
SO, YOU'RE HERE FOR OUR OTHER OFFERINGS?
I'LL ENTERTAIN YOUR REQUEST, SIR.
CLOP
REMEMBER-- NO GETTING IN THE WAY.
YES, SIR...

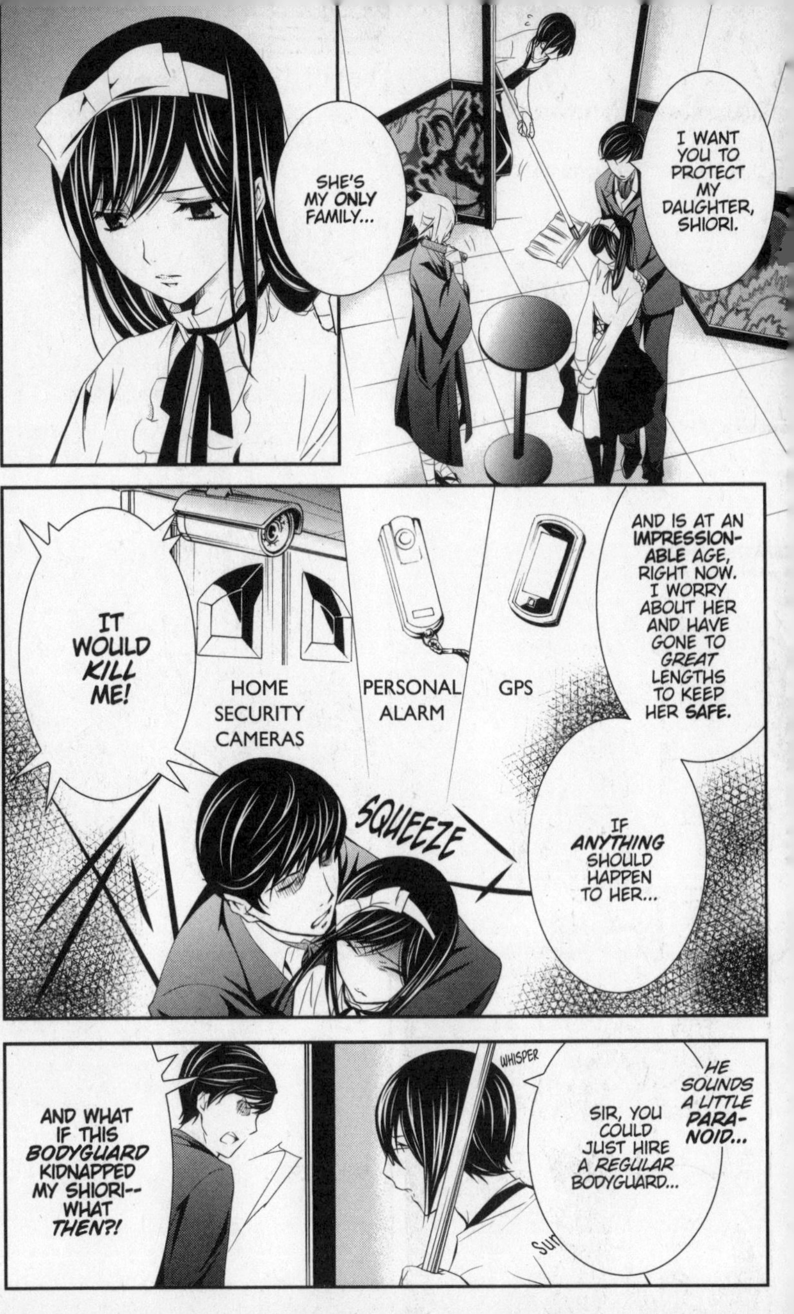
I WANT YOU TO PROTECT MY DAUGHTER, SHIORI.
SHE'S MY ONLY FAMILY...
AND IS AT AN IMPRESSIONABLE AGE, RIGHT NOW. I WORRY ABOUT HER AND HAVE GONE TO GREAT LENGTHS TO KEEP HER SAFE.
GPS
PERSONAL ALARM
HOME SECURITY CAMERAS
IF ANYTHING SHOULD HAPPEN TO HER...
SQUEEZE
IT WOULD KILL ME!
HE SOUNDS A LITTLE PARANOID...
WHISPER
SIR, YOU COULD JUST HIRE A REGULAR BODYGUARD...
AND WHAT IF THIS BODYGUARD KIDNAPPED MY SHIORI-- WHAT THEN?!

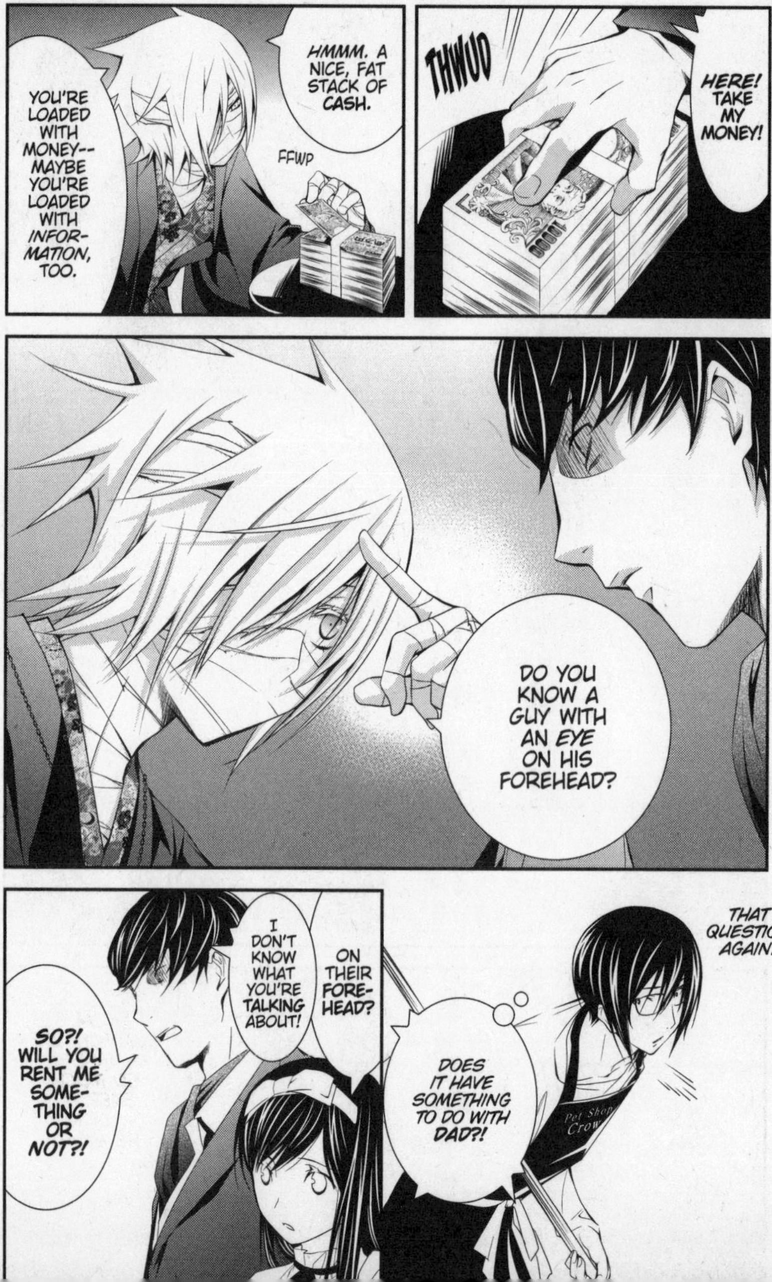
THWUD
HERE! TAKE MY MONEY!
HMMM. A NICE, FAT STACK OF CASH.
FFWP
YOU'RE LOADED WITH MONEY-- MAYBE YOU'RE LOADED WITH INFORMATION, TOO.
DO YOU KNOW A GUY WITH AN EYE ON HIS FOREHEAD?
THAT QUESTION AGAIN.
Pet Shop Crow
ON THEIR FOREHEAD?
I DON'T KNOW WHAT YOU'RE TALKING ABOUT!
DOES IT HAVE SOMETHING TO DO WITH DAD?!
SO?! WILL YOU RENT ME SOMETHING OR NOT?!

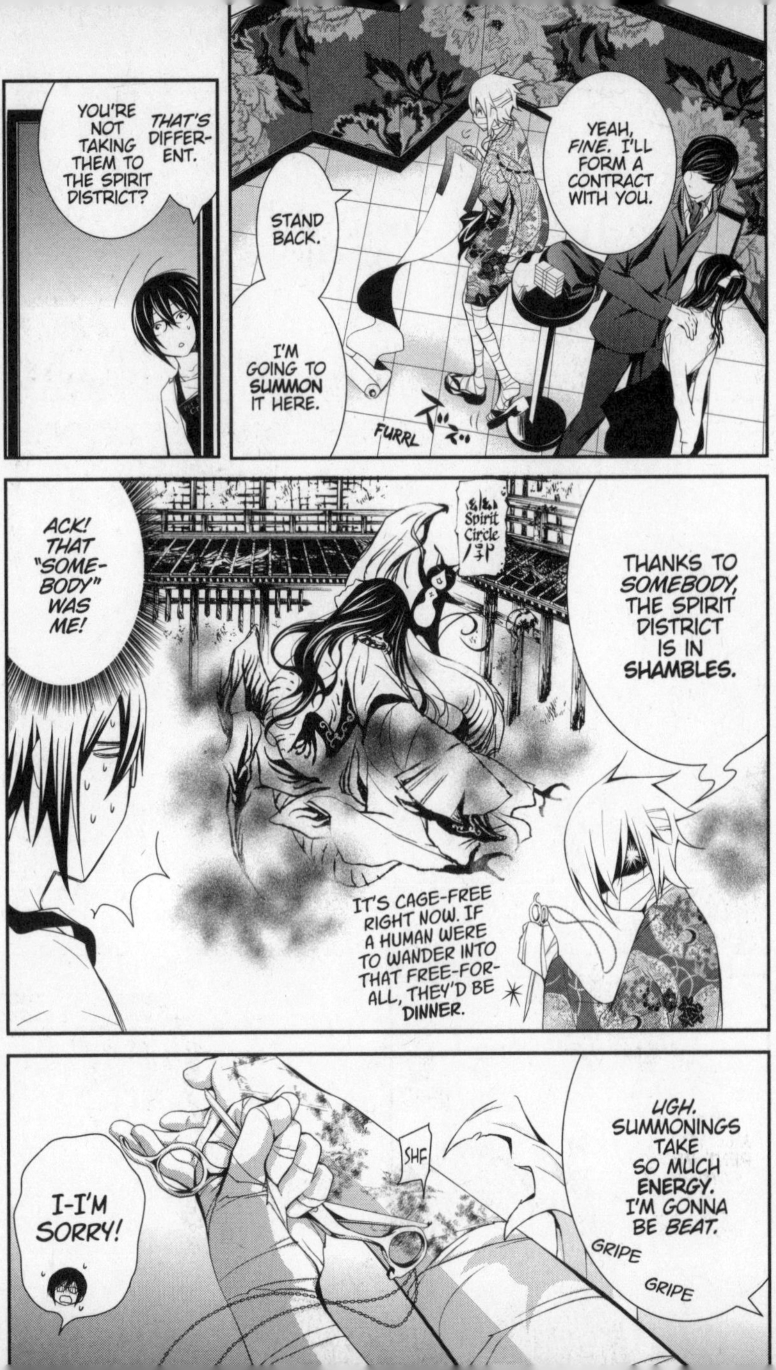
YEAH, FINE. I'LL FORM A CONTRACT WITH YOU.
STAND BACK.
I'M GOING TO SUMMON IT HERE.
FURRL
YOU'RE NOT TAKING THEM TO THE SPIRIT DISTRICT?
THAT'S DIFFERENT.
THANKS TO SOMEBODY, THE SPIRIT DISTRICT IS IN SHAMBLES.
Spirit Circle
IT'S CAGE-FREE RIGHT NOW. IF A HUMAN WERE TO WANDER INTO THAT FREE-FOR-ALL, THEY'D BE DINNER.
ACK! THAT "SOMEBODY" WAS ME!
UGH. SUMMONINGS TAKE SO MUCH ENERGY. I'M GONNA BE BEAT.
GRIPE
GRIPE
SHF
I-I'M SORRY!

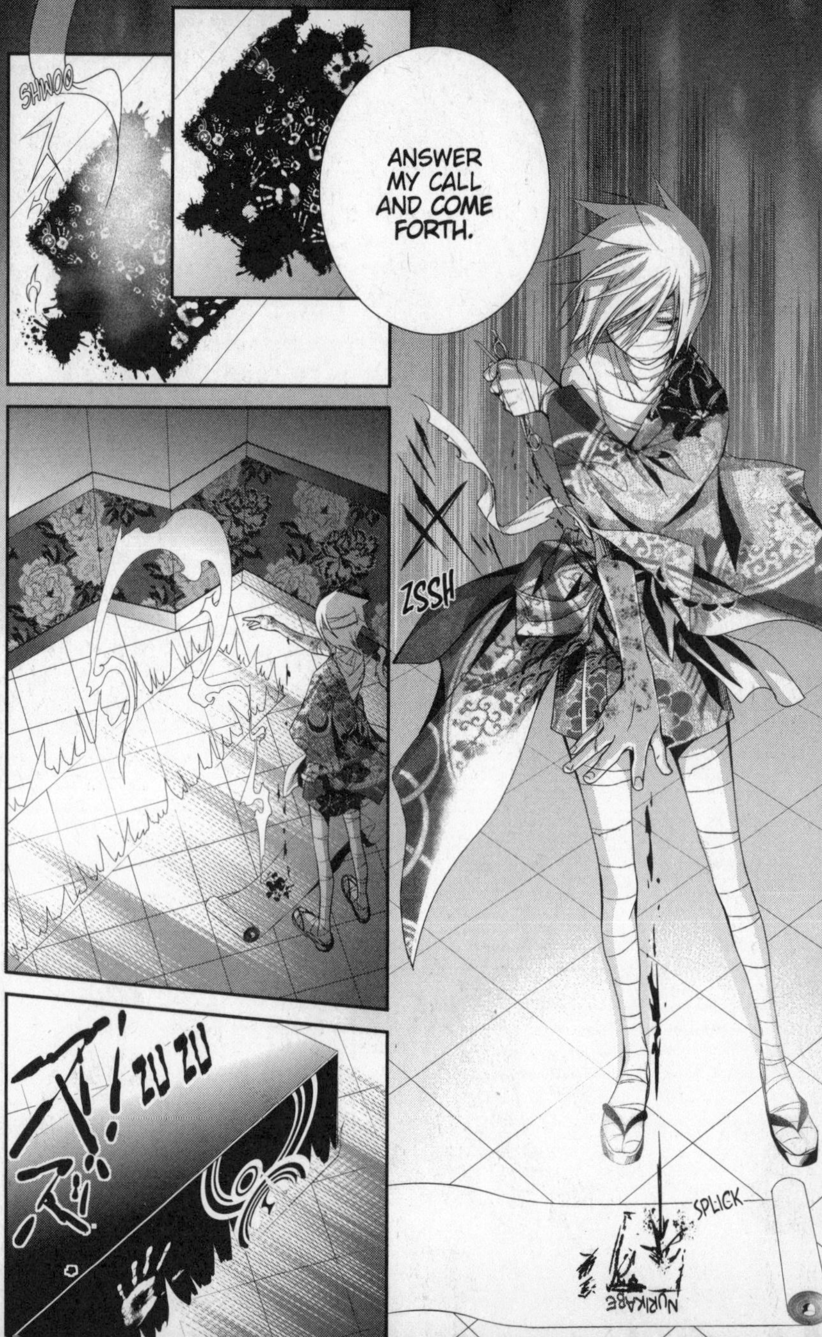
ANSWER MY CALL AND COME FORTH.
ZSSH
SPLICK
NURIKABE
SHWOO
ZU ZU

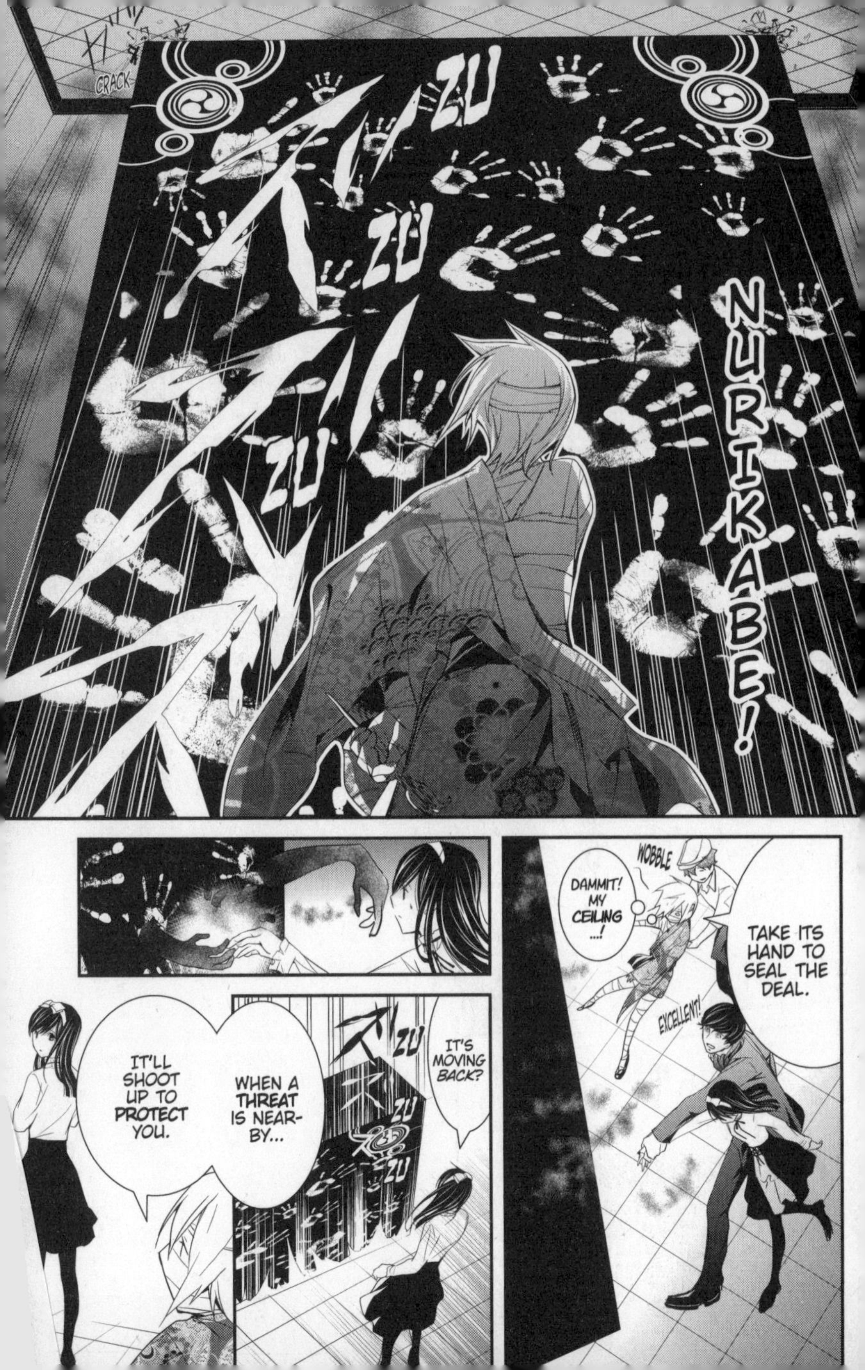

NURIKABE!
ZU
ZU
ZU
CRACK
TAKE ITS HAND TO SEAL THE DEAL.
WOBBLE
DAMMIT! MY CEILING ...!
EXCELLENT!
IT'S MOVING BACK?
ZU
ZU
ZU
WHEN A THREAT IS NEAR-BY...
IT'LL SHOOT UP TO PROTECT YOU.

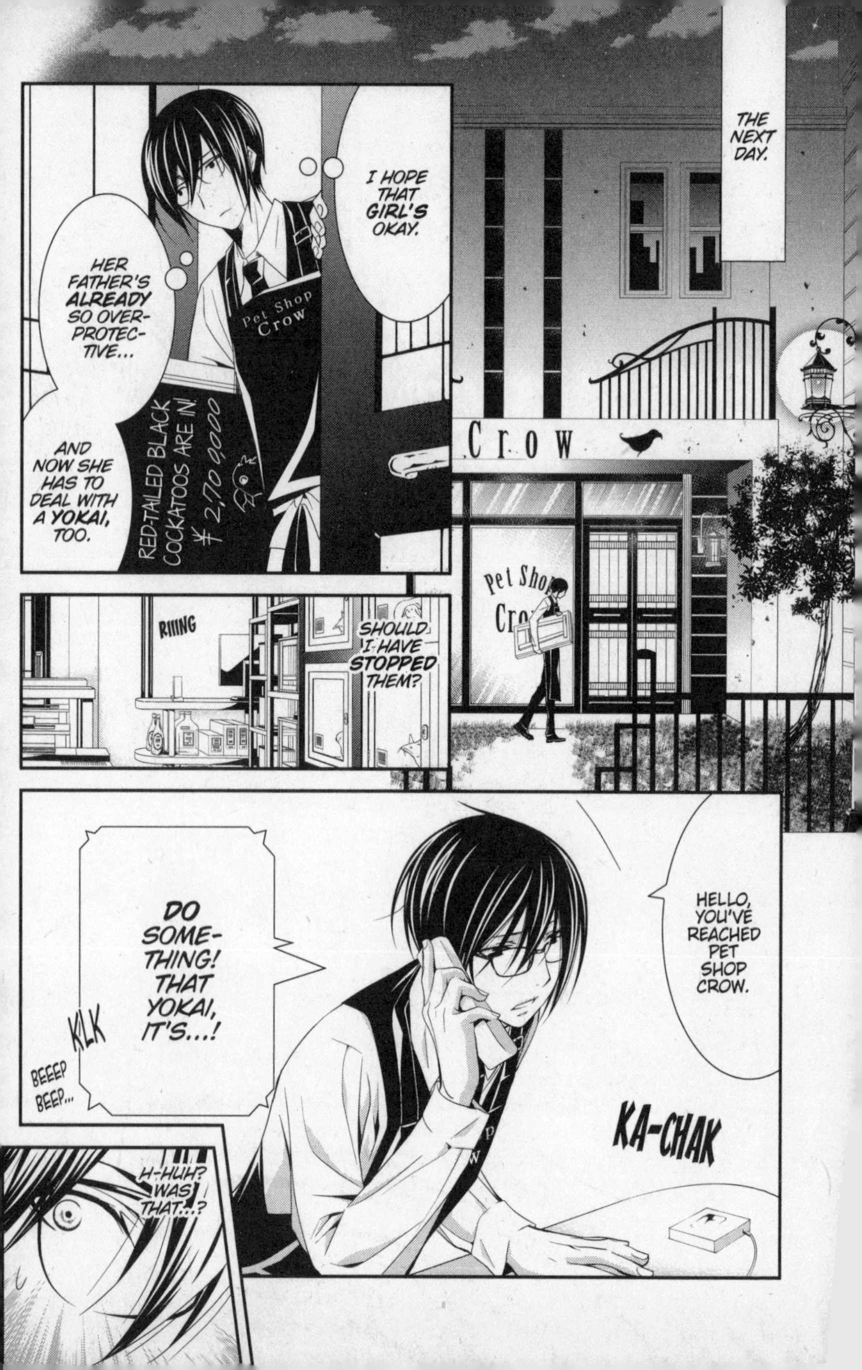
THE NEXT DAY.
Crow
Pet Shop Crow
I HOPE THAT GIRL'S OKAY.
HER FATHER'S ALREADY SO OVER-PROTECTIVE...
AND NOW SHE HAS TO DEAL WITH A YOKAI, TOO.
Pet Shop Crow
RED-TAILED BLACK COCKATOOS ARE IN! ¥2,700,000
SHOULD I HAVE STOPPED THEM?
RIIING
HELLO, YOU'VE REACHED PET SHOP CROW.
DO SOME-THING! THAT YOKAI, IT'S...!
KLK
BEEEP BEEP...
KA-CHAK
H-HUH? WAS THAT...?

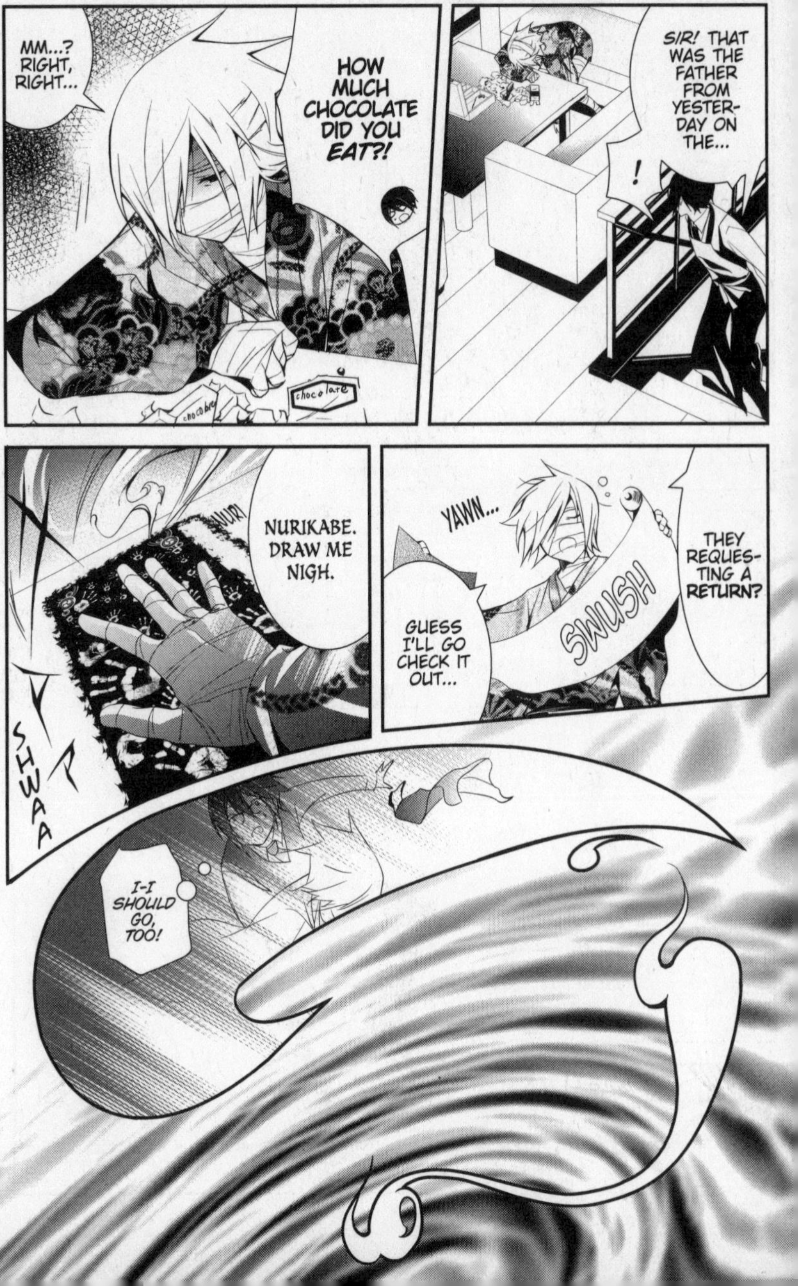
SIR! THAT WAS THE FATHER FROM YESTERDAY ON THE...
!
HOW MUCH CHOCOLATE DID YOU EAT?!
MM...? RIGHT, RIGHT...
chocolate
THEY REQUESTING A RETURN?
YAWN...
SWUSH
GUESS I'LL GO CHECK IT OUT...
NURI
NURIKABE. DRAW ME NIGH.
SHWAA
I-I SHOULD GO, TOO!

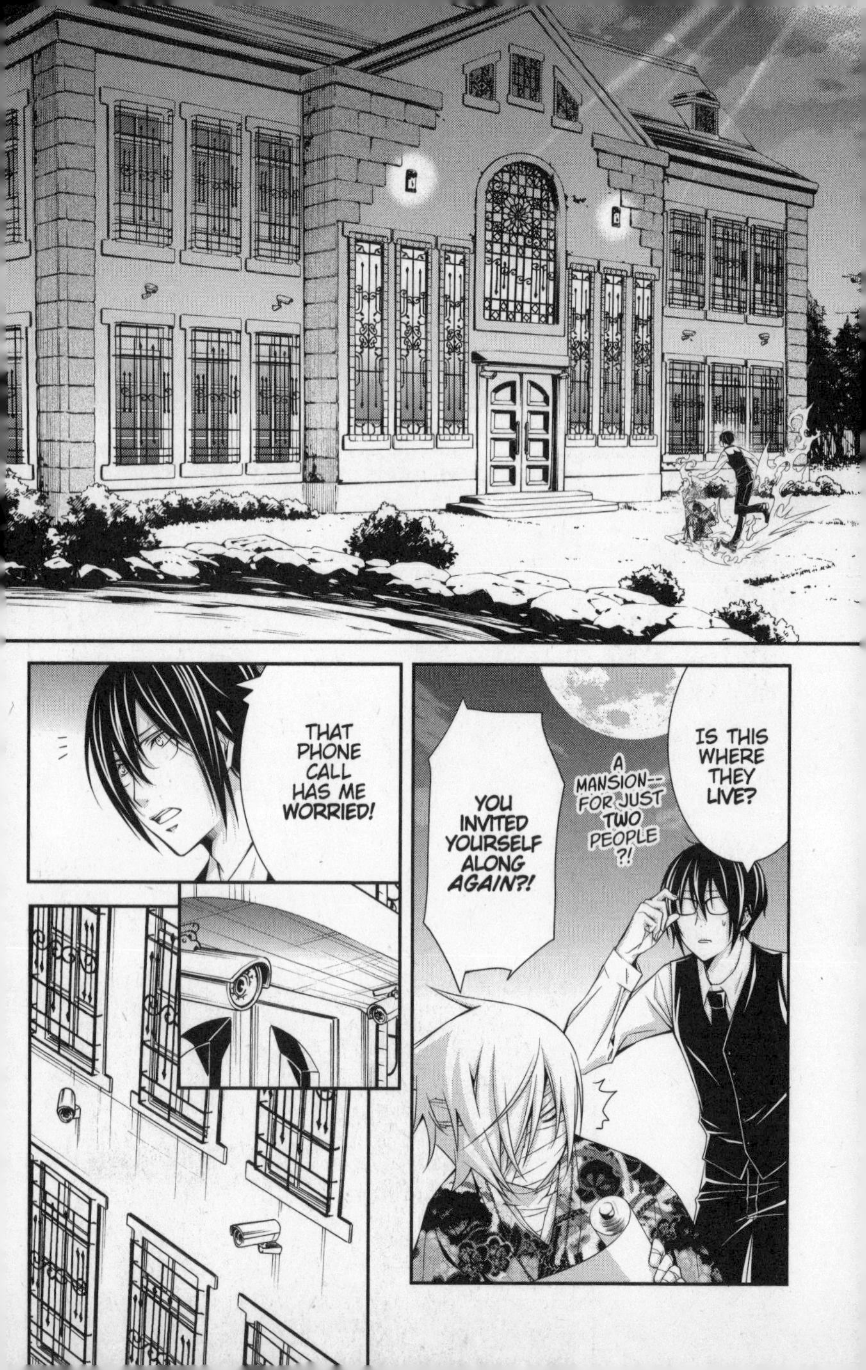
IS THIS WHERE THEY LIVE?
A MANSION-- FOR JUST TWO PEOPLE?!
YOU INVITED YOURSELF ALONG AGAIN?!
THAT PHONE CALL HAS ME WORRIED!

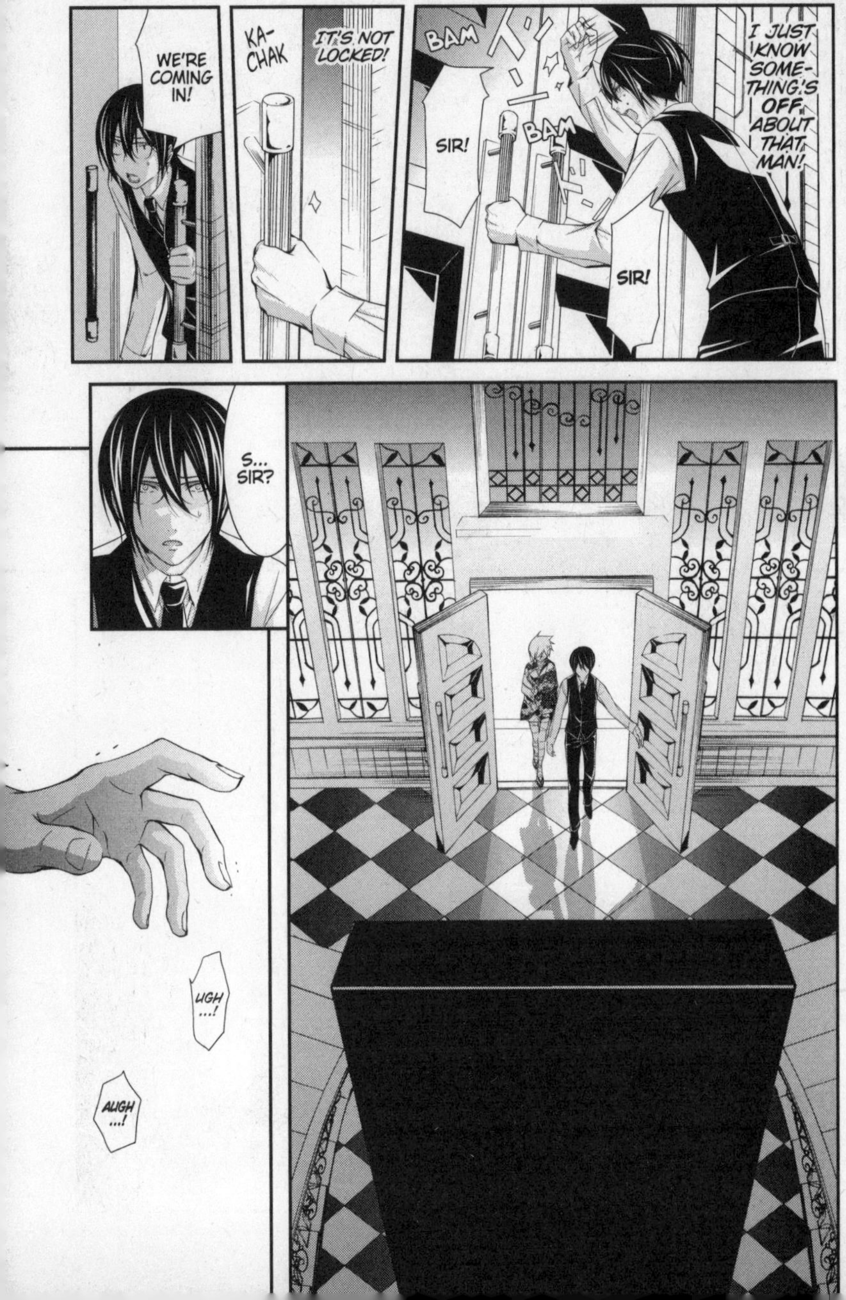
I JUST KNOW SOME-THING'S OFF ABOUT THAT MAN!
BAM
BAM
SIR!
SIR!
IT'S NOT LOCKED!
KA-CHAK
WE'RE COMING IN!
S... SIR?
UGH ...!
AUGH ...!

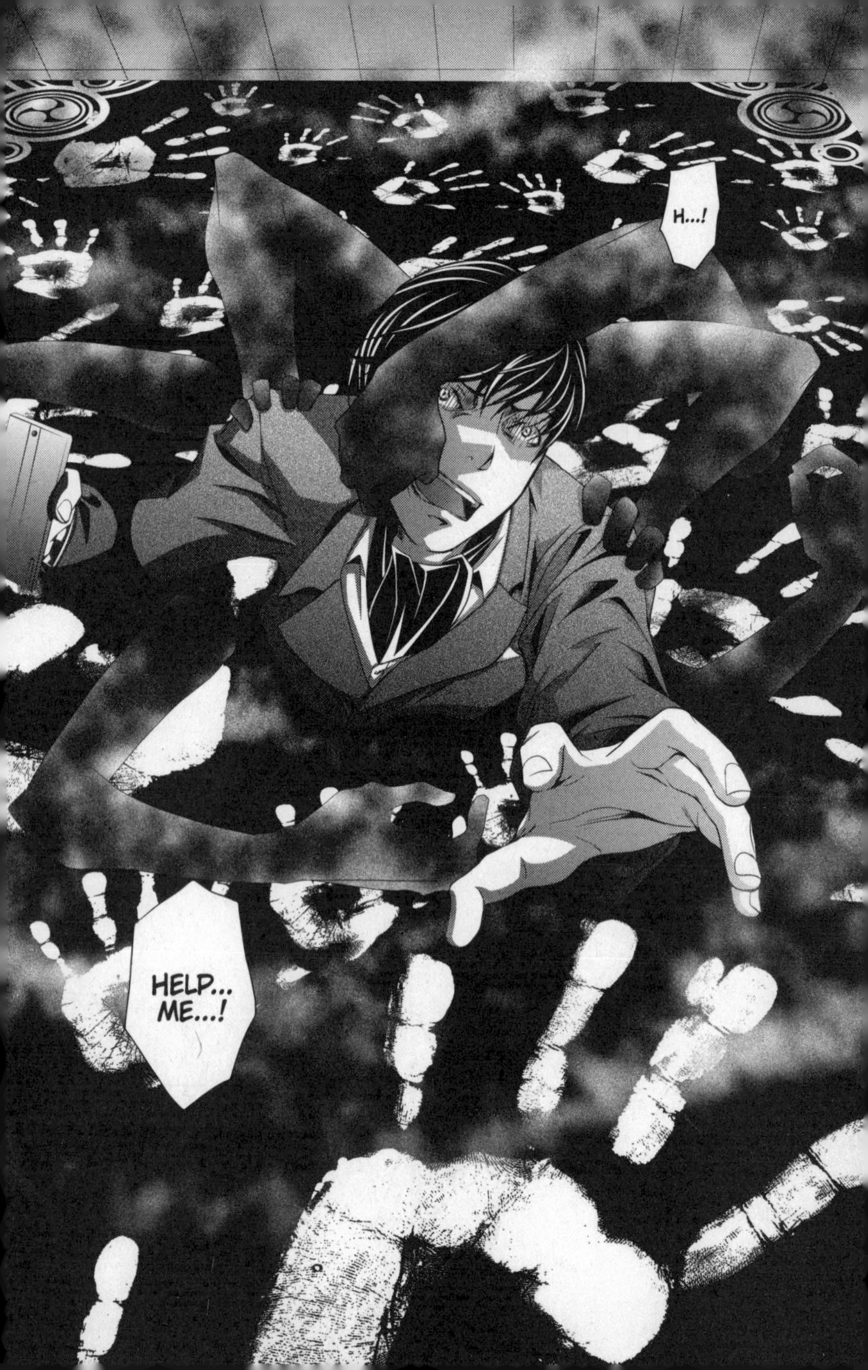
H...!
HELP... ME...!

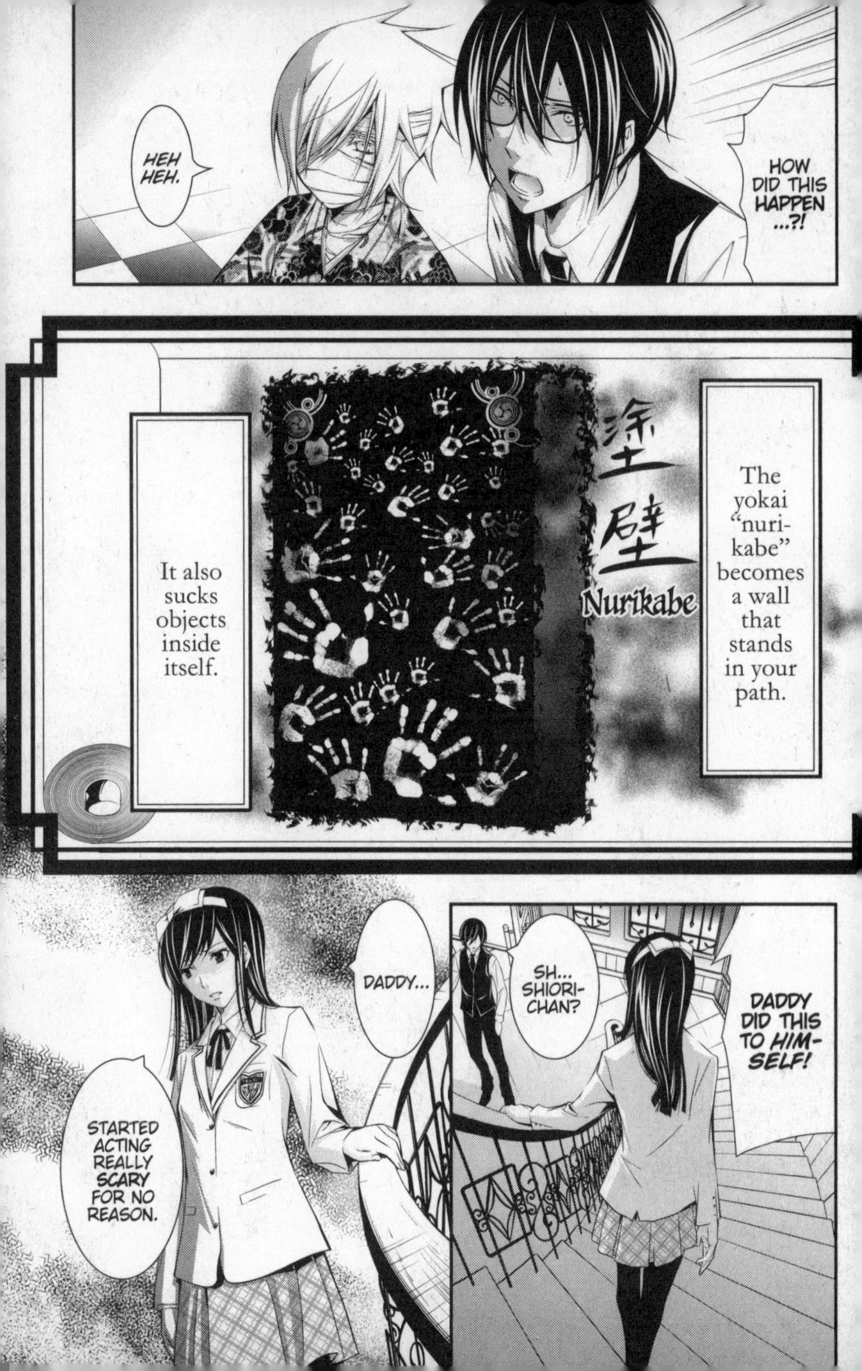
HOW DID THIS HAPPEN ...?!
HEH HEH.
The yokai "nuri-kabe" becomes a wall that stands in your path.
塗壁
Nurikabe
It also sucks objects inside itself.
SH... SHIORI-CHAN?
DADDY DID THIS TO *HIM*-SELF!
DADDY...
STARTED ACTING REALLY SCARY FOR NO REASON.

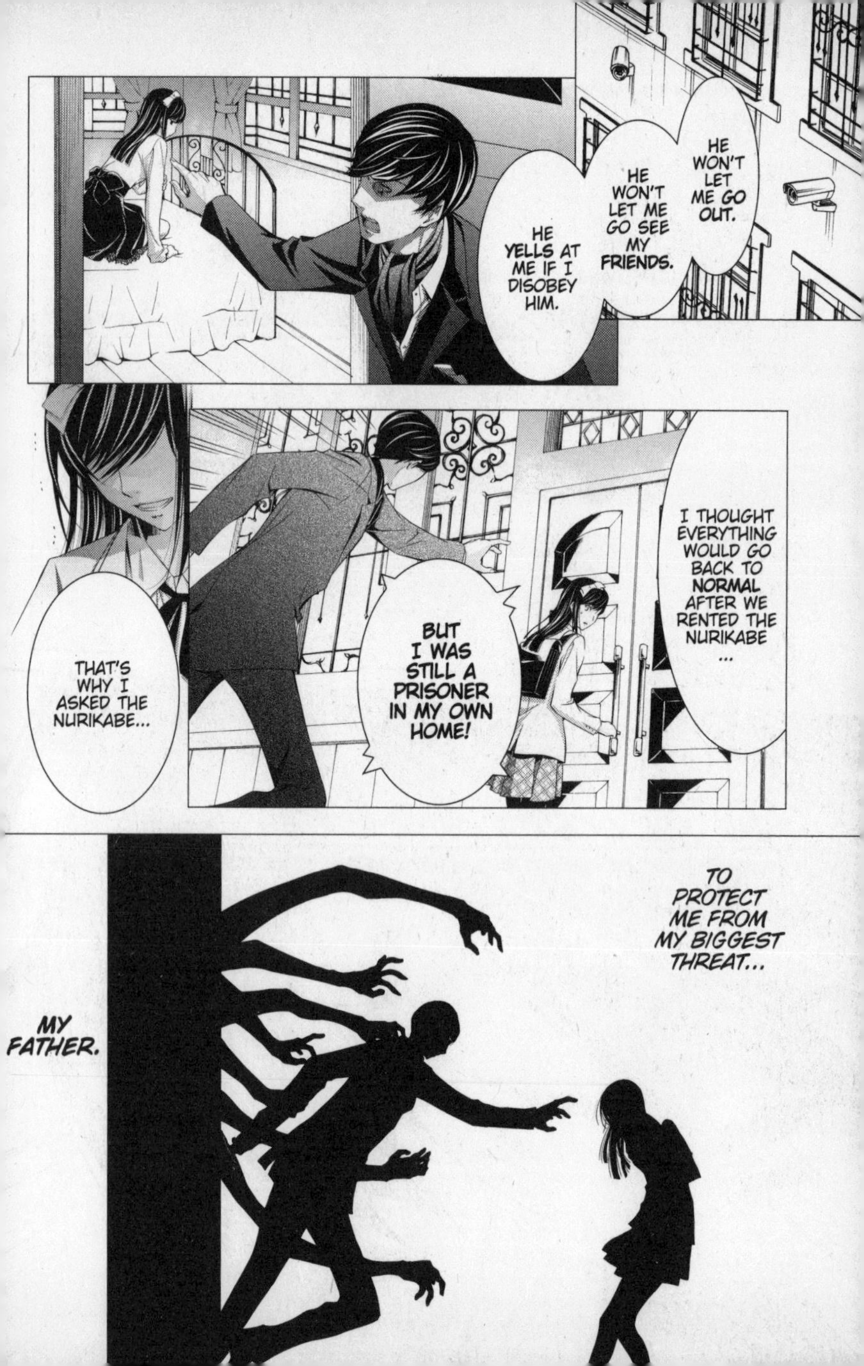
HE WON'T LET ME GO OUT.
HE WON'T LET ME GO SEE MY FRIENDS.
HE YELLS AT ME IF I DISOBEY HIM.
I THOUGHT EVERYTHING WOULD GO BACK TO NORMAL AFTER WE RENTED THE NURIKABE ...
BUT I WAS STILL A PRISONER IN MY OWN HOME!
THAT'S WHY I ASKED THE NURIKABE...
TO PROTECT ME FROM MY BIGGEST THREAT...
MY FATHER.

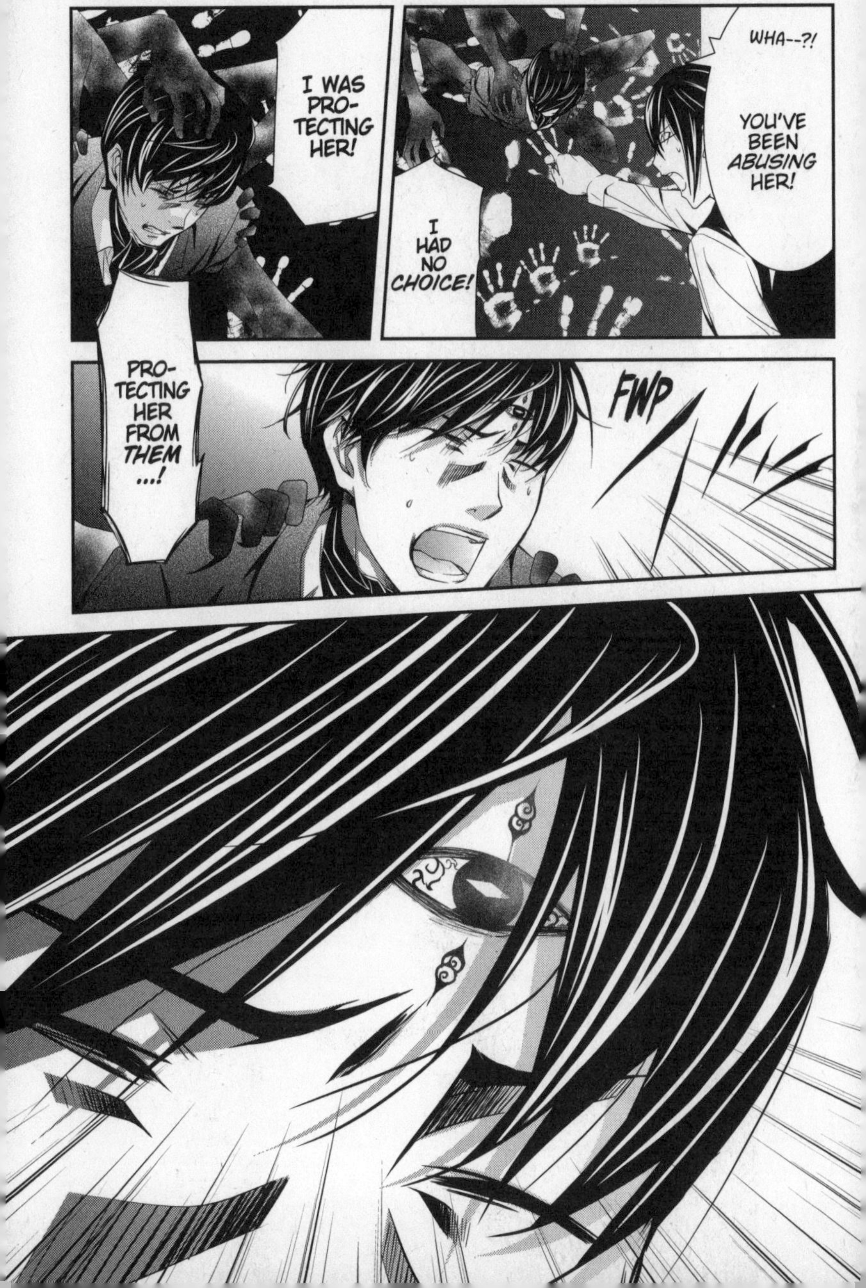
WHA--?!
YOU'VE BEEN ABUSING HER!
I HAD NO CHOICE!
I WAS PROTECTING HER!
PROTECTING HER FROM *THEM*...!
FWP

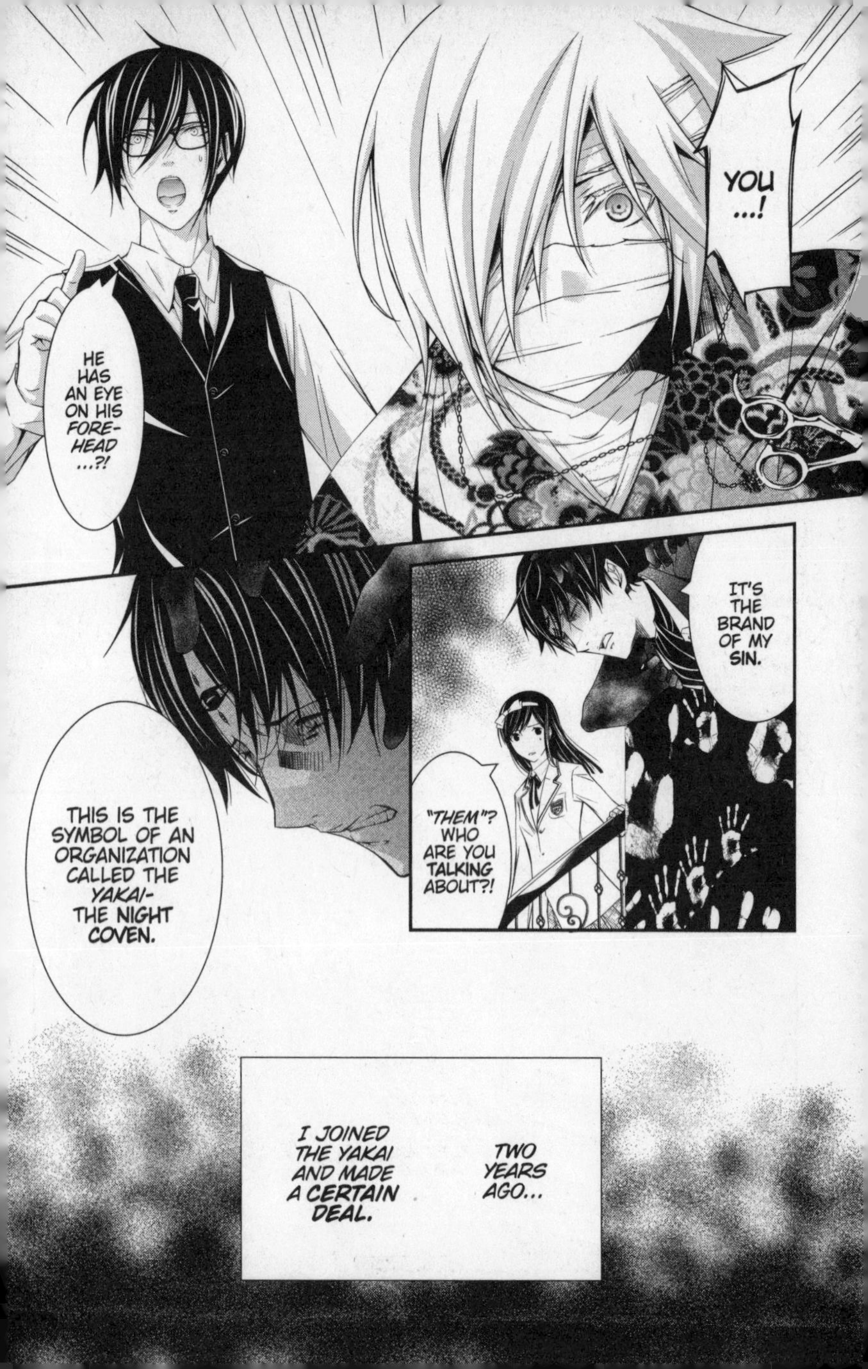
YOU ...!
HE HAS AN EYE ON HIS FORE-HEAD ...?!
IT'S THE BRAND OF MY SIN.
"THEM"? WHO ARE YOU TALKING ABOUT?!
THIS IS THE SYMBOL OF AN ORGANIZATION CALLED THE YAKAI- THE NIGHT COVEN.
TWO YEARS AGO...
I JOINED THE YAKAI AND MADE A CERTAIN DEAL.

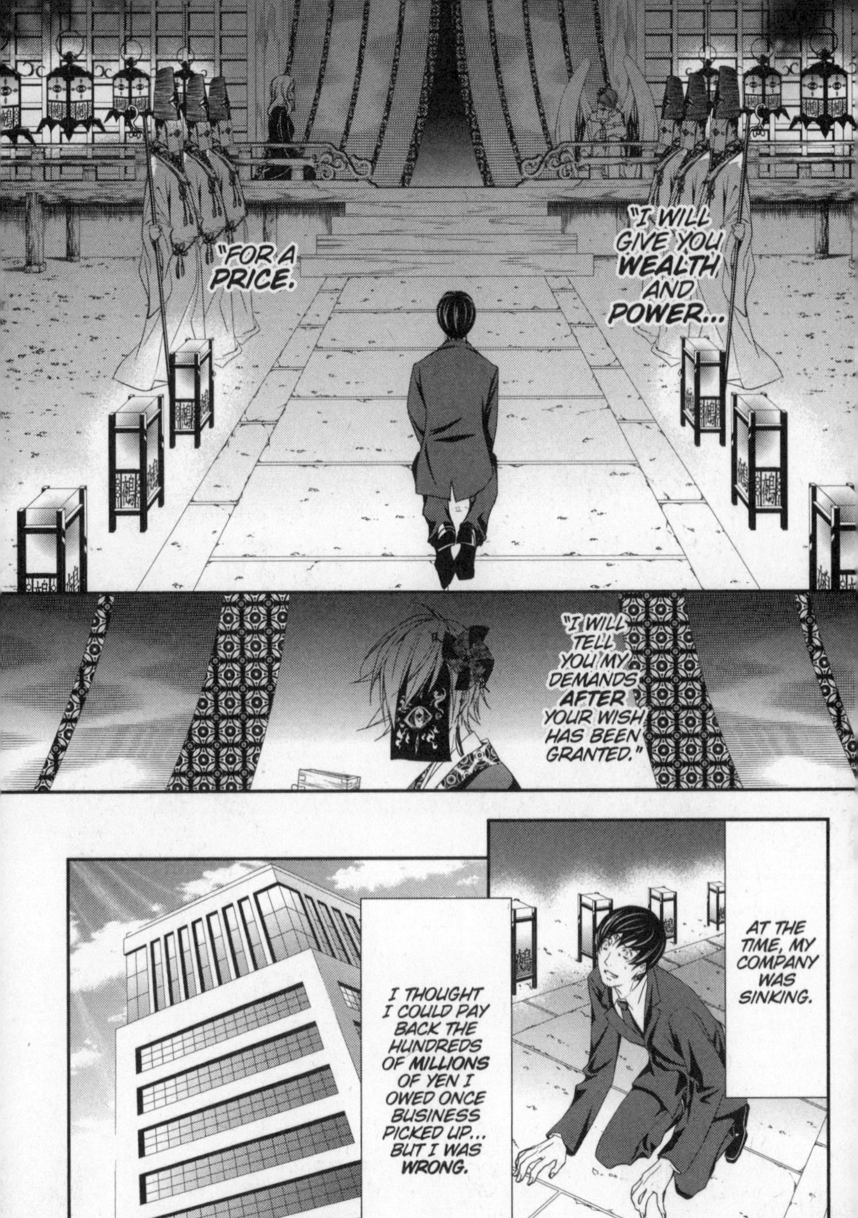
"I WILL GIVE YOU WEALTH AND POWER...
"FOR A PRICE.
"I WILL TELL YOU MY DEMANDS AFTER YOUR WISH HAS BEEN GRANTED."
AT THE TIME, MY COMPANY WAS SINKING.
I THOUGHT I COULD PAY BACK THE HUNDREDS OF MILLIONS OF YEN I OWED ONCE BUSINESS PICKED UP... BUT I WAS WRONG.

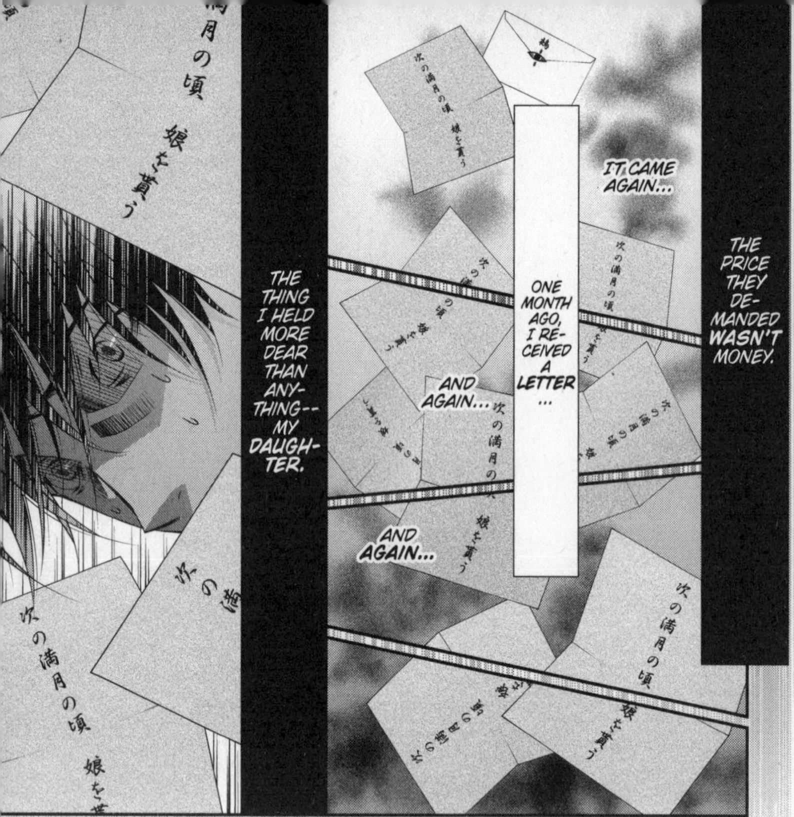
THE PRICE THEY DEMANDED WASN'T MONEY.
IT CAME AGAIN...
ONE MONTH AGO, I RECEIVED A LETTER...
次の満月の頃 娘を貰う
AND AGAIN...
AND AGAIN...
THE THING I HELD MORE DEAR THAN ANYTHING--MY DAUGHTER.

Letter: "On the next full moon, we will take your daughter."

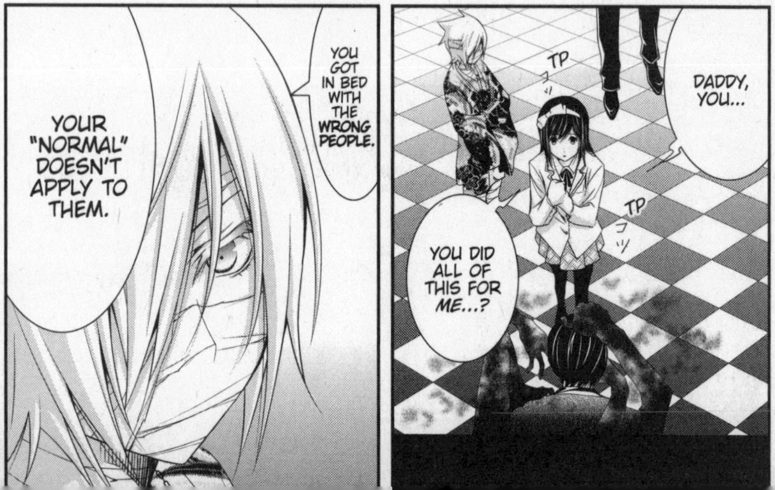
DADDY, YOU...
TP
コッ
YOU DID ALL OF THIS FOR ME...?
TP
コッ
YOU GOT IN BED WITH THE WRONG PEOPLE.
YOUR "NORMAL" DOESN'T APPLY TO THEM.

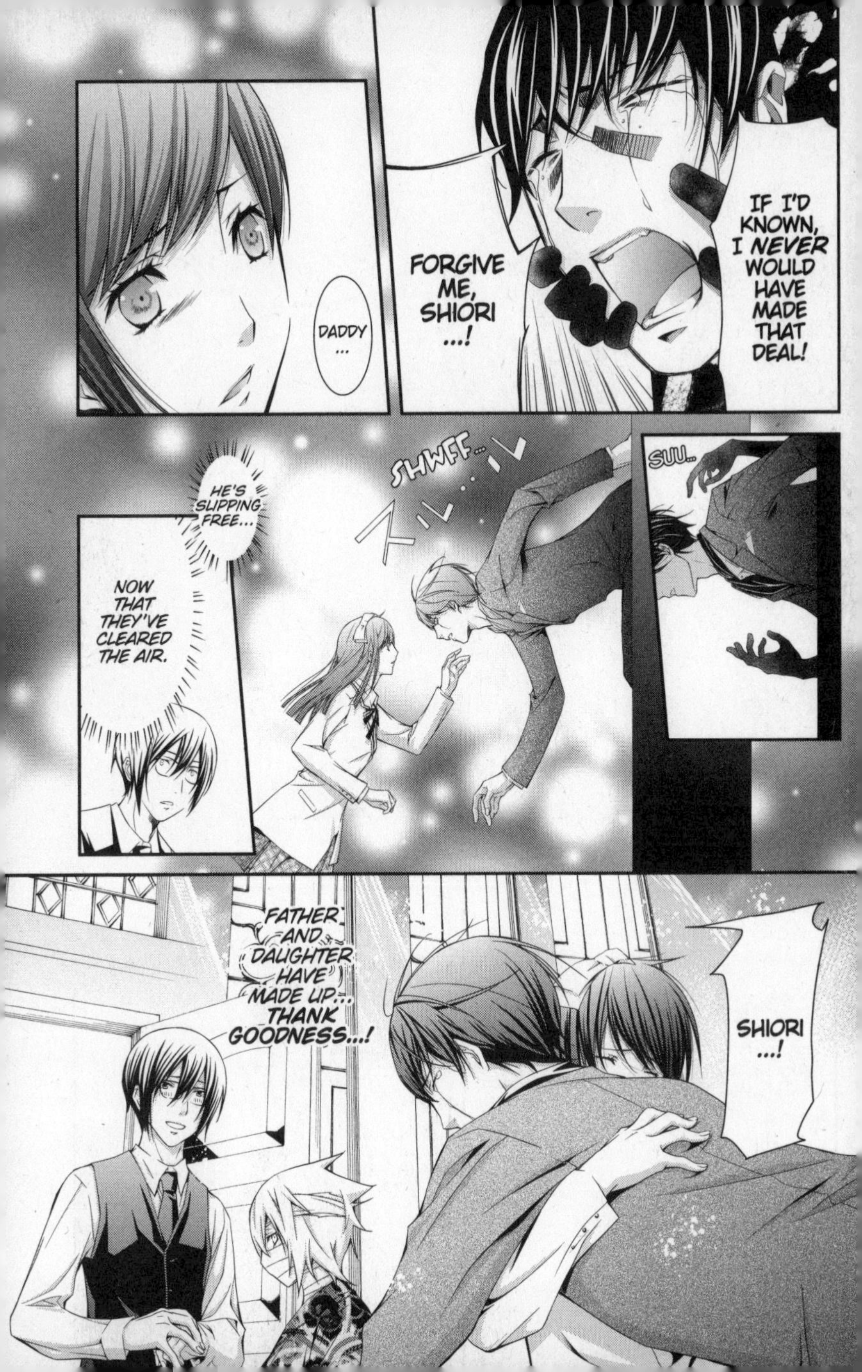
IF I'D KNOWN, I *NEVER* WOULD HAVE MADE THAT DEAL!
FORGIVE ME, SHIORI ...!
DADDY ...
SUU...
SHWFF...
HE'S SLIPPING FREE...
NOW THAT THEY'VE CLEARED THE AIR.
SHIORI ...!
FATHER AND DAUGHTER HAVE MADE UP... THANK GOODNESS...!

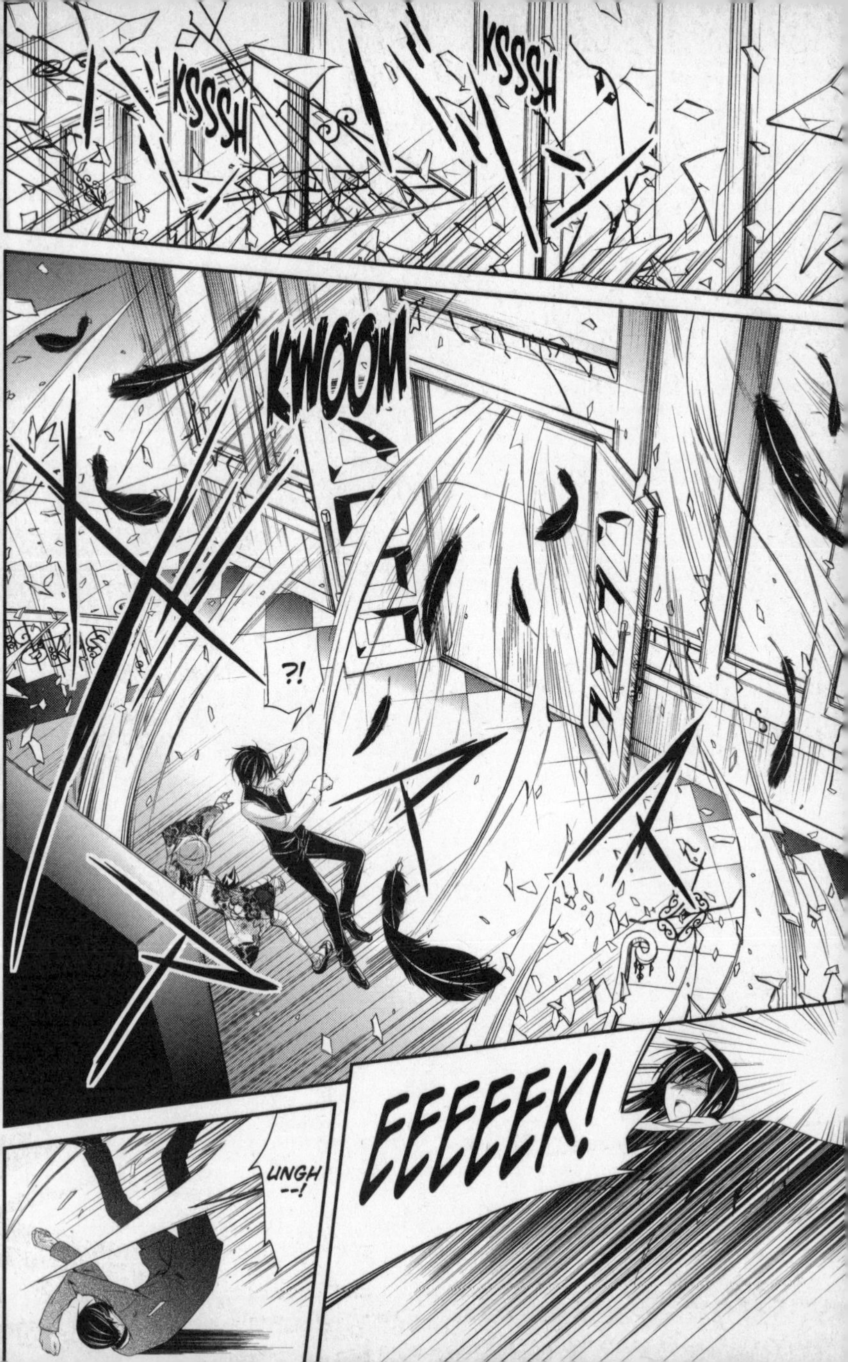
KSSSH
KSSSH
KWOOM
?!
EEEEEK!
UNGH --!

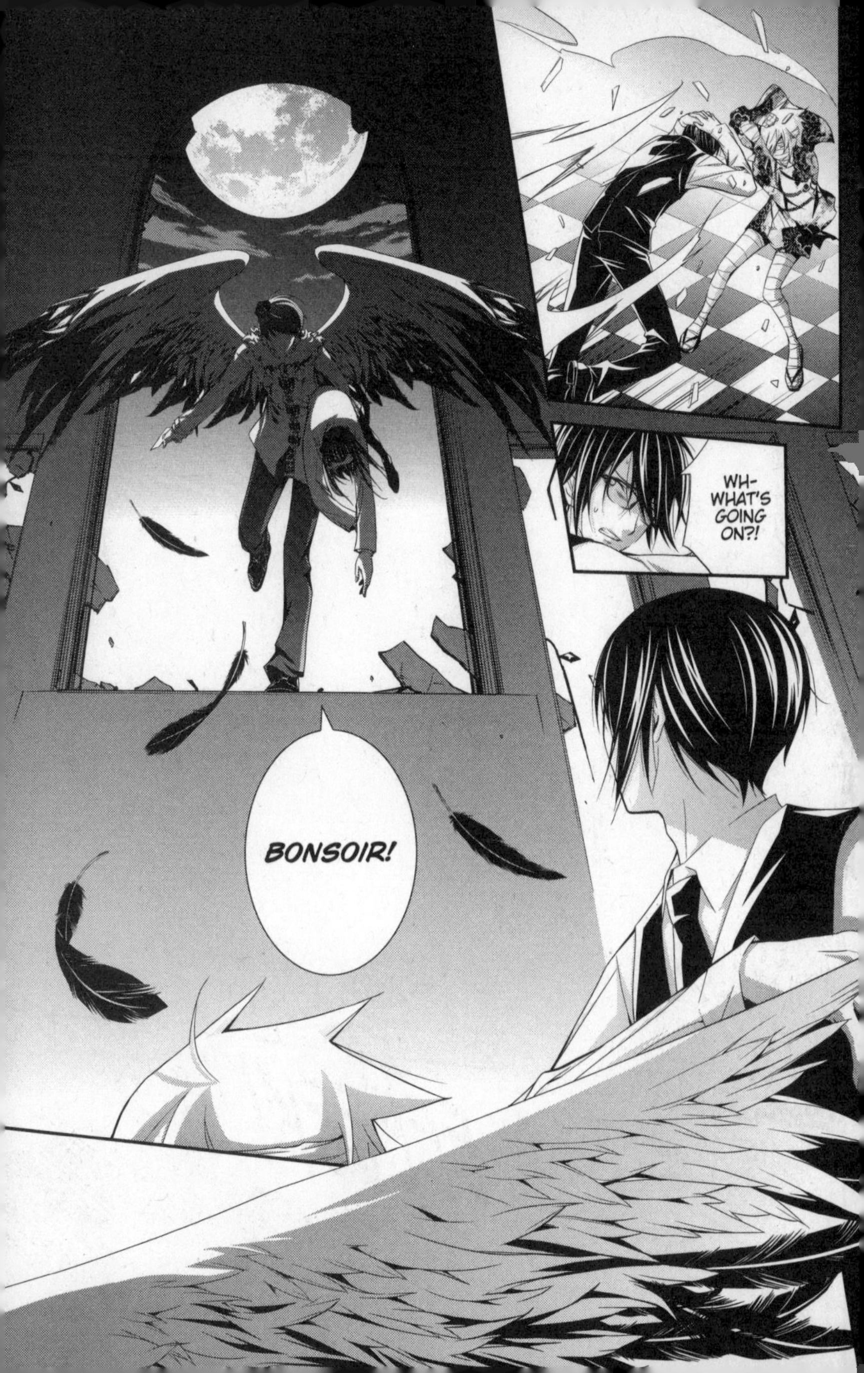
WH-WHAT'S GOING ON?!
BONSOIR!

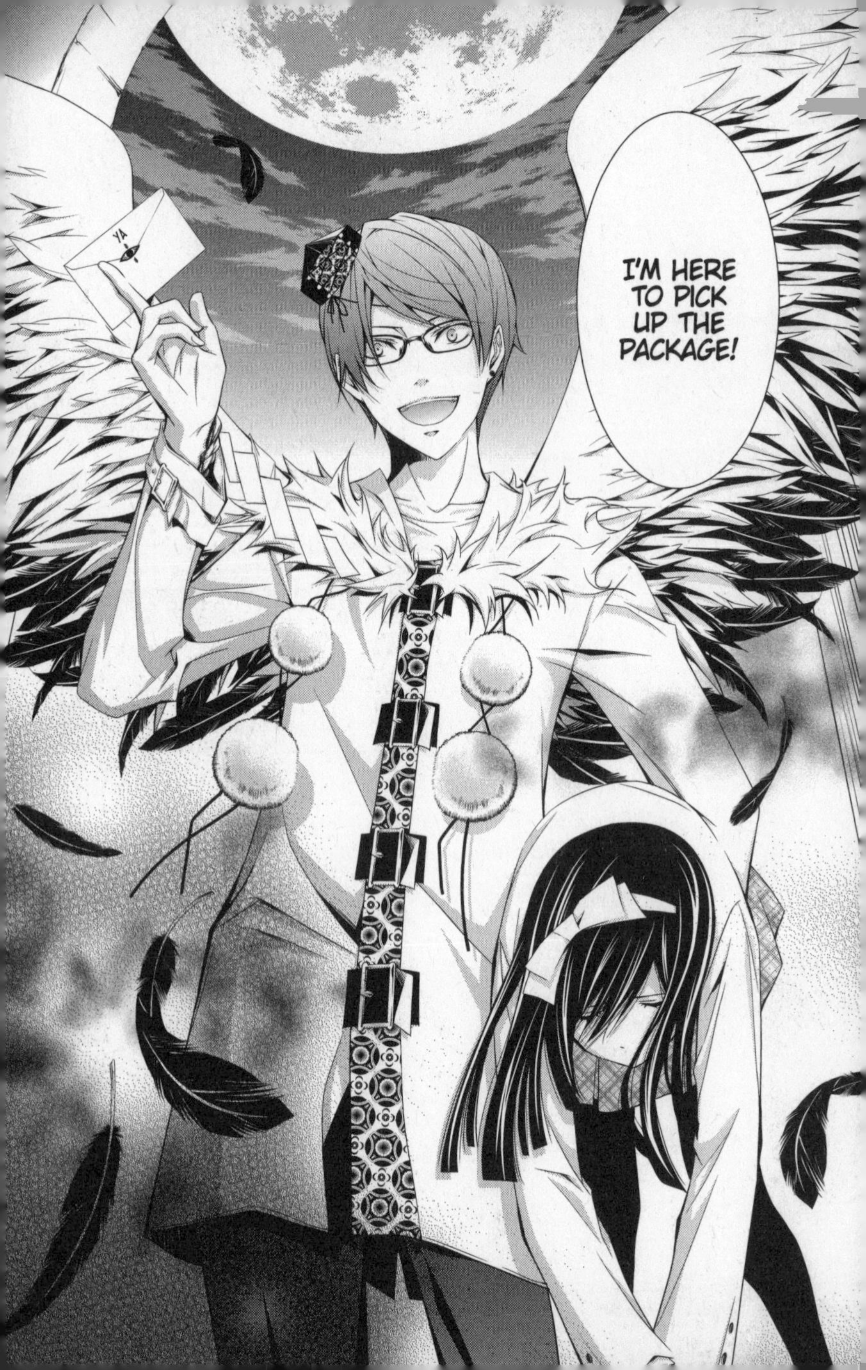
I'M HERE TO PICK UP THE PACKAGE!
YA

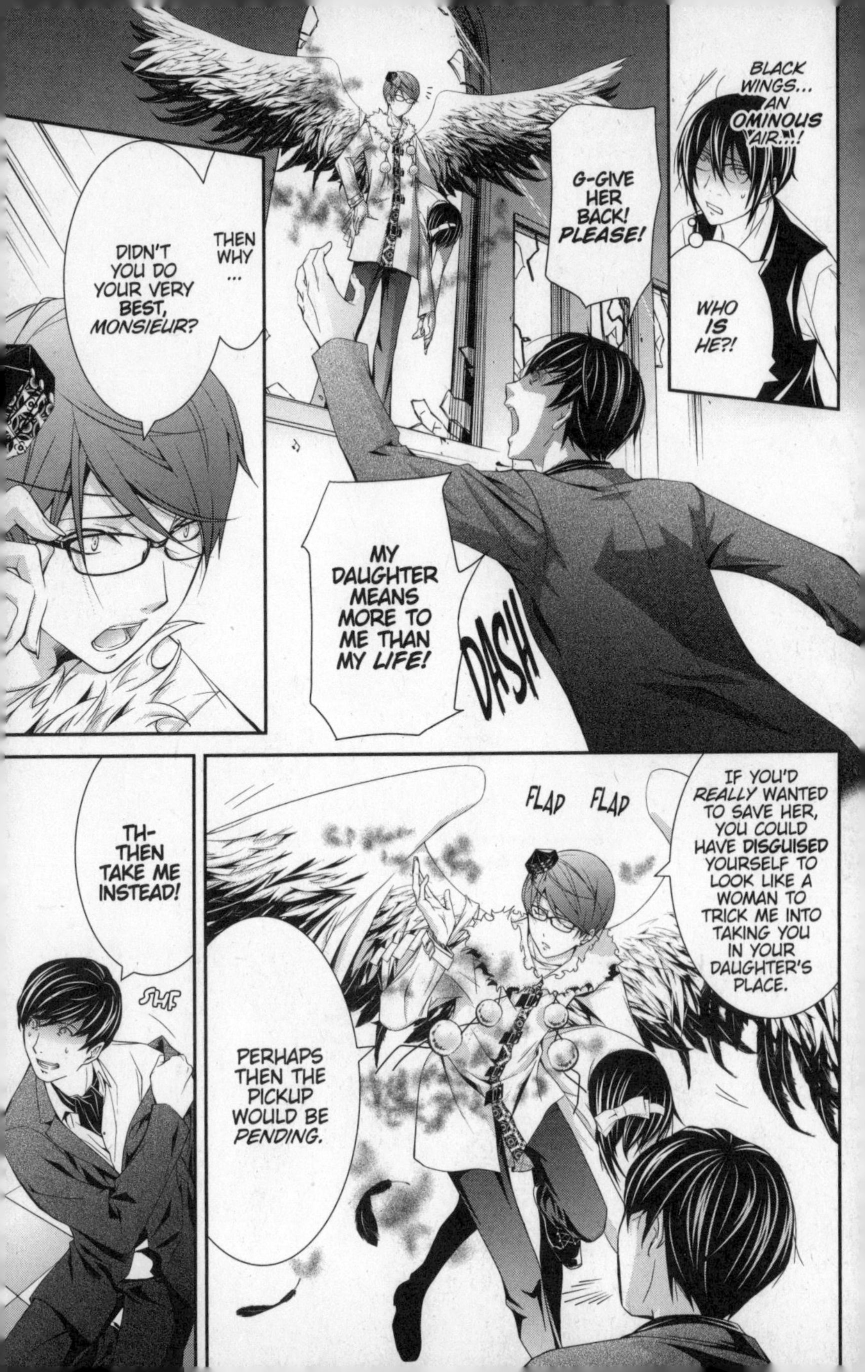
BLACK WINGS... AN OMINOUS AIR...!
WHO IS HE?!
G-GIVE HER BACK! PLEASE!
MY DAUGHTER MEANS MORE TO ME THAN MY LIFE!
DASH
THEN WHY ...
DIDN'T YOU DO YOUR VERY BEST, MONSIEUR?
FLAP FLAP
IF YOU'D REALLY WANTED TO SAVE HER, YOU COULD HAVE DISGUISED YOURSELF TO LOOK LIKE A WOMAN TO TRICK ME INTO TAKING YOU IN YOUR DAUGHTER'S PLACE.
PERHAPS THEN THE PICKUP WOULD BE PENDING.
TH-THEN TAKE ME INSTEAD!
SHF

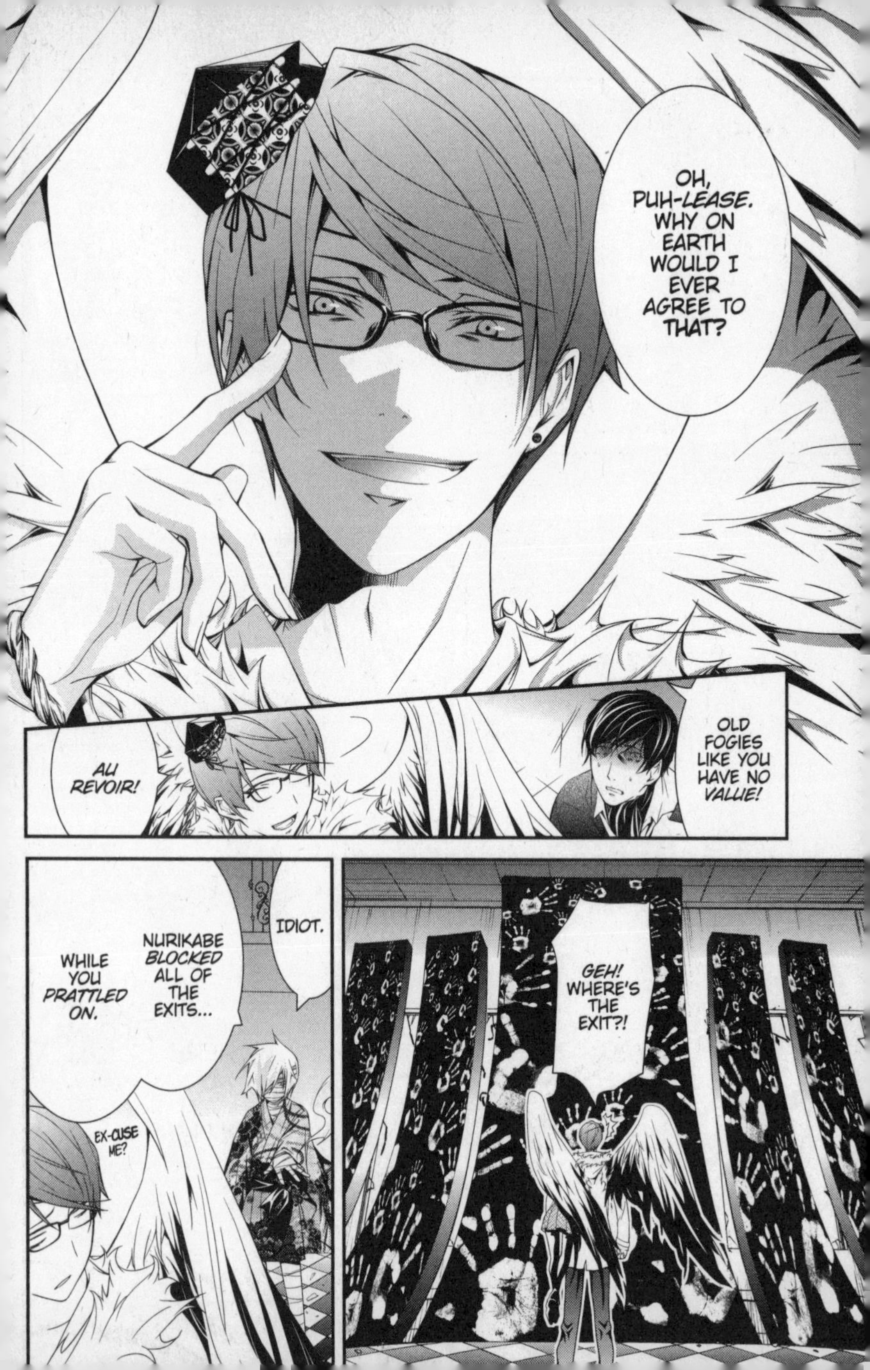
OH, PUH-*LEASE*. WHY ON EARTH WOULD I EVER AGREE TO THAT?
OLD FOGIES LIKE YOU HAVE NO *VALUE!*
AU REVOIR!
GEH! WHERE'S THE EXIT?!
IDIOT.
NURIKABE *BLOCKED* ALL OF THE EXITS...
WHILE YOU *PRATTLED* ON.
EX-CUSE ME?

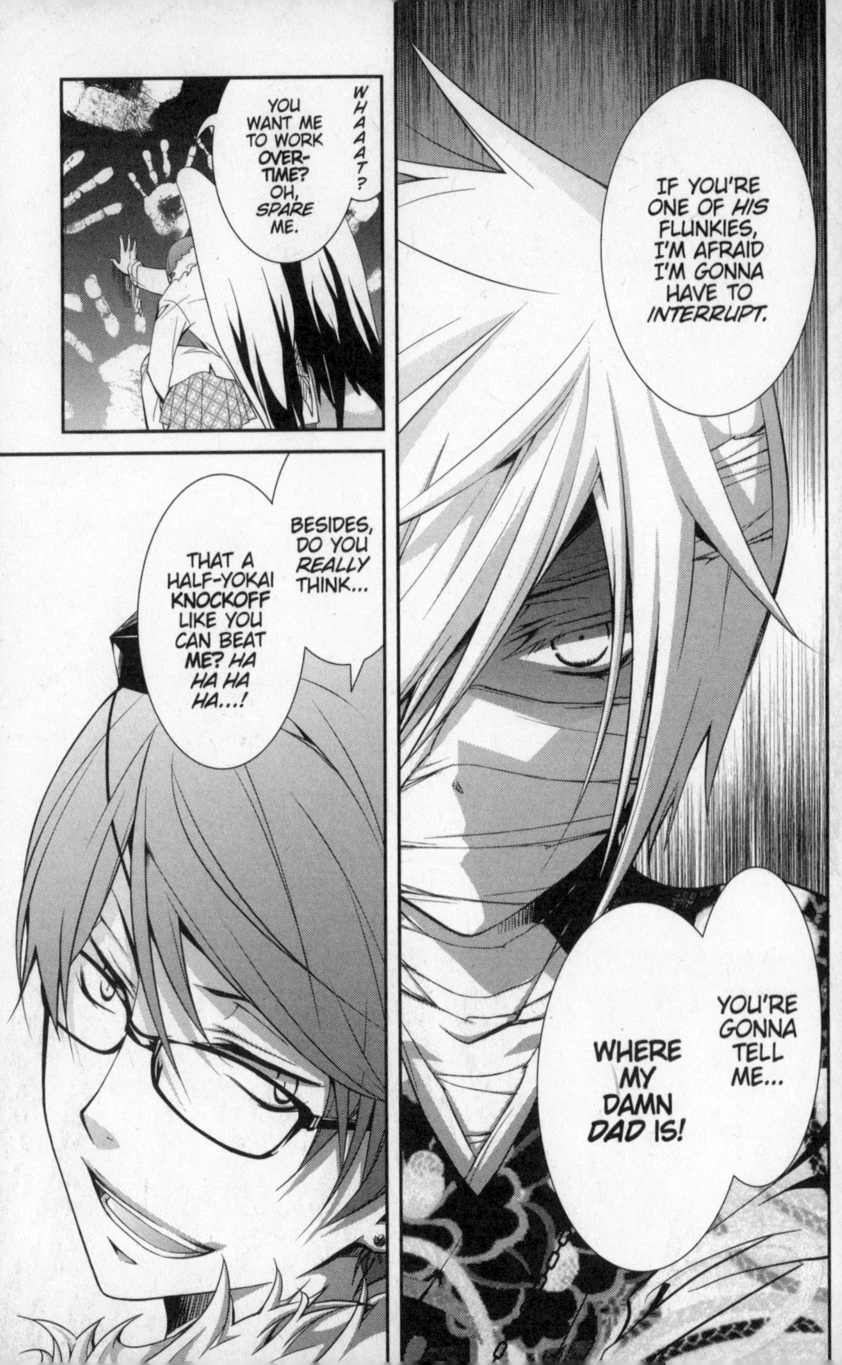
IF YOU'RE ONE OF *HIS* FLUNKIES, I'M AFRAID I'M GONNA HAVE TO *INTERRUPT.*
YOU'RE GONNA TELL ME...
WHERE MY DAMN *DAD* IS!
WHAAAAT?
YOU WANT ME TO WORK OVER-TIME? OH, *SPARE* ME.
BESIDES, DO YOU *REALLY* THINK...
THAT A HALF-YOKAI KNOCKOFF LIKE YOU CAN BEAT ME? *HA HA HA HA...!*

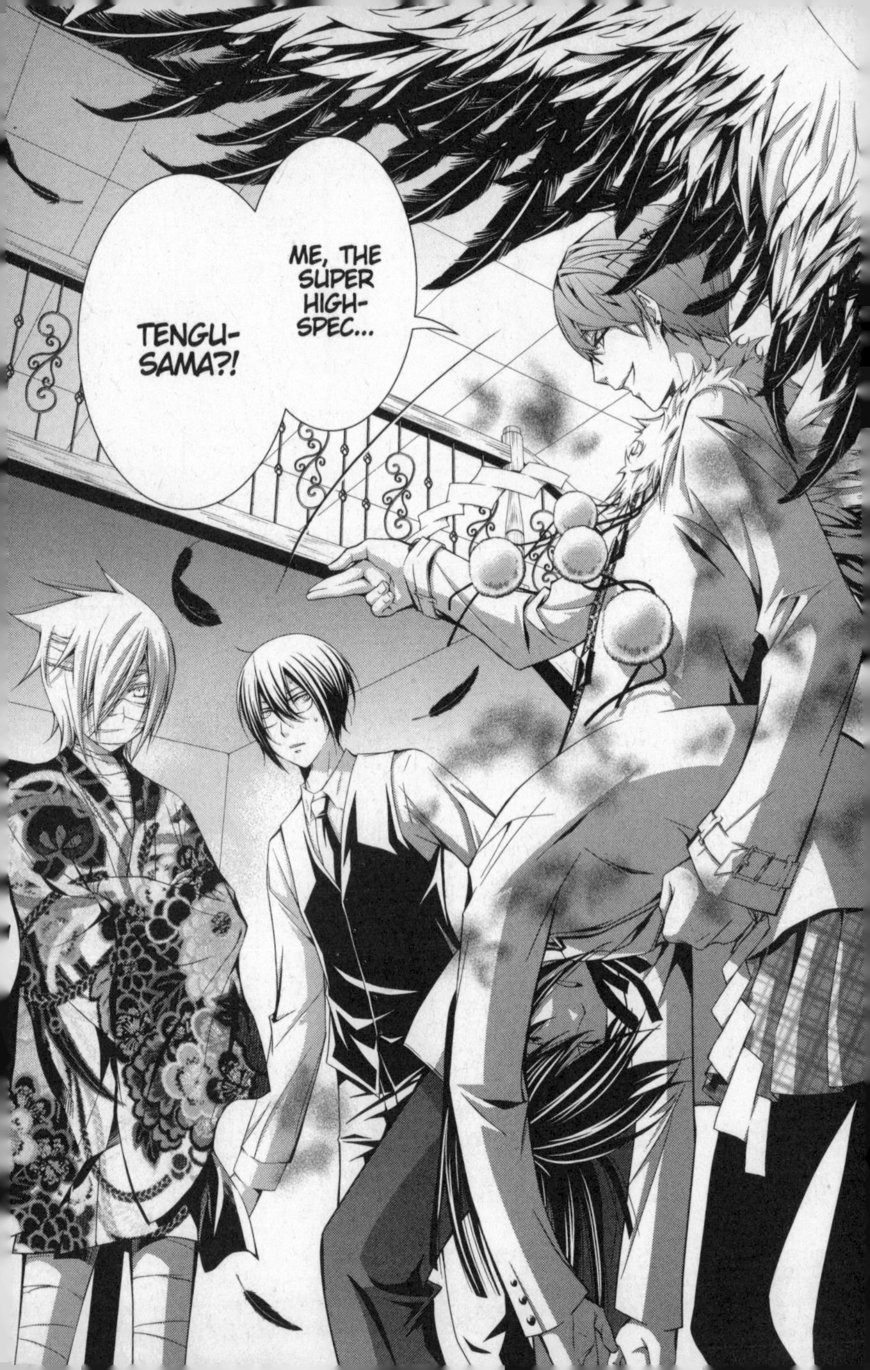
ME, THE SUPER HIGH-SPEC...
TENGU-SAMA?!

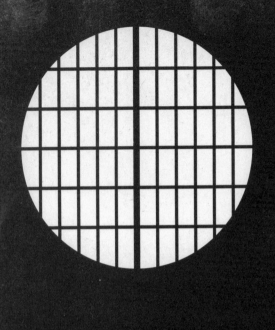

Yōkai Rental Shop

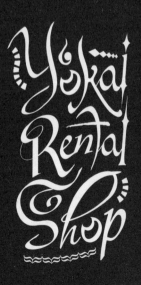

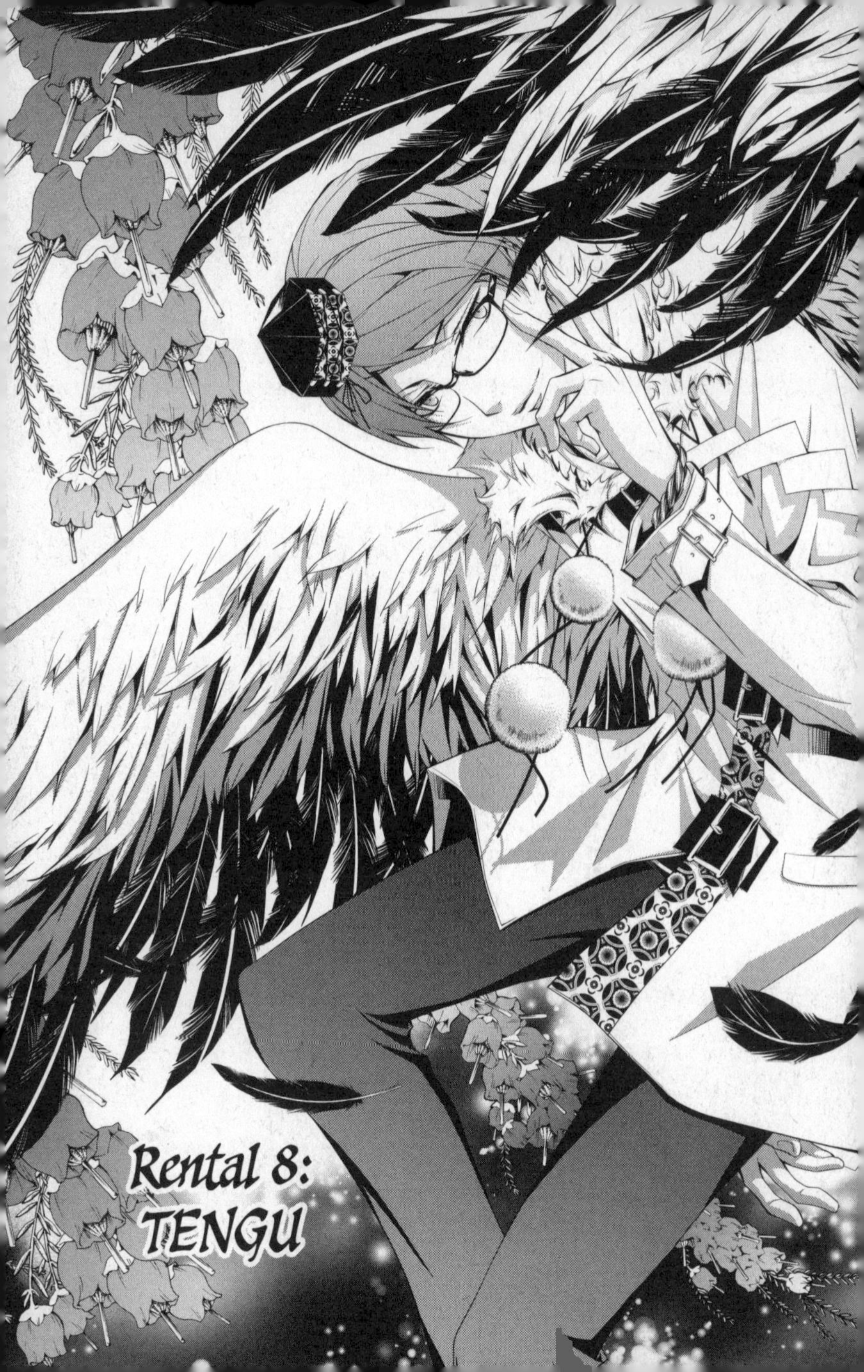
Rental 8:
TENGU

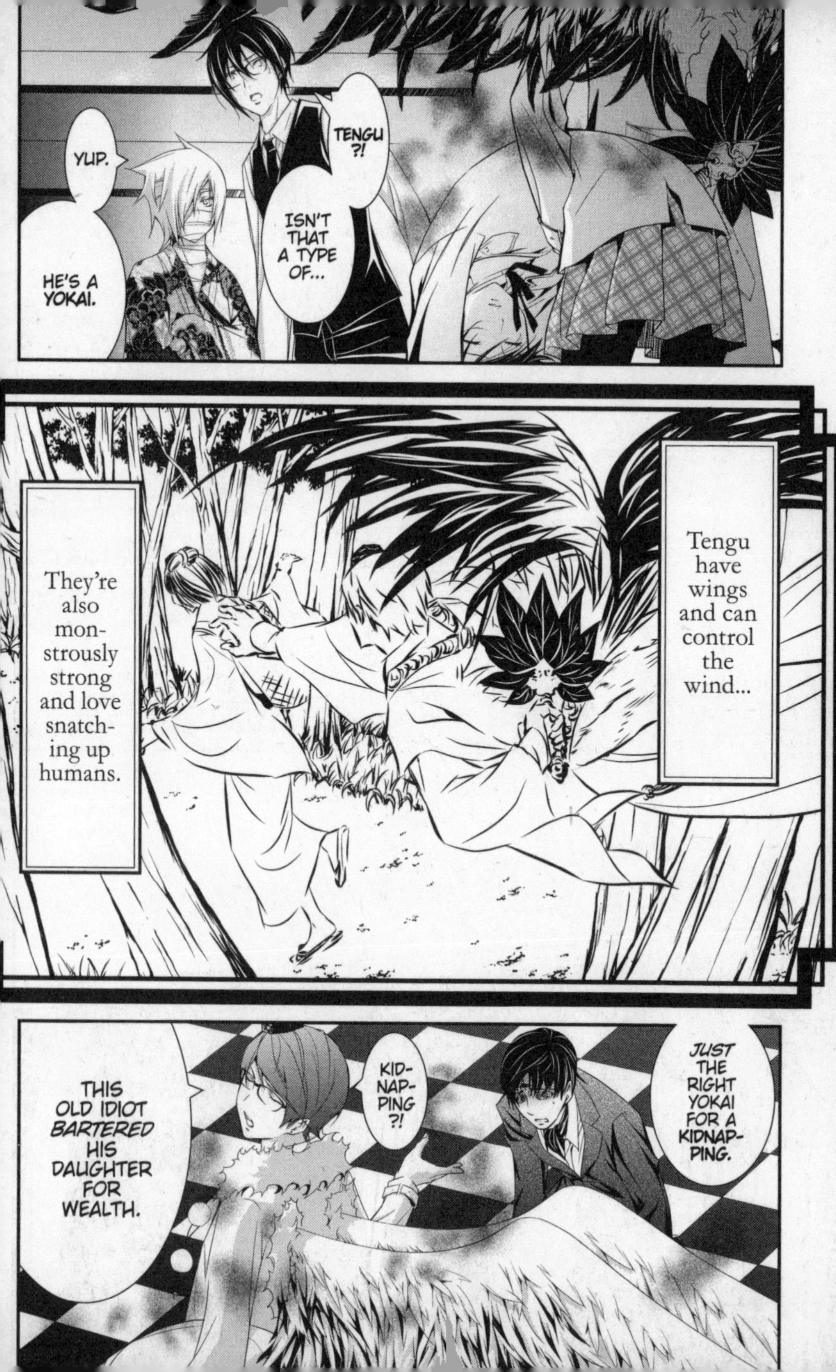
TENGU?!
ISN'T THAT A TYPE OF...
YUP.
HE'S A YOKAI.
Tengu have wings and can control the wind...
They're also monstrously strong and love snatching up humans.
JUST THE RIGHT YOKAI FOR A KIDNAPPING.
KIDNAPPING?!
THIS OLD IDIOT *BARTERED* HIS DAUGHTER FOR WEALTH.

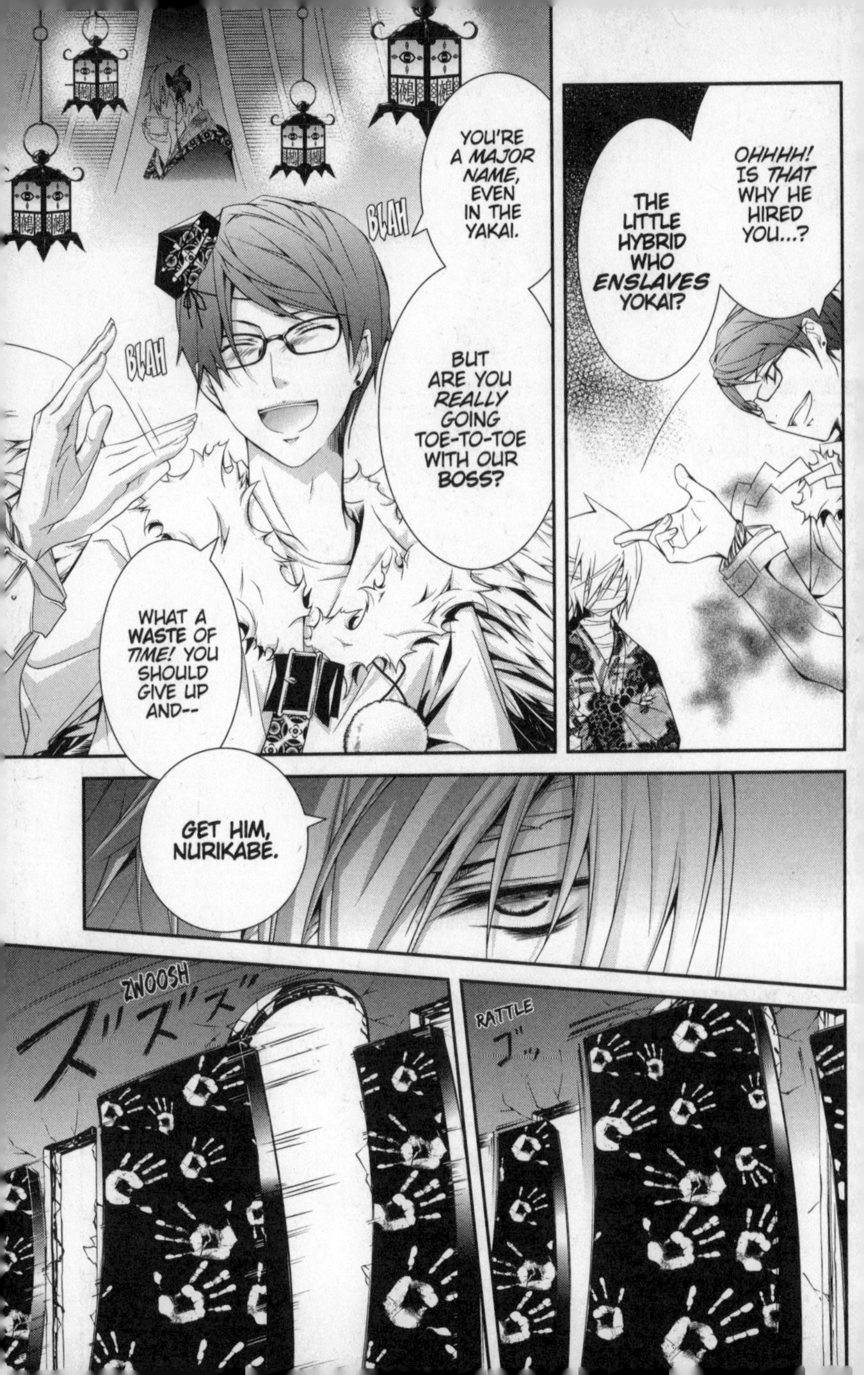

OHHHH! IS THAT WHY HE HIRED YOU...?
THE LITTLE HYBRID WHO ENSLAVES YOKAI?
YOU'RE A MAJOR NAME, EVEN IN THE YAKAI.
BLAH
BUT ARE YOU REALLY GOING TOE-TO-TOE WITH OUR BOSS?
BLAH
WHAT A WASTE OF TIME! YOU SHOULD GIVE UP AND--
GET HIM, NURIKABE.
RATTLE
ZWOOSH

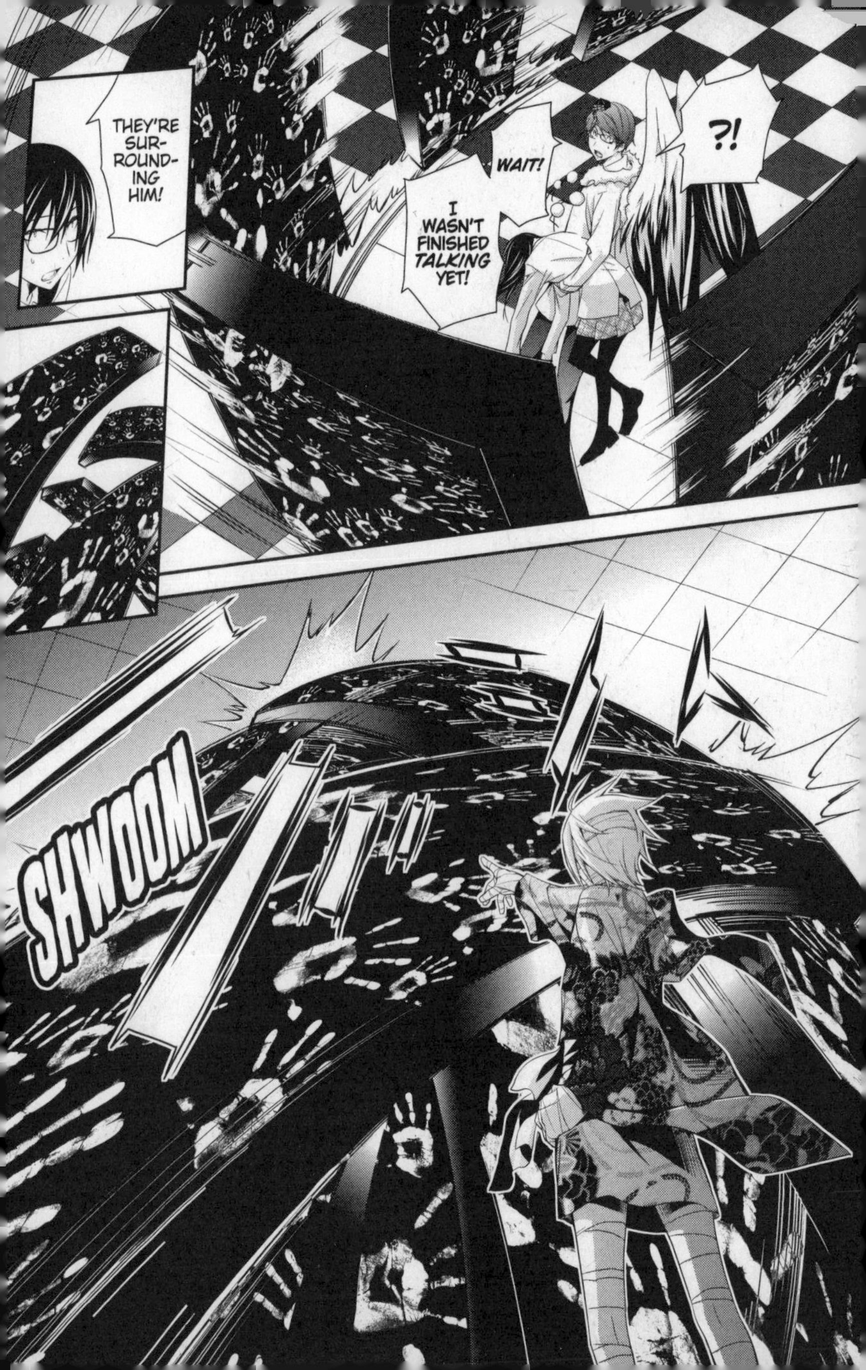
?!
WAIT!
I WASN'T FINISHED TALKING YET!
THEY'RE SUR-ROUND-ING HIM!
SHWOOM

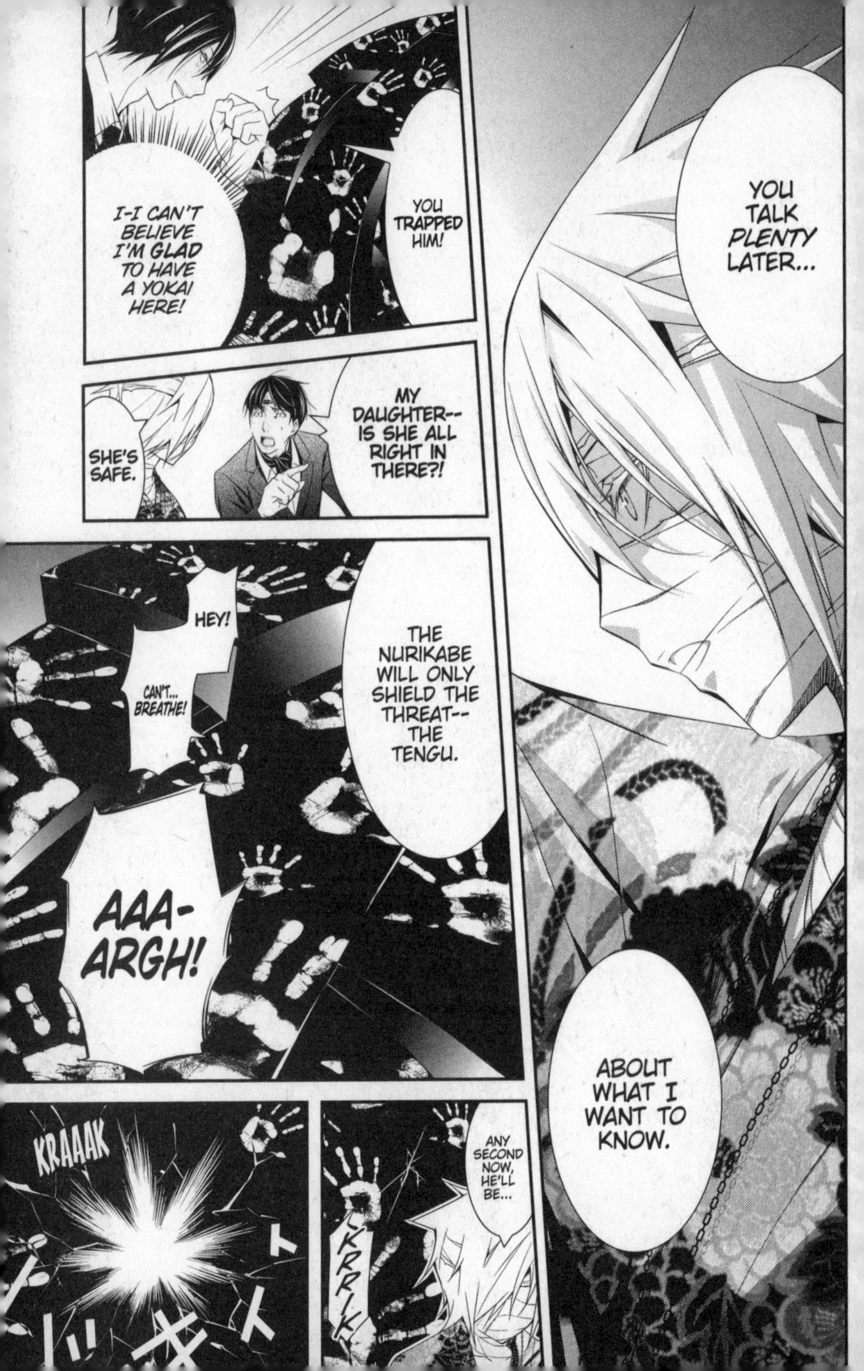
YOU TALK PLENTY LATER...
ABOUT WHAT I WANT TO KNOW.
YOU TRAPPED HIM!
I-I CAN'T BELIEVE I'M GLAD TO HAVE A YOKAI HERE!
MY DAUGHTER-- IS SHE ALL RIGHT IN THERE?!
SHE'S SAFE.
THE NURIKABE WILL ONLY SHIELD THE THREAT-- THE TENGU.
HEY!
CAN'T... BREATHE!
AAA-ARGH!
ANY SECOND NOW, HE'LL BE...
KRRIK
KRAAAK

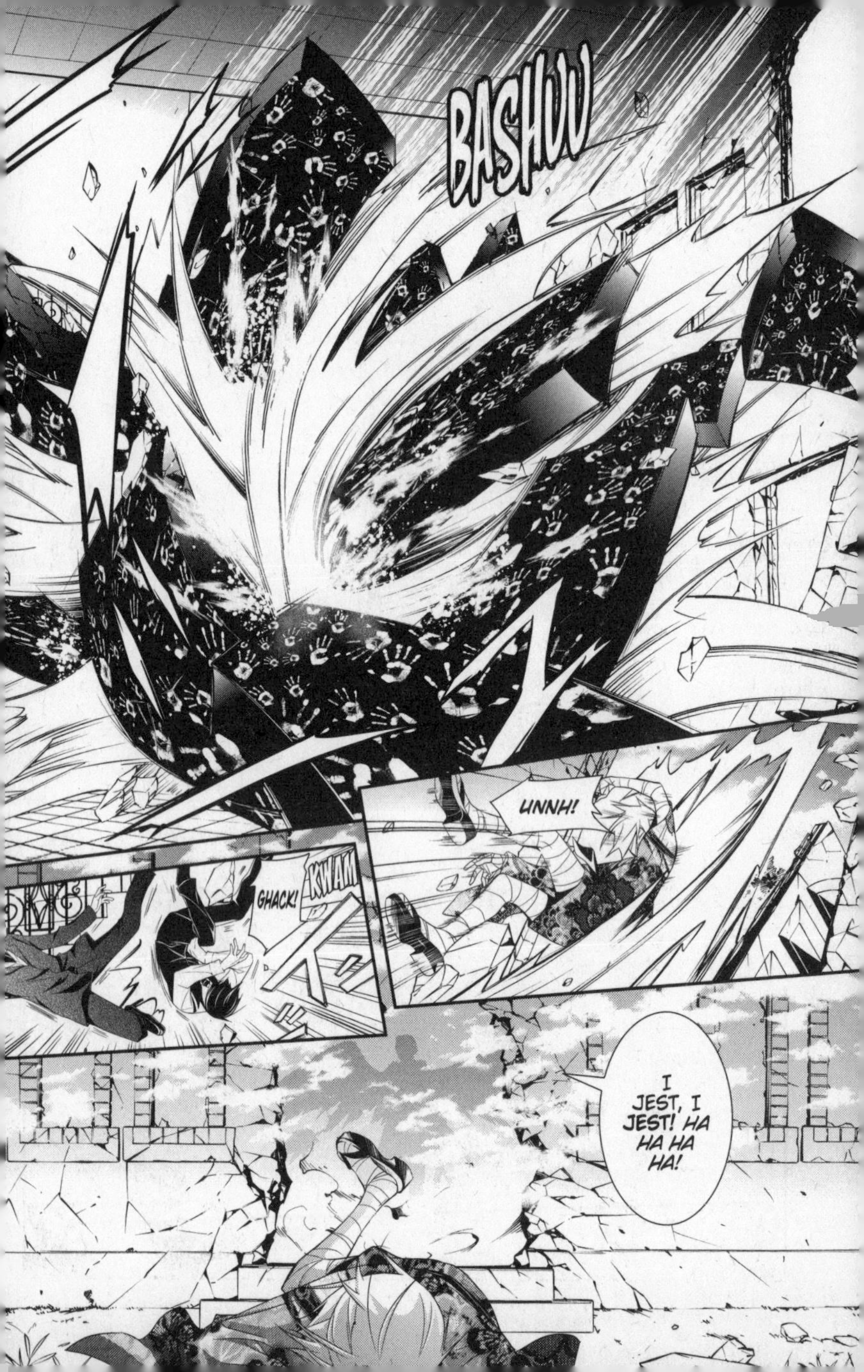
BASHUU
UNNH!
KWAM
GHACK!
I JEST, I JEST! HA HA HA HA!

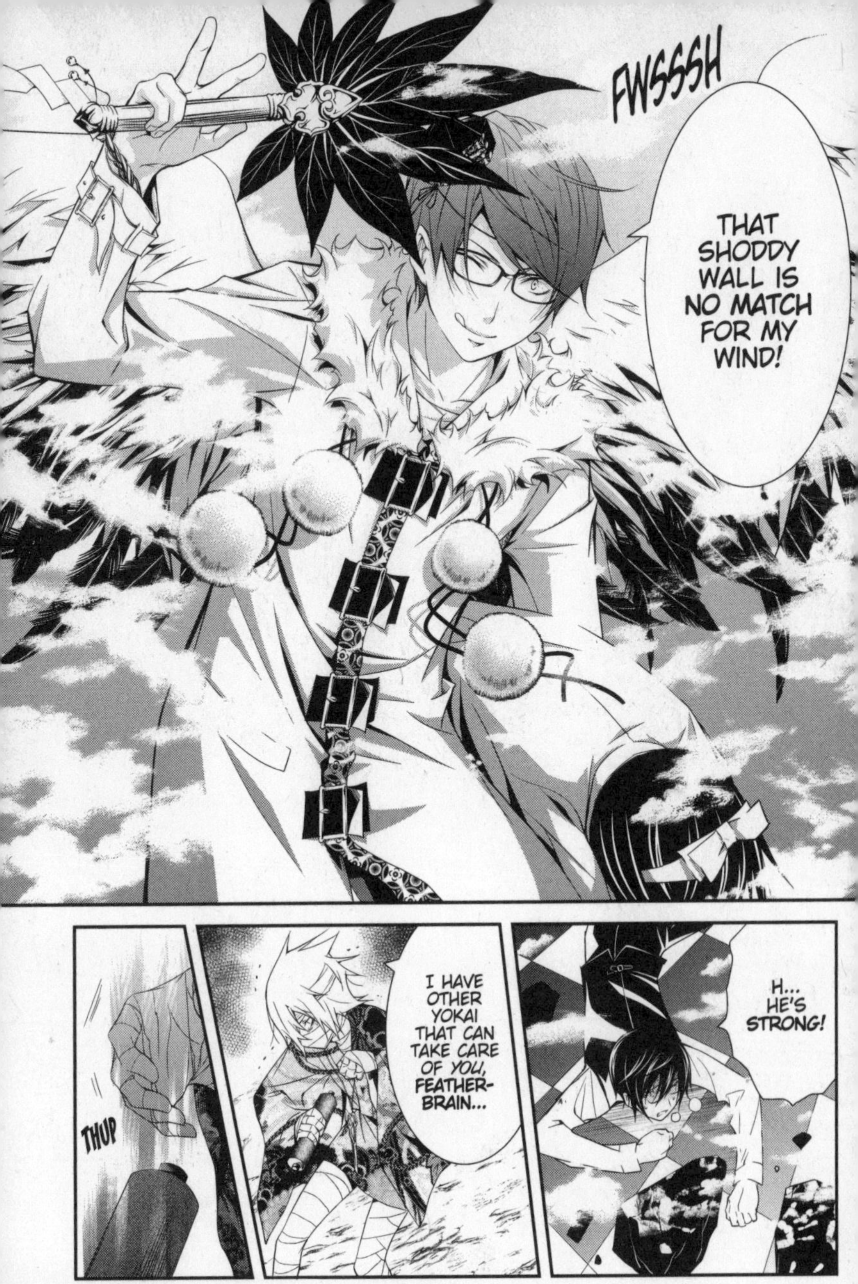
THAT SHODDY WALL IS NO MATCH FOR MY WIND!
FWSSSH
H... HE'S STRONG!
I HAVE OTHER YOKAI THAT CAN TAKE CARE OF *YOU*, FEATHER-BRAIN...
THUP

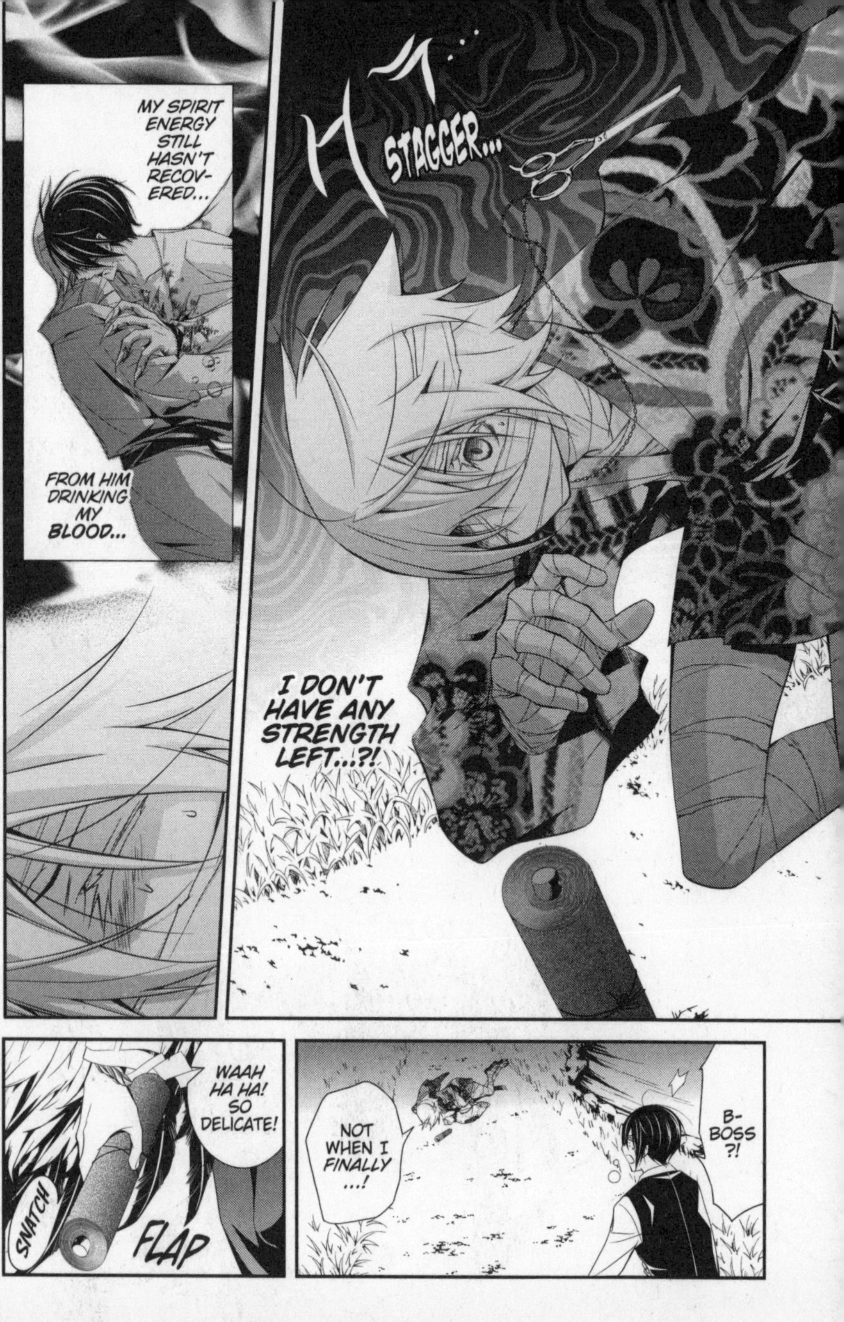
STAGGER...
I DON'T HAVE ANY STRENGTH LEFT...?!
MY SPIRIT ENERGY STILL HASN'T RECOVERED...
FROM HIM DRINKING MY BLOOD...
B-BOSS?!
NOT WHEN I FINALLY...!
WAAH HA HA! SO DELICATE!
SNATCH
FLAP

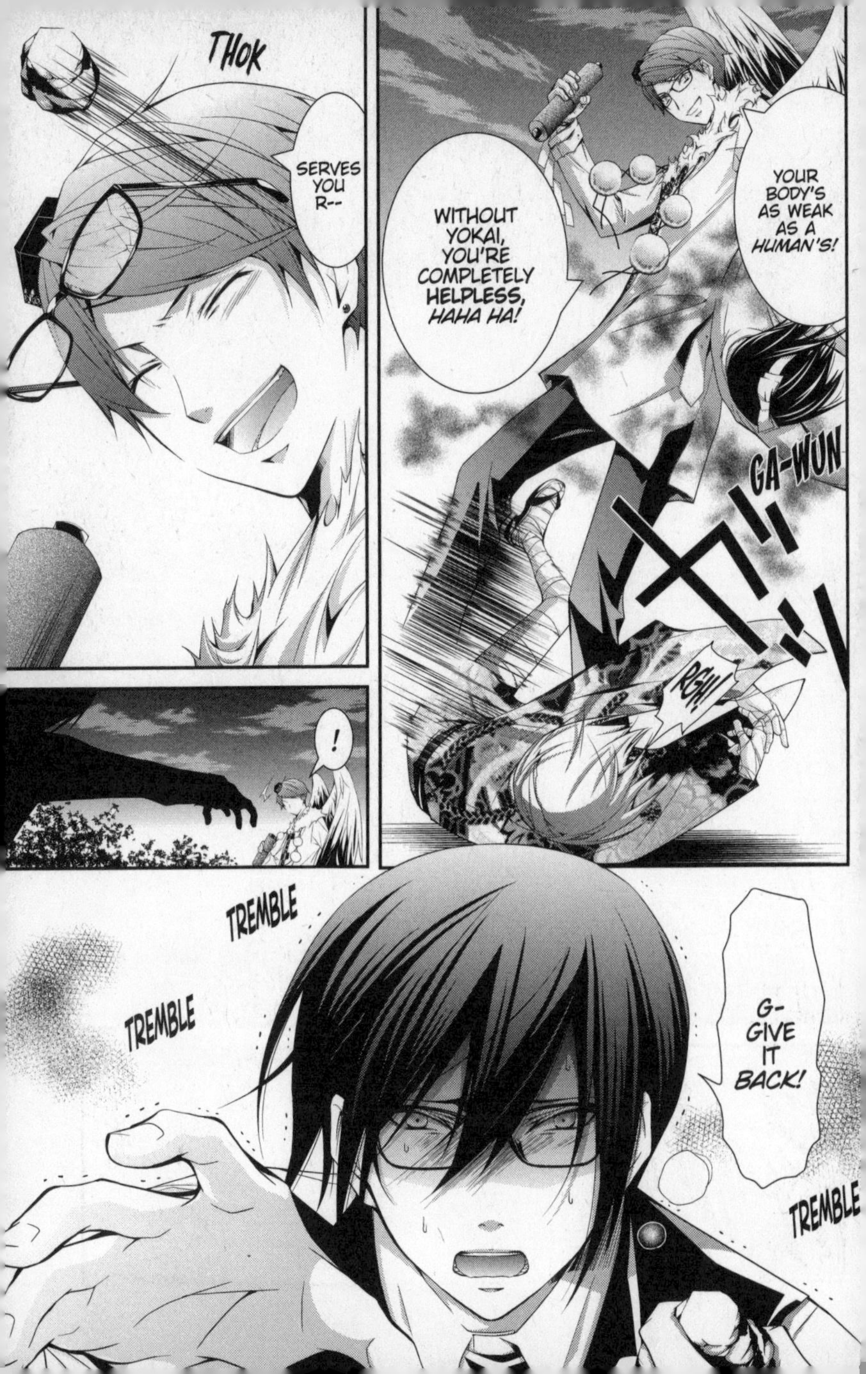
YOUR BODY'S AS WEAK AS A HUMAN'S!
WITHOUT YOKAI, YOU'RE COMPLETELY HELPLESS, HAHA HA!
GA-WUN
RGH!
THOK
SERVES YOU R--
!
G- GIVE IT BACK!
TREMBLE
TREMBLE
TREMBLE

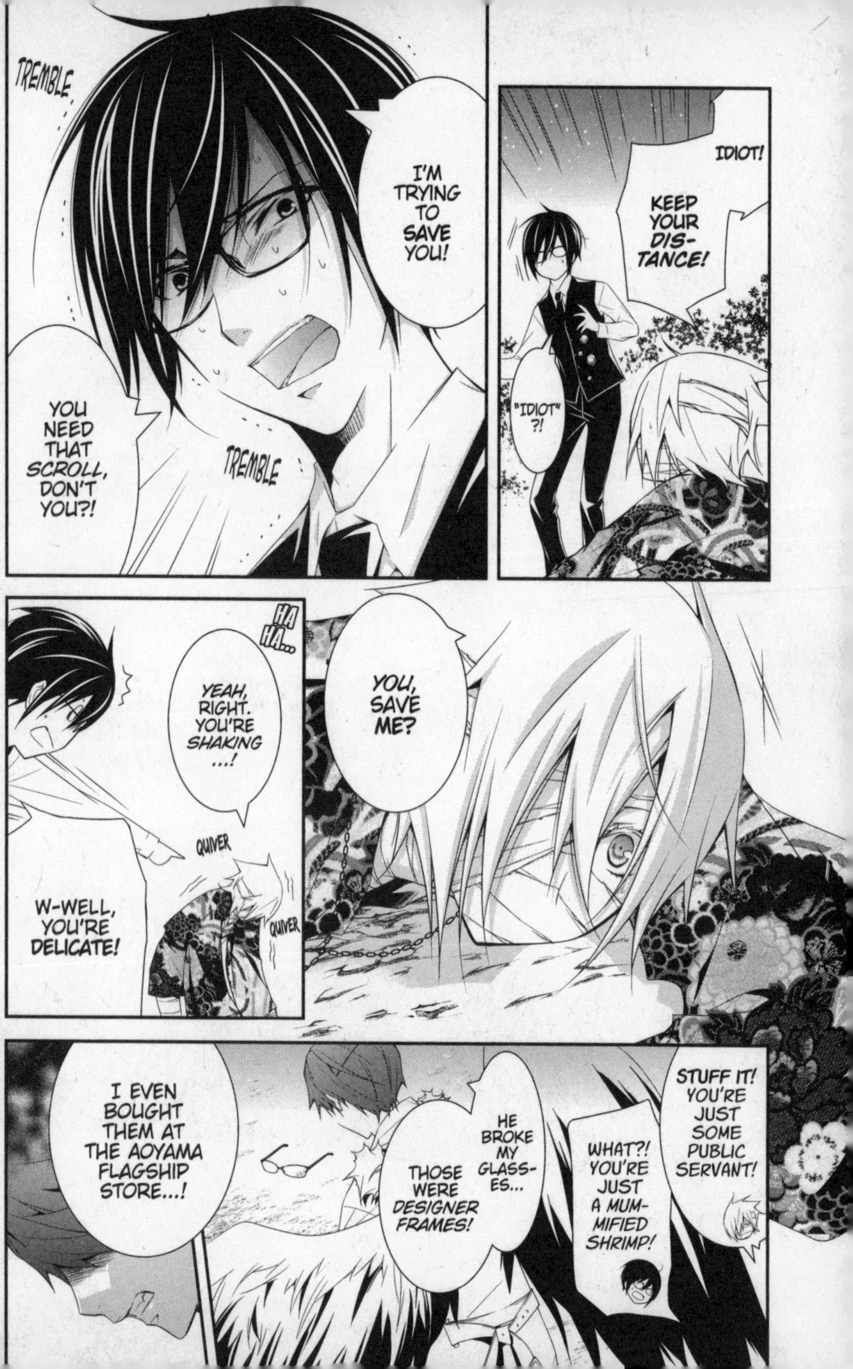
IDIOT!
KEEP YOUR DIS-TANCE!
"IDIOT" ?!
TREMBLE
I'M TRYING TO SAVE YOU!
YOU NEED THAT SCROLL, DON'T YOU?!
TREMBLE
YOU, SAVE ME?
HA HA...
YEAH, RIGHT. YOU'RE SHAKING ...!
QUIVER
QUIVER
W-WELL, YOU'RE DELICATE!
STUFF IT! YOU'RE JUST SOME PUBLIC SERVANT!
WHAT?! YOU'RE JUST A MUM-MIFIED SHRIMP!
HE BROKE MY GLASS-ES...
THOSE WERE DESIGNER FRAMES!
I EVEN BOUGHT THEM AT THE AOYAMA FLAGSHIP STORE...!

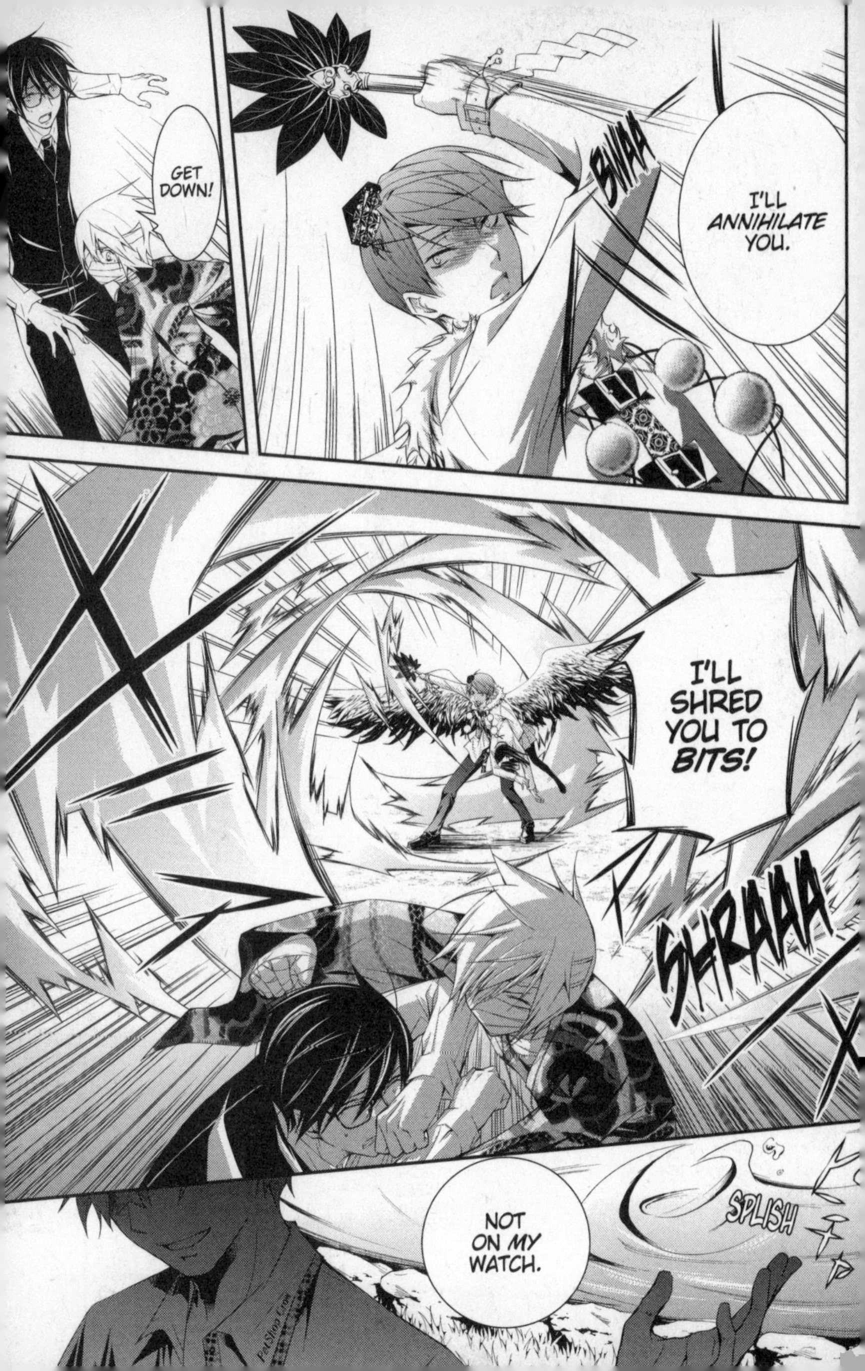
I'LL ANNIHILATE YOU.
SWAA
GET DOWN!
I'LL SHRED YOU TO BITS!
SHRAAA
SPLISH
NOT ON MY WATCH.

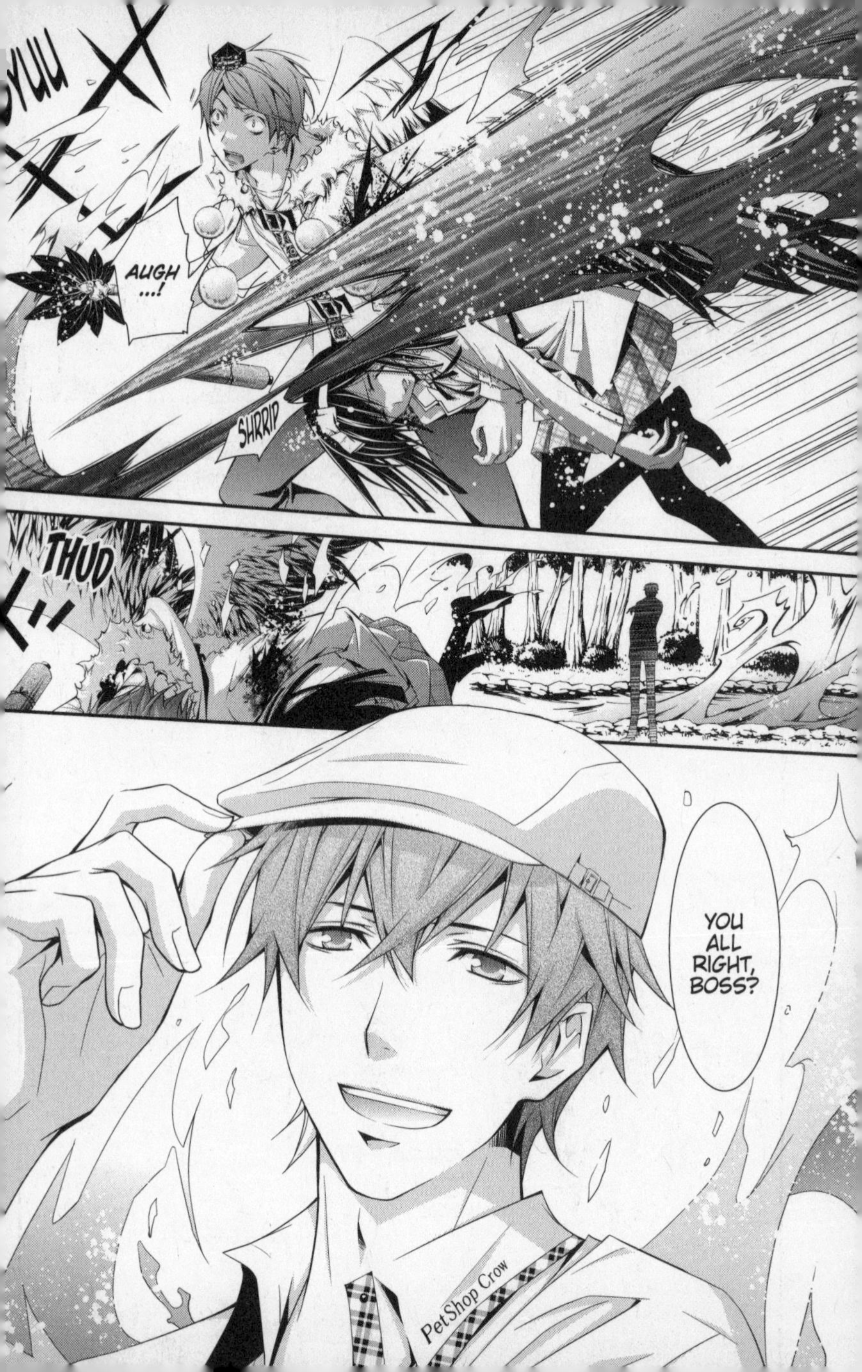
AUGH ...!
SHRRIP
THUD
YOU ALL RIGHT, BOSS?
PetShop Crow

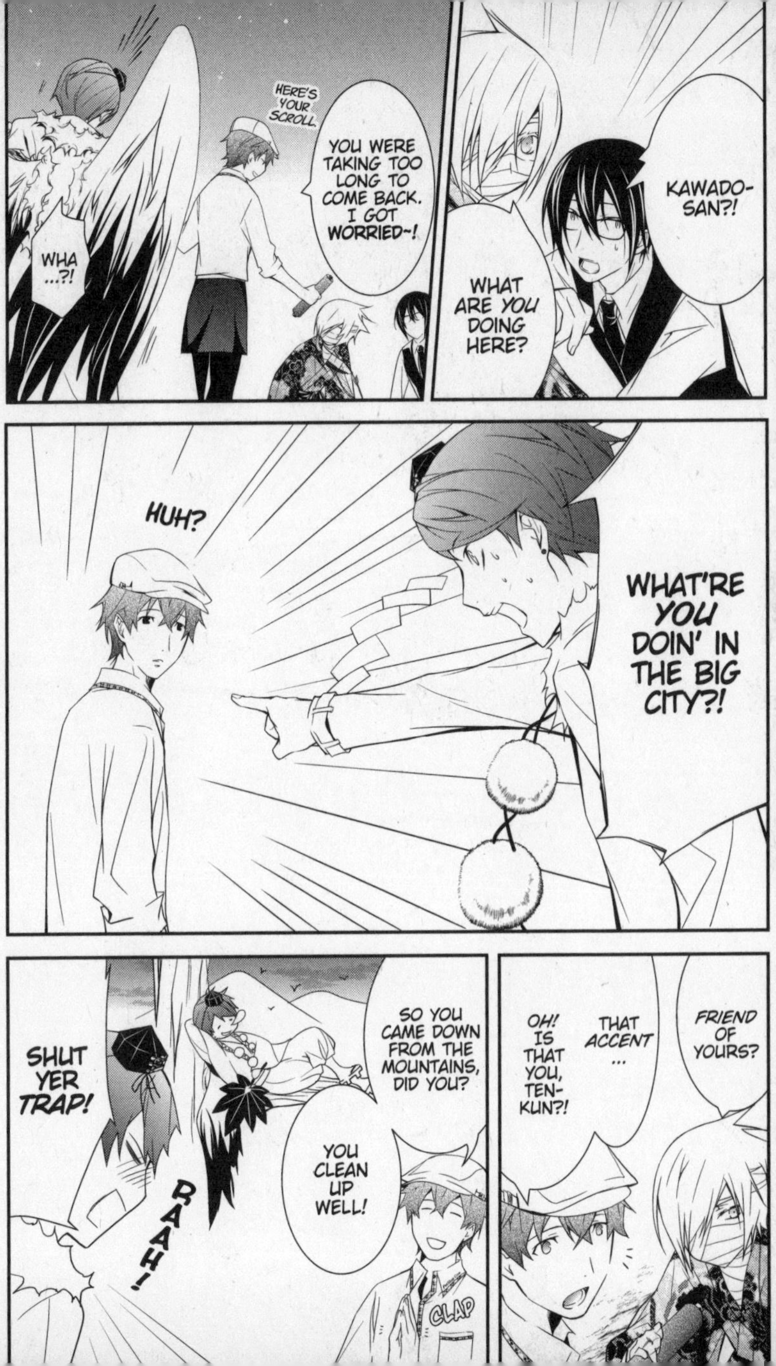
KAWADO-SAN?!
WHAT ARE YOU DOING HERE?
YOU WERE TAKING TOO LONG TO COME BACK. I GOT WORRIED~!
HERE'S YOUR SCROLL.
WHA ...?!
WHAT'RE YOU DOIN' IN THE BIG CITY?!
HUH?
FRIEND OF YOURS?
THAT ACCENT ...
OH! IS THAT YOU, TEN-KUN?!
SO YOU CAME DOWN FROM THE MOUNTAINS, DID YOU?
YOU CLEAN UP WELL!
CLAP
SHUT YER TRAP!
RAAH!

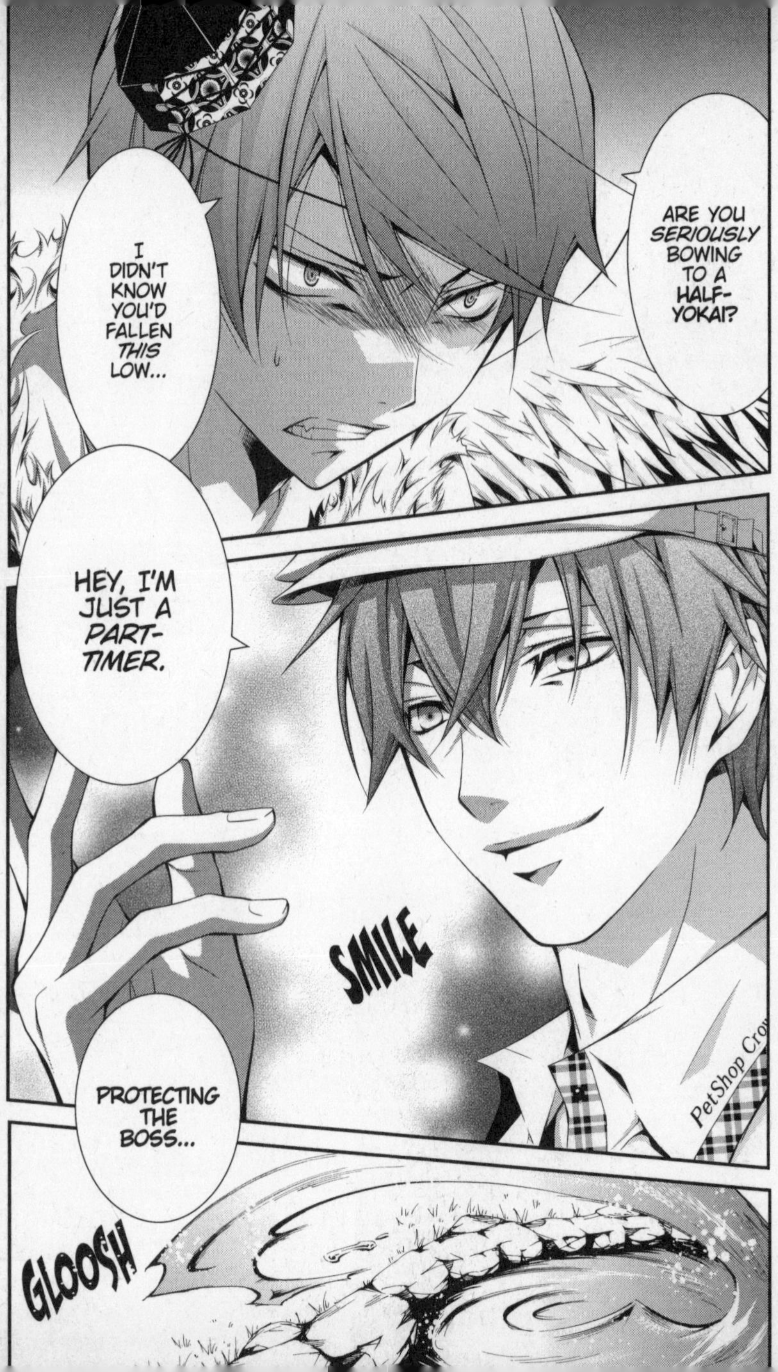
ARE YOU SERIOUSLY BOWING TO A HALF-YOKAI?
I DIDN'T KNOW YOU'D FALLEN *THIS* LOW...
HEY, I'M JUST A *PART-TIMER.*
SMILE
PetShop Crow
PROTECTING THE BOSS...
GLOOSH

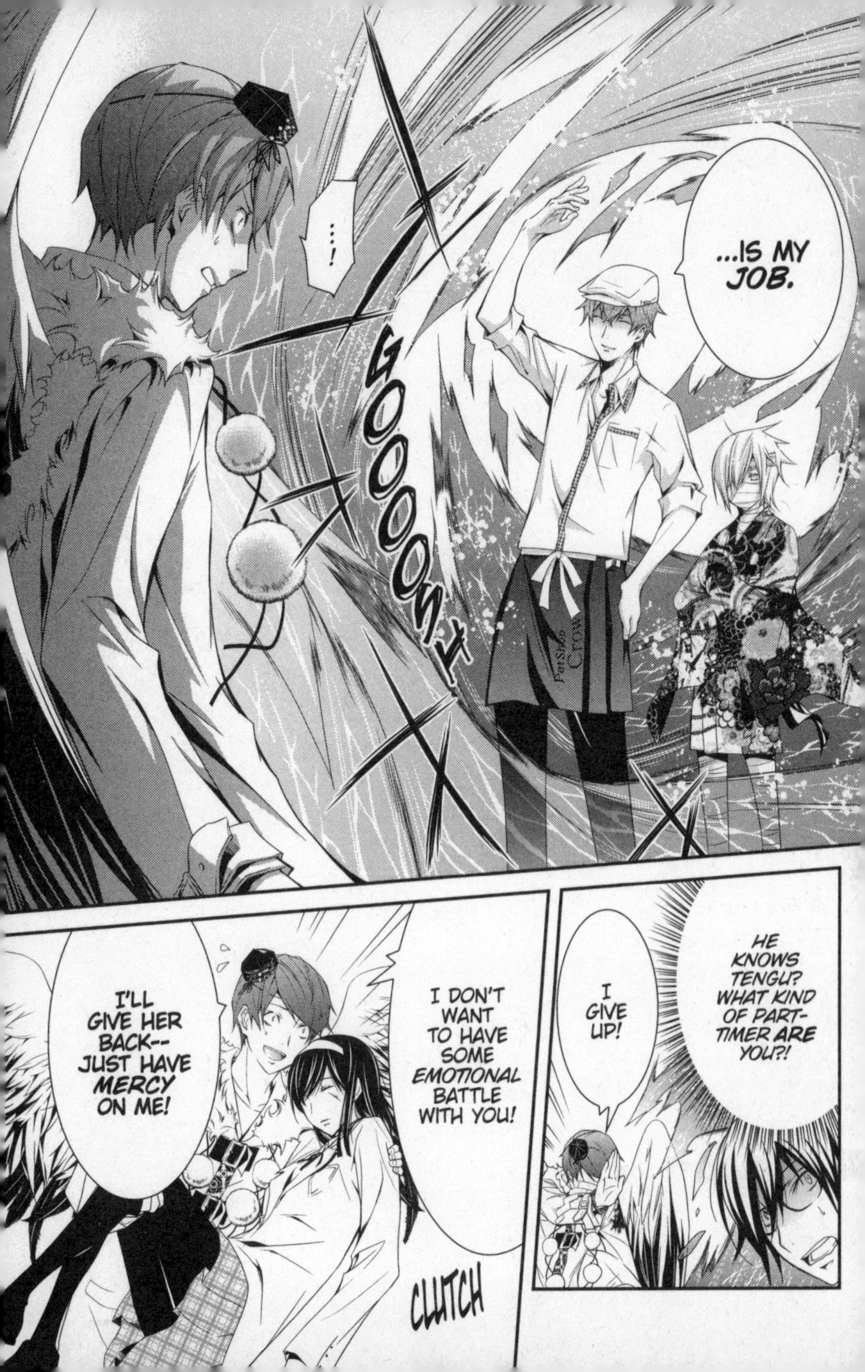
...IS MY JOB.
GOOOOSH
...!
HE KNOWS TENGU? WHAT KIND OF PART-TIMER ARE YOU?!
I GIVE UP!
I DON'T WANT TO HAVE SOME EMOTIONAL BATTLE WITH YOU!
I'LL GIVE HER BACK-- JUST HAVE MERCY ON ME!
CLUTCH

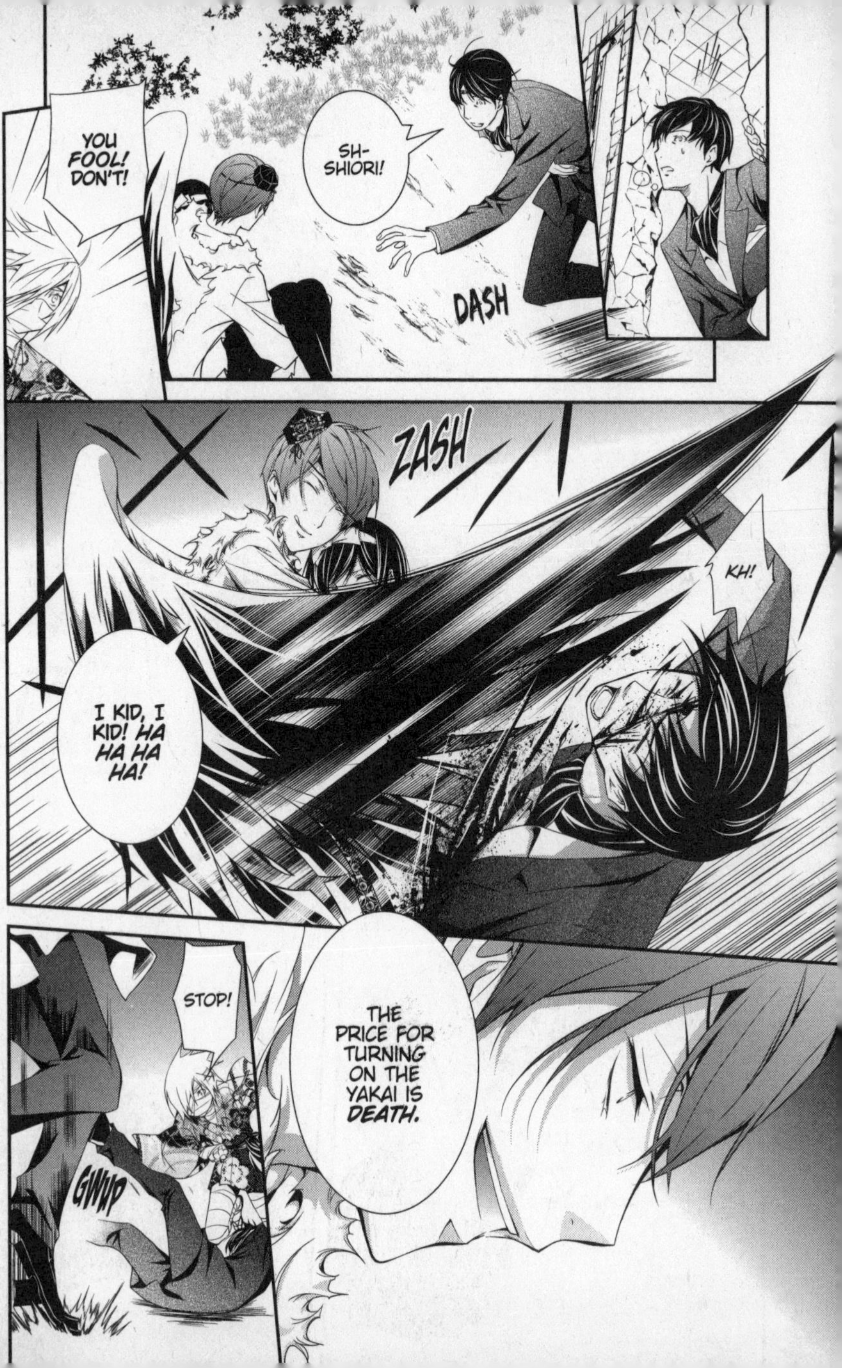
SH-SHIORI!
DASH
YOU FOOL! DON'T!
ZASH
KH!
I KID, I KID! HA HA HA HA!
THE PRICE FOR TURNING ON THE YAKAI IS DEATH.
STOP!
GWUP

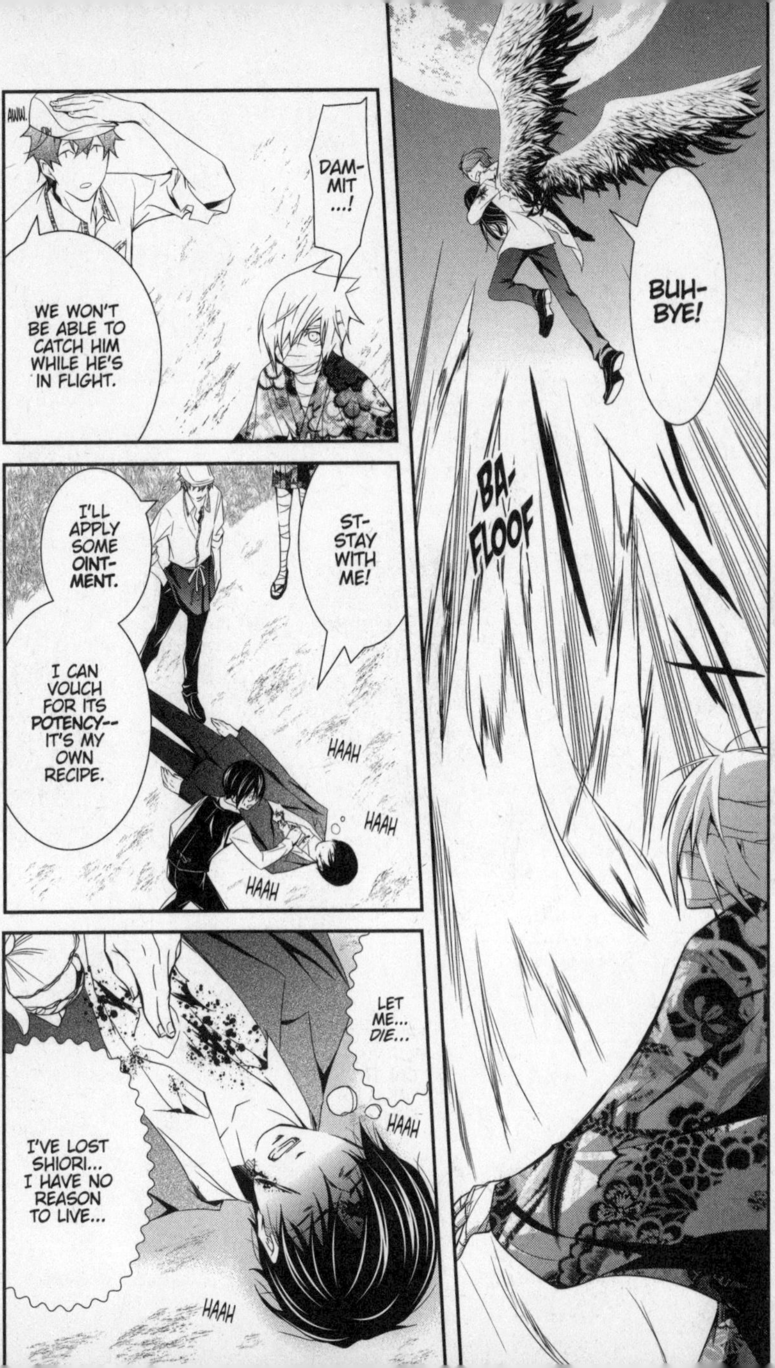
BUH-BYE!
BA-FLOOF
DAM-MIT ...!
AWW.
WE WON'T BE ABLE TO CATCH HIM WHILE HE'S IN FLIGHT.
ST-STAY WITH ME!
I'LL APPLY SOME OINT-MENT.
I CAN VOUCH FOR ITS POTENCY-- IT'S MY OWN RECIPE.
HAAH
HAAH
HAAH
LET ME... DIE...
HAAH
I'VE LOST SHIORI... I HAVE NO REASON TO LIVE...
HAAH

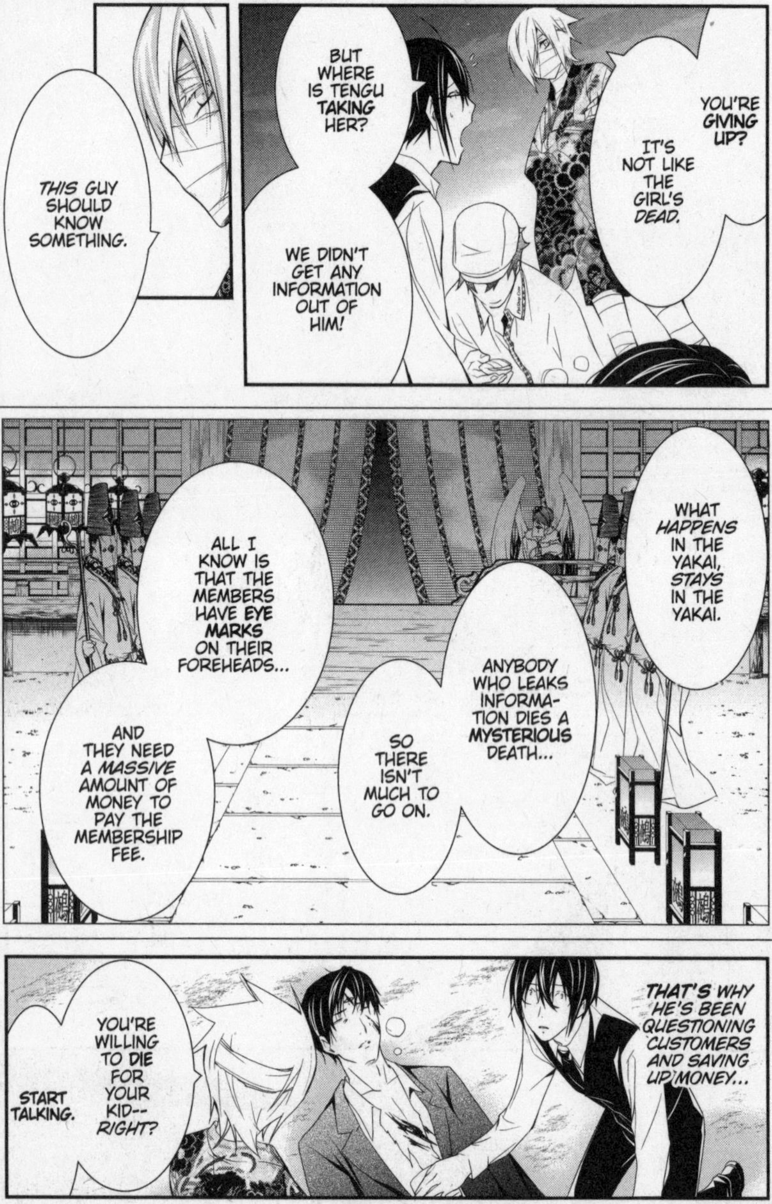
YOU'RE GIVING UP?
IT'S NOT LIKE THE GIRL'S DEAD.
BUT WHERE IS TENGU TAKING HER?
WE DIDN'T GET ANY INFORMATION OUT OF HIM!
THIS GUY SHOULD KNOW SOMETHING.
WHAT HAPPENS IN THE YAKAI, STAYS IN THE YAKAI.
ANYBODY WHO LEAKS INFORMATION DIES A MYSTERIOUS DEATH...
SO THERE ISN'T MUCH TO GO ON.
ALL I KNOW IS THAT THE MEMBERS HAVE EYE MARKS ON THEIR FOREHEADS...
AND THEY NEED A MASSIVE AMOUNT OF MONEY TO PAY THE MEMBERSHIP FEE.
THAT'S WHY HE'S BEEN QUESTIONING CUSTOMERS AND SAVING UP MONEY...
YOU'RE WILLING TO DIE FOR YOUR KID-- RIGHT?
START TALKING.

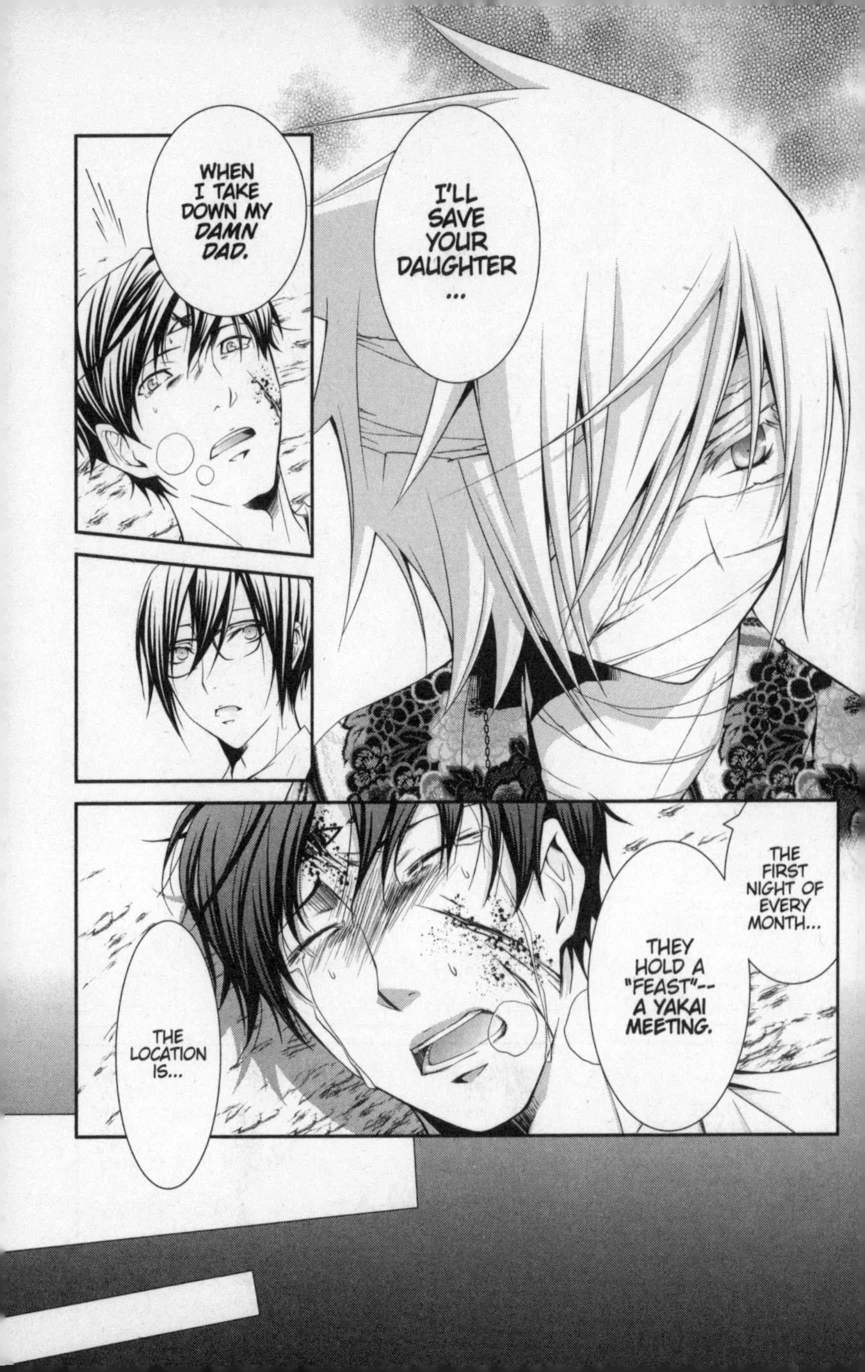
I'LL SAVE YOUR DAUGHTER ...
WHEN I TAKE DOWN MY DAMN DAD.
THE FIRST NIGHT OF EVERY MONTH...
THEY HOLD A "FEAST"-- A YAKAI MEETING.
THE LOCATION IS...

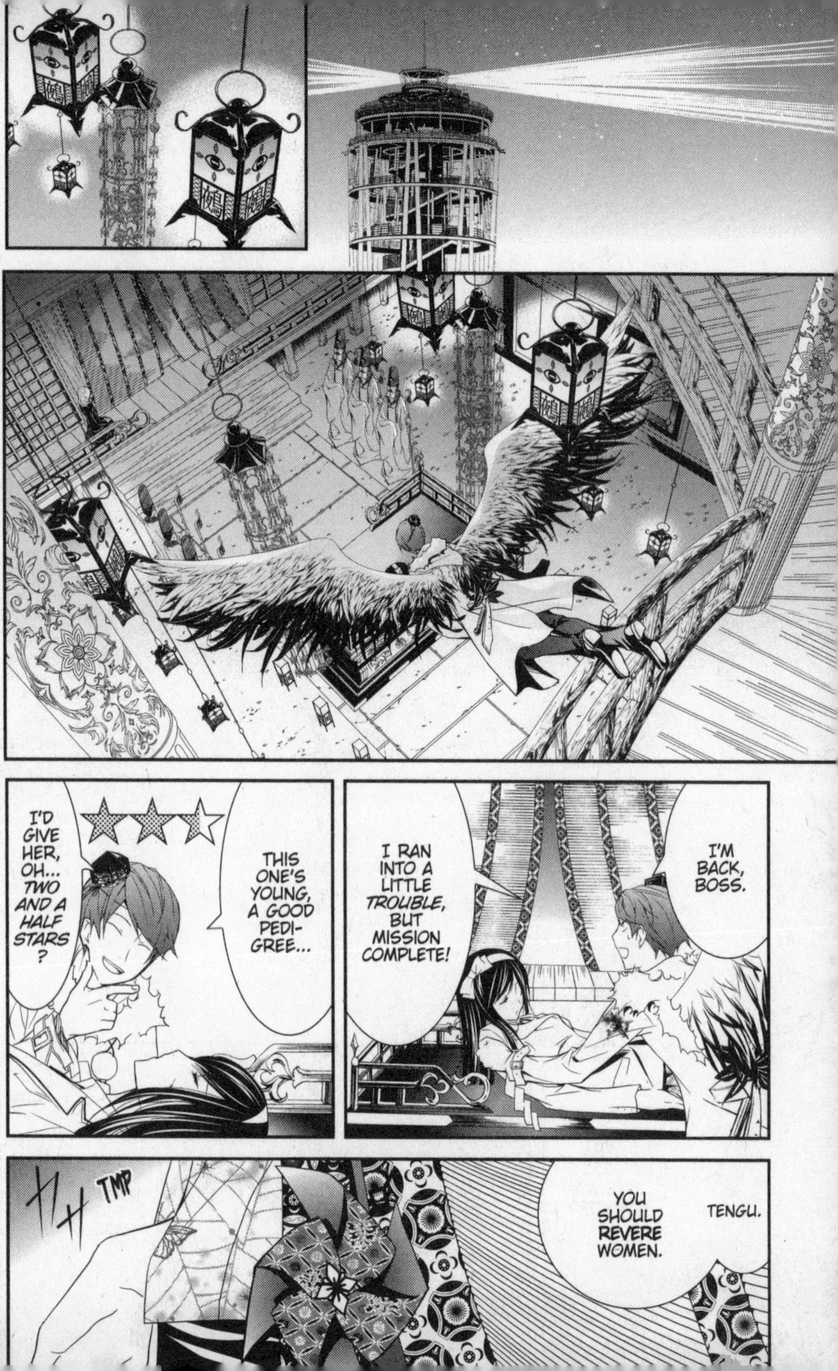
I'M BACK, BOSS.
I RAN INTO A LITTLE TROUBLE, BUT MISSION COMPLETE!
THIS ONE'S YOUNG, A GOOD PEDIGREE...
I'D GIVE HER, OH... TWO AND A HALF STARS?
TENGU.
YOU SHOULD REVERE WOMEN.
TMP

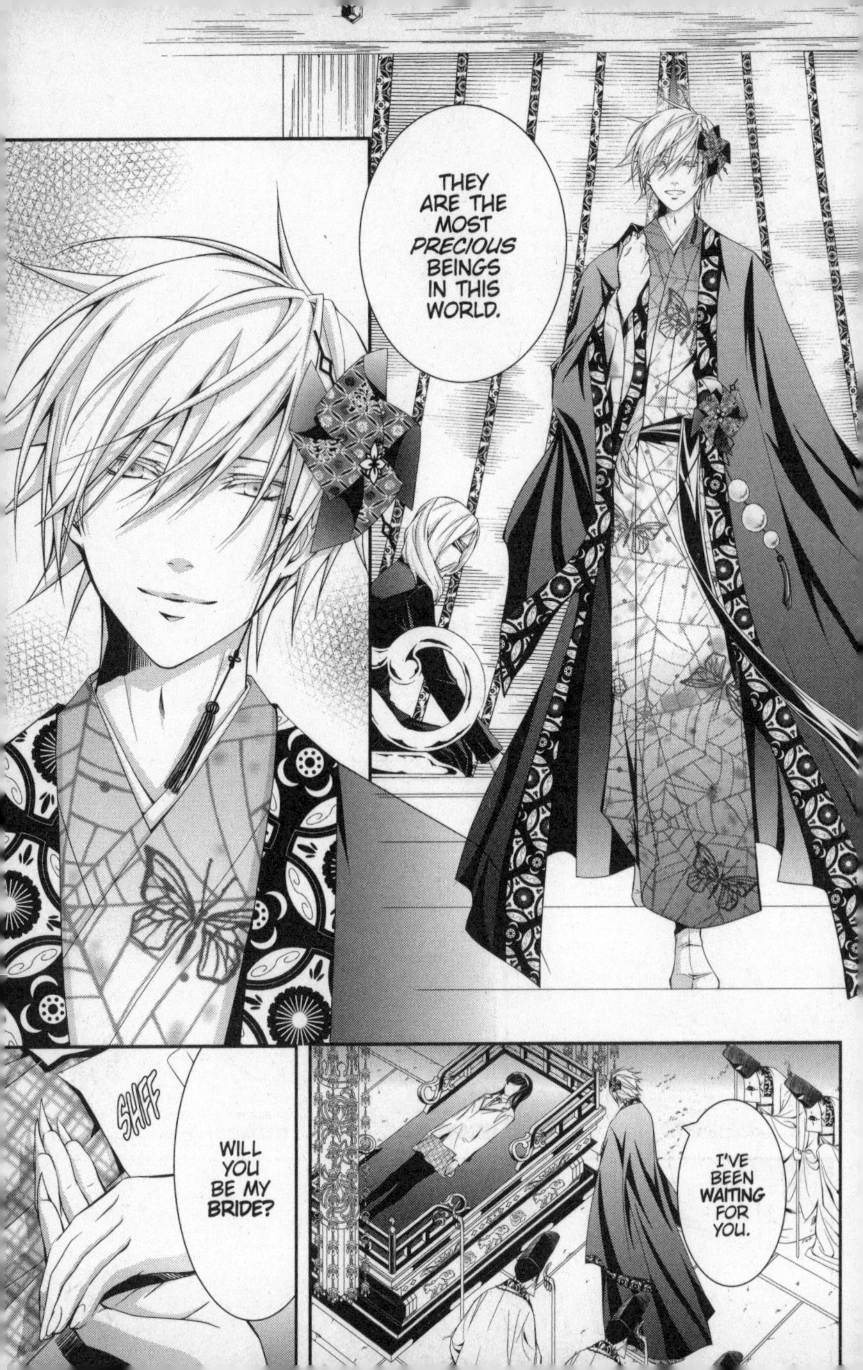
THEY ARE THE MOST *PRECIOUS* BEINGS IN THIS WORLD.
I'VE BEEN WAITING FOR YOU.
SHFF
WILL YOU BE MY BRIDE?

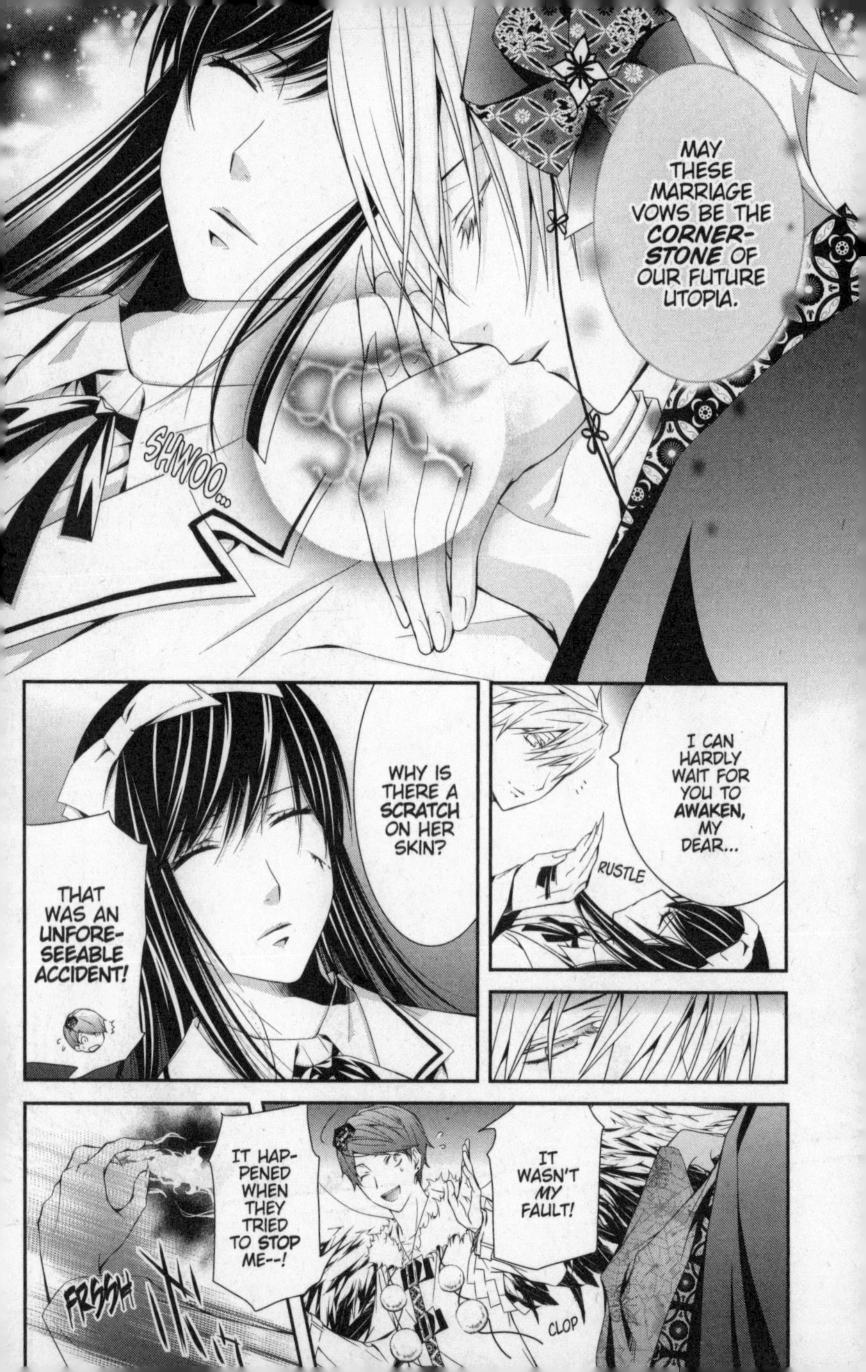
MAY THESE MARRIAGE VOWS BE THE CORNER-STONE OF OUR FUTURE UTOPIA.
SHWOO...
I CAN HARDLY WAIT FOR YOU TO AWAKEN, MY DEAR...
RUSTLE
WHY IS THERE A SCRATCH ON HER SKIN?
THAT WAS AN UNFORE-SEEABLE ACCIDENT!
IT WASN'T MY FAULT!
IT HAP-PENED WHEN THEY TRIED TO STOP ME--!
CLOP
FRSSH

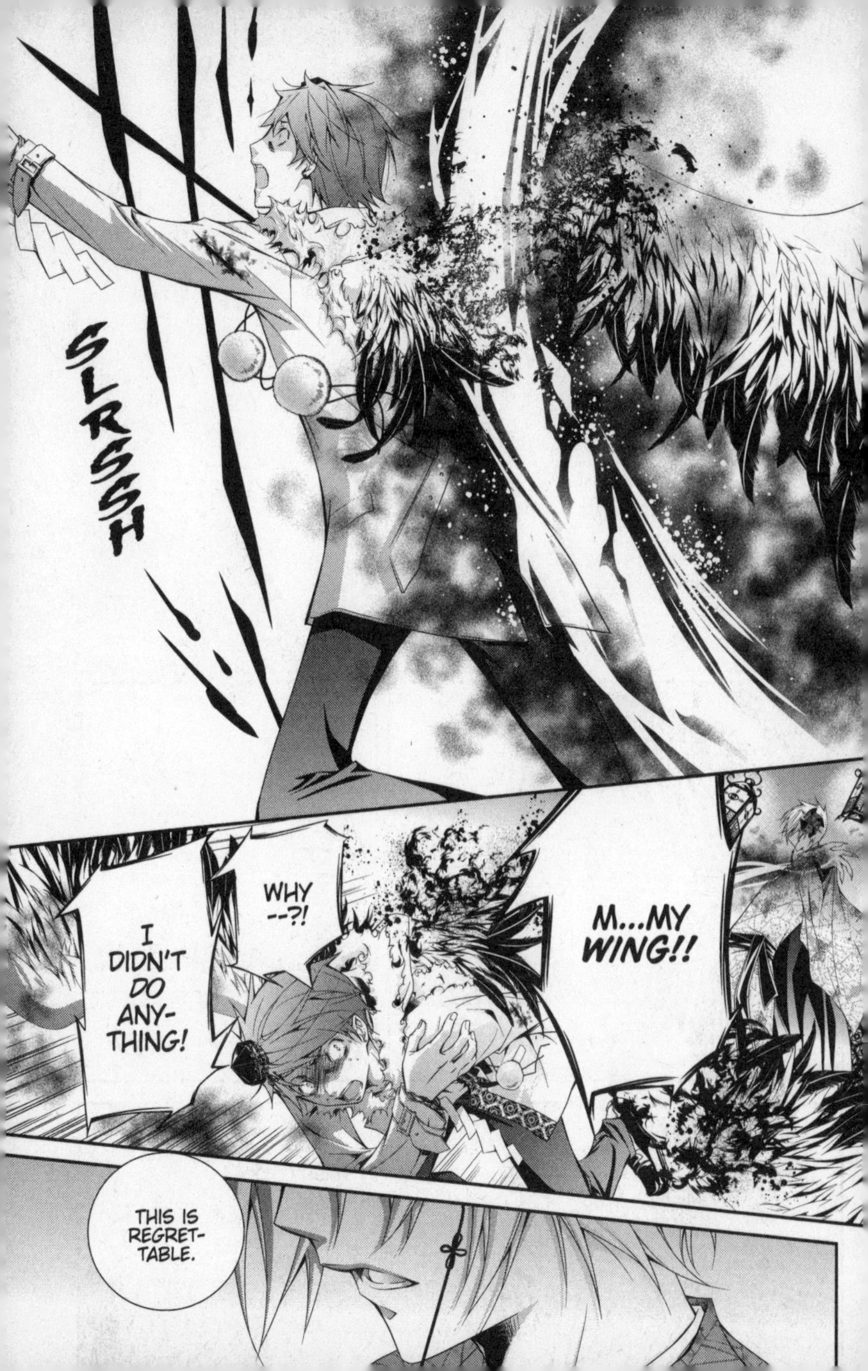
SLRSSH
M...MY WING!!
WHY --?!
I DIDN'T DO ANYTHING!
THIS IS REGRET-TABLE.

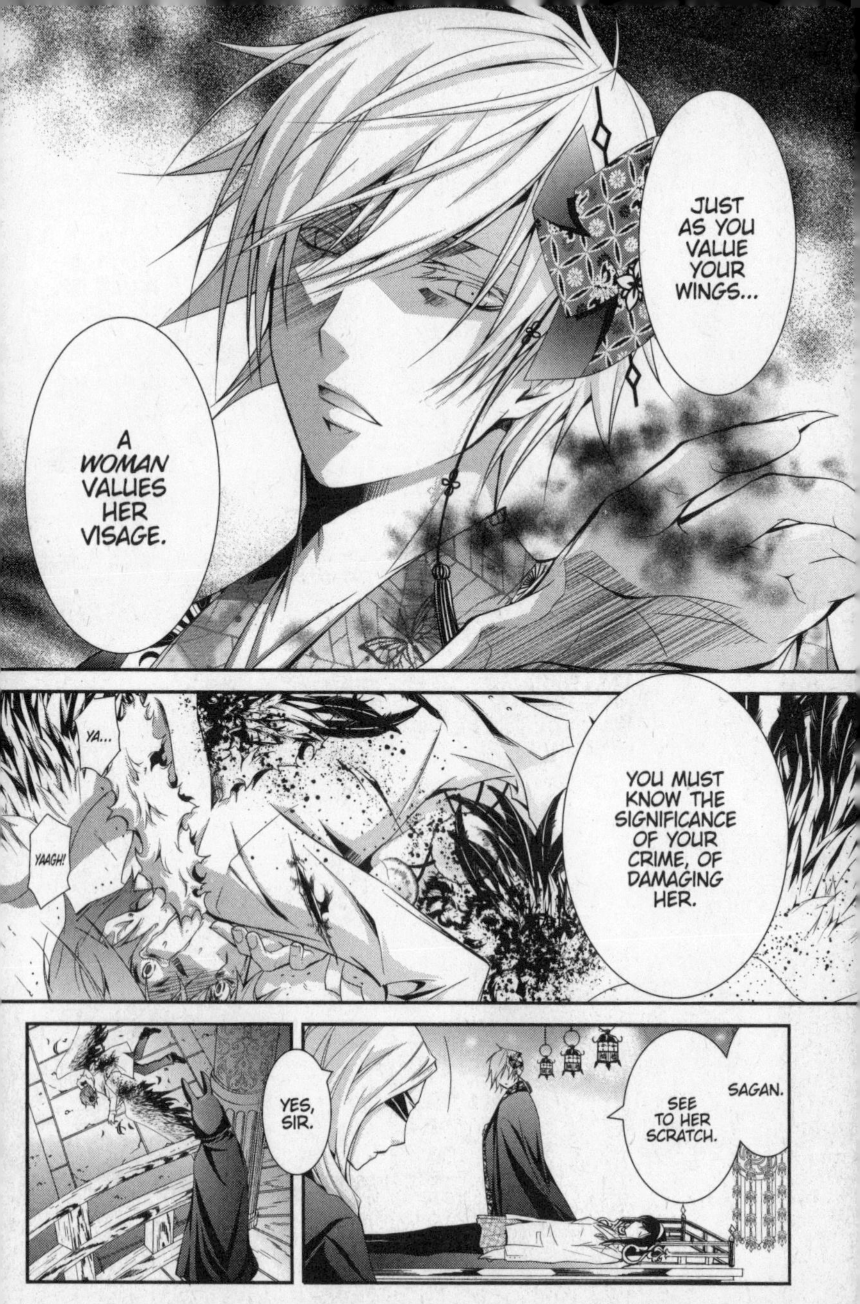
JUST AS YOU VALUE YOUR WINGS...
A WOMAN VALUES HER VISAGE.
YOU MUST KNOW THE SIGNIFICANCE OF YOUR CRIME, OF DAMAGING HER.
YA...
YAAGH!
SAGAN.
SEE TO HER SCRATCH.
YES, SIR.

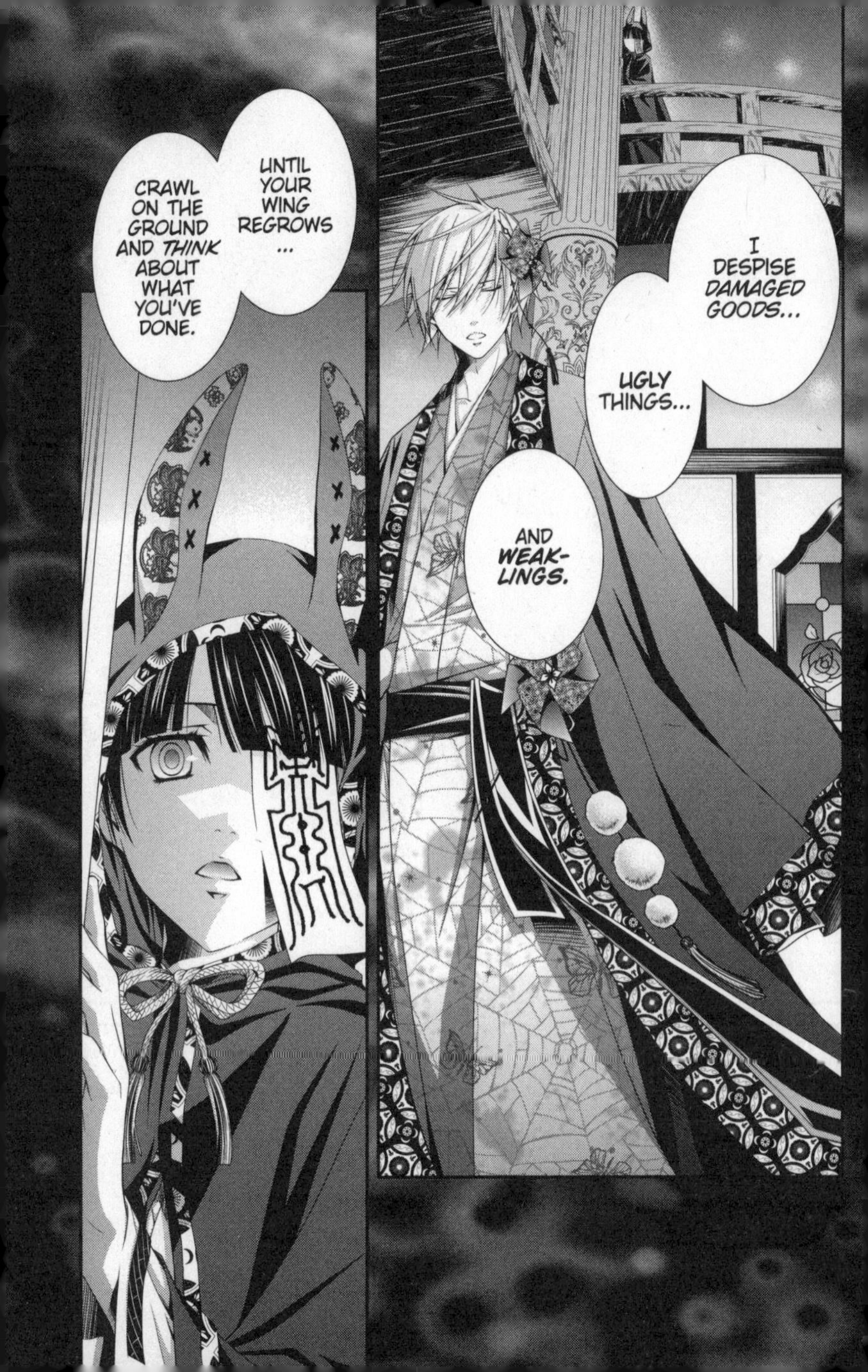
I DESPISE DAMAGED GOODS...
UGLY THINGS...
AND WEAK-LINGS.
UNTIL YOUR WING REGROWS ...
CRAWL ON THE GROUND AND THINK ABOUT WHAT YOU'VE DONE.

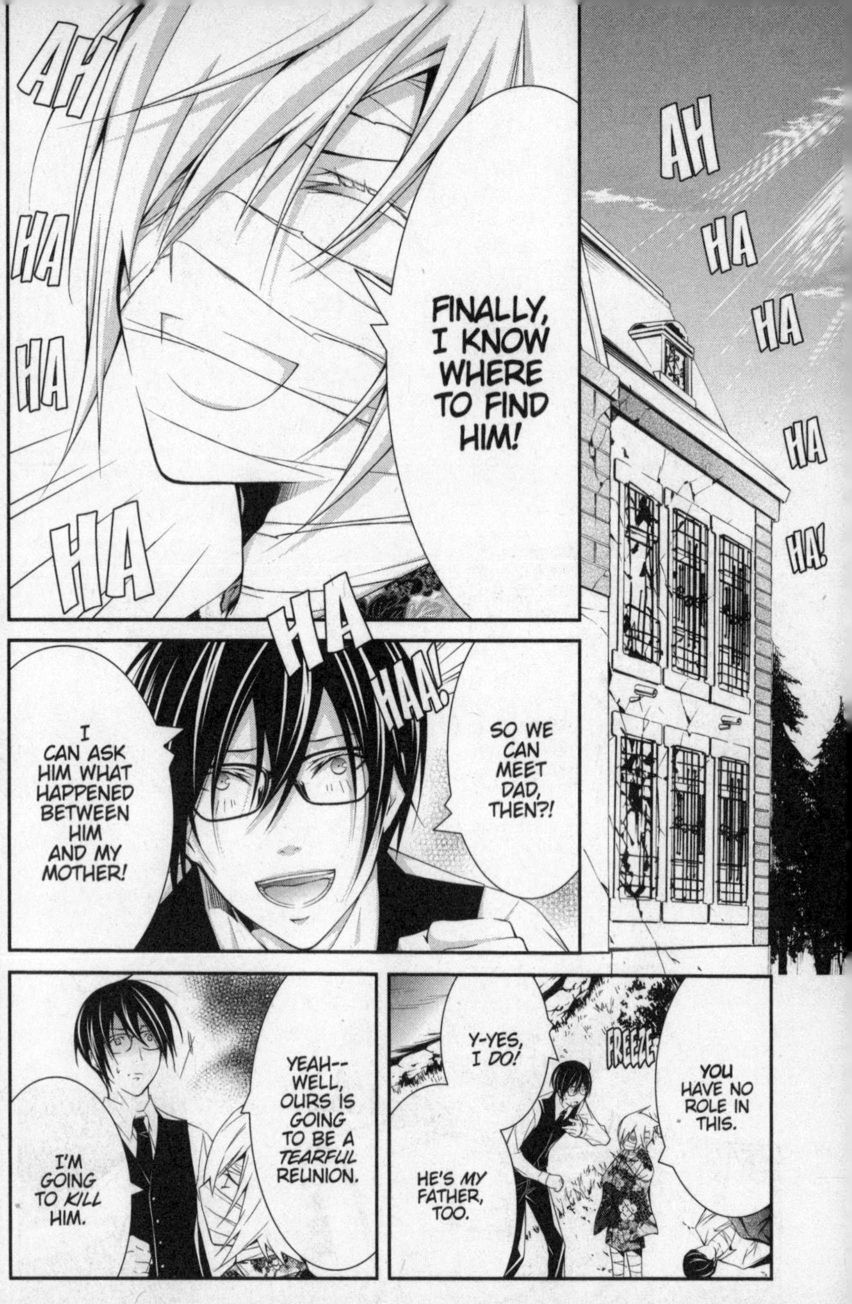
AH
HA
HA
HA
HA!
FINALLY, I KNOW WHERE TO FIND HIM!
AH
HA
HA
HA
HA
HAA!
SO WE CAN MEET DAD, THEN?!
I CAN ASK HIM WHAT HAPPENED BETWEEN HIM AND MY MOTHER!
YOU HAVE NO ROLE IN THIS.
FREEZE
Y-YES, I DO!
HE'S *MY* FATHER, TOO.
YEAH--WELL, OURS IS GOING TO BE A *TEARFUL* REUNION.
I'M GOING TO *KILL* HIM.

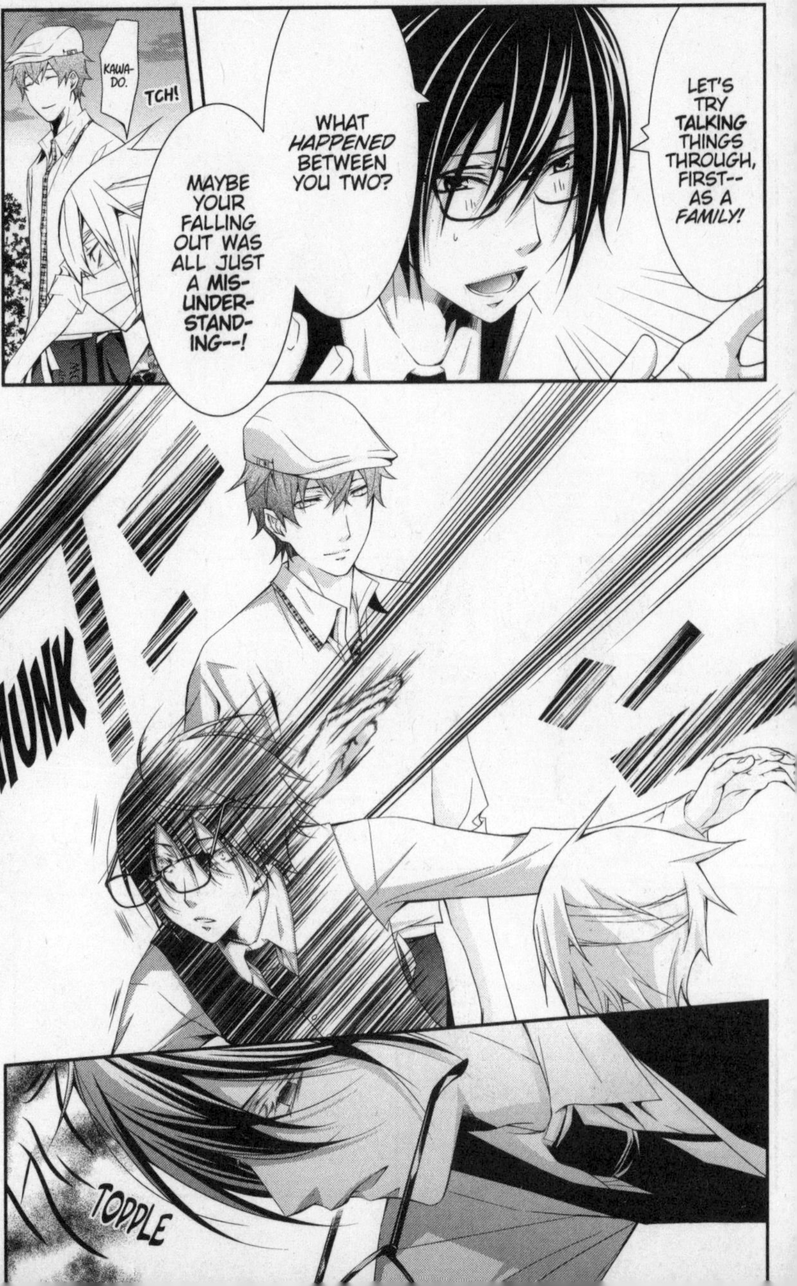

LET'S TRY TALKING THINGS THROUGH, FIRST-- AS A FAMILY!
WHAT HAPPENED BETWEEN YOU TWO?
MAYBE YOUR FALLING OUT WAS ALL JUST A MIS-UNDER-STAND-ING--!
KAWA-DO.
TCH!
WHUNK
TOPPLE

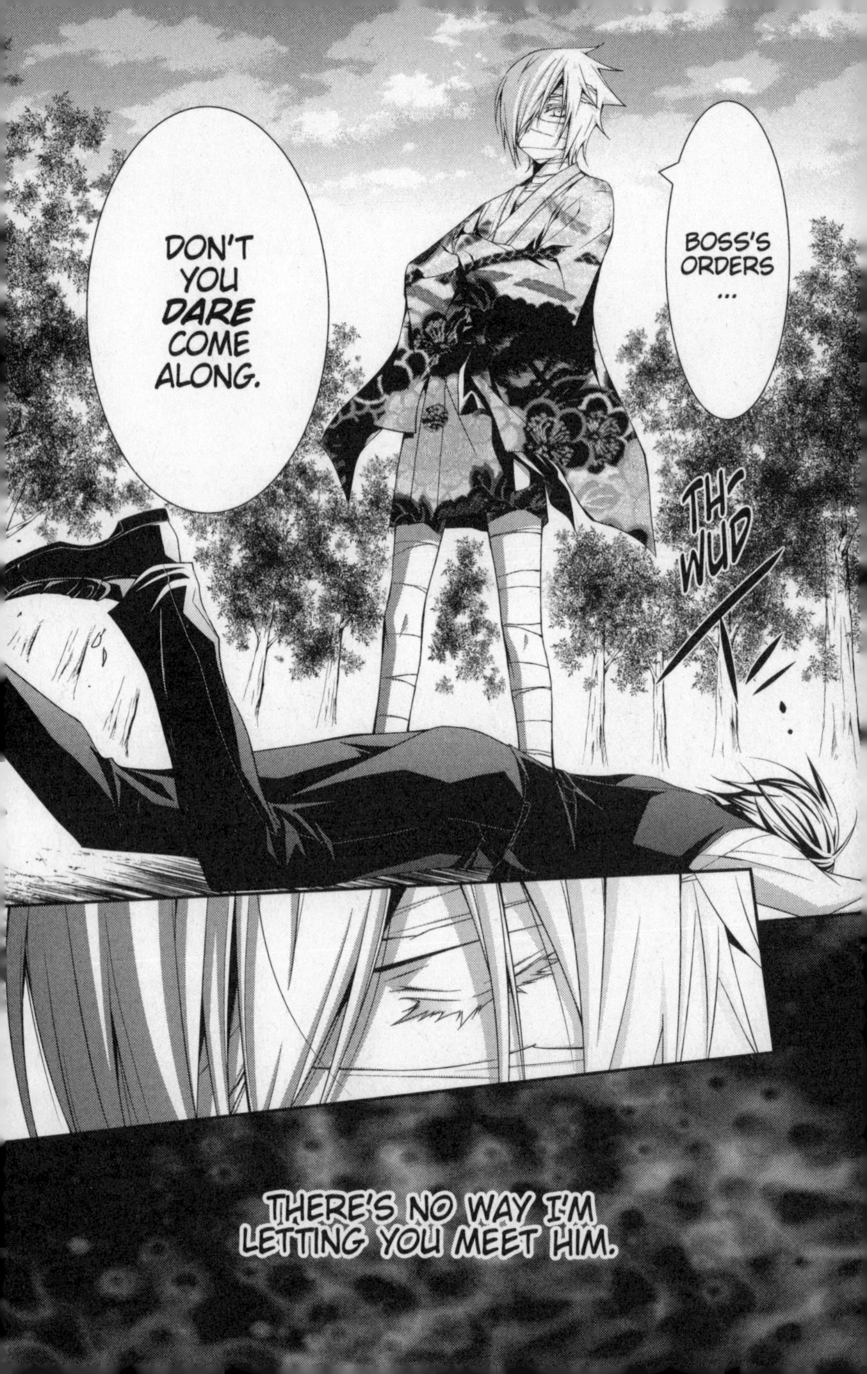
BOSS'S ORDERS ...
DON'T YOU DARE COME ALONG.
TH-WUD
THERE'S NO WAY I'M LETTING YOU MEET HIM.

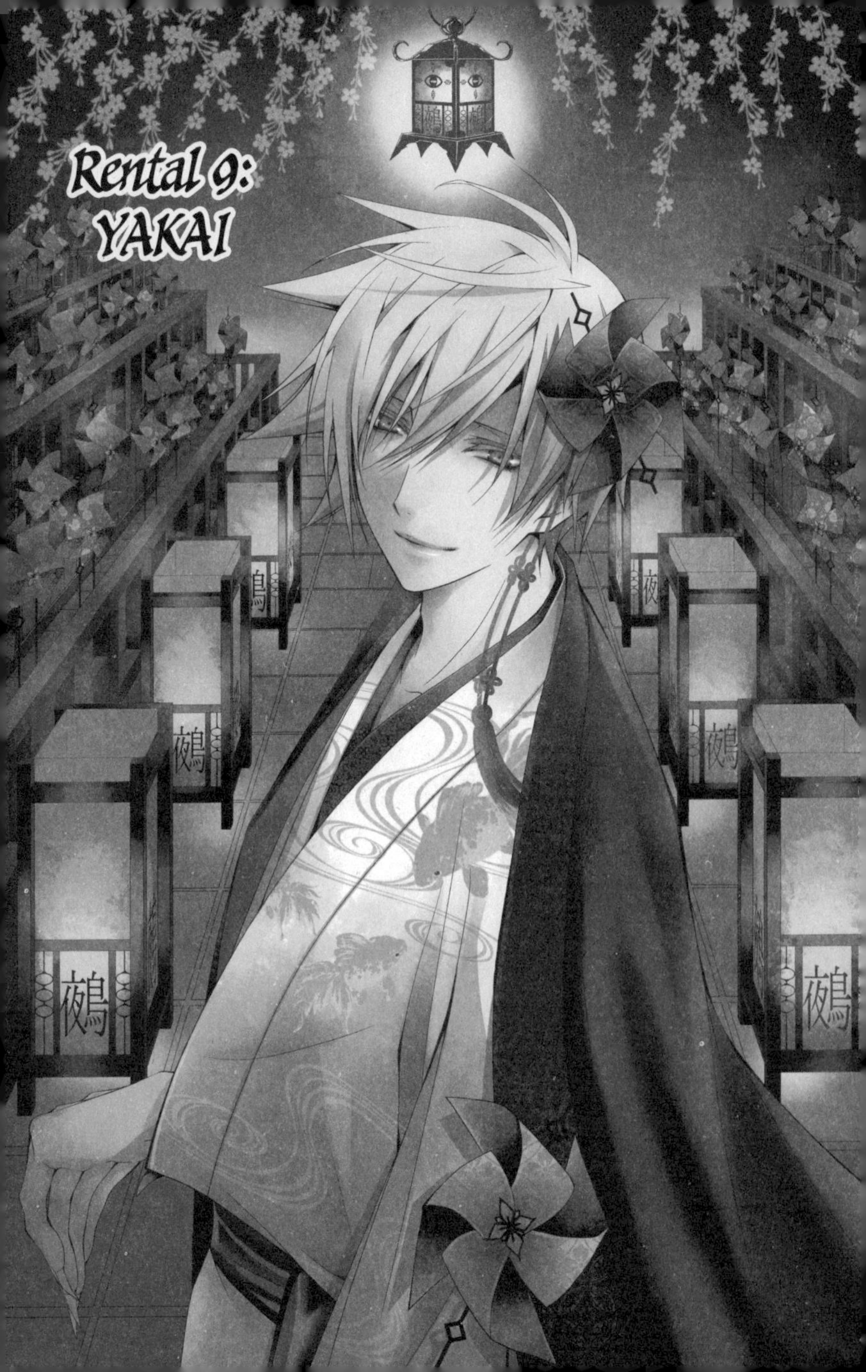
Rental 9:
YAKAI

Yōkai Rental Shop

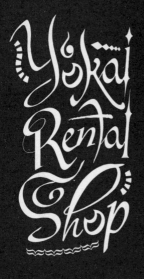

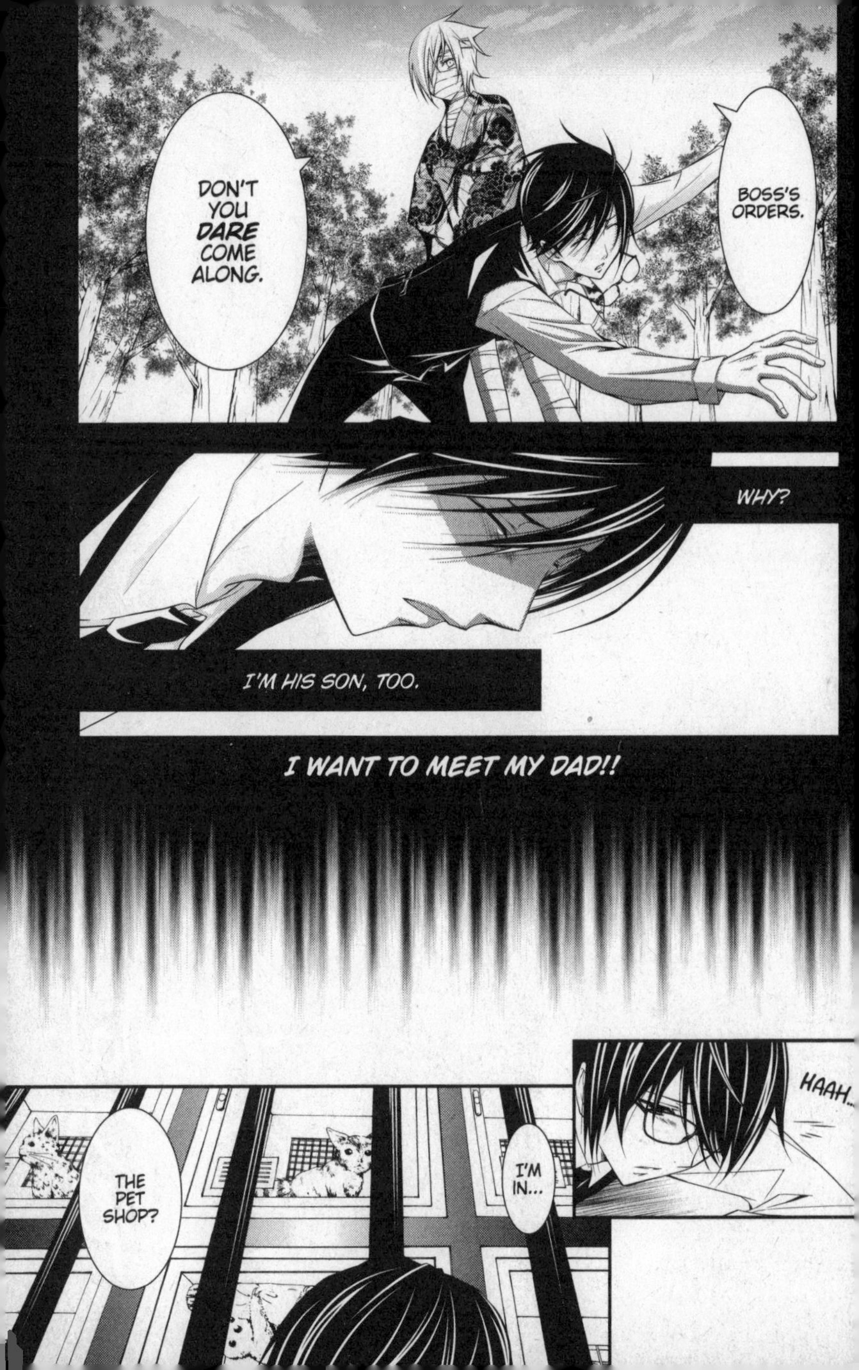
BOSS'S ORDERS.
DON'T YOU DARE COME ALONG.
WHY?
I'M HIS SON, TOO.
I WANT TO MEET MY DAD!!
HAAH...
I'M IN...
THE PET SHOP?

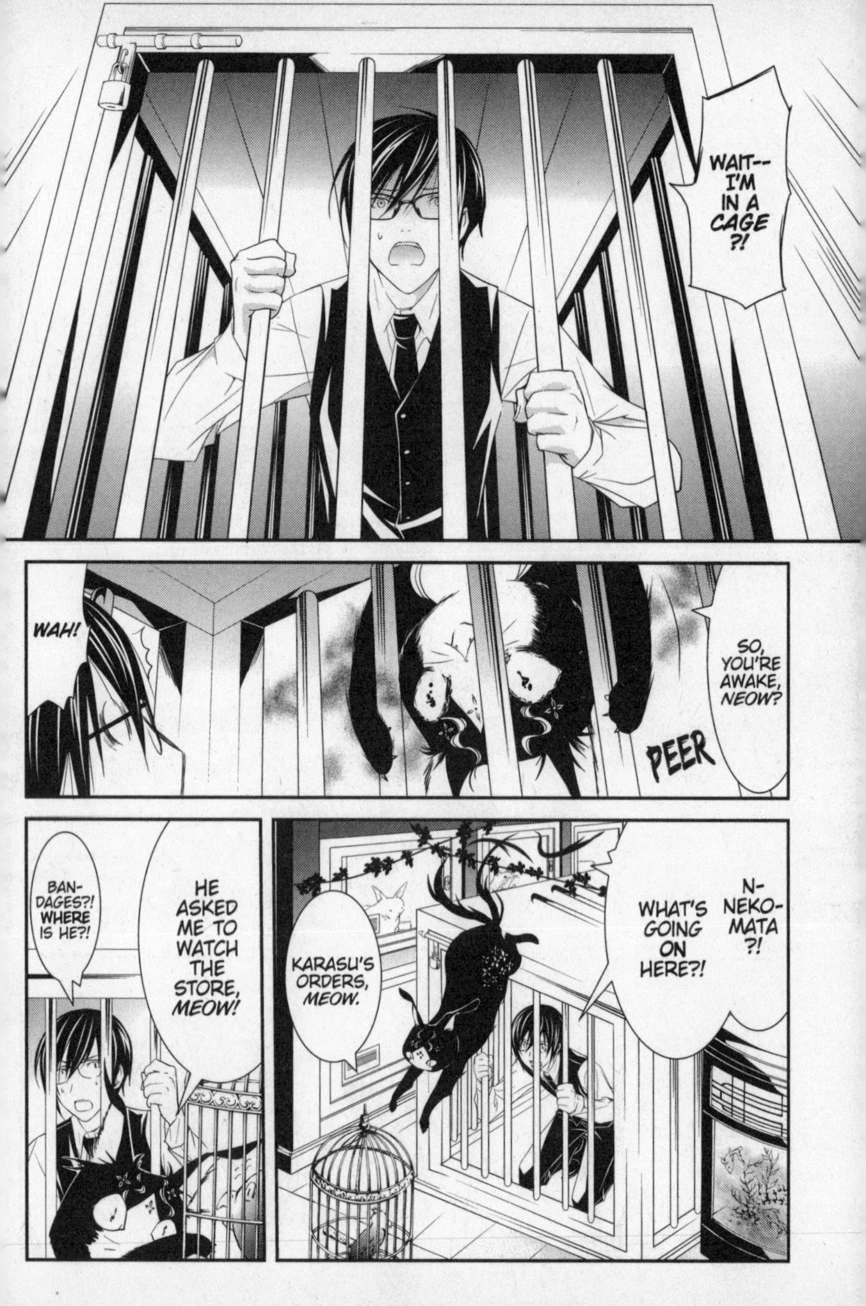
WAIT-- I'M IN A CAGE?!
SO, YOU'RE AWAKE, *NEOW?*
PEER
WAH!
N-NEKO-MATA?!
WHAT'S GOING ON HERE?!
KARASU'S ORDERS, *MEOW.*
HE ASKED ME TO WATCH THE STORE, *MEOW!*
BAN-DAGES?! WHERE IS HE?!

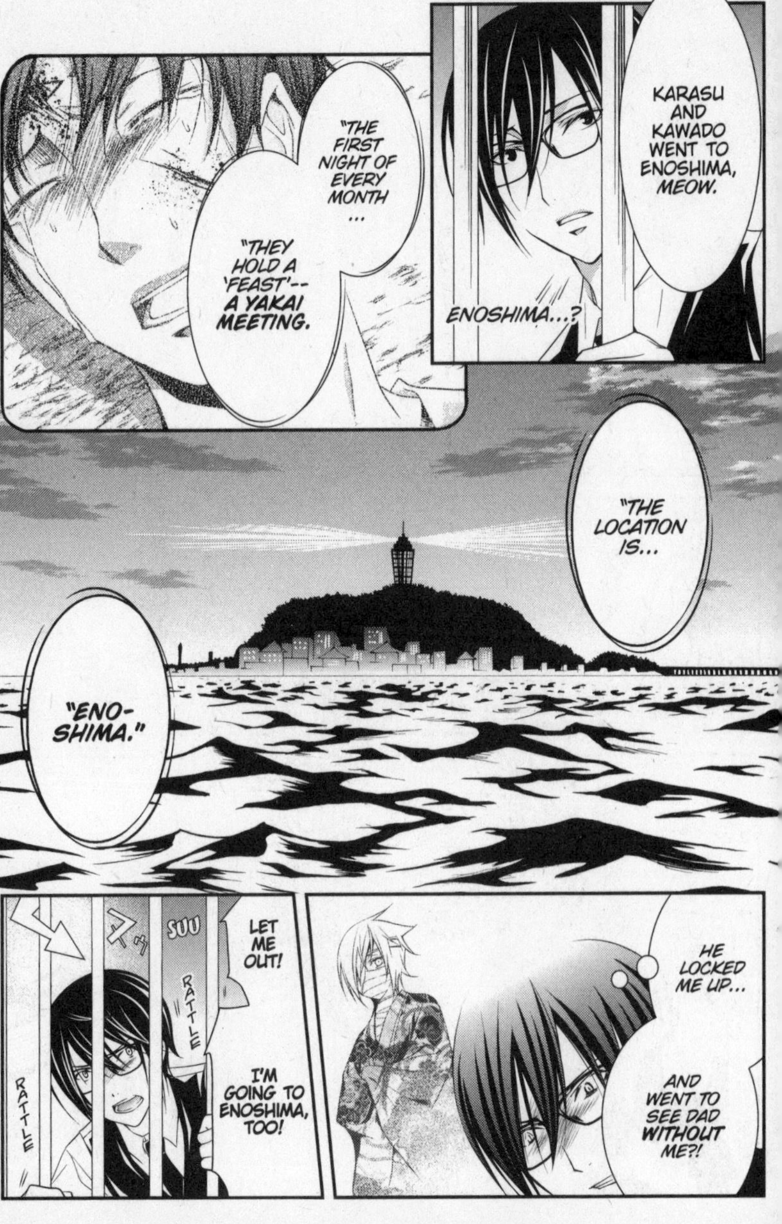
KARASU AND KAWADO WENT TO ENOSHIMA, MEOW.
ENOSHIMA...?
"THE FIRST NIGHT OF EVERY MONTH ...
"THEY HOLD A 'FEAST'-- A YAKAI MEETING.
"THE LOCATION IS...
"ENO-SHIMA."
HE LOCKED ME UP...
AND WENT TO SEE DAD WITHOUT ME?!
スッ
SUU
LET ME OUT!
RATTLE
I'M GOING TO ENOSHIMA, TOO!
RATTLE

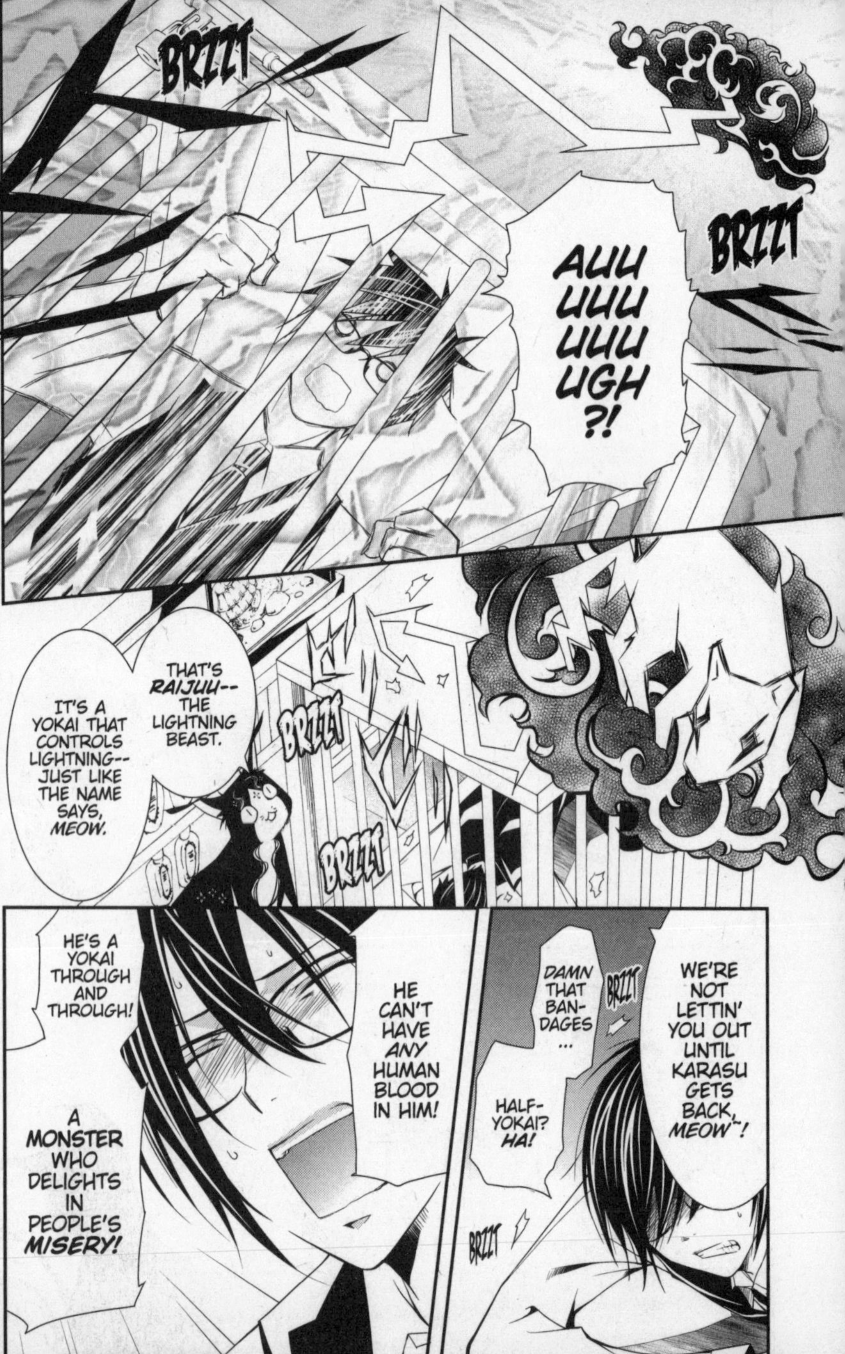
BRZZT
AUUUUUUUUUUGH?!
BRZZT
THAT'S *RAIJUU*-- THE LIGHTNING BEAST.
IT'S A YOKAI THAT CONTROLS LIGHTNING-- JUST LIKE THE NAME SAYS, *MEOW.*
BRZZT
BRZZT
WE'RE NOT LETTIN' YOU OUT UNTIL KARASU GETS BACK, *MEOW*~!
DAMN THAT BANDAGES...
BRZZT
HALF-YOKAI? *HA!*
BRZZT
HE CAN'T HAVE *ANY* HUMAN BLOOD IN HIM!
HE'S A YOKAI THROUGH AND THROUGH!
A MONSTER WHO DELIGHTS IN PEOPLE'S *MISERY!*

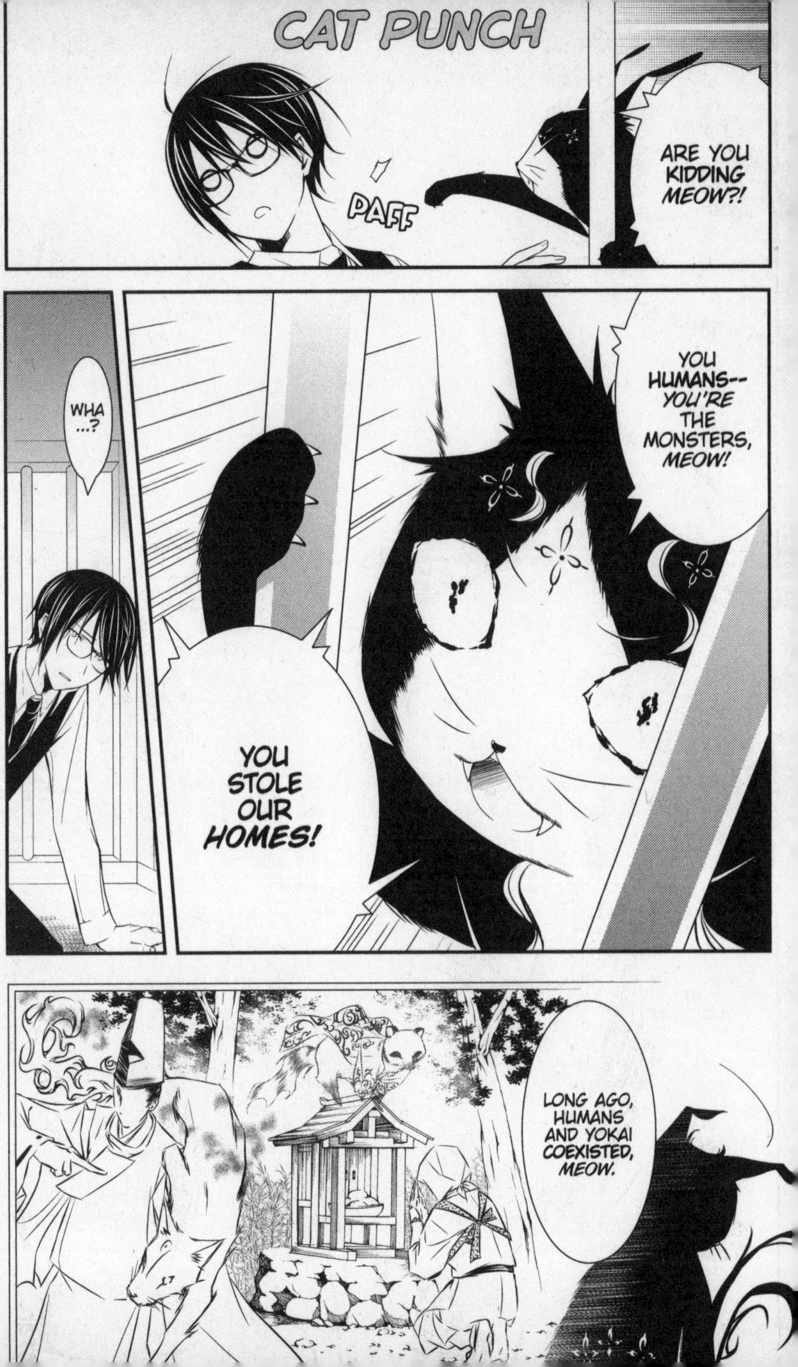
CAT PUNCH
ARE YOU KIDDING MEOW?!
PAFF
YOU HUMANS-- YOU'RE THE MONSTERS, MEOW!
YOU STOLE OUR HOMES!
WHA ...?
LONG AGO, HUMANS AND YOKAI COEXISTED, MEOW.

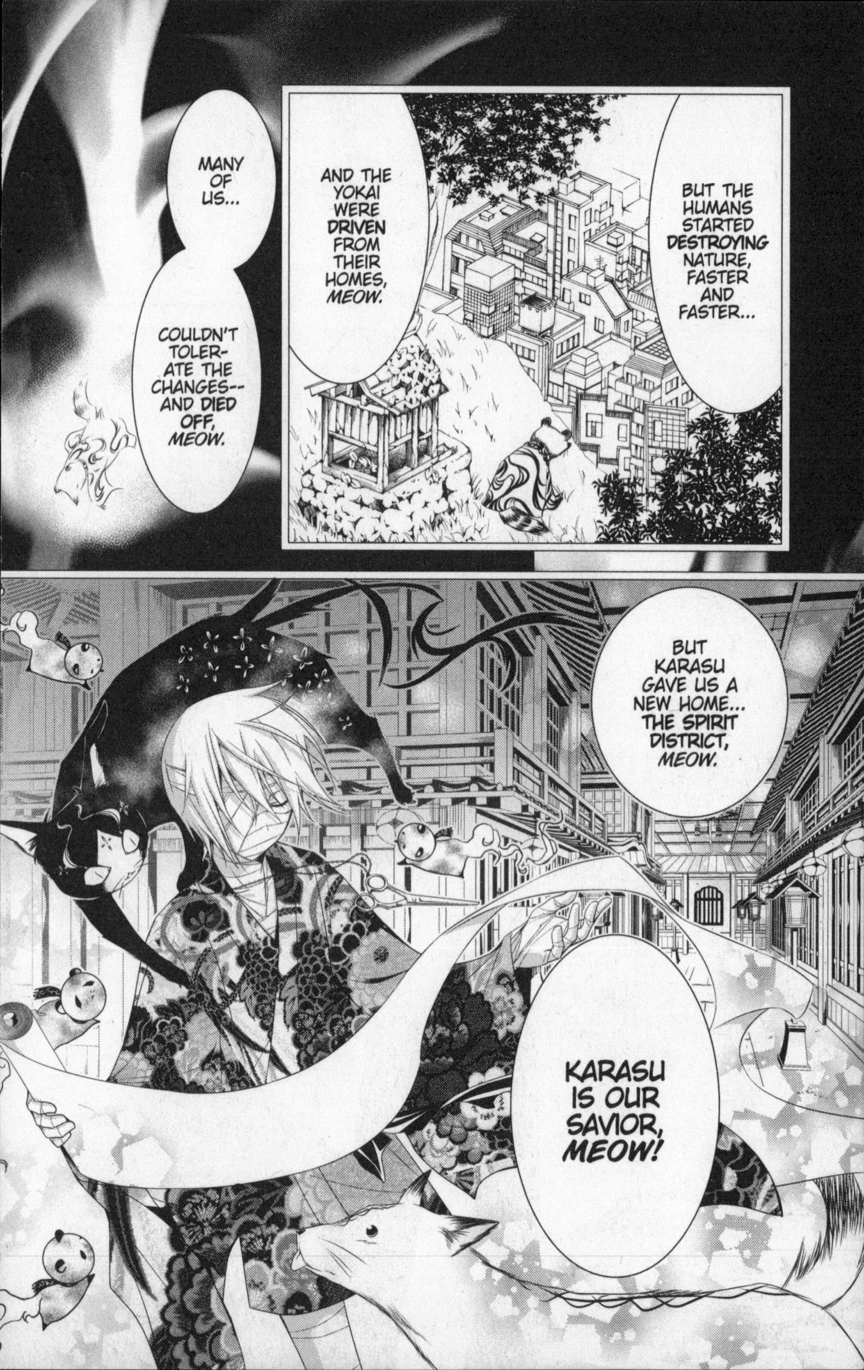
BUT THE HUMANS STARTED DESTROYING NATURE, FASTER AND FASTER...
AND THE YOKAI WERE DRIVEN FROM THEIR HOMES, MEOW.
MANY OF US...
COULDN'T TOLER-ATE THE CHANGES--AND DIED OFF, MEOW.
BUT KARASU GAVE US A NEW HOME... THE SPIRIT DISTRICT, MEOW.
KARASU IS OUR SAVIOR, MEOW!

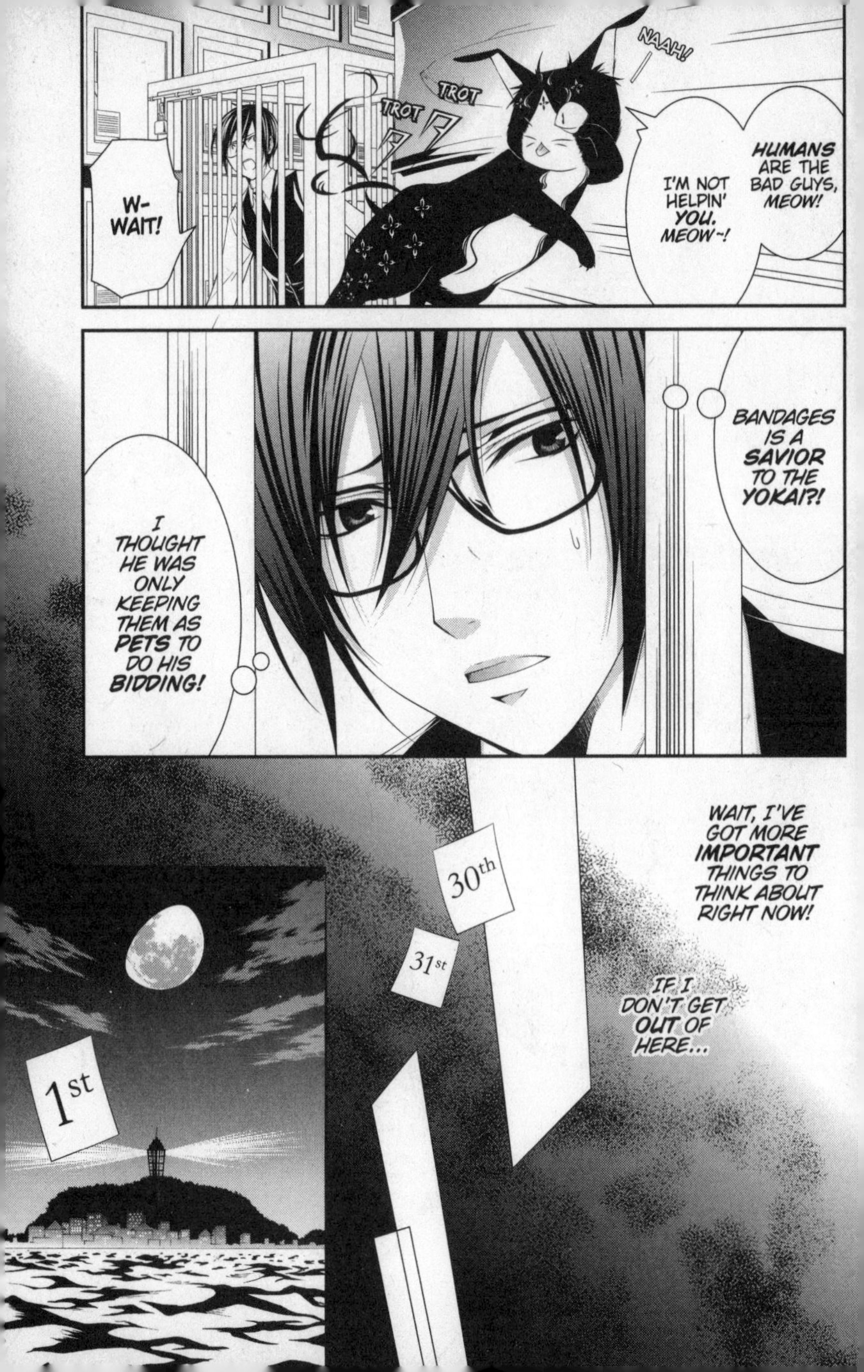
NAAH!
HUMANS ARE THE BAD GUYS, MEOW!
I'M NOT HELPIN' YOU. MEOW~!
TROT
TROT
W-WAIT!
BANDAGES IS A SAVIOR TO THE YOKAI?!
I THOUGHT HE WAS ONLY KEEPING THEM AS PETS TO DO HIS BIDDING!
WAIT, I'VE GOT MORE IMPORTANT THINGS TO THINK ABOUT RIGHT NOW!
30th
31st
IF I DON'T GET OUT OF HERE...
1st

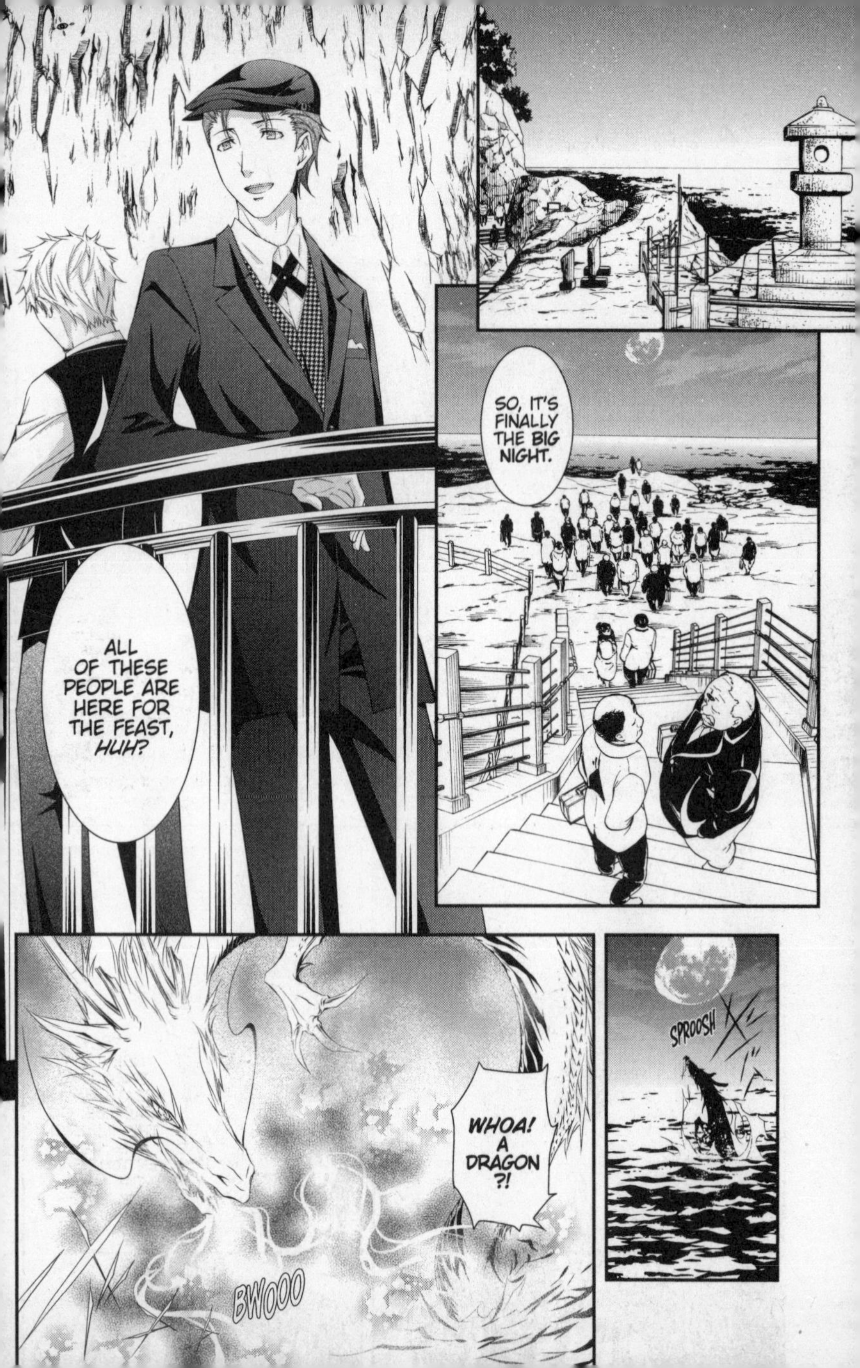
SO, IT'S FINALLY THE BIG NIGHT.
ALL OF THESE PEOPLE ARE HERE FOR THE FEAST, *HUH?*
SPROOSH
WHOA! A DRAGON ?!
BWOOO

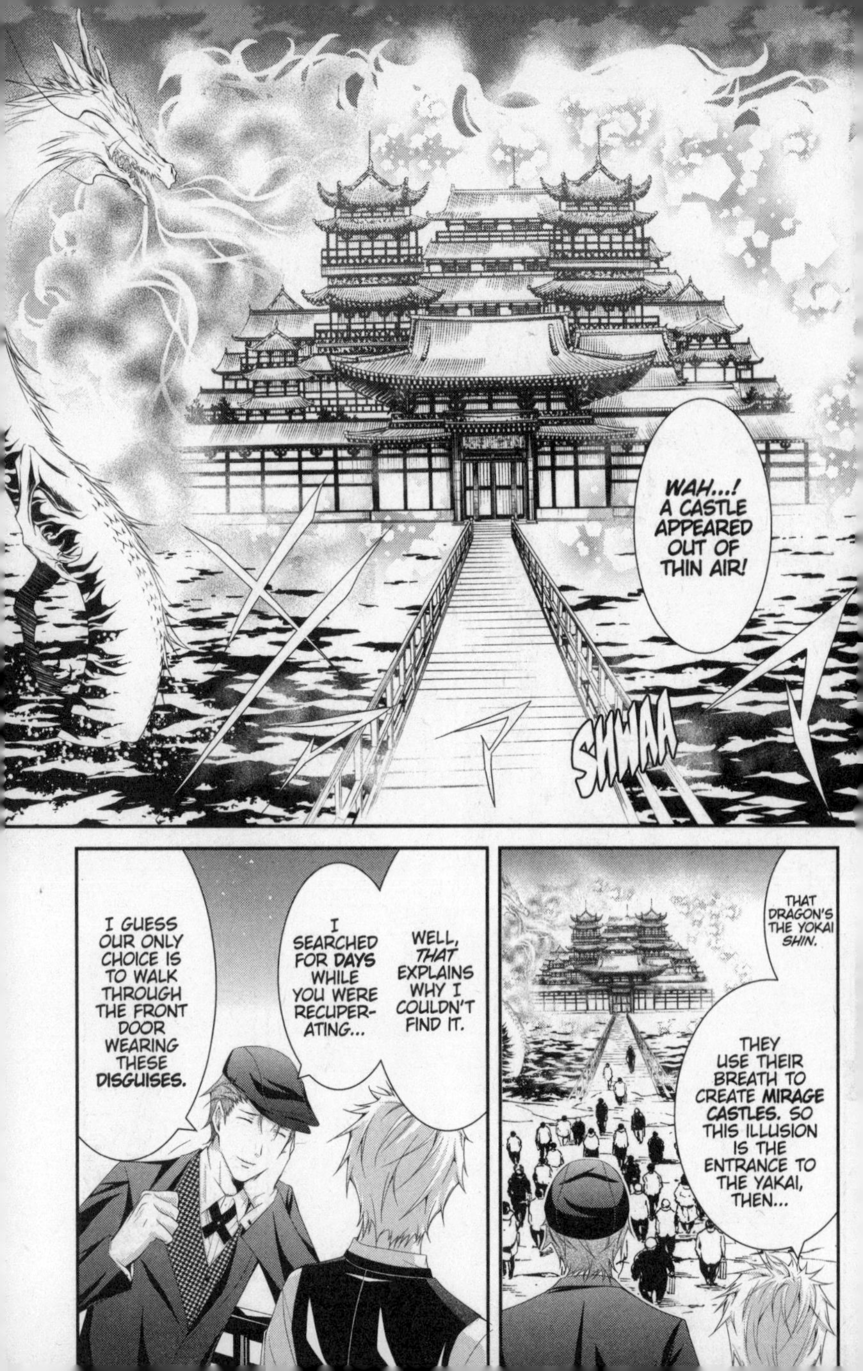
WAH...! A CASTLE APPEARED OUT OF THIN AIR!
SHWAA
THAT DRAGON'S THE YOKAI SHIN.
THEY USE THEIR BREATH TO CREATE MIRAGE CASTLES. SO THIS ILLUSION IS THE ENTRANCE TO THE YAKAI, THEN...
WELL, THAT EXPLAINS WHY I COULDN'T FIND IT.
I SEARCHED FOR DAYS WHILE YOU WERE RECUPERATING...
I GUESS OUR ONLY CHOICE IS TO WALK THROUGH THE FRONT DOOR WEARING THESE DISGUISES.

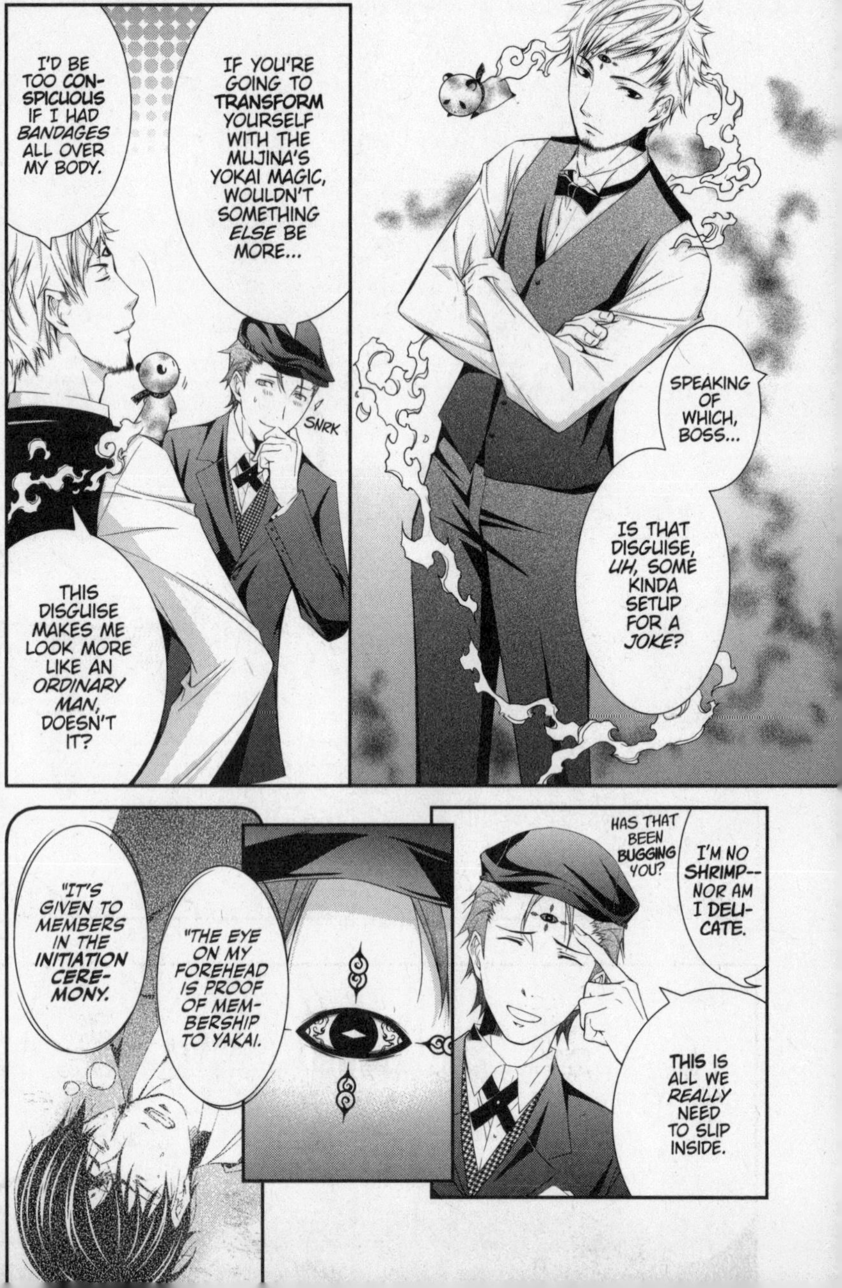
SPEAKING OF WHICH, BOSS...
IS THAT DISGUISE, UH, SOME KINDA SETUP FOR A JOKE?
IF YOU'RE GOING TO TRANSFORM YOURSELF WITH THE MUJINA'S YOKAI MAGIC, WOULDN'T SOMETHING ELSE BE MORE...
I'D BE TOO CONSPICUOUS IF I HAD BANDAGES ALL OVER MY BODY.
SNRK
THIS DISGUISE MAKES ME LOOK MORE LIKE AN ORDINARY MAN, DOESN'T IT?
HAS THAT BEEN BUGGING YOU?
I'M NO SHRIMP--NOR AM I DELICATE.
THIS IS ALL WE REALLY NEED TO SLIP INSIDE.
"THE EYE ON MY FOREHEAD IS PROOF OF MEMBERSHIP TO YAKAI.
"IT'S GIVEN TO MEMBERS IN THE INITIATION CEREMONY.

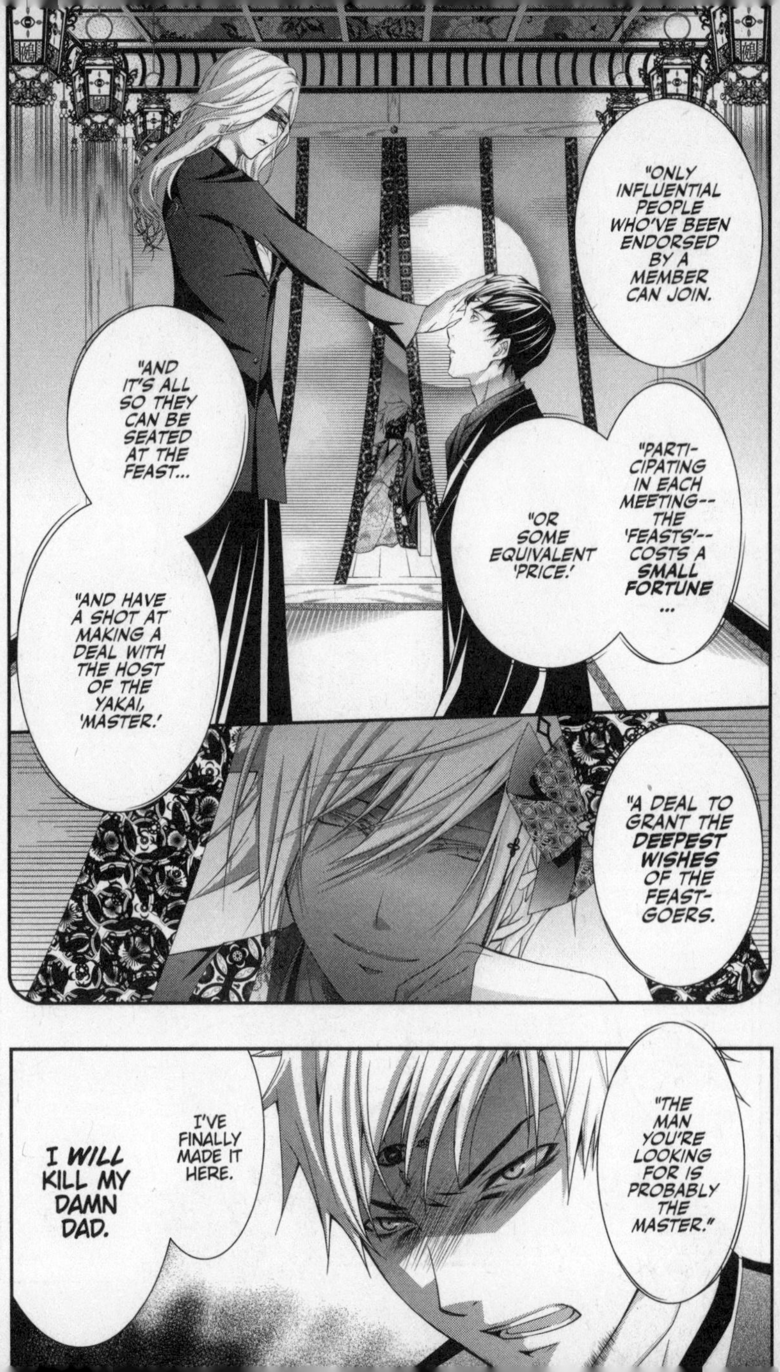
"ONLY INFLUENTIAL PEOPLE WHO'VE BEEN ENDORSED BY A MEMBER CAN JOIN.
"PARTICIPATING IN EACH MEETING--THE 'FEASTS'--COSTS A **SMALL FORTUNE**...
"OR SOME EQUIVALENT 'PRICE.'
"AND IT'S ALL SO THEY CAN BE SEATED AT THE FEAST...
"AND HAVE A SHOT AT MAKING A DEAL WITH THE HOST OF THE YAKAI, 'MASTER.'
"A DEAL TO GRANT THE **DEEPEST WISHES** OF THE FEAST-GOERS.
"THE MAN YOU'RE LOOKING FOR IS PROBABLY THE MASTER."
I'VE FINALLY MADE IT HERE.
I *WILL* KILL MY DAMN DAD.

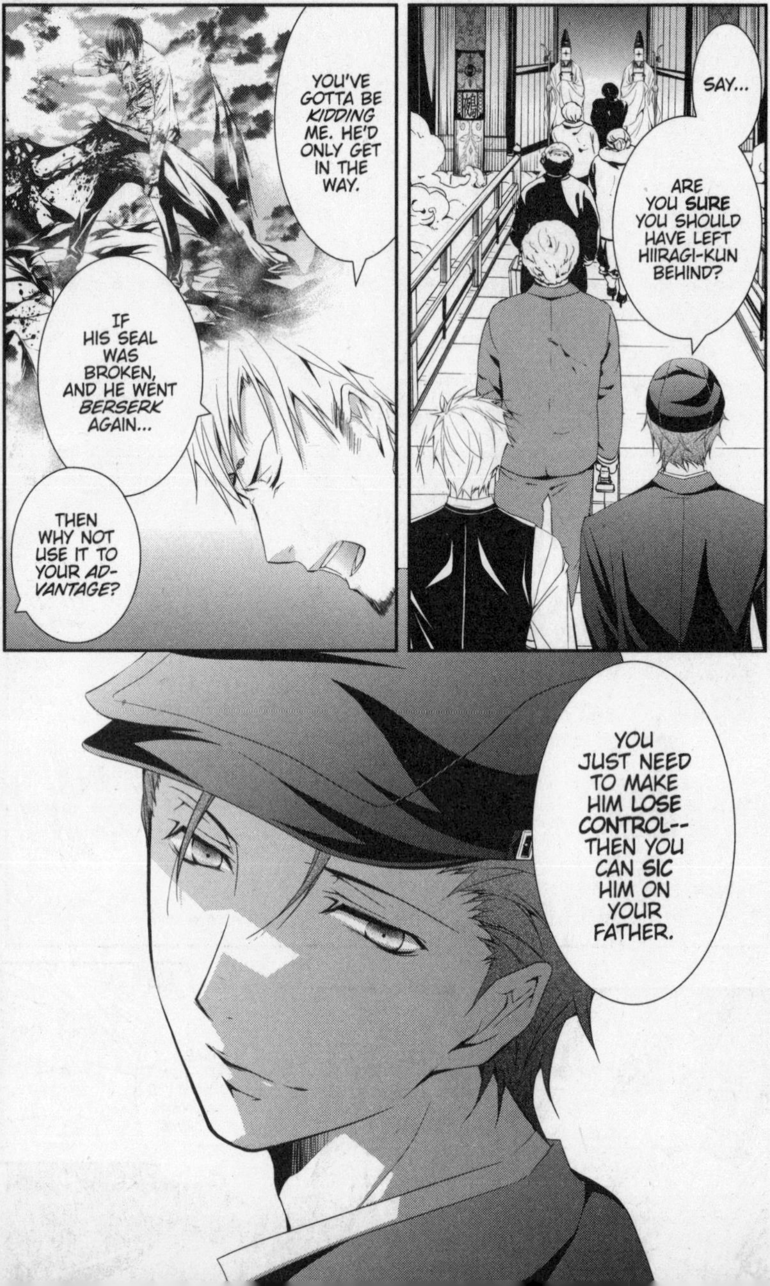
SAY...
ARE YOU SURE YOU SHOULD HAVE LEFT HIIRAGI-KUN BEHIND?
YOU'VE GOTTA BE *KIDDING* ME. HE'D ONLY GET IN THE WAY.
IF HIS SEAL WAS BROKEN, AND HE WENT *BERSERK* AGAIN...
THEN WHY NOT USE IT TO YOUR *AD-VANTAGE?*
YOU JUST NEED TO MAKE HIM LOSE CONTROL-- THEN YOU CAN SIC HIM ON YOUR FATHER.

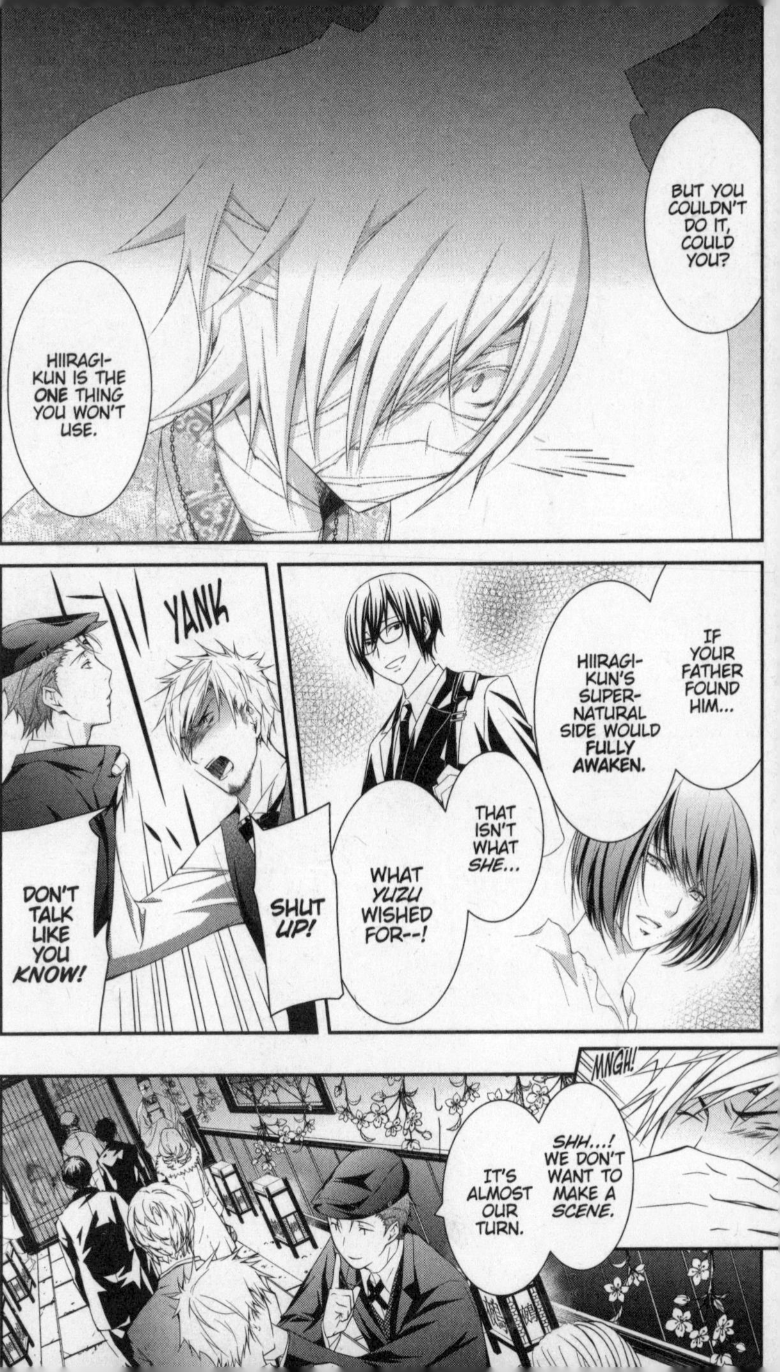
BUT YOU COULDN'T DO IT, COULD YOU?
HIIRAGI-KUN IS THE ONE THING YOU WON'T USE.
IF YOUR FATHER FOUND HIM...
HIIRAGI-KUN'S SUPER-NATURAL SIDE WOULD FULLY AWAKEN.
THAT ISN'T WHAT SHE...
WHAT YUZU WISHED FOR--!
YANK
SHUT UP!
DON'T TALK LIKE YOU KNOW!
MNGH!
SHH...! WE DON'T WANT TO MAKE A SCENE.
IT'S ALMOST OUR TURN.

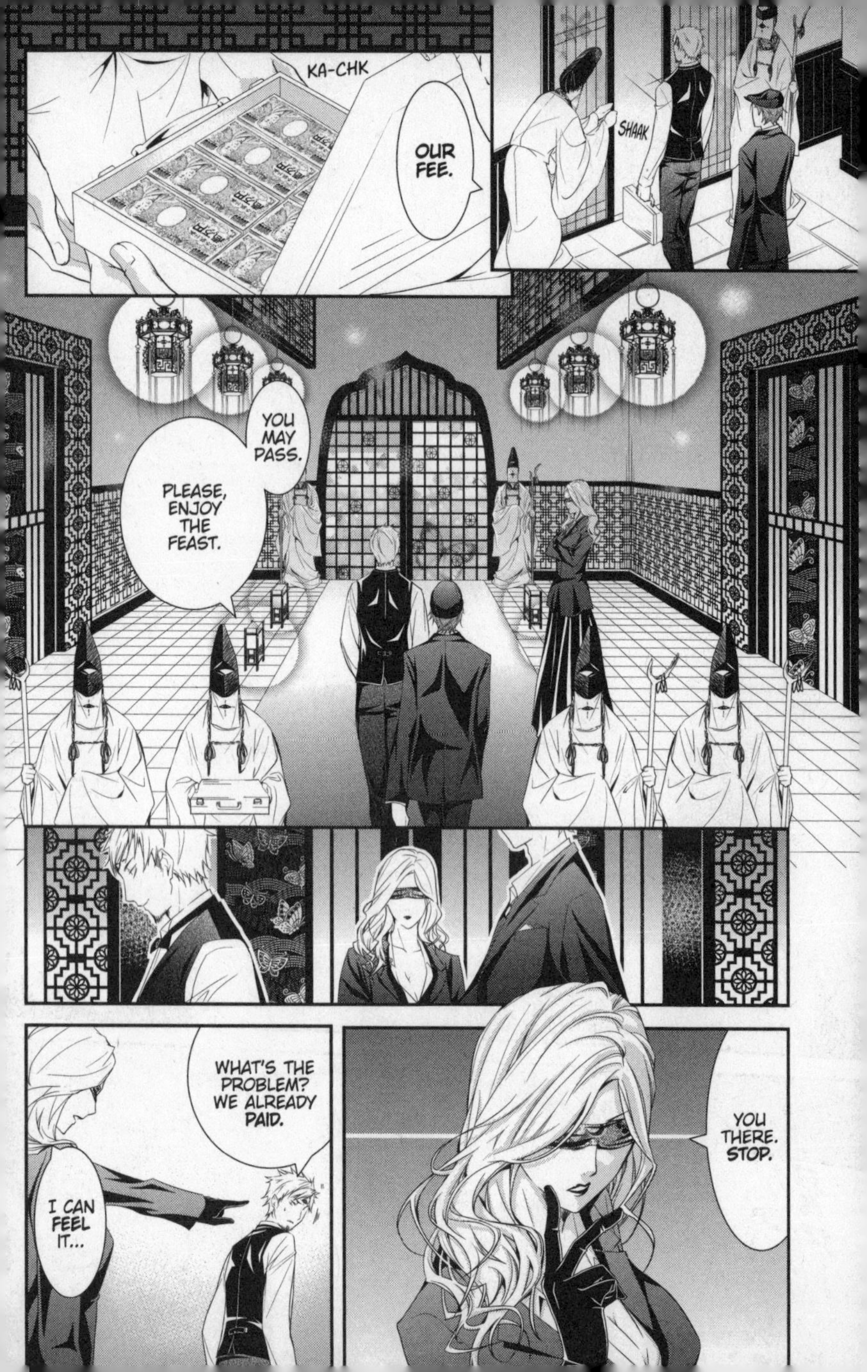
SHAAK
KA-CHK
OUR FEE.
YOU MAY PASS.
PLEASE, ENJOY THE FEAST.
YOU THERE. STOP.
WHAT'S THE PROBLEM? WE ALREADY PAID.
I CAN FEEL IT...

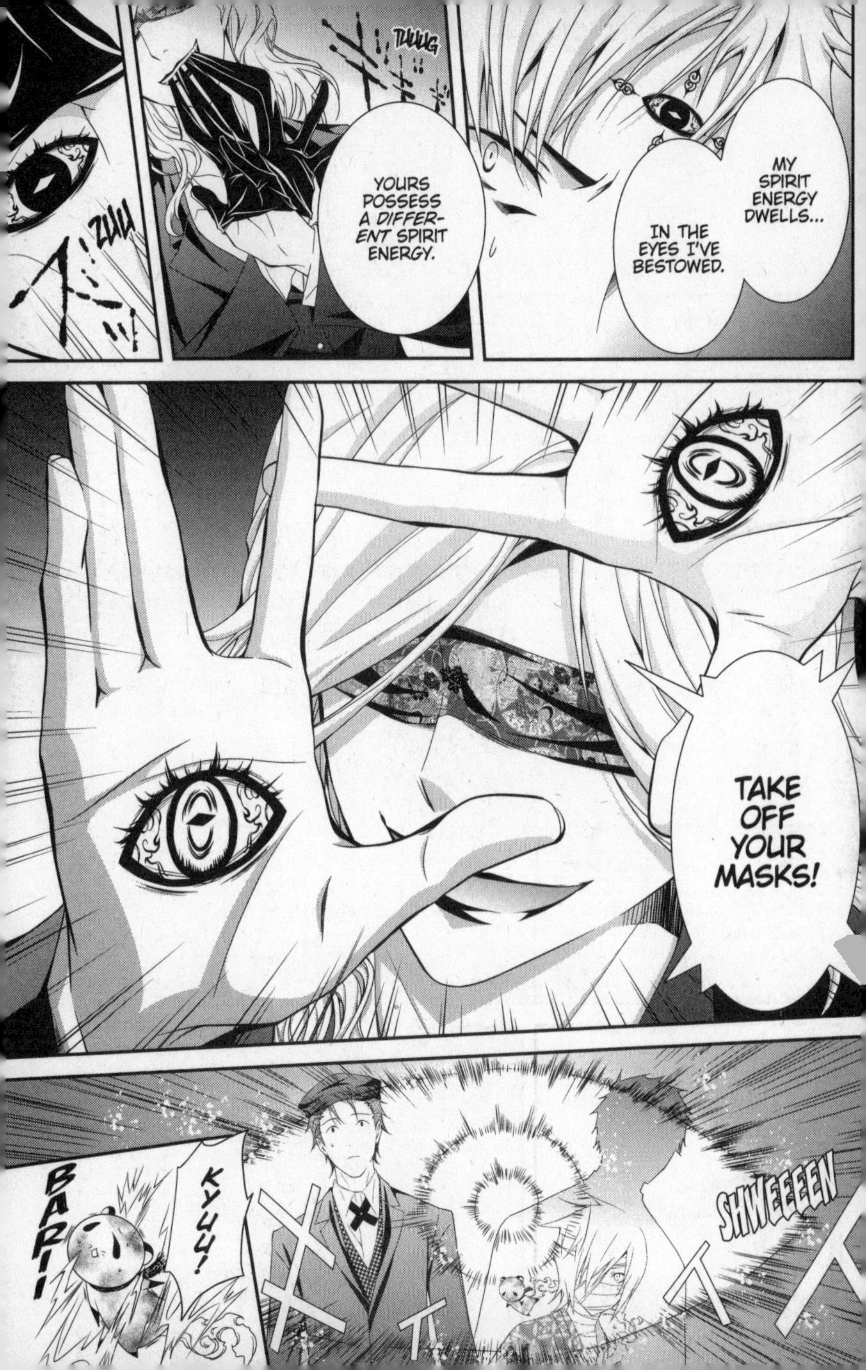
MY SPIRIT ENERGY DWELLS...
IN THE EYES I'VE BESTOWED.
THUUG
YOURS POSSESS A *DIFFERENT* SPIRIT ENERGY.
ZUU
TAKE OFF YOUR MASKS!
SHWEEEEN
KYUU!
BARI

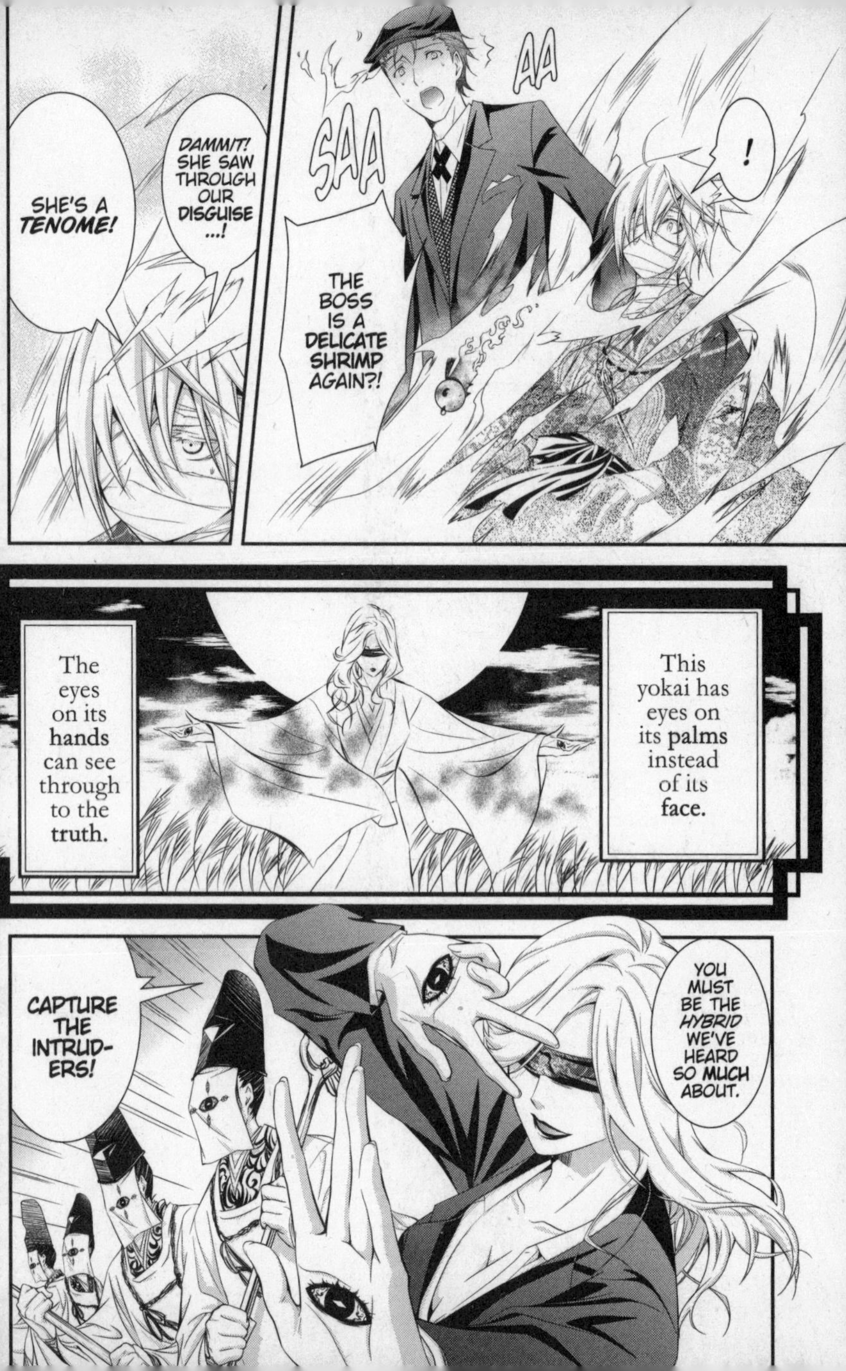
!
AA
SAA
THE BOSS IS A DELICATE SHRIMP AGAIN?!
DAMMIT! SHE SAW THROUGH OUR DISGUISE ...!
SHE'S A *TENOME!*
This yokai has eyes on its **palms** instead of its **face.**
The eyes on its **hands** can see through to the **truth.**
YOU MUST BE THE *HYBRID* WE'VE HEARD SO MUCH ABOUT.
CAPTURE THE INTRUDERS!

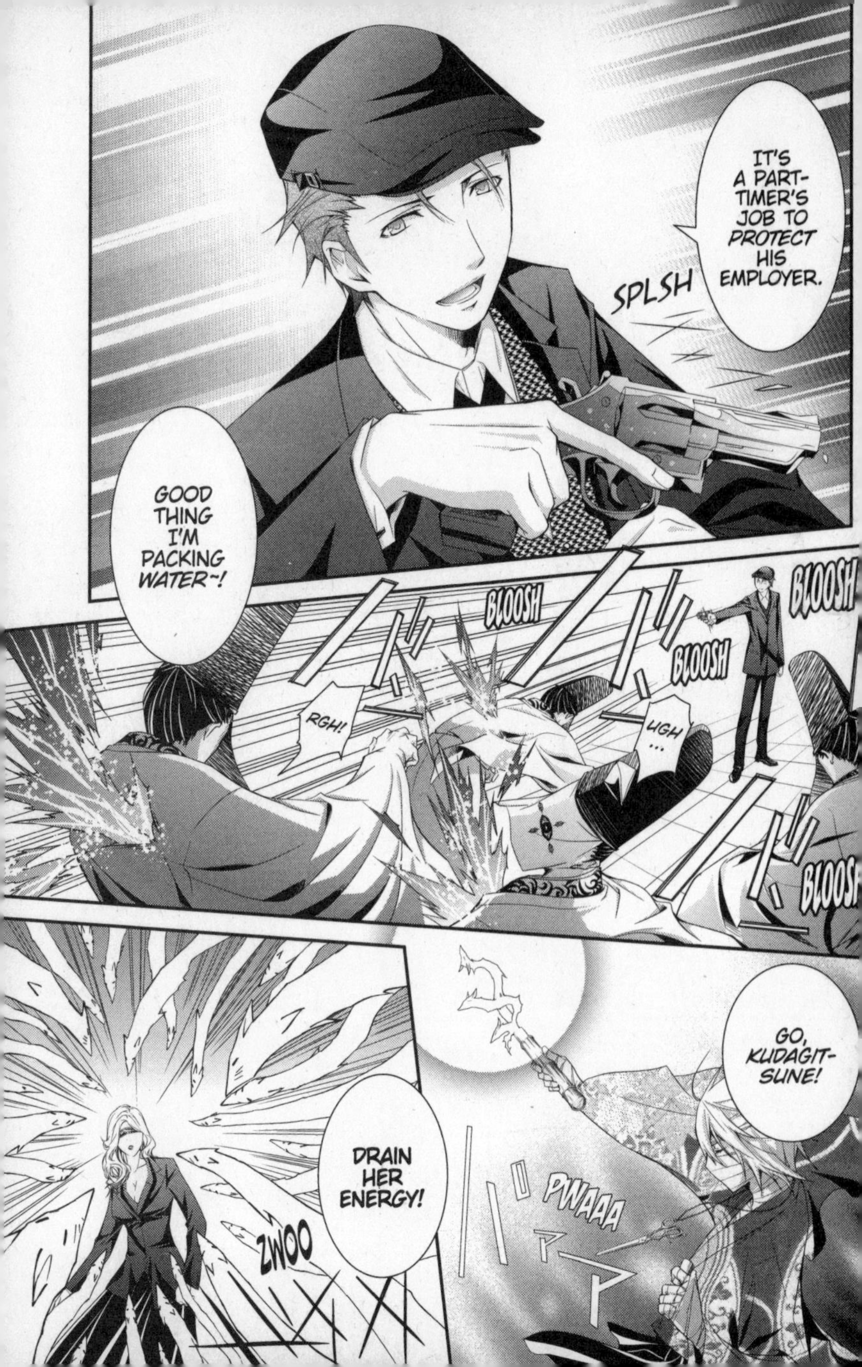
IT'S A PART-TIMER'S JOB TO PROTECT HIS EMPLOYER.
SPLSH
GOOD THING I'M PACKING WATER~!
BLOOSH
BLOOSH
BLOOSH
UGH...
RGH!
BLOOSH
GO, KUDAGITSUNE!
DRAIN HER ENERGY!
PWAAA
ZWOO

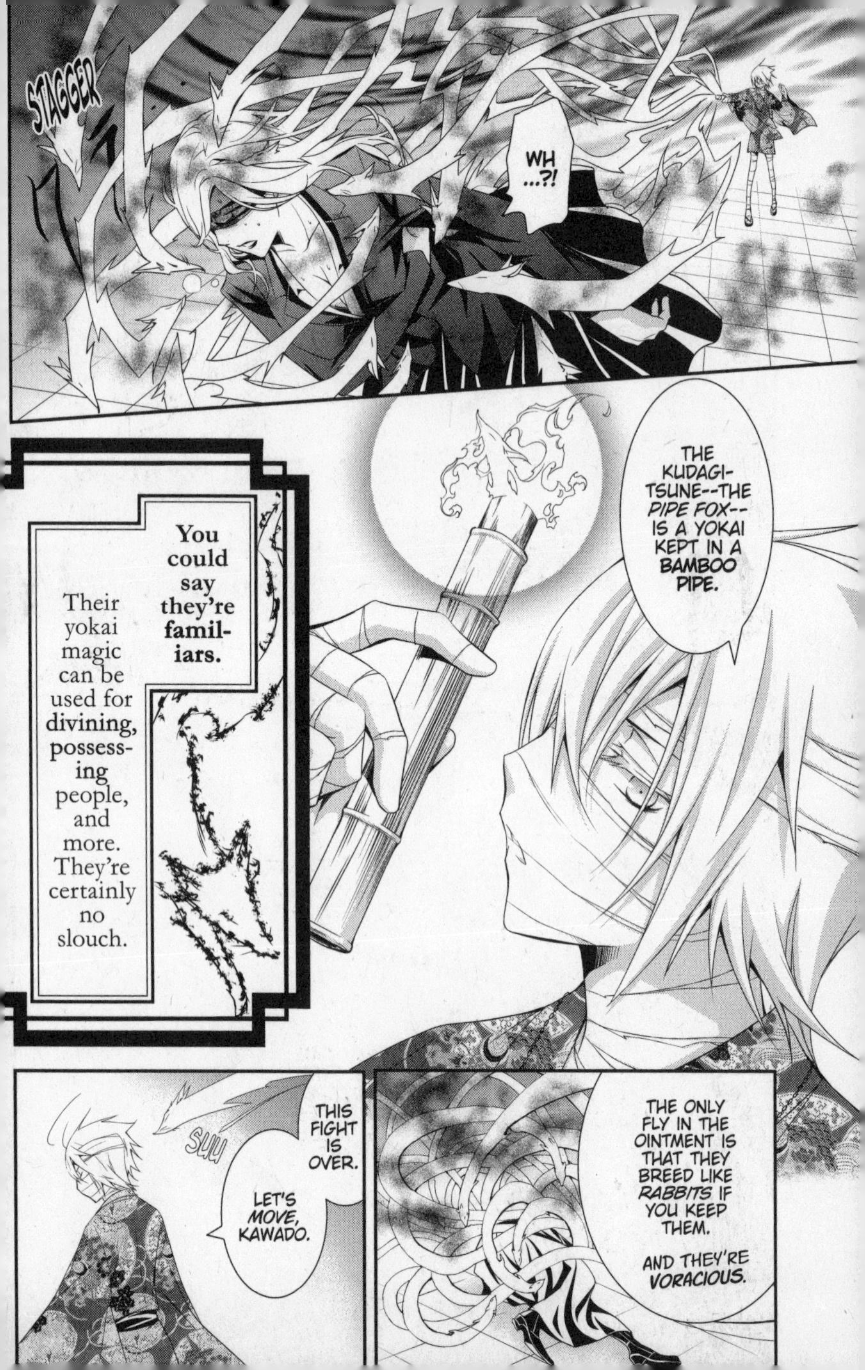
WH ...?!
STAGGER
THE KUDAGI-TSUNE--THE *PIPE FOX*--IS A YOKAI KEPT IN A BAMBOO PIPE.
You could say they're familiars.
Their yokai magic can be used for divining, possessing people, and more. They're certainly no slouch.
THE ONLY FLY IN THE OINTMENT IS THAT THEY BREED LIKE *RABBITS* IF YOU KEEP THEM.
AND THEY'RE *VORACIOUS*.
SUU
THIS FIGHT IS OVER.
LET'S *MOVE*, KAWADO.

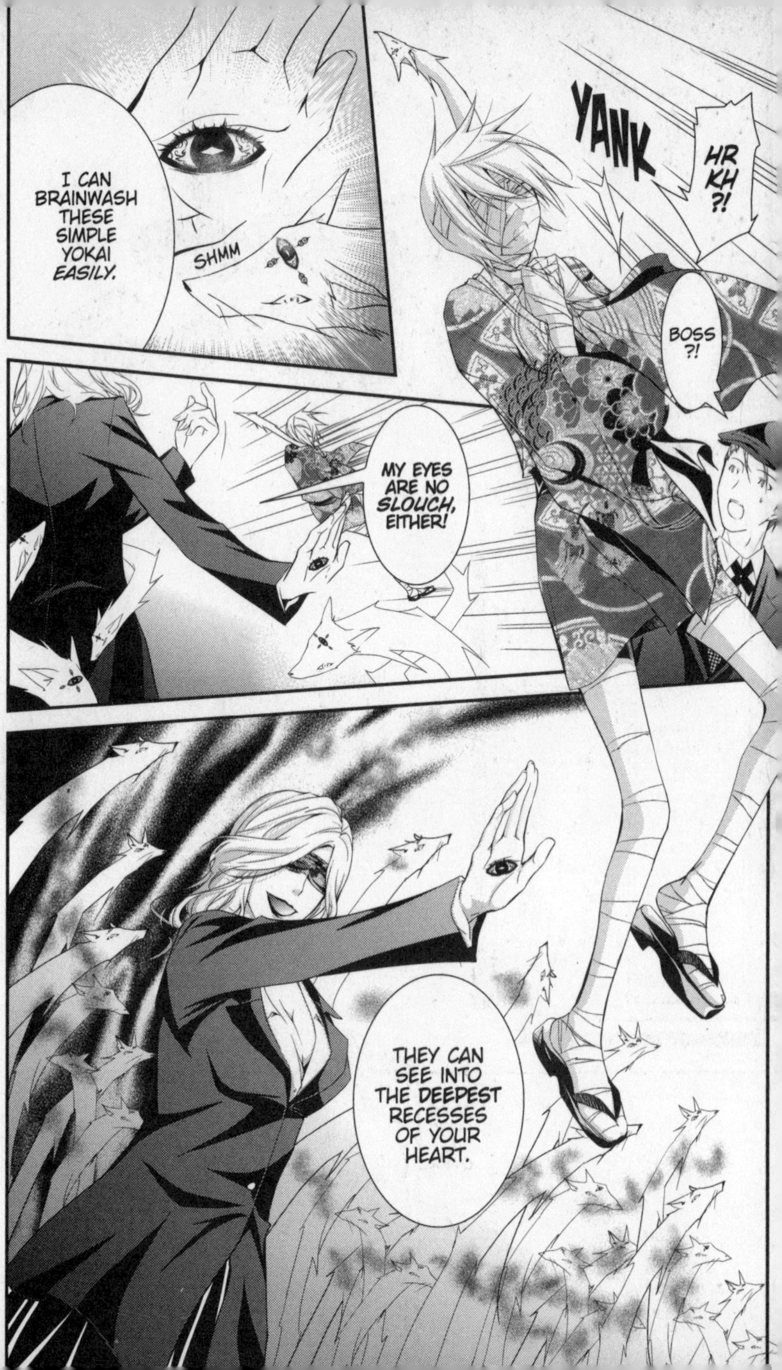
YANK
HRKH?!
BOSS?!
I CAN BRAINWASH THESE SIMPLE YOKAI *EASILY.*
SHMM
MY EYES ARE NO *SLOUCH,* EITHER!
THEY CAN SEE INTO THE DEEPEST RECESSES OF YOUR HEART.

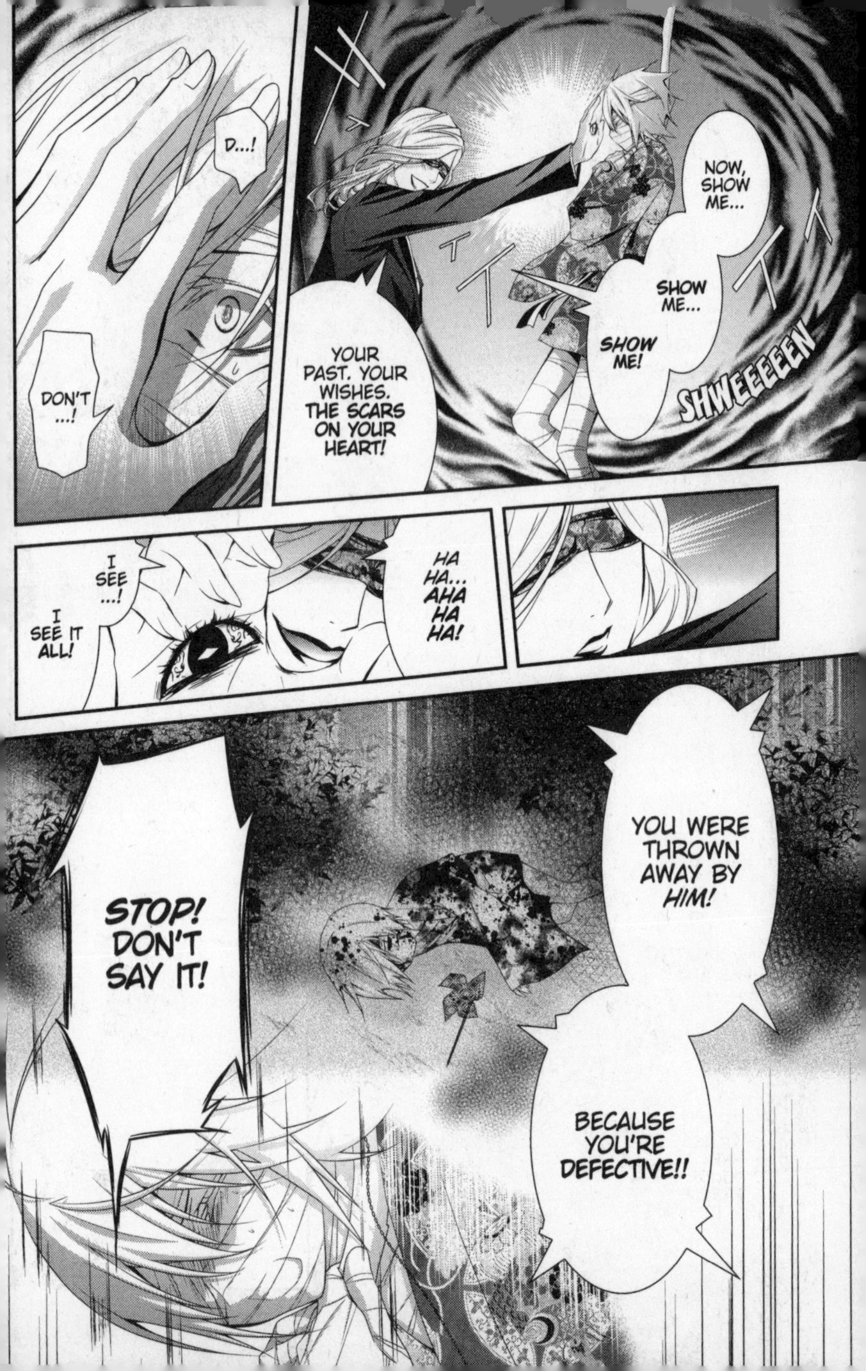
NOW, SHOW ME...
SHOW ME...
SHOW ME!
SHWEEEEEN
YOUR PAST. YOUR WISHES. THE SCARS ON YOUR HEART!
D...!
DON'T ...!
HA HA... AHA HA HA!
I SEE ...!
I SEE IT ALL!
YOU WERE THROWN AWAY BY HIM!
BECAUSE YOU'RE DEFECTIVE!!
STOP! DON'T SAY IT!

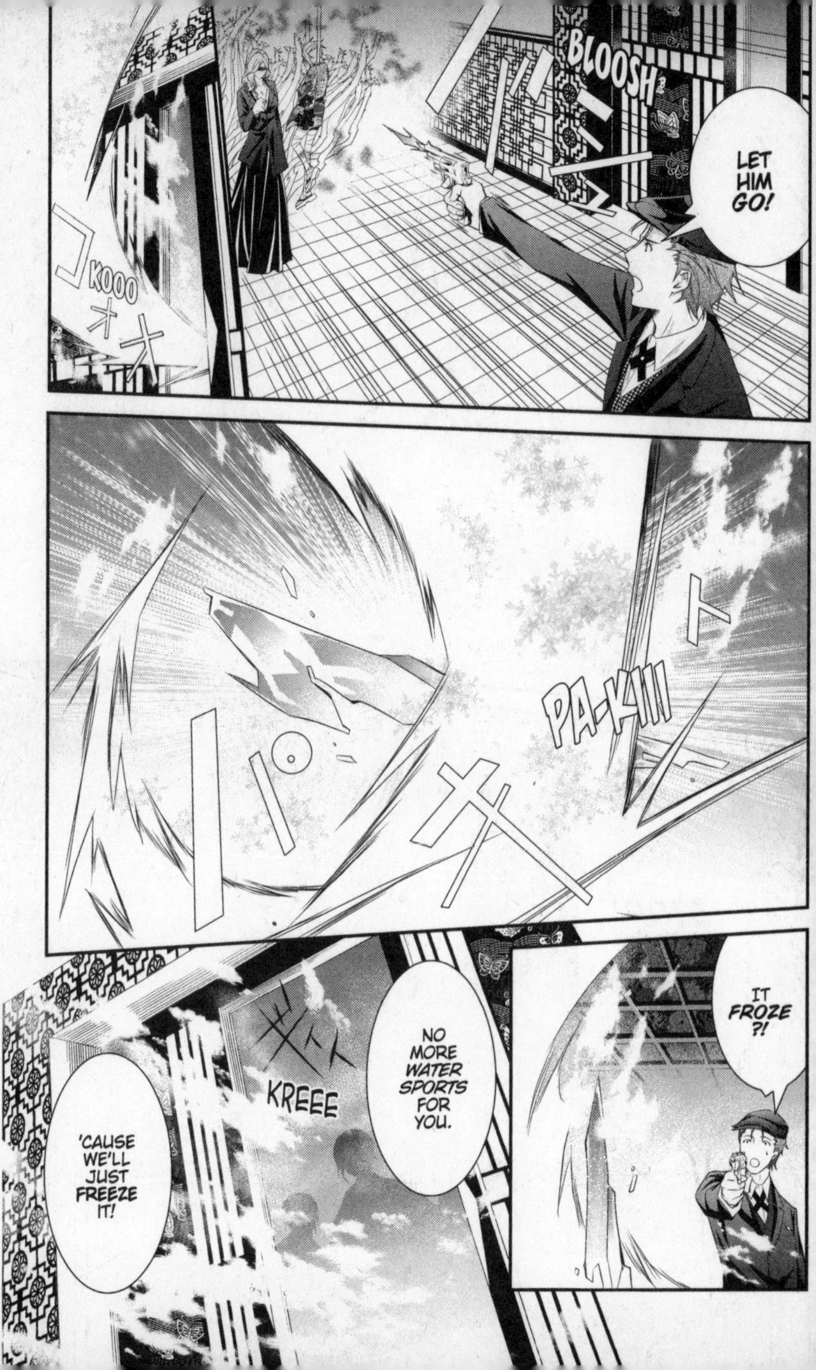
BLOOSH
LET HIM GO!
KOOO
PA-KIIN
IT FROZE?!
NO MORE WATER SPORTS FOR YOU.
KREEE
'CAUSE WE'LL JUST FREEZE IT!

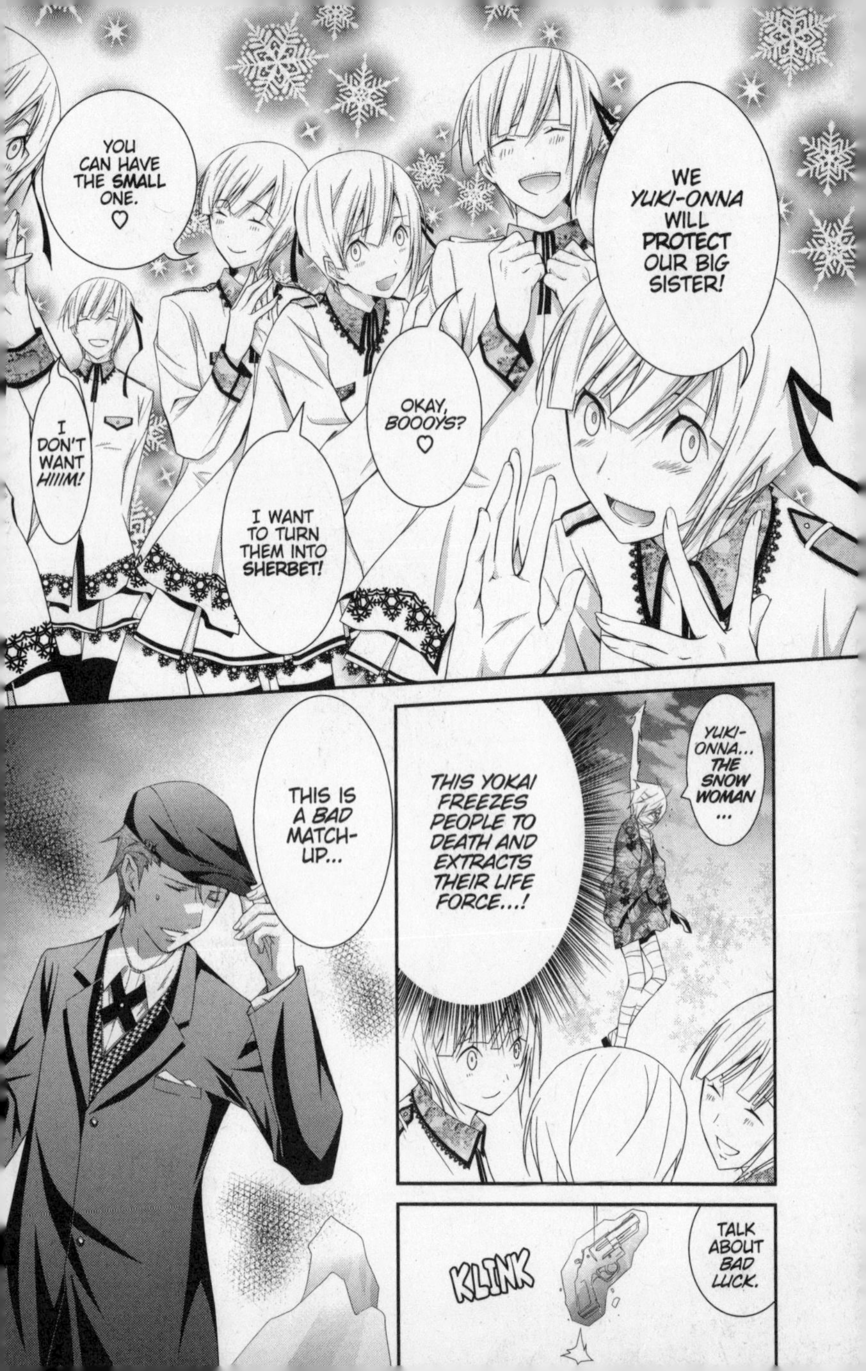
WE YUKI-ONNA WILL PROTECT OUR BIG SISTER!
OKAY, BOOOYS? ♡
YOU CAN HAVE THE SMALL ONE. ♡
I WANT TO TURN THEM INTO SHERBET!
I DON'T WANT HIIIM!
YUKI-ONNA... THE SNOW WOMAN ...
THIS YOKAI FREEZES PEOPLE TO DEATH AND EXTRACTS THEIR LIFE FORCE...!
TALK ABOUT BAD LUCK.
KLINK
THIS IS A BAD MATCH-UP...

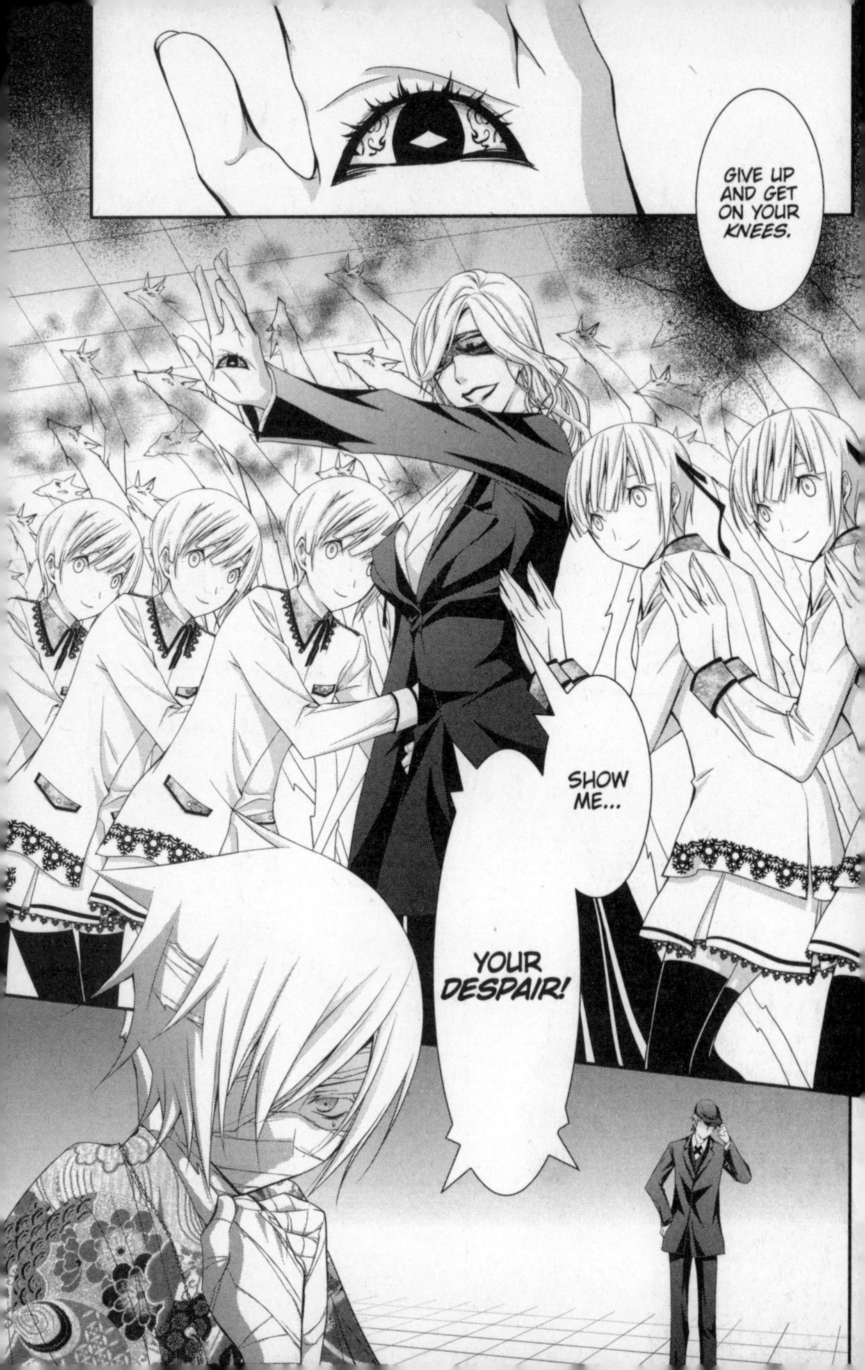
GIVE UP AND GET ON YOUR KNEES.
SHOW ME...
YOUR DESPAIR!

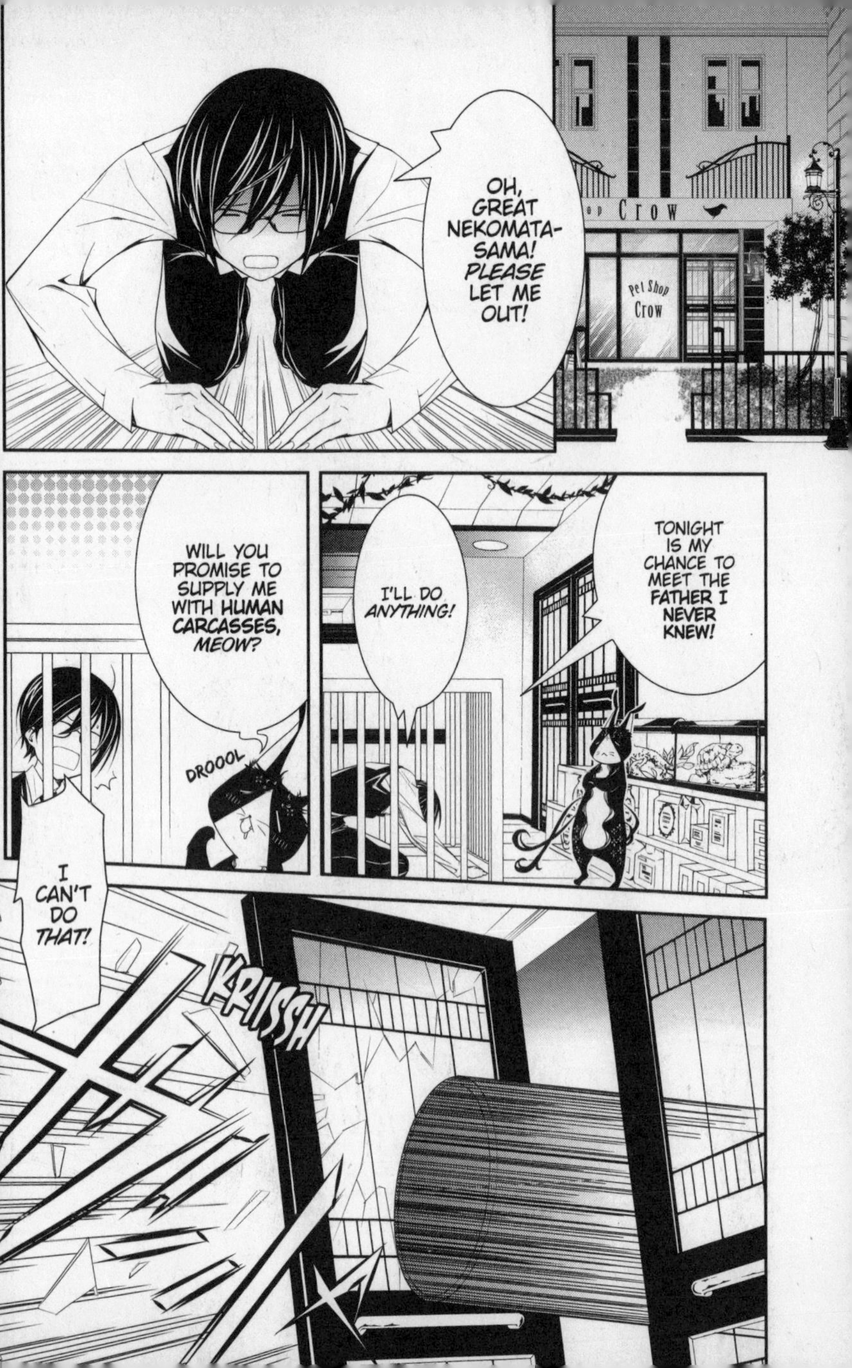

Pet Shop Crow
OH, GREAT NEKOMATA-SAMA! PLEASE LET ME OUT!
TONIGHT IS MY CHANCE TO MEET THE FATHER I NEVER KNEW!
I'LL DO *ANYTHING*!
WILL YOU PROMISE TO SUPPLY ME WITH HUMAN CARCASSES, *MEOW*?
DROOOL
I CAN'T DO *THAT*!
KRIISH

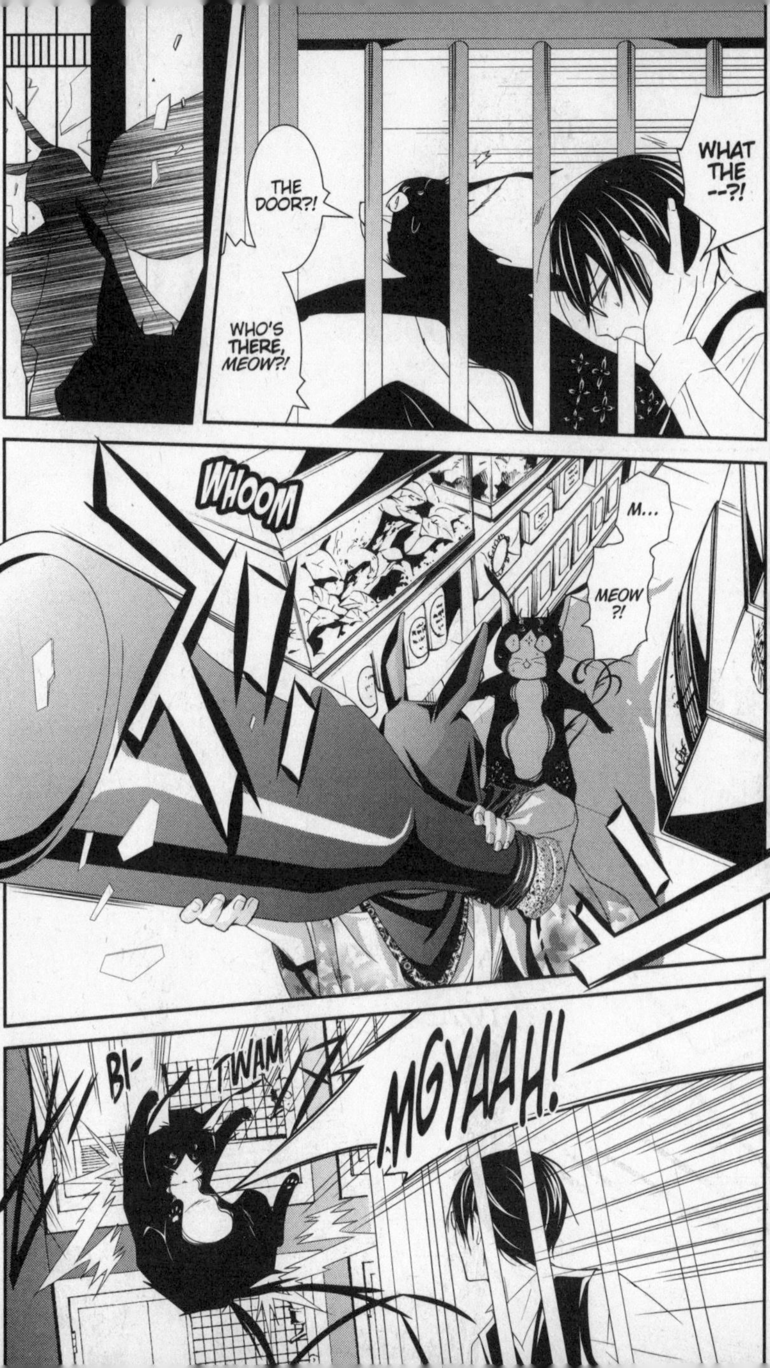
WHAT THE --?!
THE DOOR?!
WHO'S THERE, MEOW?!
M...
MEOW ?!
WHOOM
MGYAAH!
BI-
TWAM

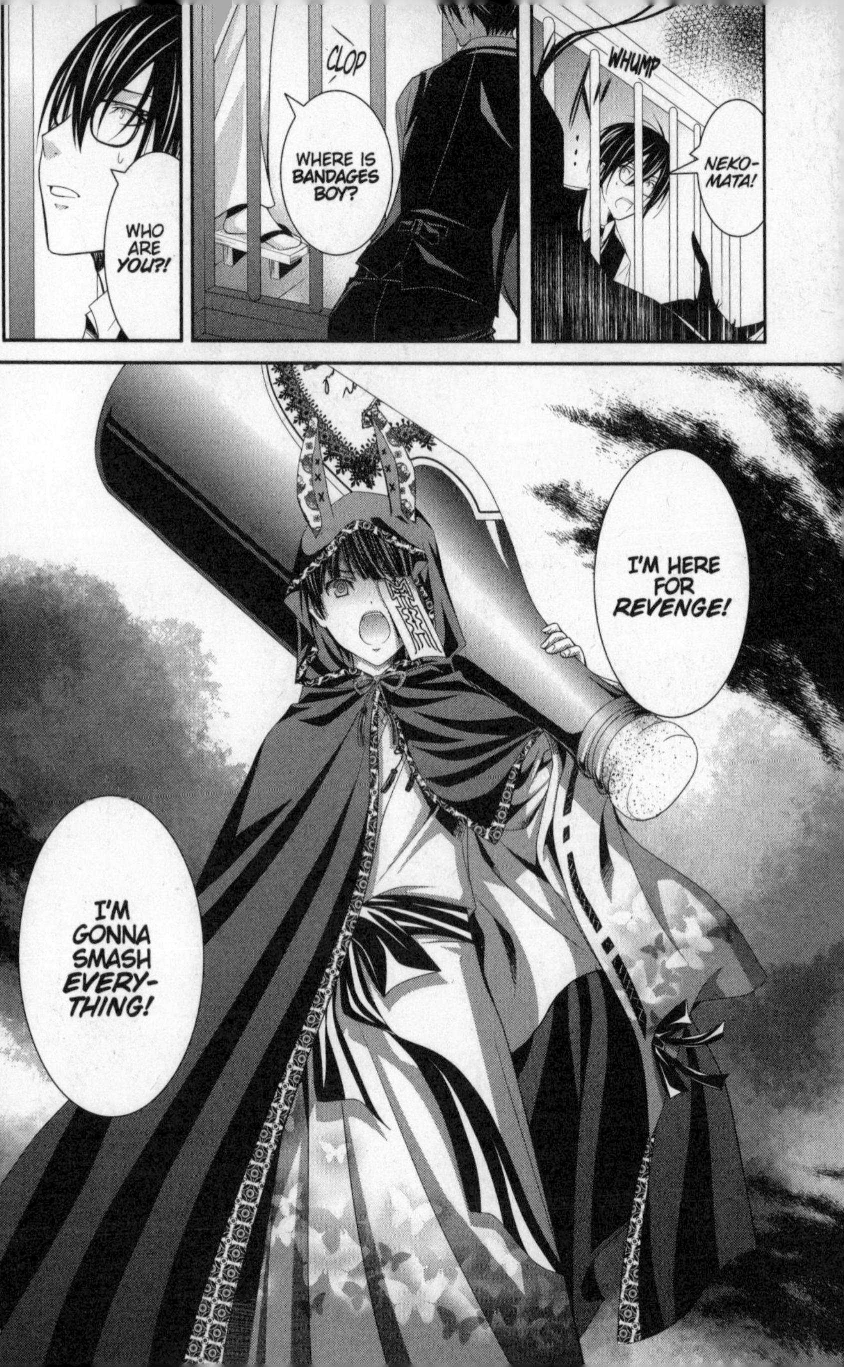
WHUMP
NEKO-MATA!
CLOP
WHERE IS BANDAGES BOY?
WHO ARE YOU?!
I'M HERE FOR REVENGE!
I'M GONNA SMASH EVERYTHING!

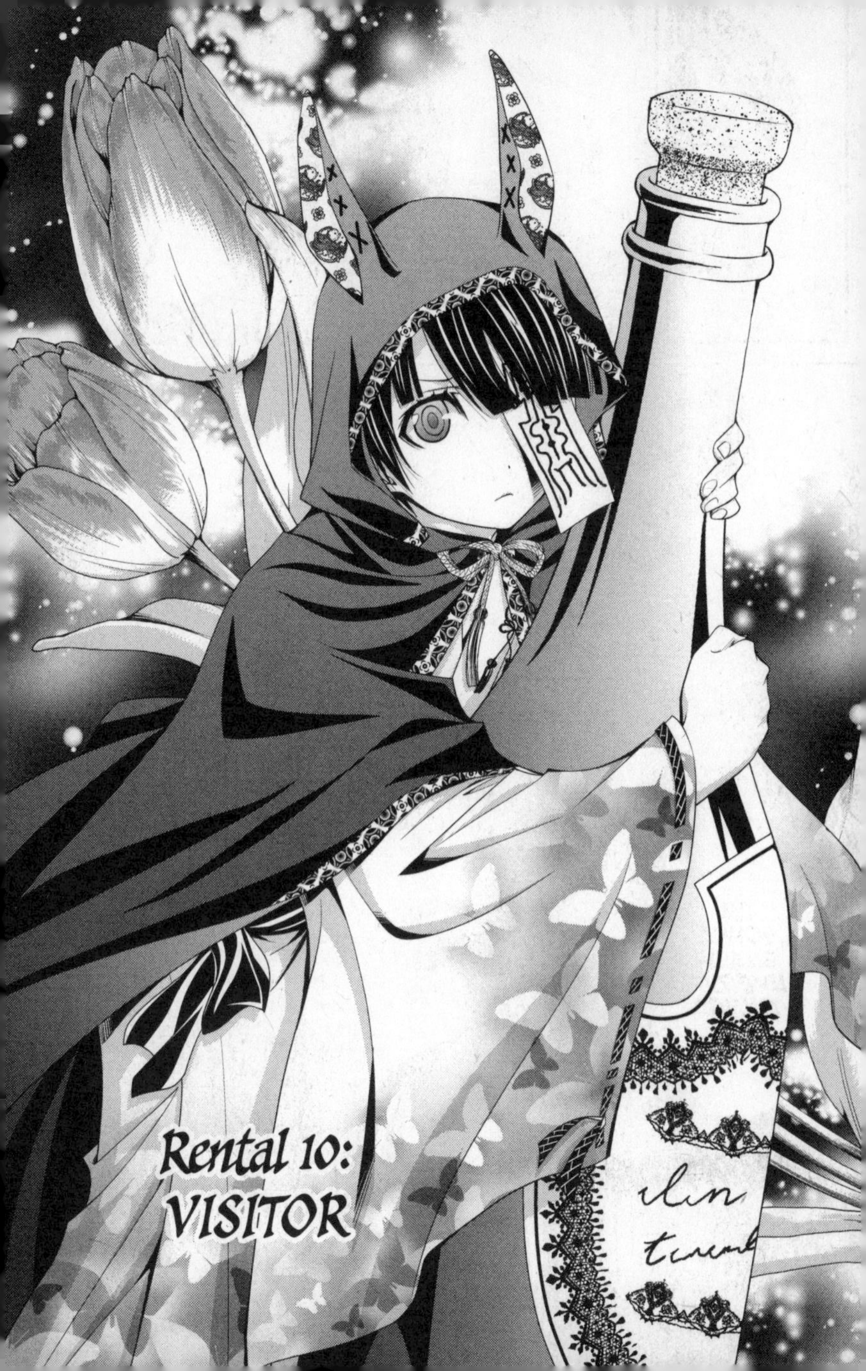
Rental 10:
VISITOR

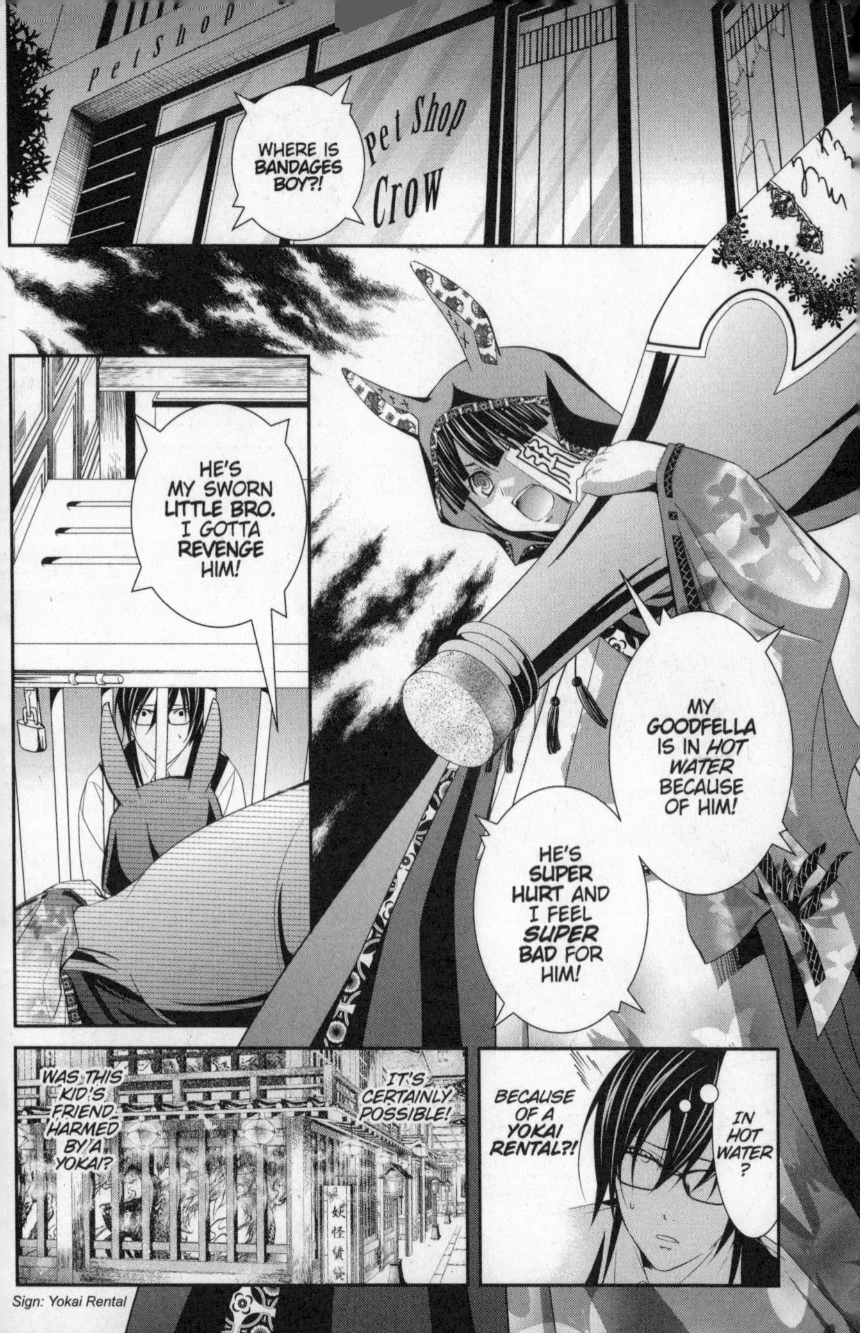
Pet Shop
Pet Shop Crow
WHERE IS BANDAGES BOY?!
MY GOODFELLA IS IN *HOT WATER* BECAUSE OF HIM!
HE'S SUPER HURT AND I FEEL *SUPER* BAD FOR HIM!
HE'S MY SWORN LITTLE BRO. I GOTTA REVENGE HIM!
IN HOT WATER?
BECAUSE OF A YOKAI RENTAL?!
IT'S CERTAINLY POSSIBLE!
WAS THIS KID'S FRIEND HARMED BY A YOKAI?

Sign: Yokai Rental

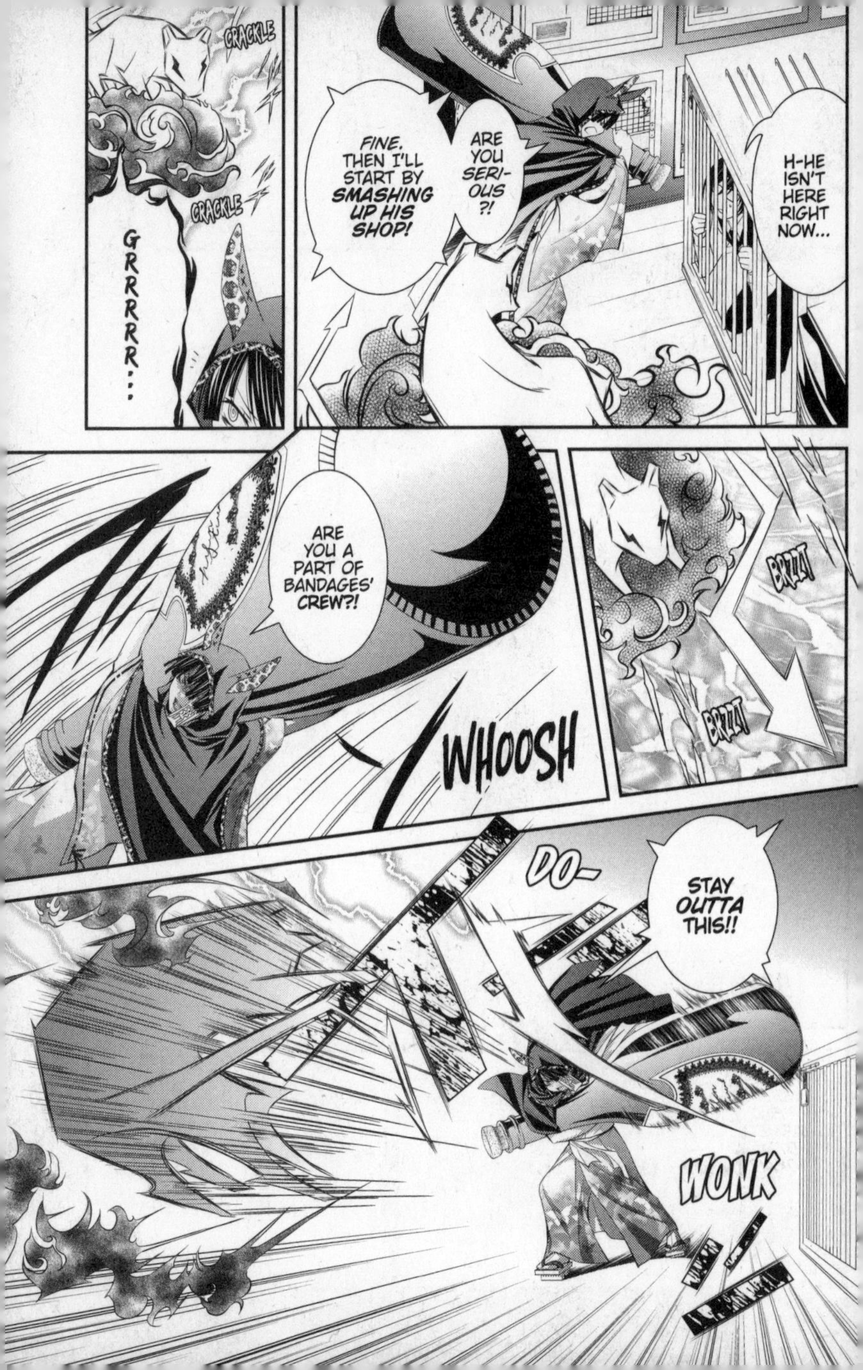
H-HE ISN'T HERE RIGHT NOW...
ARE YOU SERI-OUS?!
FINE. THEN I'LL START BY SMASHING UP HIS SHOP!
CRACKLE
CRACKLE
GRRRRRR...
BRZZT
BRZZT
ARE YOU A PART OF BANDAGES' CREW?!
WHOOSH
STAY OUTTA THIS!!
DO-
WONK

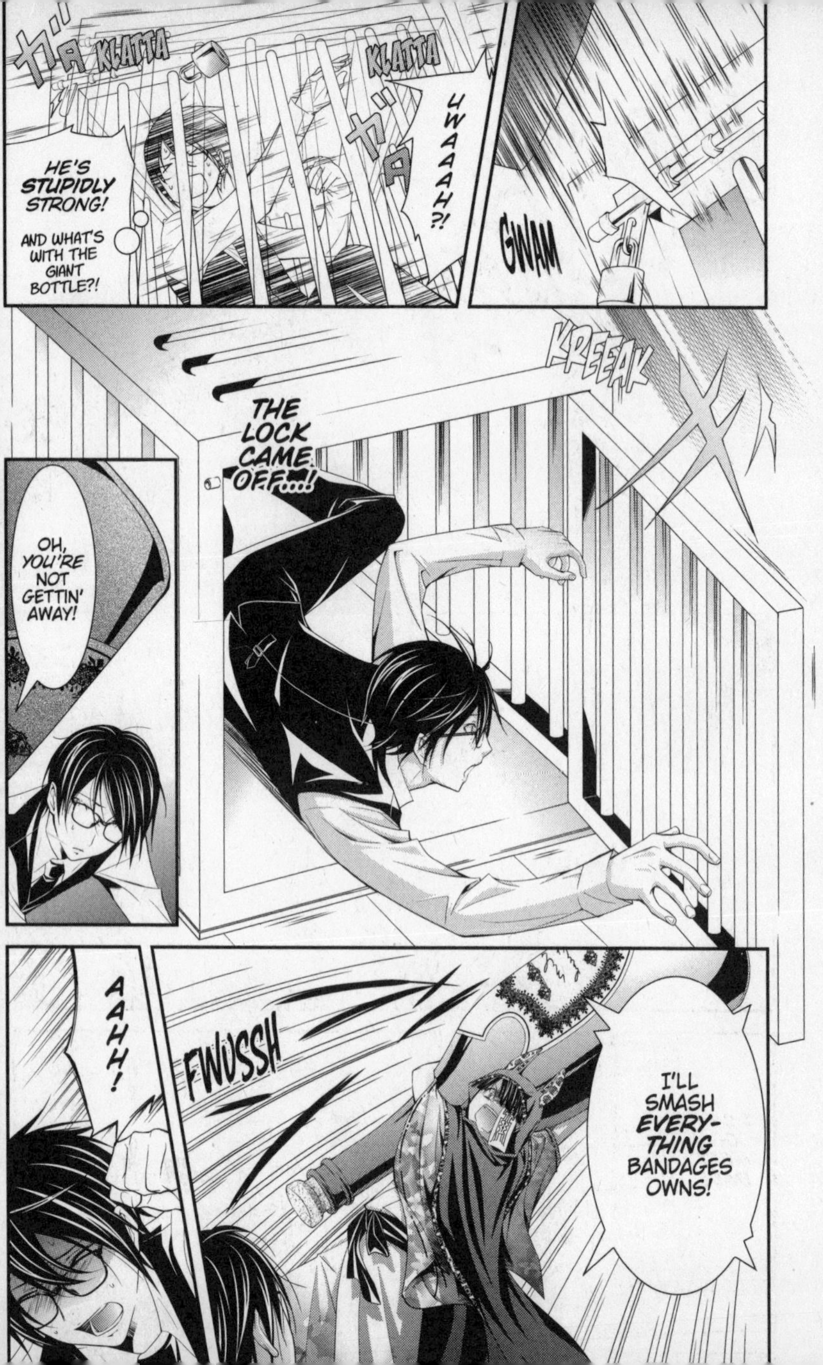
GWAM
KLATTA
UWAAAAH?!
KLATTA
HE'S STUPIDLY STRONG!
AND WHAT'S WITH THE GIANT BOTTLE?!
KREEAK
THE LOCK CAME OFF...!
OH, YOU'RE NOT GETTIN' AWAY!
I'LL SMASH EVERYTHING BANDAGES OWNS!
FWUSSH
AAHH!

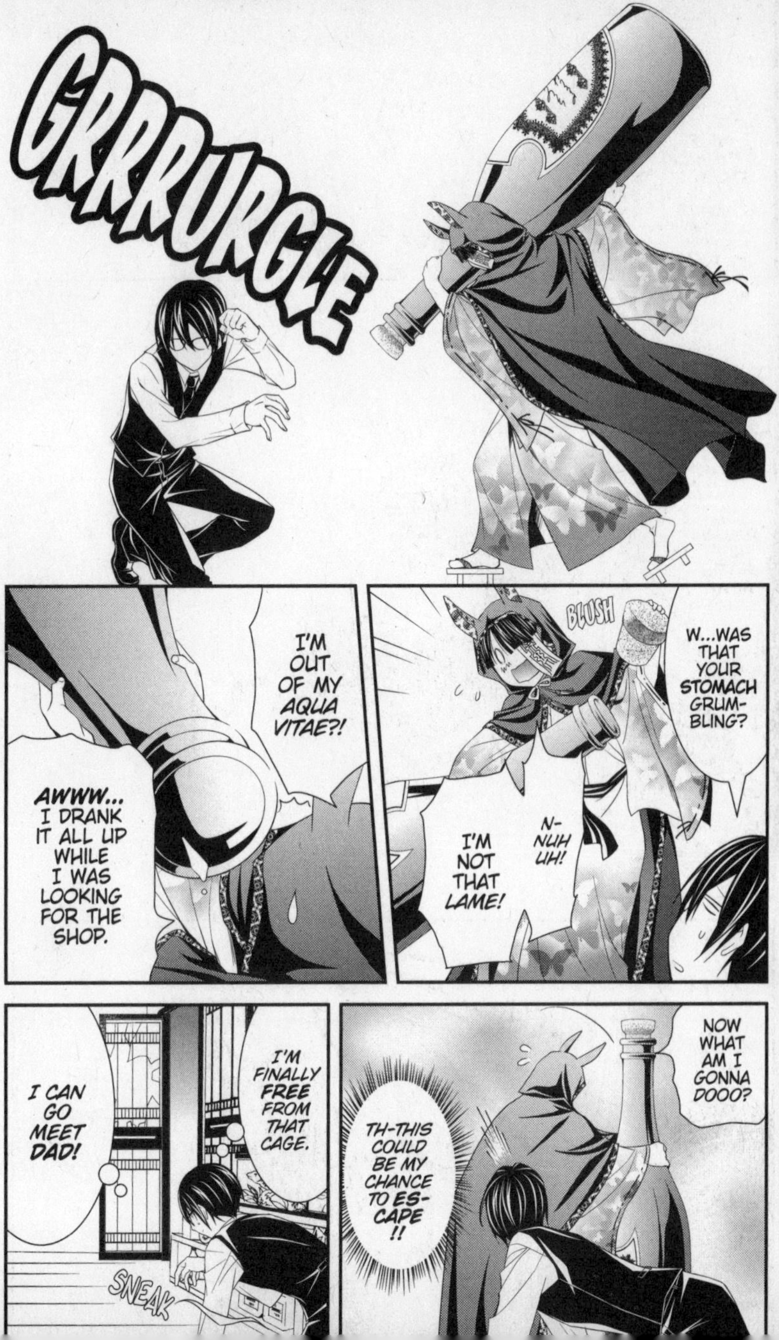
GRRRURGLE
BLUSH
W...WAS THAT YOUR STOMACH GRUM-BLING?
N-NUH UH!
I'M NOT THAT LAME!
I'M OUT OF MY AQUA VITAE?!
AWWW... I DRANK IT ALL UP WHILE I WAS LOOKING FOR THE SHOP.
NOW WHAT AM I GONNA DOOO?
TH-THIS COULD BE MY CHANCE TO ES-CAPE !!
I'M FINALLY FREE FROM THAT CAGE.
I CAN GO MEET DAD!
SNEAK

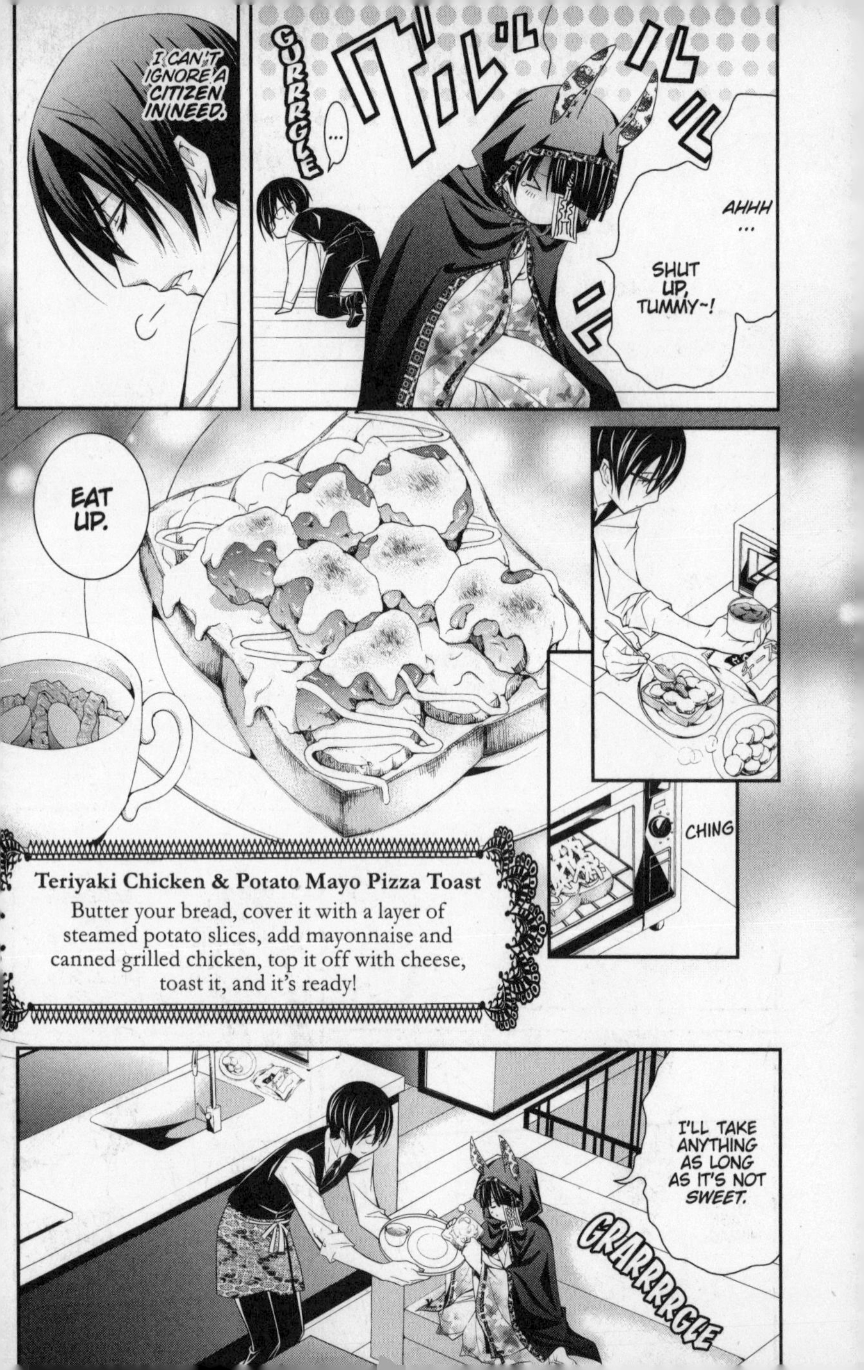
AHHH ...
SHUT UP, TUMMY~!
GURRGLE
...
I CAN'T IGNORE A CITIZEN IN NEED.
CHING
EAT UP.
Teriyaki Chicken & Potato Mayo Pizza Toast
Butter your bread, cover it with a layer of steamed potato slices, add mayonnaise and canned grilled chicken, top it off with cheese, toast it, and it's ready!
I'LL TAKE ANYTHING AS LONG AS IT'S NOT SWEET.
GRARRRRGLE

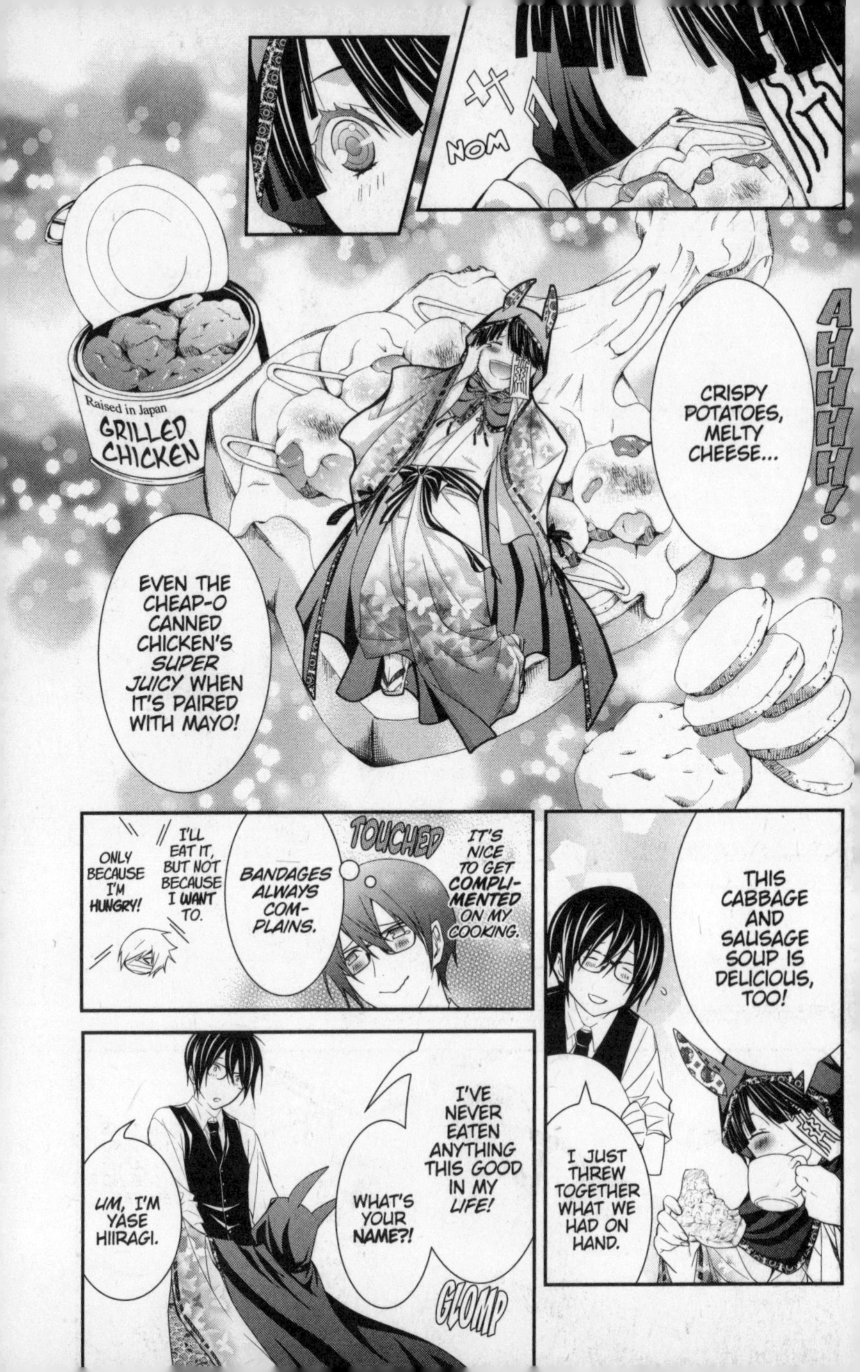
NOM
AHHHHHH!
CRISPY POTATOES, MELTY CHEESE...
Raised in Japan GRILLED CHICKEN
EVEN THE CHEAP-O CANNED CHICKEN'S SUPER JUICY WHEN IT'S PAIRED WITH MAYO!
THIS CABBAGE AND SAUSAGE SOUP IS DELICIOUS, TOO!
IT'S NICE TO GET COMPLIMENTED ON MY COOKING.
TOUCHED
BANDAGES ALWAYS COMPLAINS.
I'LL EAT IT, BUT NOT BECAUSE I WANT TO.
ONLY BECAUSE I'M HUNGRY!
I JUST THREW TOGETHER WHAT WE HAD ON HAND.
I'VE NEVER EATEN ANYTHING THIS GOOD IN MY LIFE!
GLOMP
WHAT'S YOUR NAME?!
UM, I'M YASE HIIRAGI.

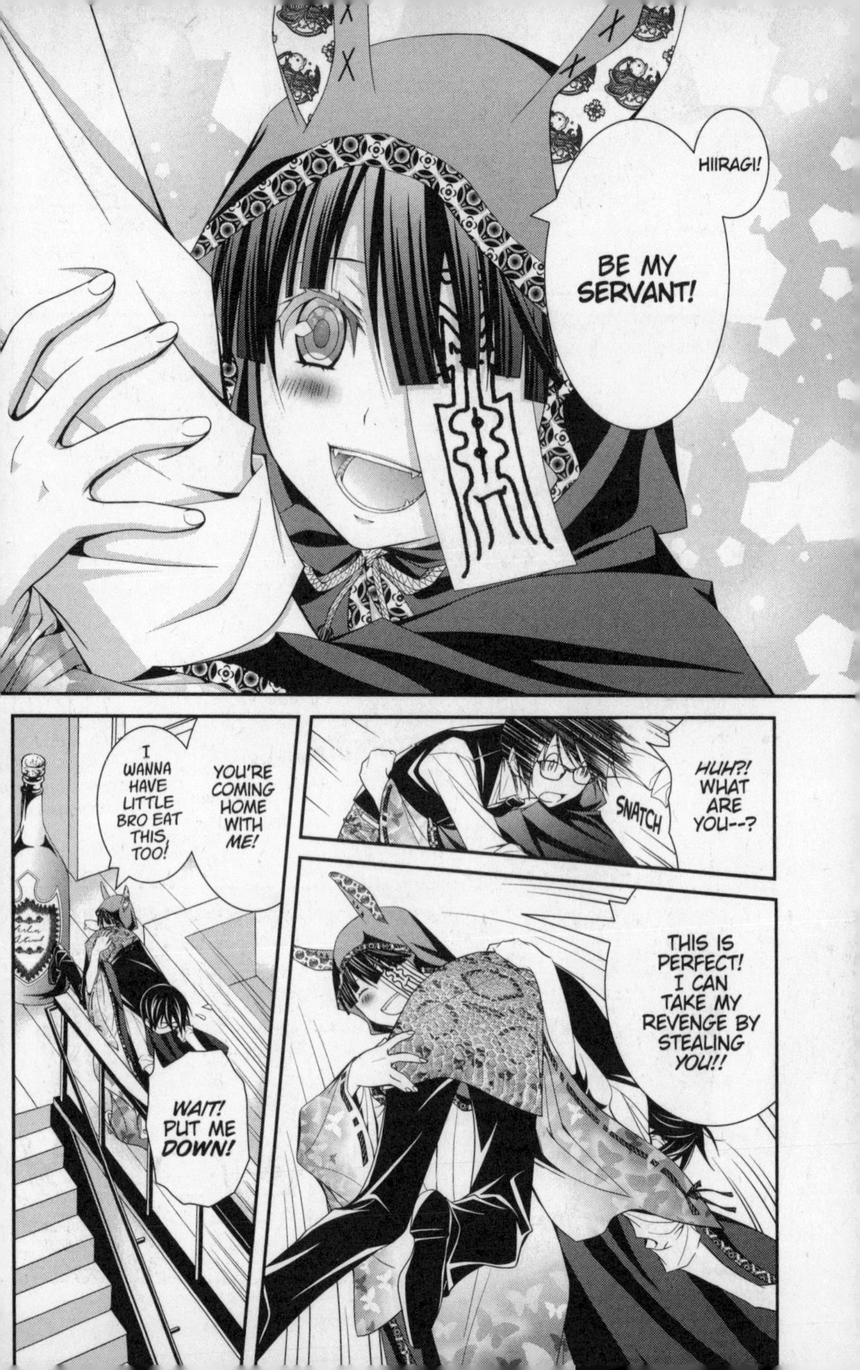
HIIRAGI!
BE MY SERVANT!
HUH?! WHAT ARE YOU--?
SNATCH
THIS IS PERFECT! I CAN TAKE MY REVENGE BY STEALING YOU!!
YOU'RE COMING HOME WITH ME!
I WANNA HAVE LITTLE BRO EAT THIS, TOO!
WAIT! PUT ME DOWN!

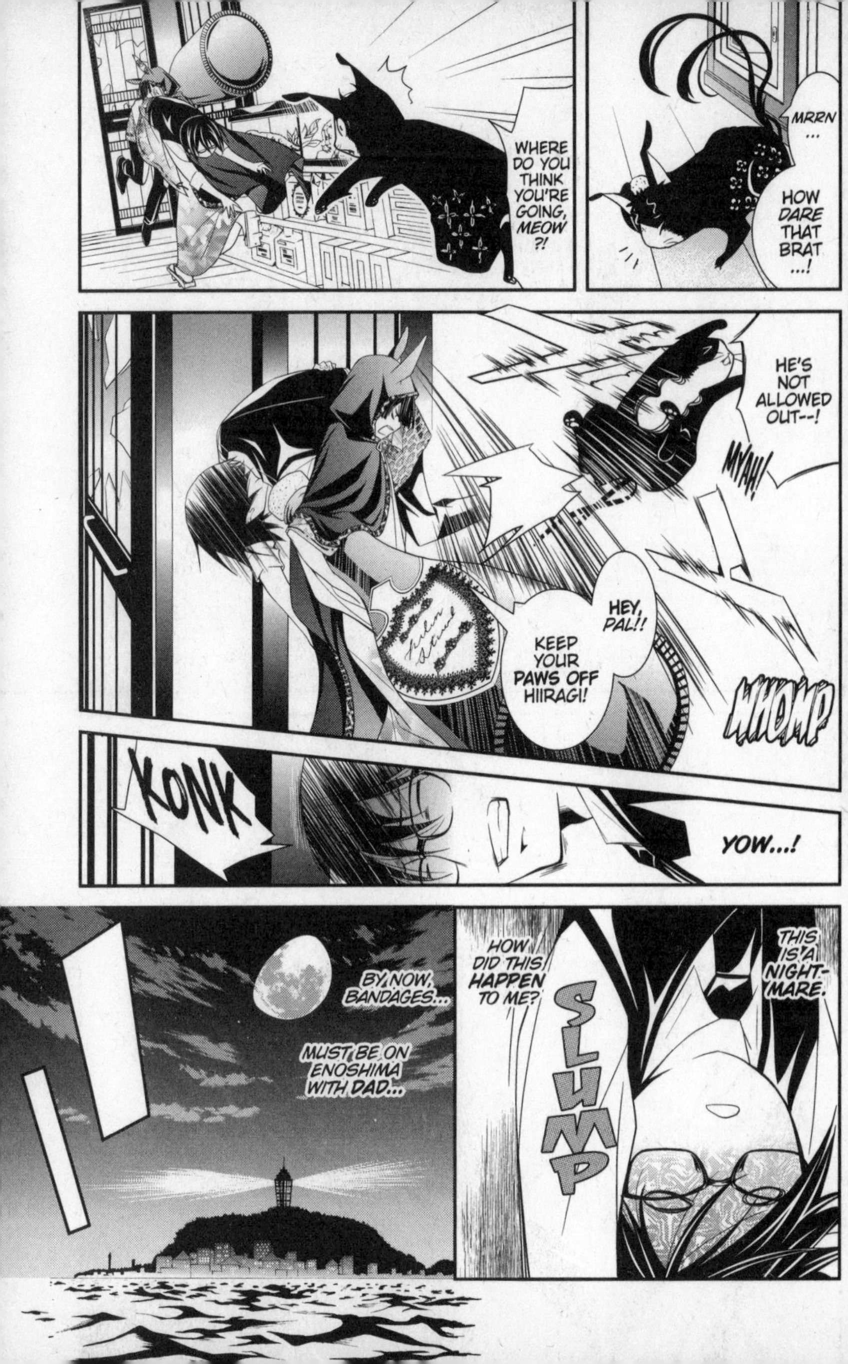
MRRN ...
HOW DARE THAT BRAT ...!
WHERE DO YOU THINK YOU'RE GOING, MEOW ?!
HE'S NOT ALLOWED OUT--!
MYAH!
HEY, PAL!!
KEEP YOUR PAWS OFF HIIRAGI!
WHOMP
YOW...!
KONK
THIS IS A NIGHT-MARE.
HOW DID THIS HAPPEN TO ME?
SLUMP
BY NOW, BANDAGES...
MUST BE ON ENOSHIMA WITH DAD...

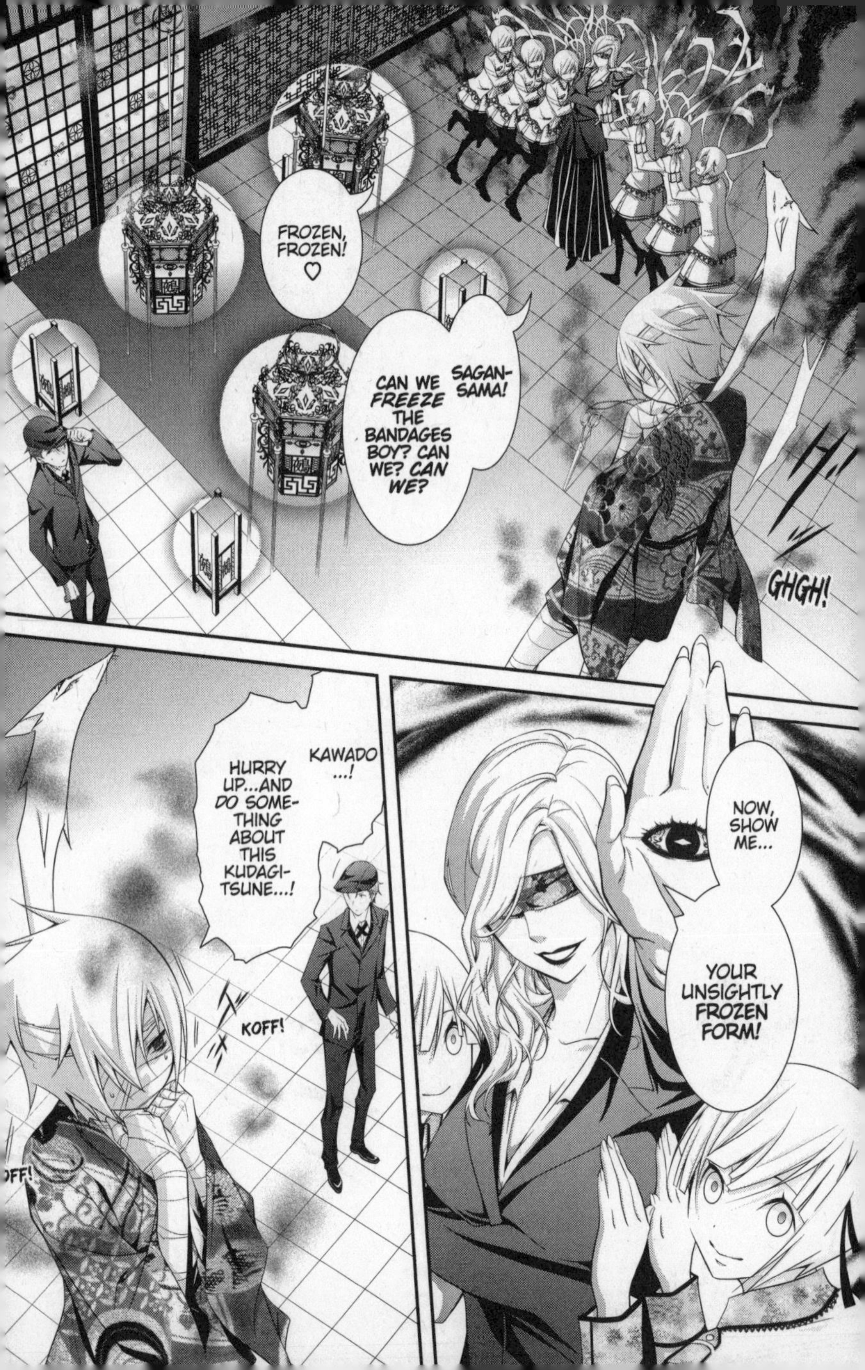
SAGAN-SAMA!
CAN WE FREEZE THE BANDAGES BOY? CAN WE? CAN WE?
FROZEN, FROZEN! ♡
GHGH!
NOW, SHOW ME...
YOUR UNSIGHTLY FROZEN FORM!
KAWADO ...!
HURRY UP...AND DO SOME-THING ABOUT THIS KUDAGI-TSUNE...!
KOFF!
OFF!

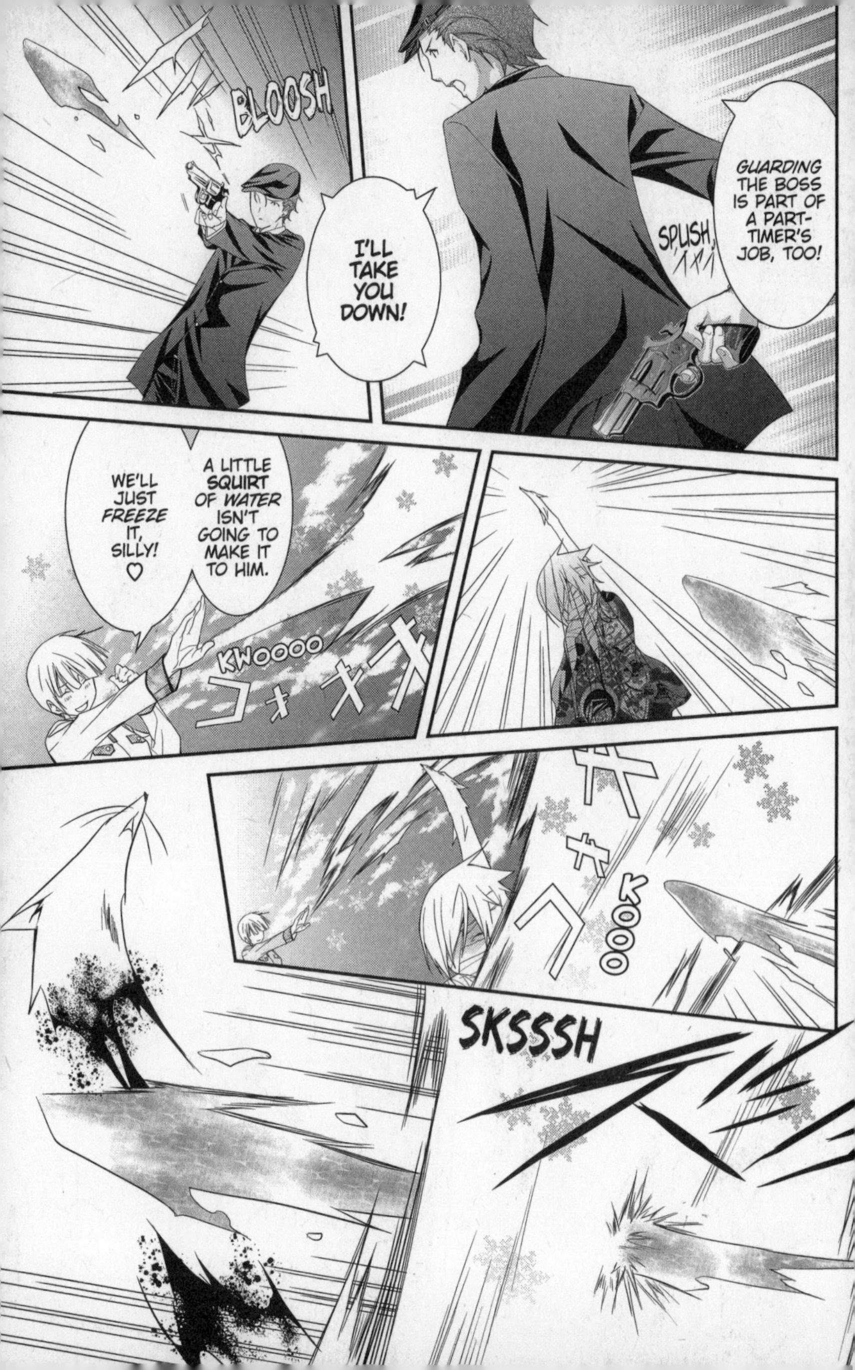
GUARDING THE BOSS IS PART OF A PART-TIMER'S JOB, TOO!
SPLISH,
I'LL TAKE YOU DOWN!
BLOOSH
A LITTLE SQUIRT OF WATER ISN'T GOING TO MAKE IT TO HIM.
WE'LL JUST FREEZE IT, SILLY! ♡
KWOOOO
KOOOO
SKSSSH

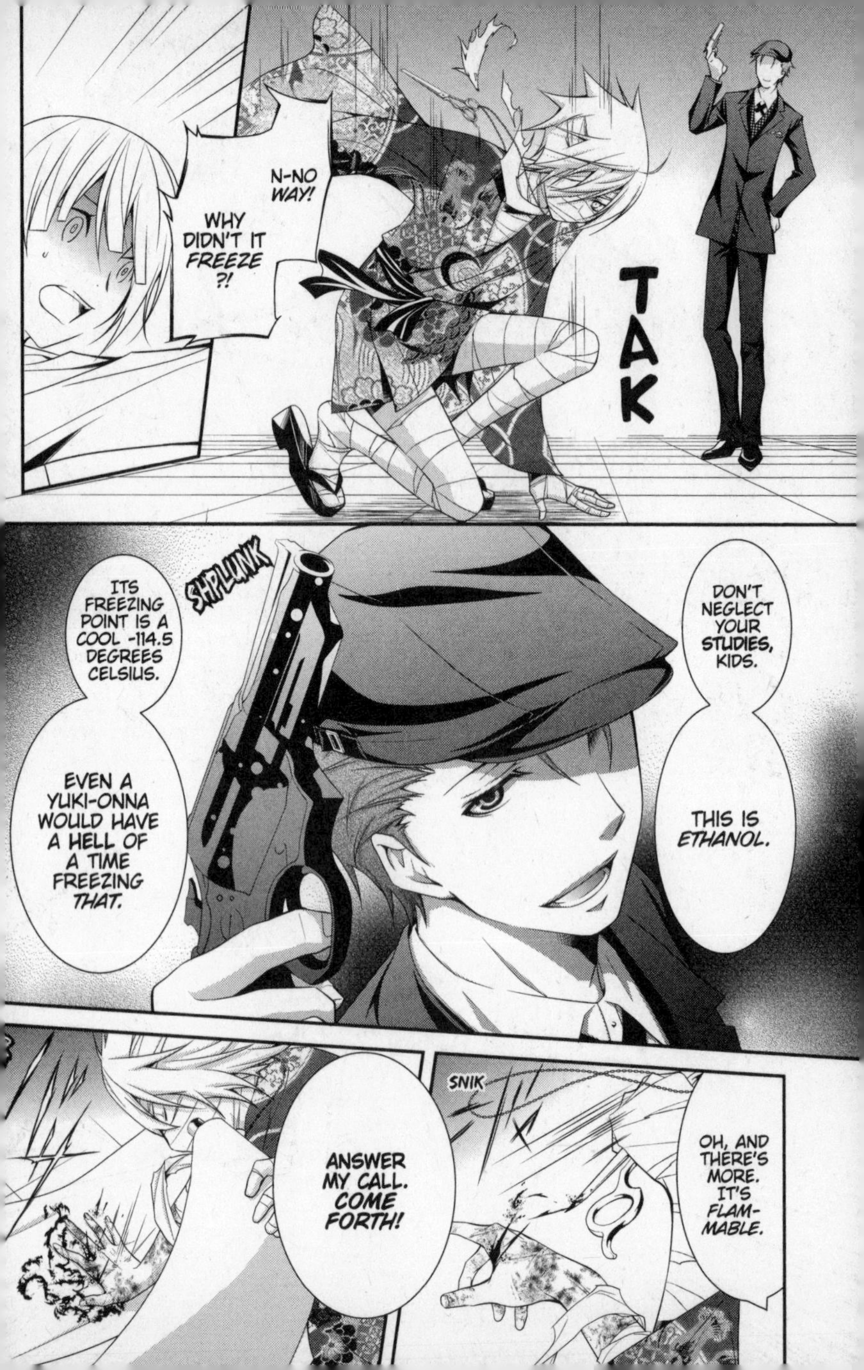

TAK
N-NO WAY!
WHY DIDN'T IT FREEZE ?!
DON'T NEGLECT YOUR STUDIES, KIDS.
THIS IS ETHANOL.
SHPLUNK
ITS FREEZING POINT IS A COOL -114.5 DEGREES CELSIUS.
EVEN A YUKI-ONNA WOULD HAVE A HELL OF A TIME FREEZING THAT.
SNIK
OH, AND THERE'S MORE. IT'S FLAM-MABLE.
ANSWER MY CALL. COME FORTH!

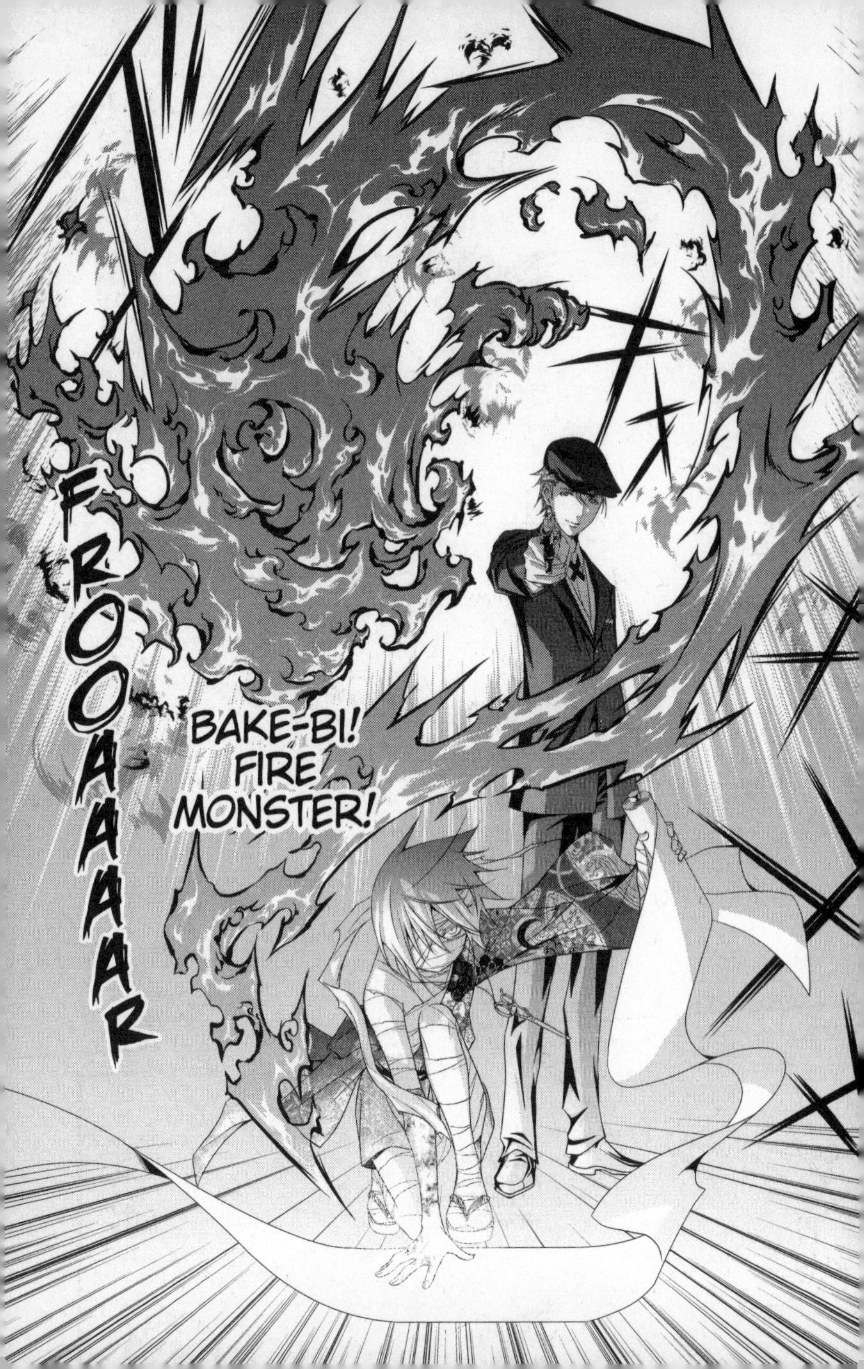
FROOAAAAR
BAKE-BI! FIRE MONSTER!

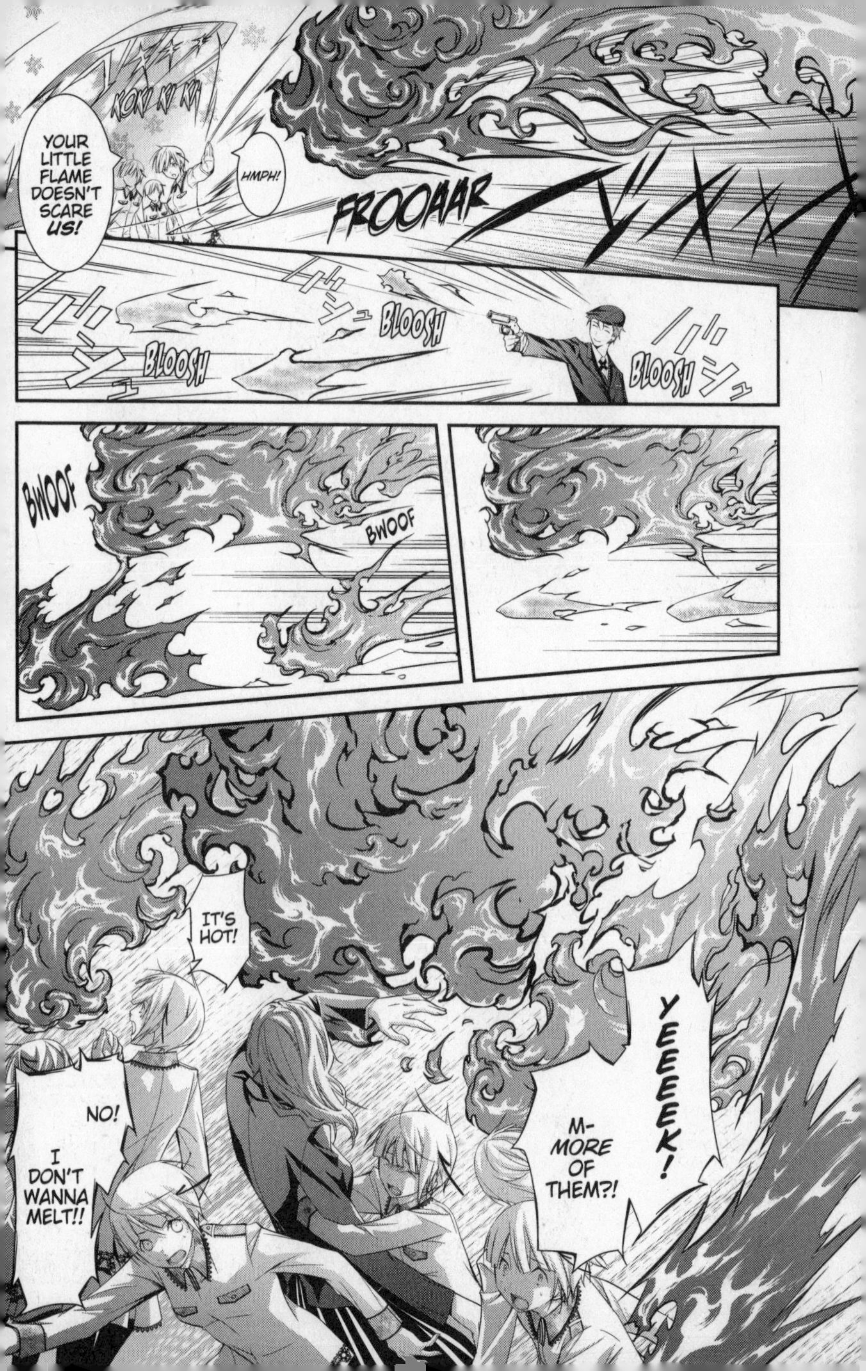
FROOAAR
HMPH!
KOKI KI KI
YOUR LITTLE FLAME DOESN'T SCARE US!
BLOOSH
BLOOSH
BLOOSH
BWOOF
BWOOF
YEEEEK!
M-MORE OF THEM?!
IT'S HOT!
NO!
I DON'T WANNA MELT!!

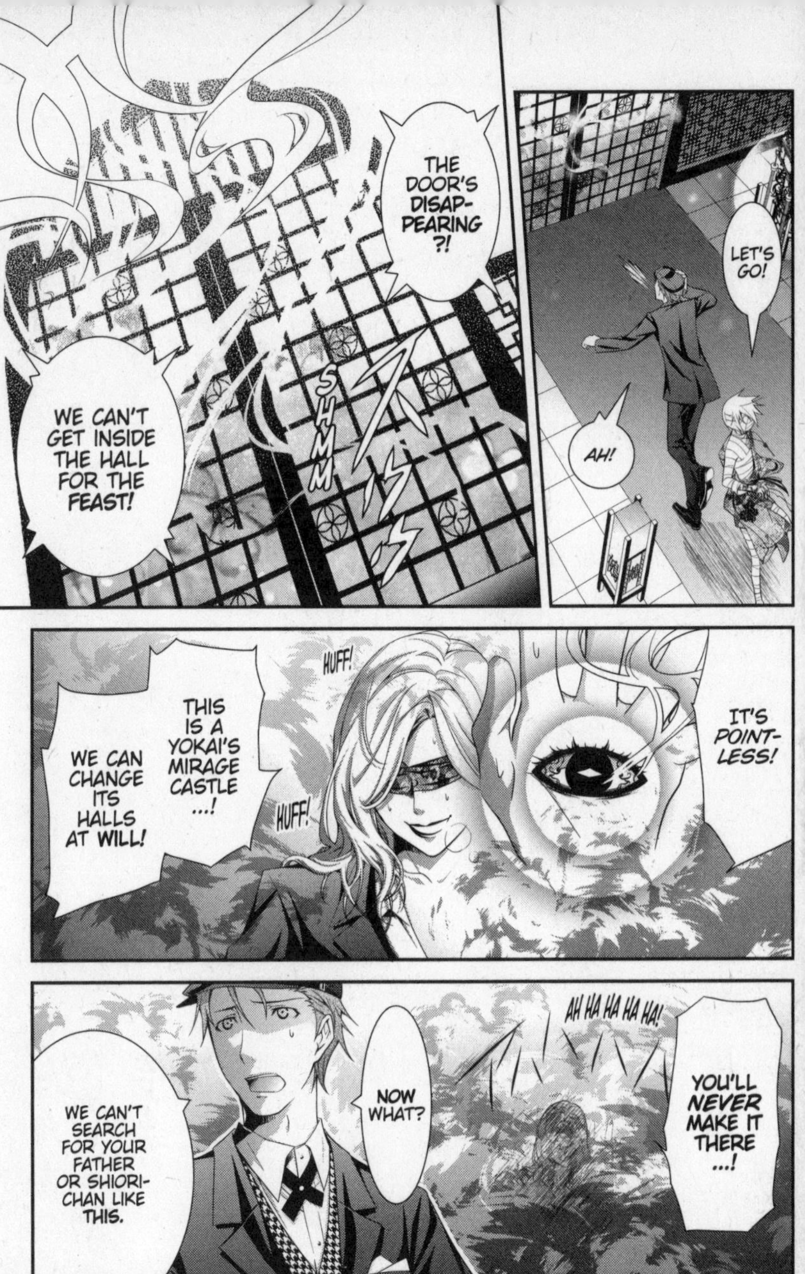
LET'S GO!
AH!
THE DOOR'S DISAPPEARING?!
SHMM
WE CAN'T GET INSIDE THE HALL FOR THE FEAST!
IT'S POINTLESS!
HUFF!
THIS IS A YOKAI'S MIRAGE CASTLE ...!
HUFF!
WE CAN CHANGE ITS HALLS AT WILL!
YOU'LL NEVER MAKE IT THERE ...!
AH HA HA HA HA!
NOW WHAT?
WE CAN'T SEARCH FOR YOUR FATHER OR SHIORI-CHAN LIKE THIS.

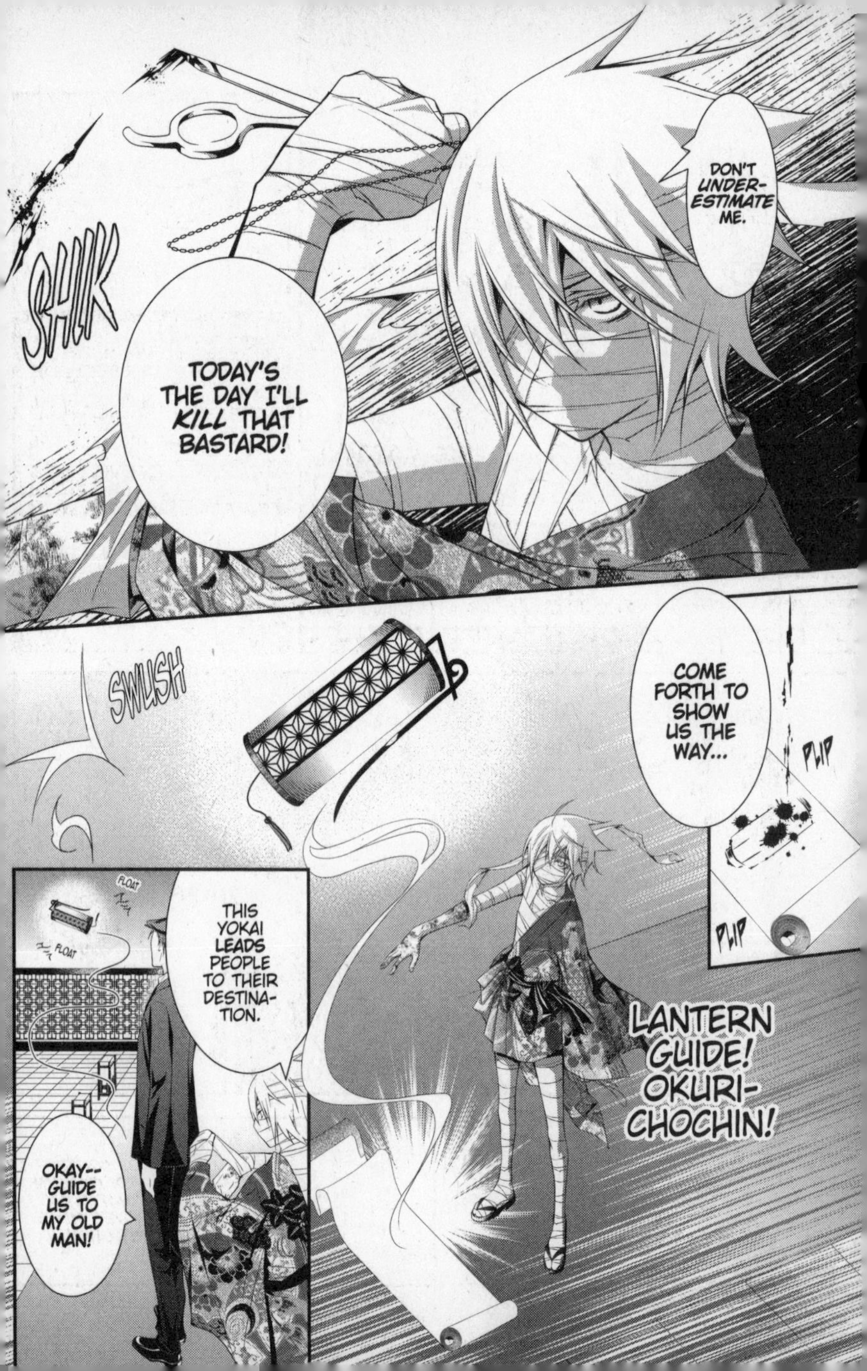
DON'T UNDER-ESTIMATE ME.
TODAY'S THE DAY I'LL *KILL* THAT BASTARD!
SHIK
COME FORTH TO SHOW US THE WAY...
PLIP
PLIP
SWISH
LANTERN GUIDE! OKURI-CHOCHIN!
FLOAT
FLOAT
THIS YOKAI LEADS PEOPLE TO THEIR DESTINA-TION.
OKAY--GUIDE US TO MY OLD MAN!

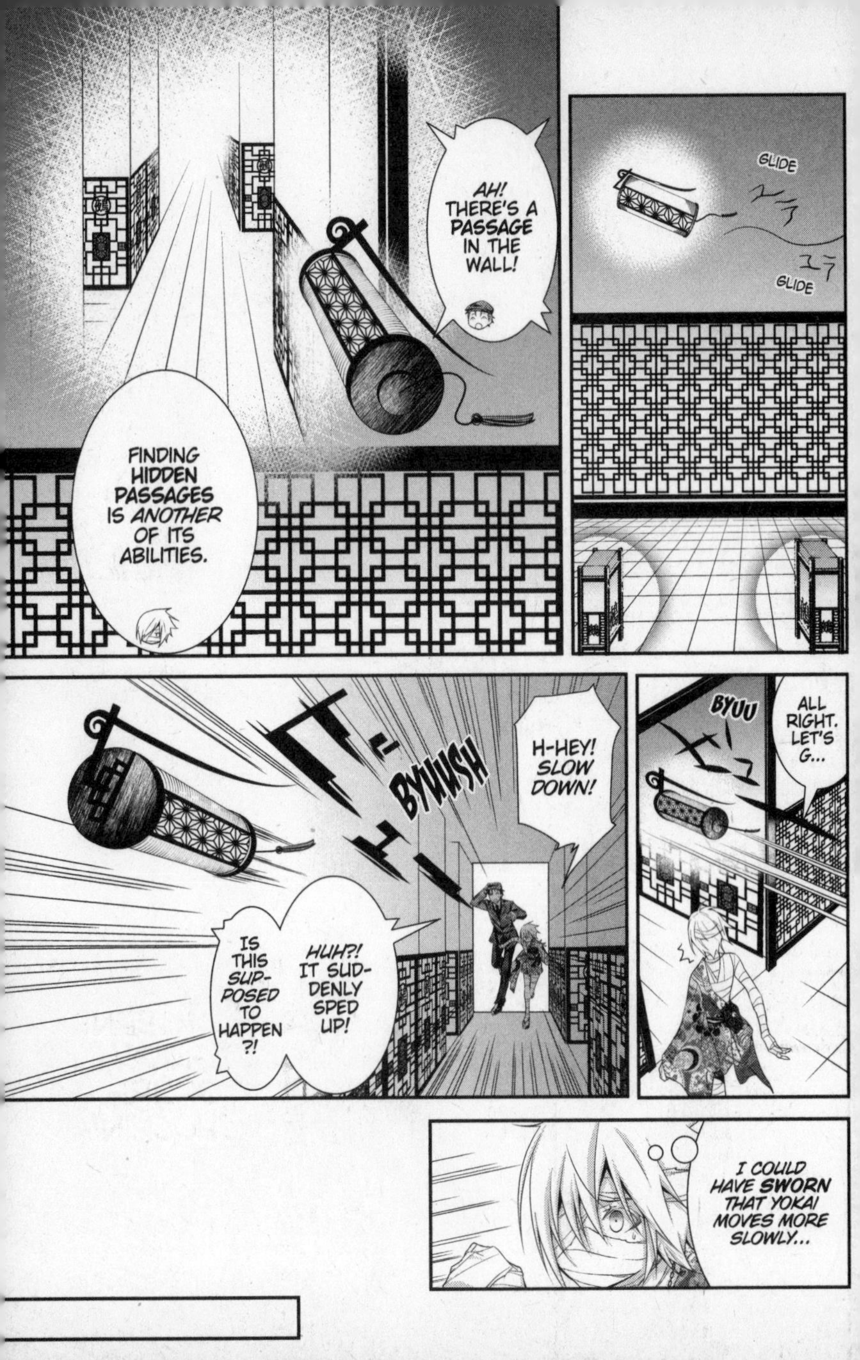
GLIDE
GLIDE
AH! THERE'S A PASSAGE IN THE WALL!
FINDING HIDDEN PASSAGES IS ANOTHER OF ITS ABILITIES.
ALL RIGHT. LET'S G...
BYUU
H-HEY! SLOW DOWN!
BYUUSH
HUH?! IT SUDDENLY SPED UP!
IS THIS SUPPOSED TO HAPPEN?!
I COULD HAVE SWORN THAT YOKAI MOVES MORE SLOWLY...

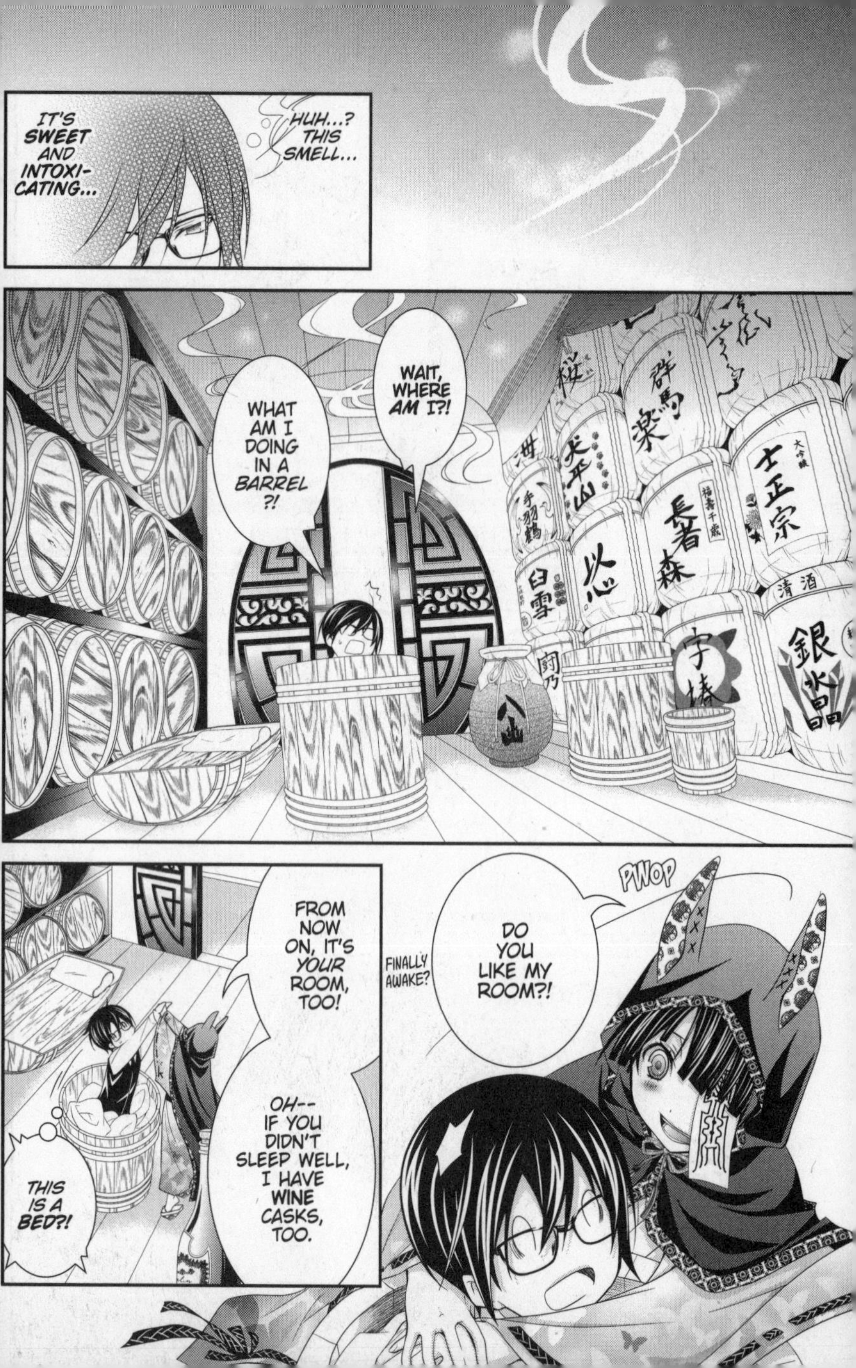
HUH...? THIS SMELL...
IT'S SWEET AND INTOXI-CATING...
WAIT, WHERE AM I?!
WHAT AM I DOING IN A BARREL?!
PWOP
DO YOU LIKE MY ROOM?!
FINALLY AWAKE?
FROM NOW ON, IT'S YOUR ROOM, TOO!
OH-- IF YOU DIDN'T SLEEP WELL, I HAVE WINE CASKS, TOO.
THIS IS A BED?!

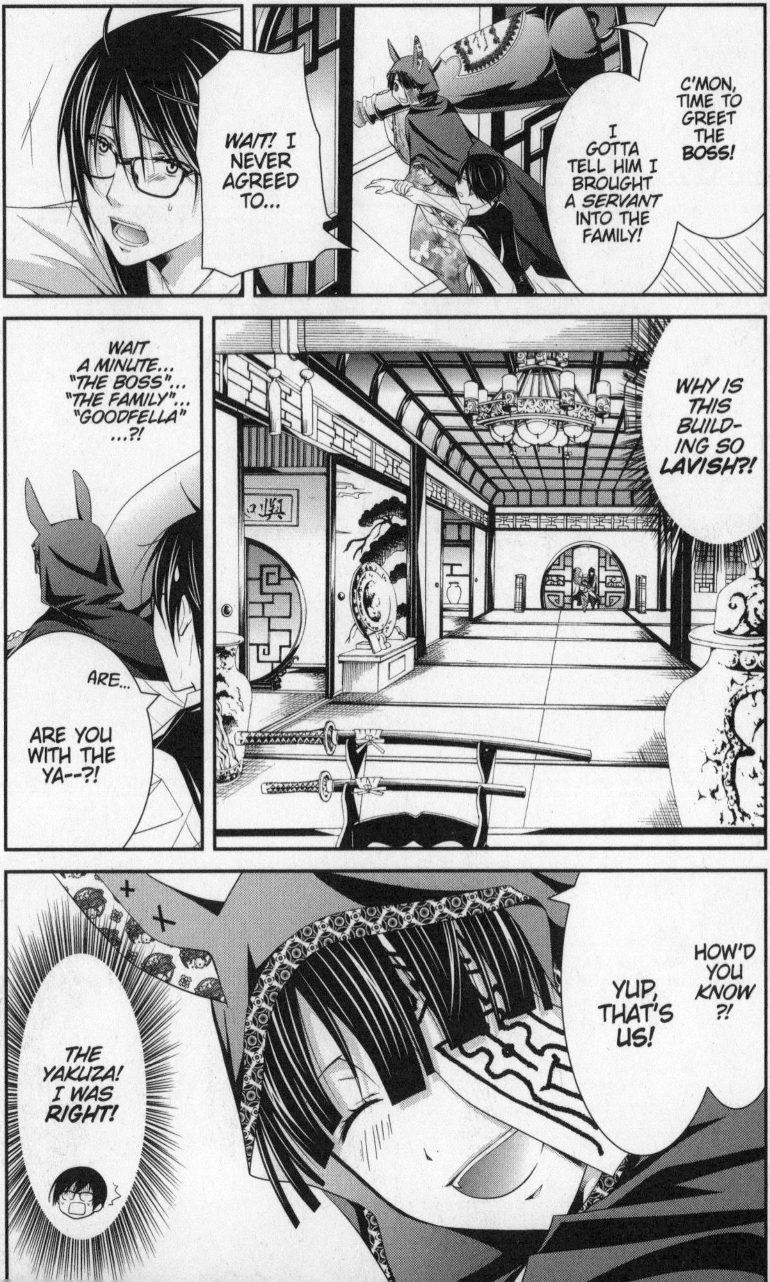
C'MON, TIME TO GREET THE BOSS!
I GOTTA TELL HIM I BROUGHT A SERVANT INTO THE FAMILY!
WAIT! I NEVER AGREED TO...
WHY IS THIS BUILD-ING SO LAVISH?!
WAIT A MINUTE... "THE BOSS"... "THE FAMILY"... "GOODFELLA" ...?!
ARE...
ARE YOU WITH THE YA--?!
HOW'D YOU KNOW ?!
YUP, THAT'S US!
THE YAKUZA! I WAS RIGHT!

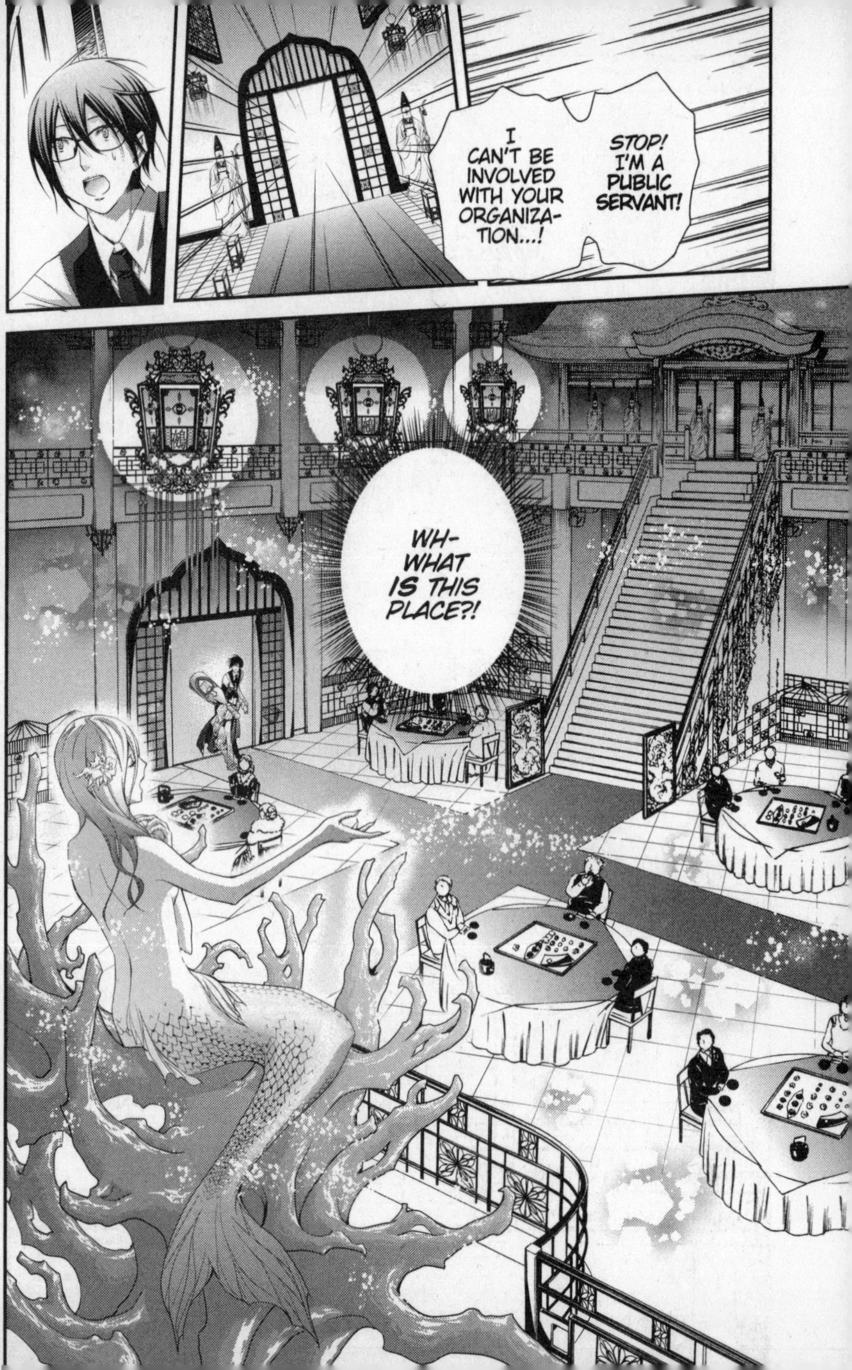
STOP! I'M A PUBLIC SERVANT!
I CAN'T BE INVOLVED WITH YOUR ORGANIZATION...!
WH-WHAT IS THIS PLACE?!

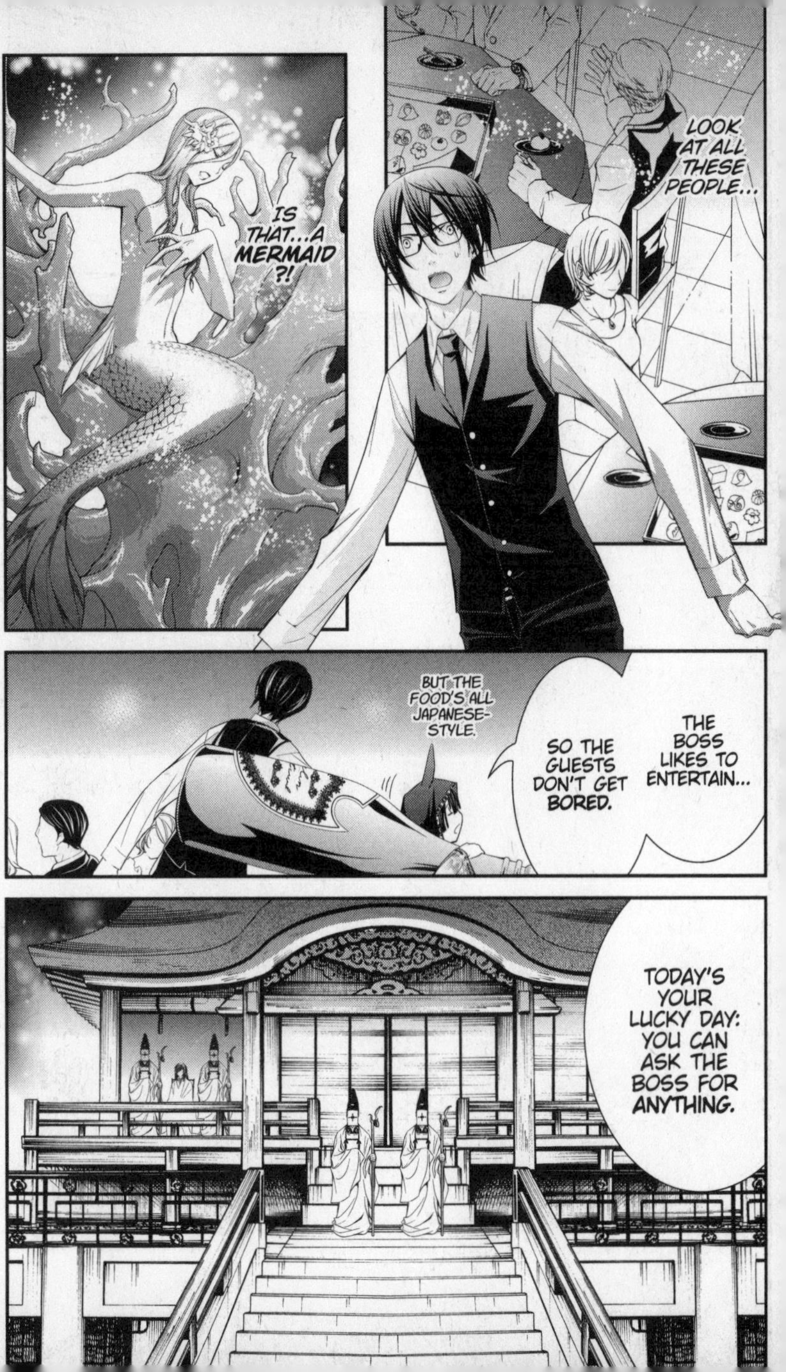
LOOK AT ALL THESE PEOPLE...
IS THAT...A MERMAID?!
THE BOSS LIKES TO ENTERTAIN...
SO THE GUESTS DON'T GET BORED.
BUT THE FOOD'S ALL JAPANESE-STYLE.
TODAY'S YOUR LUCKY DAY: YOU CAN ASK THE BOSS FOR ANYTHING.

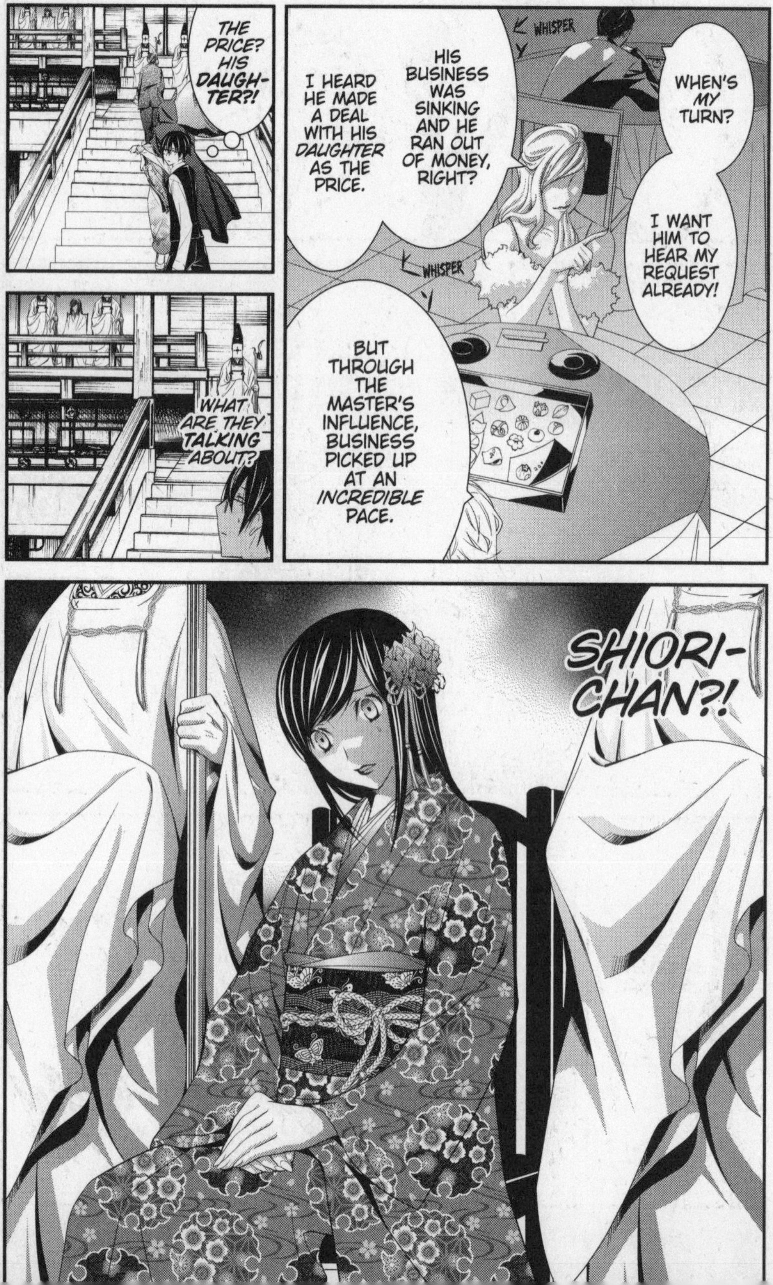
WHEN'S MY TURN?
I WANT HIM TO HEAR MY REQUEST ALREADY!
WHISPER
HIS BUSINESS WAS SINKING AND HE RAN OUT OF MONEY, RIGHT?
I HEARD HE MADE A DEAL WITH HIS DAUGHTER AS THE PRICE.
WHISPER
BUT THROUGH THE MASTER'S INFLUENCE, BUSINESS PICKED UP AT AN INCREDIBLE PACE.
THE PRICE? HIS DAUGHTER?!
WHAT ARE THEY TALKING ABOUT?
SHIORI-CHAN?!

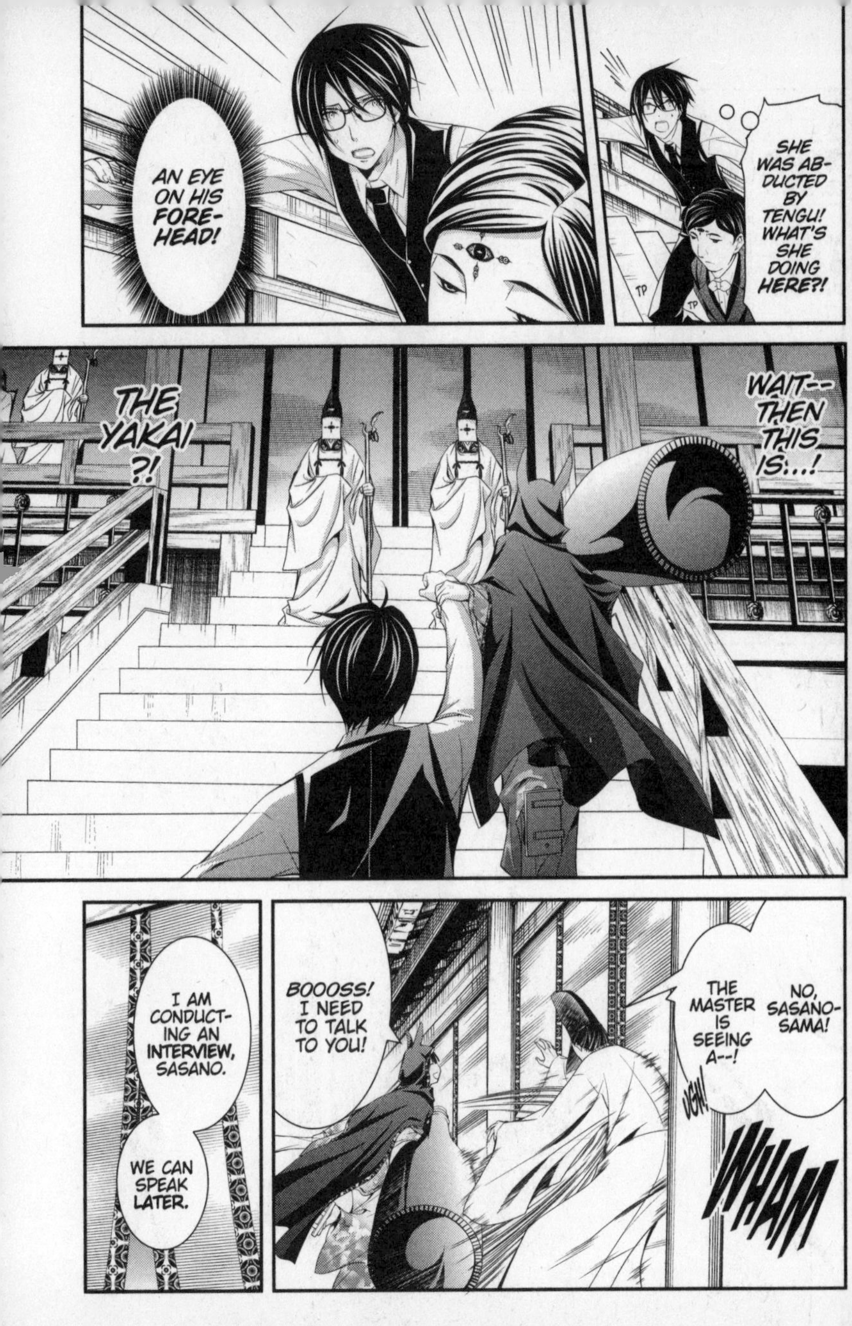
SHE WAS AB-DUCTED BY TENGU! WHAT'S SHE DOING HERE?!
TP
TP
AN EYE ON HIS FORE-HEAD!
WAIT-- THEN THIS IS...!
THE YAKAI ?!
NO, SASANO-SAMA!
THE MASTER IS SEEING A--!
UGH!
WHAM
BOOOSS! I NEED TO TALK TO YOU!
I AM CONDUCTING AN INTERVIEW, SASANO.
WE CAN SPEAK LATER.

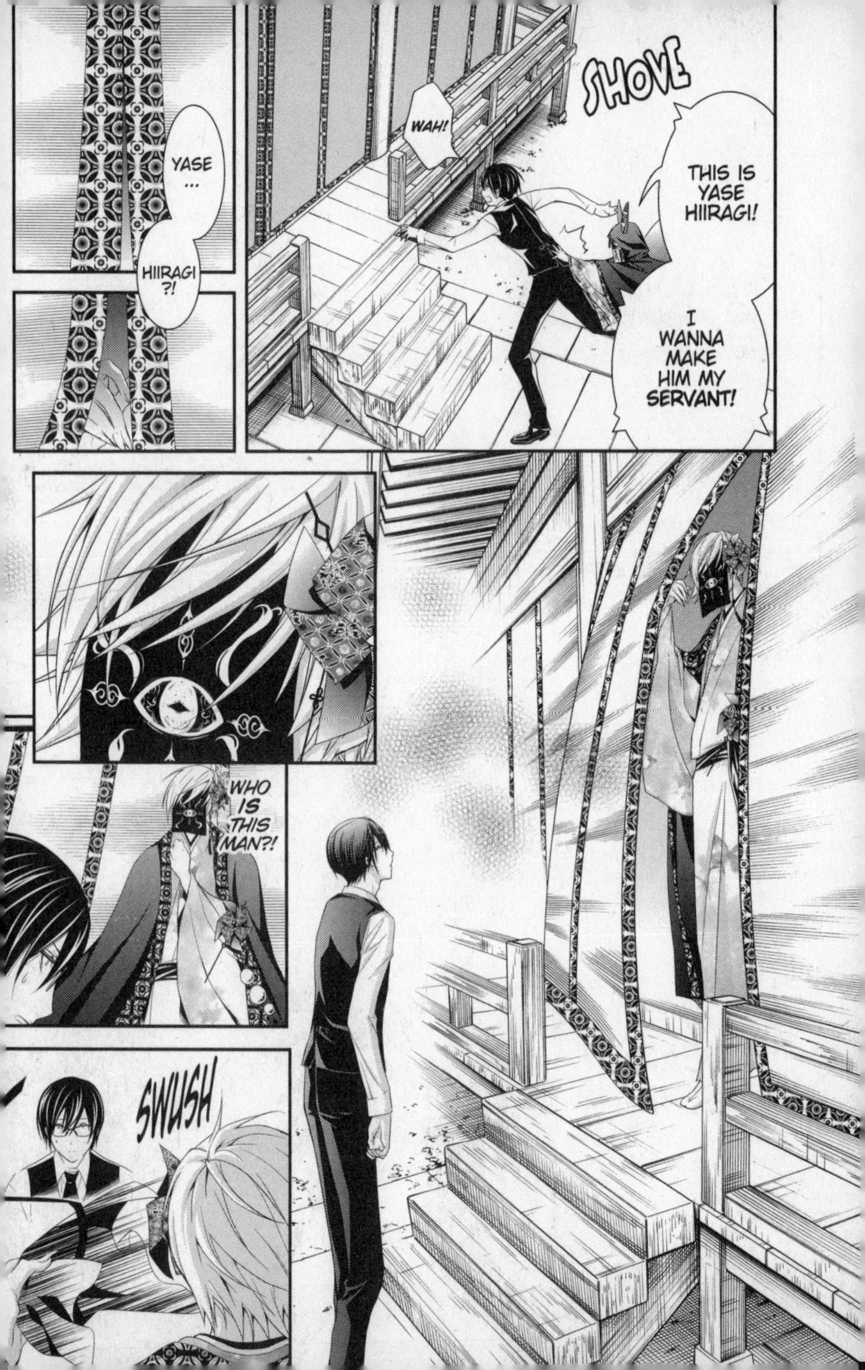
SHOVE
THIS IS YASE HIIRAGI!
WAH!
I WANNA MAKE HIM MY SERVANT!
YASE ...
HIIRAGI ?!
WHO IS THIS MAN?!
SWUSH

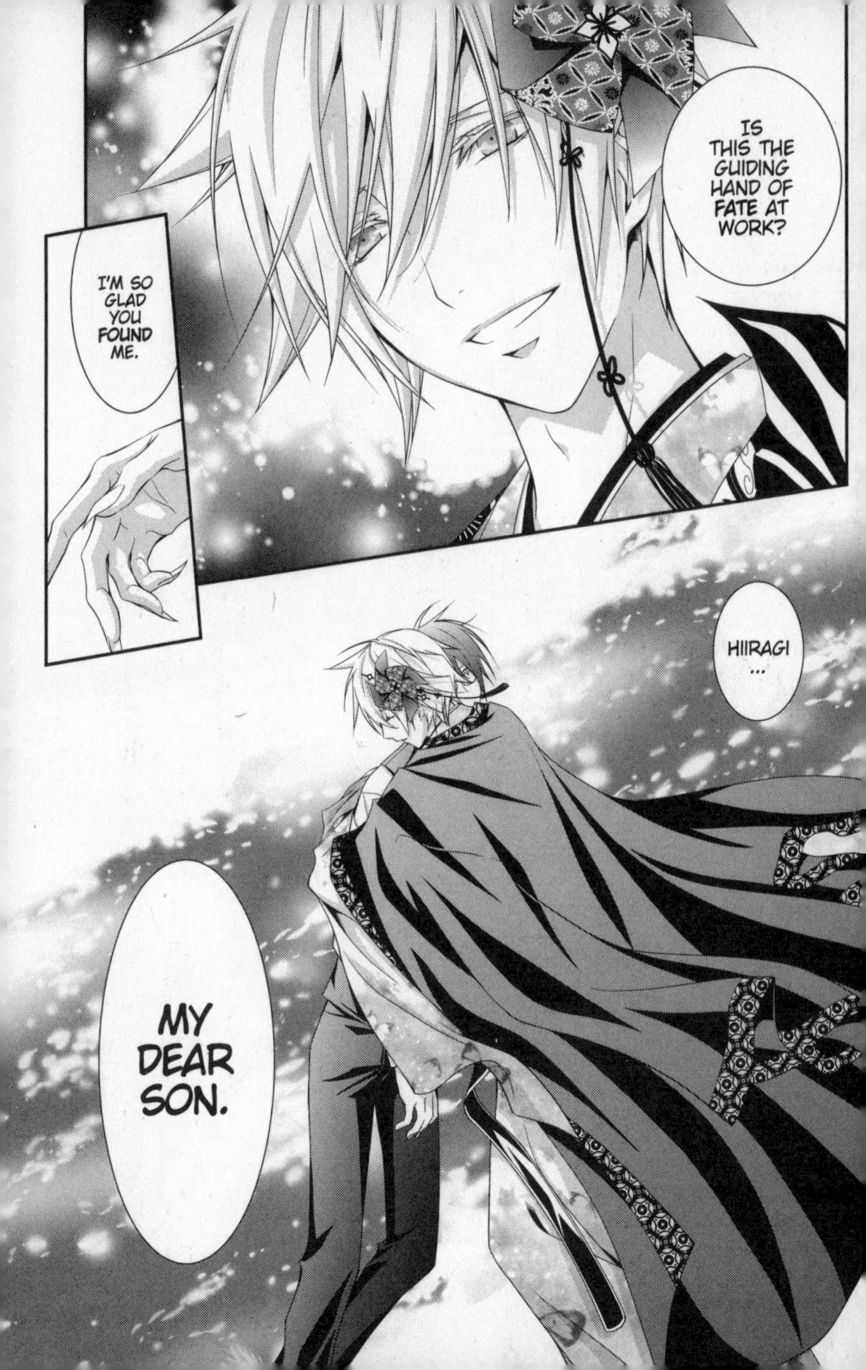
IS THIS THE GUIDING HAND OF FATE AT WORK?
I'M SO GLAD YOU FOUND ME.
HIIRAGI...
MY DEAR SON.

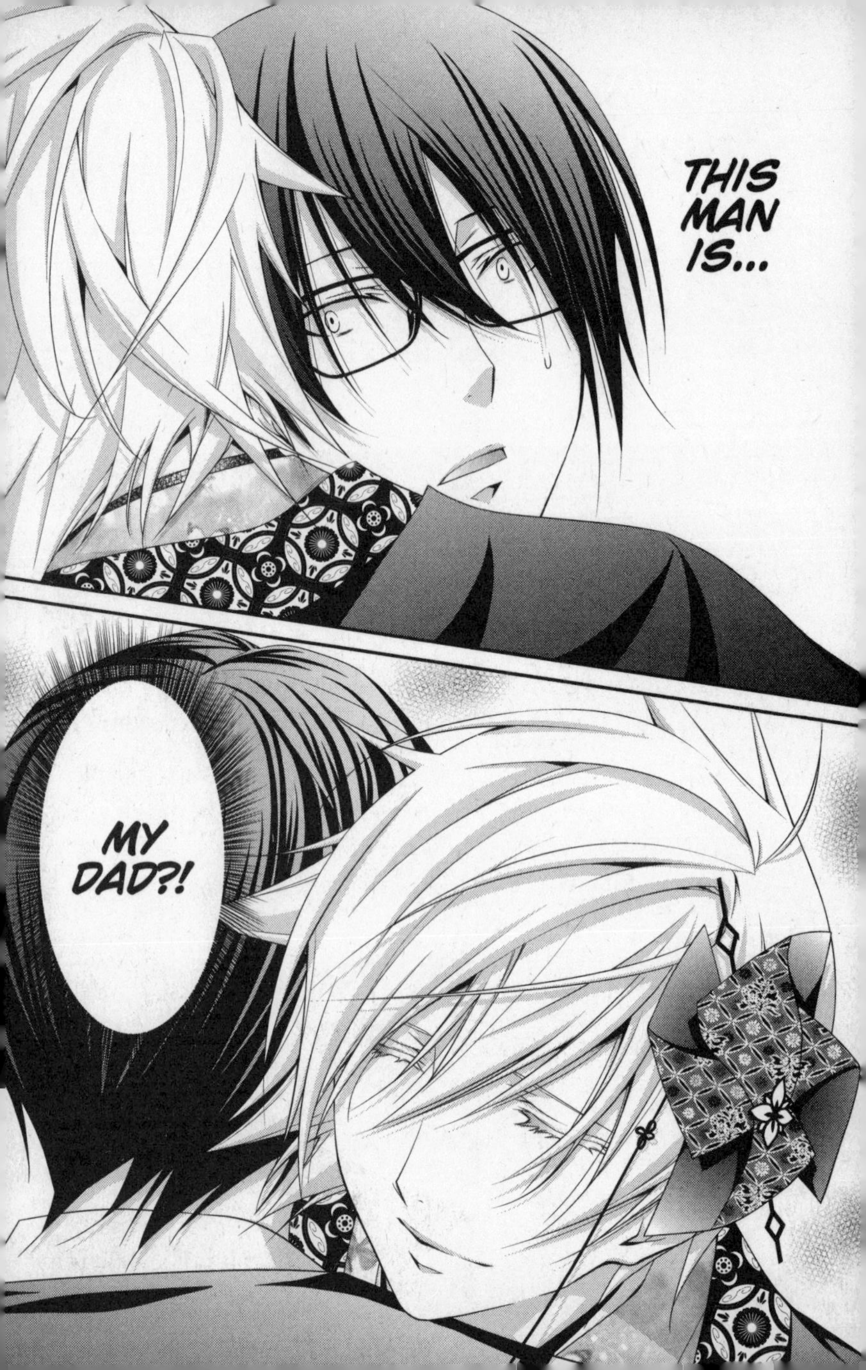
THIS MAN IS...
MY DAD?!

Rental 11: CHANCE MEETING

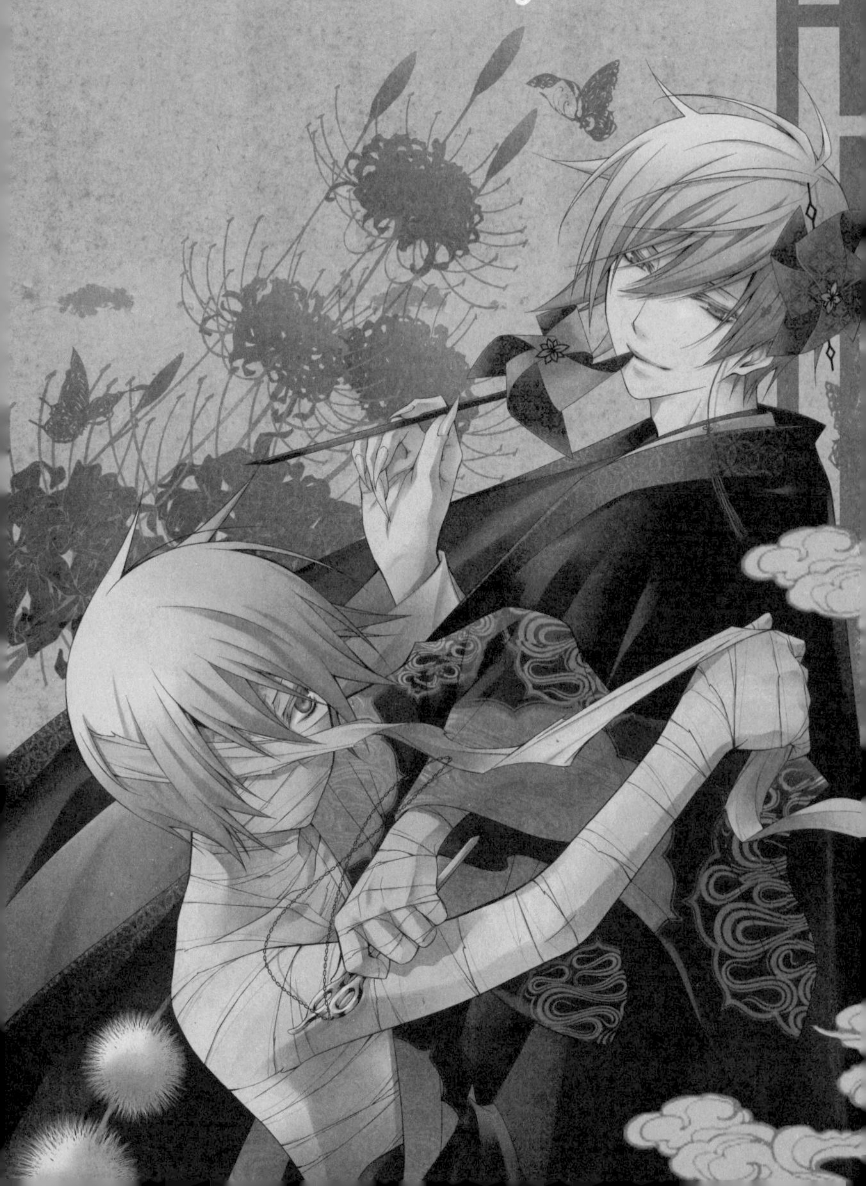

Yōkai Rental Shop

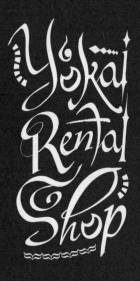

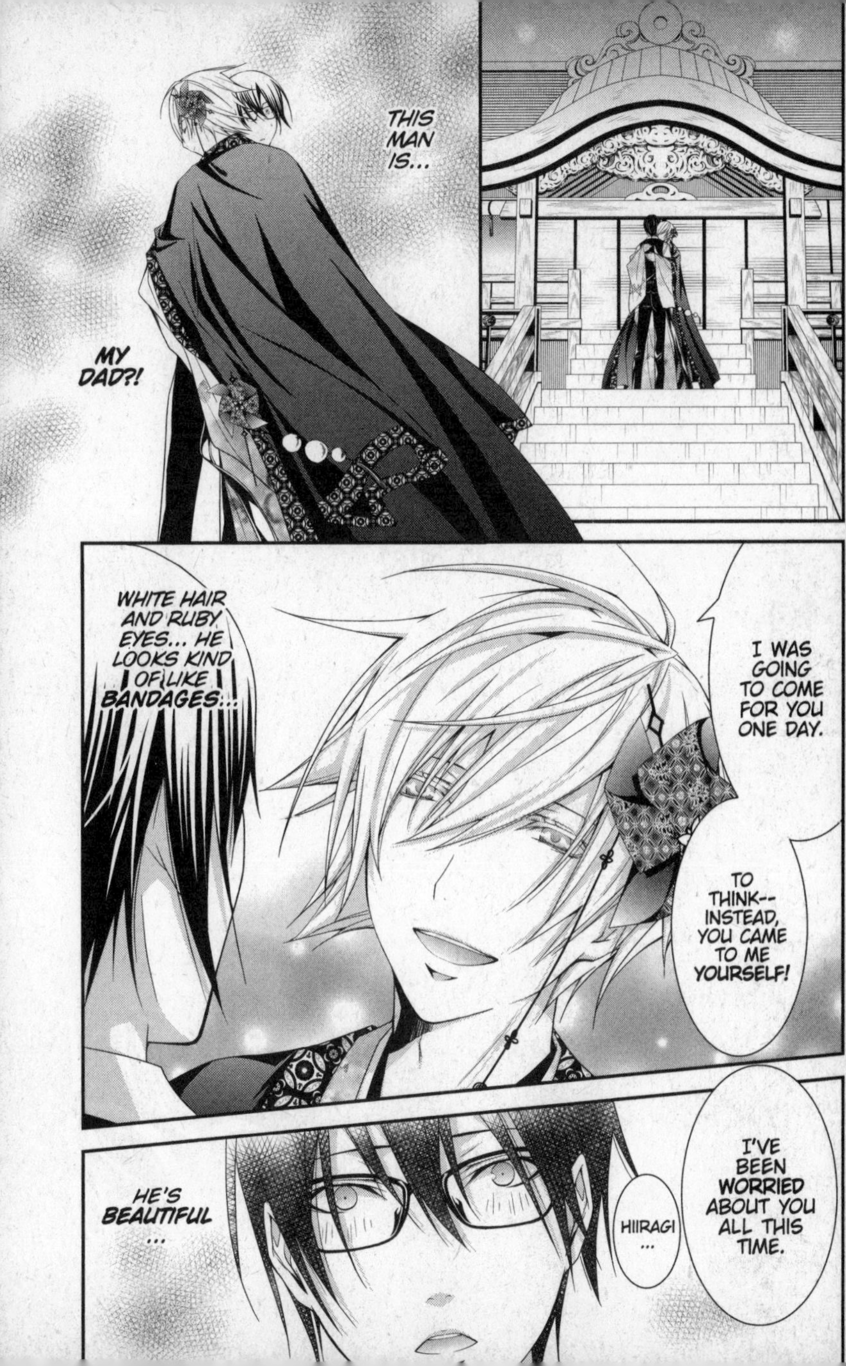
THIS MAN IS...
MY DAD?!
I WAS GOING TO COME FOR YOU ONE DAY.
TO THINK-- INSTEAD, YOU CAME TO ME YOURSELF!
WHITE HAIR AND RUBY EYES... HE LOOKS KIND OF LIKE BANDAGES...
I'VE BEEN WORRIED ABOUT YOU ALL THIS TIME.
HIIRAGI...
HE'S BEAUTIFUL...

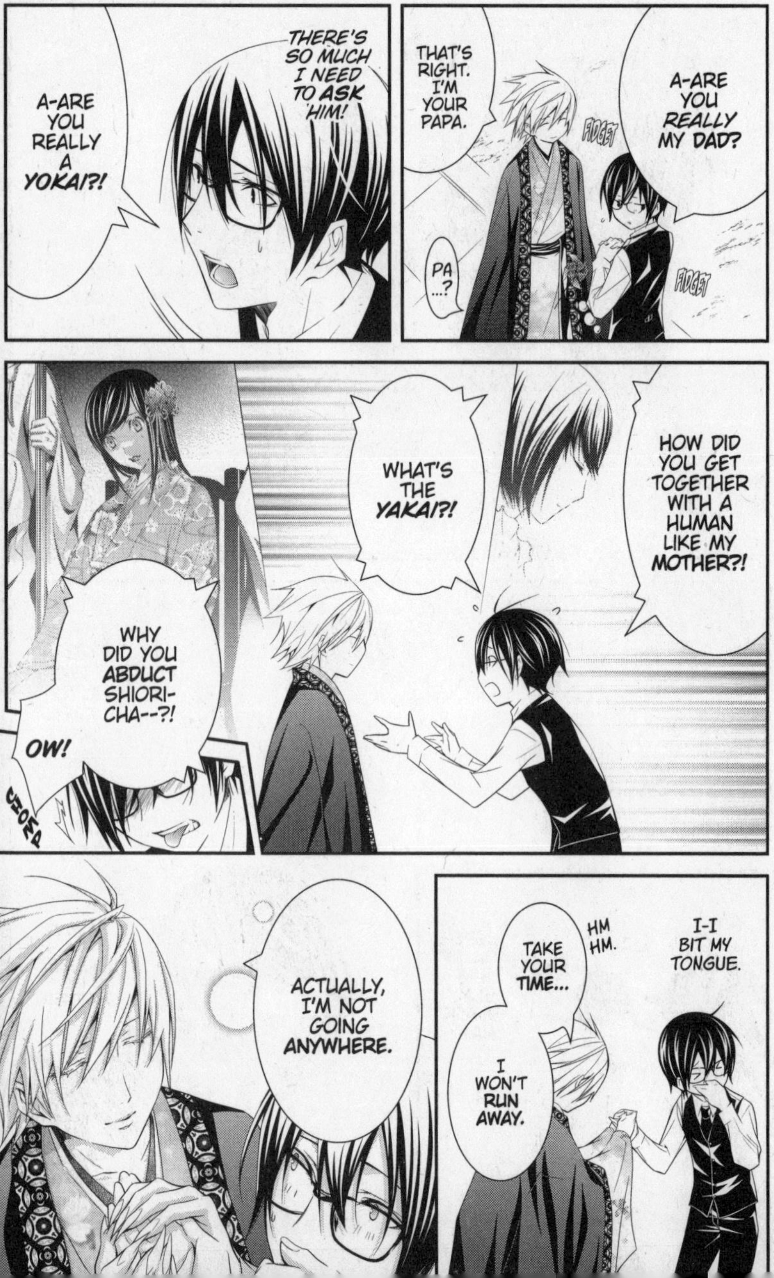
A-ARE YOU REALLY MY DAD?
FIDGET
FIDGET
THAT'S RIGHT. I'M YOUR PAPA.
PA ...?
THERE'S SO MUCH I NEED TO ASK HIM!
A-ARE YOU REALLY A YOKAI?!
HOW DID YOU GET TOGETHER WITH A HUMAN LIKE MY MOTHER?!
WHAT'S THE YAKAI?!
WHY DID YOU ABDUCT SHIORI-CHA--?!
OW!
I-I BIT MY TONGUE.
HM HM.
TAKE YOUR TIME...
I WON'T RUN AWAY.
ACTUALLY, I'M NOT GOING ANYWHERE.

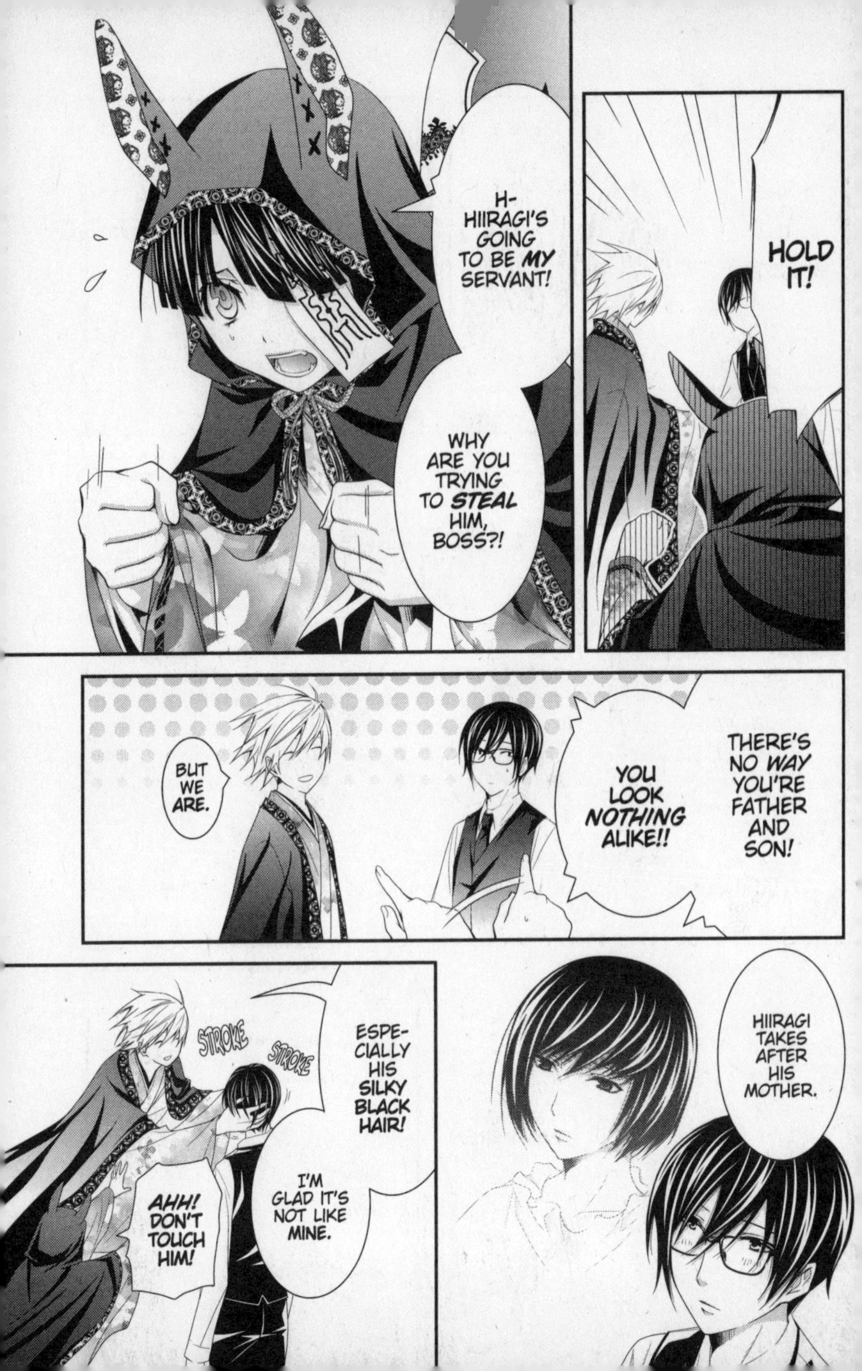
HOLD IT!
H-HIIRAGI'S GOING TO BE MY SERVANT!
WHY ARE YOU TRYING TO STEAL HIM, BOSS?!
THERE'S NO WAY YOU'RE FATHER AND SON!
YOU LOOK NOTHING ALIKE!!
BUT WE ARE.
HIIRAGI TAKES AFTER HIS MOTHER.
ESPE-CIALLY HIS SILKY BLACK HAIR!
STROKE
STROKE
I'M GLAD IT'S NOT LIKE MINE.
AHH! DON'T TOUCH HIM!

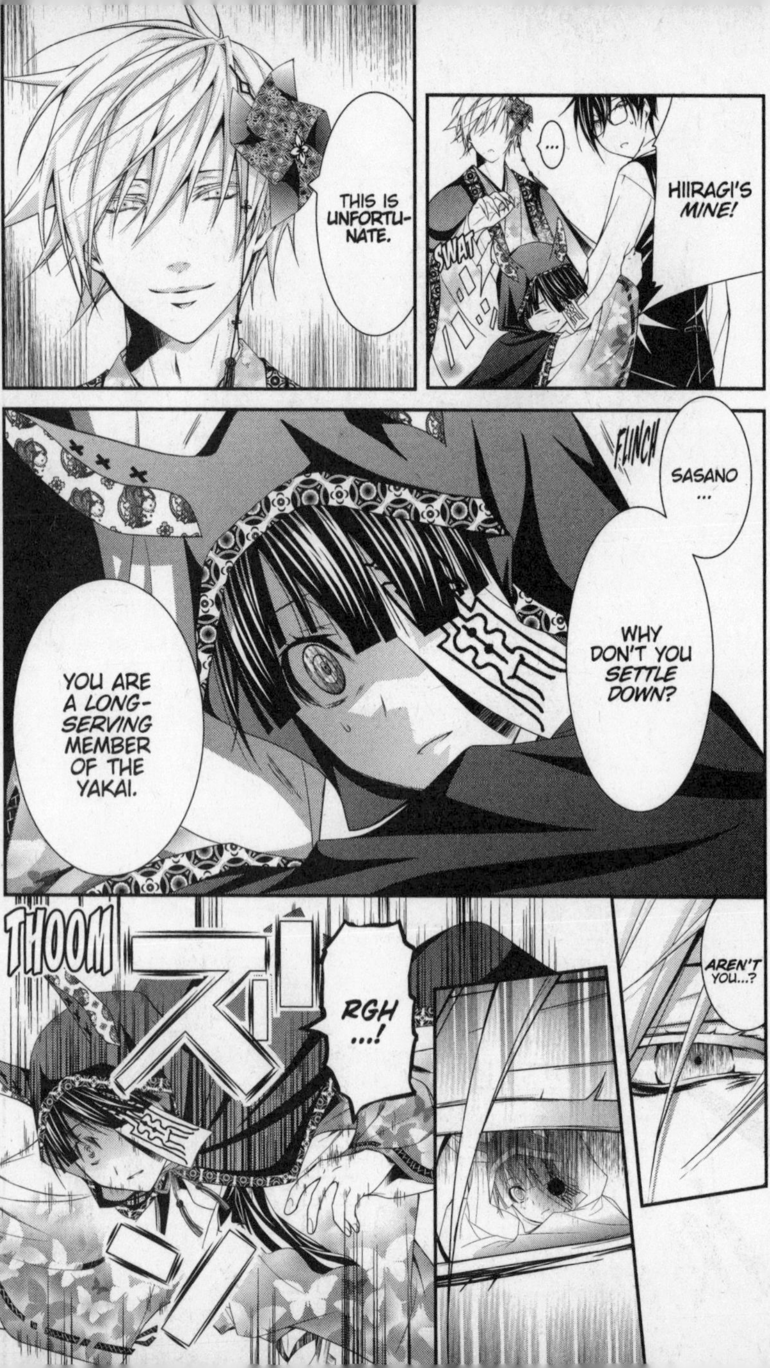
...
HIIRAGI'S MINE!
SWAT
THIS IS UNFORTUNATE.
FLINCH
SASANO ...
WHY DON'T YOU SETTLE DOWN?
YOU ARE A LONG-SERVING MEMBER OF THE YAKAI.
AREN'T YOU...?
THOOM
RGH ...!

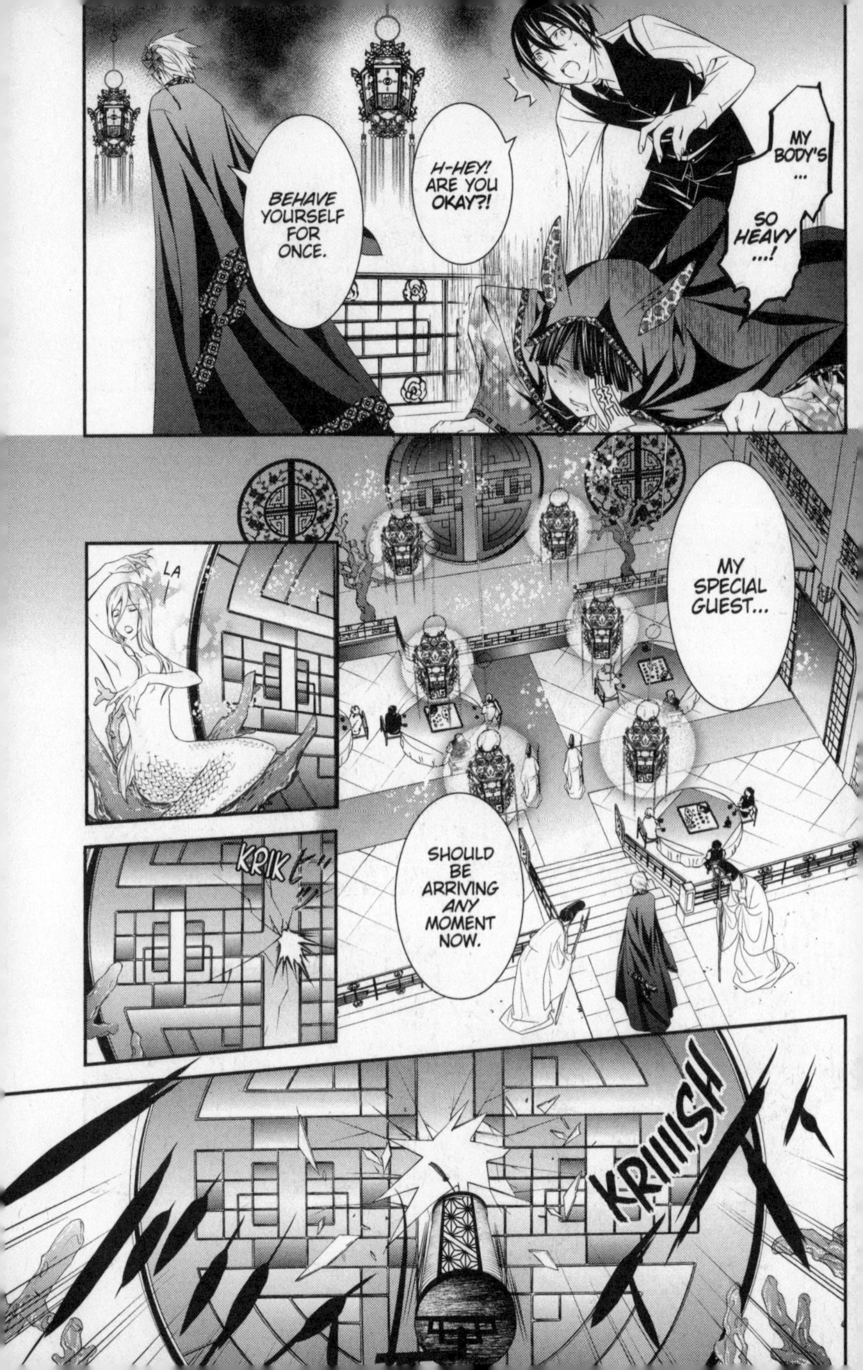
MY BODY'S ...
SO HEAVY ...!
H-HEY! ARE YOU OKAY?!
BEHAVE YOURSELF FOR ONCE.
MY SPECIAL GUEST...
SHOULD BE ARRIVING ANY MOMENT NOW.
LA
KRIK
KRIIISH

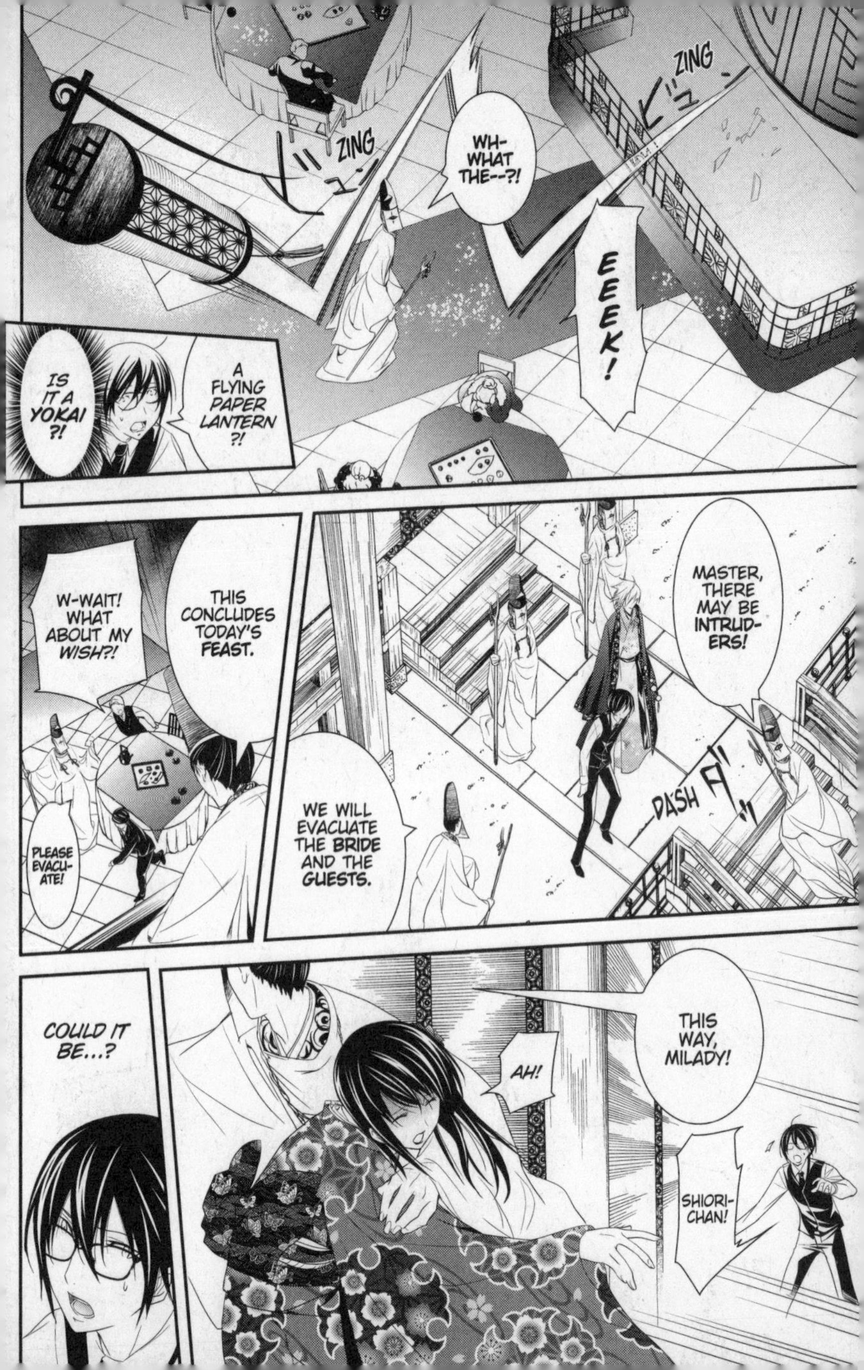
ZING
WH- WHAT THE--?!
ZING
EEEK!
A FLYING PAPER LANTERN?!
IS IT A YOKAI?!
MASTER, THERE MAY BE INTRUD- ERS!
DASH
WE WILL EVACUATE THE BRIDE AND THE GUESTS.
THIS CONCLUDES TODAY'S FEAST.
W-WAIT! WHAT ABOUT MY WISH?!
PLEASE EVACU- ATE!
THIS WAY, MILADY!
AH!
SHIORI- CHAN!
COULD IT BE...?

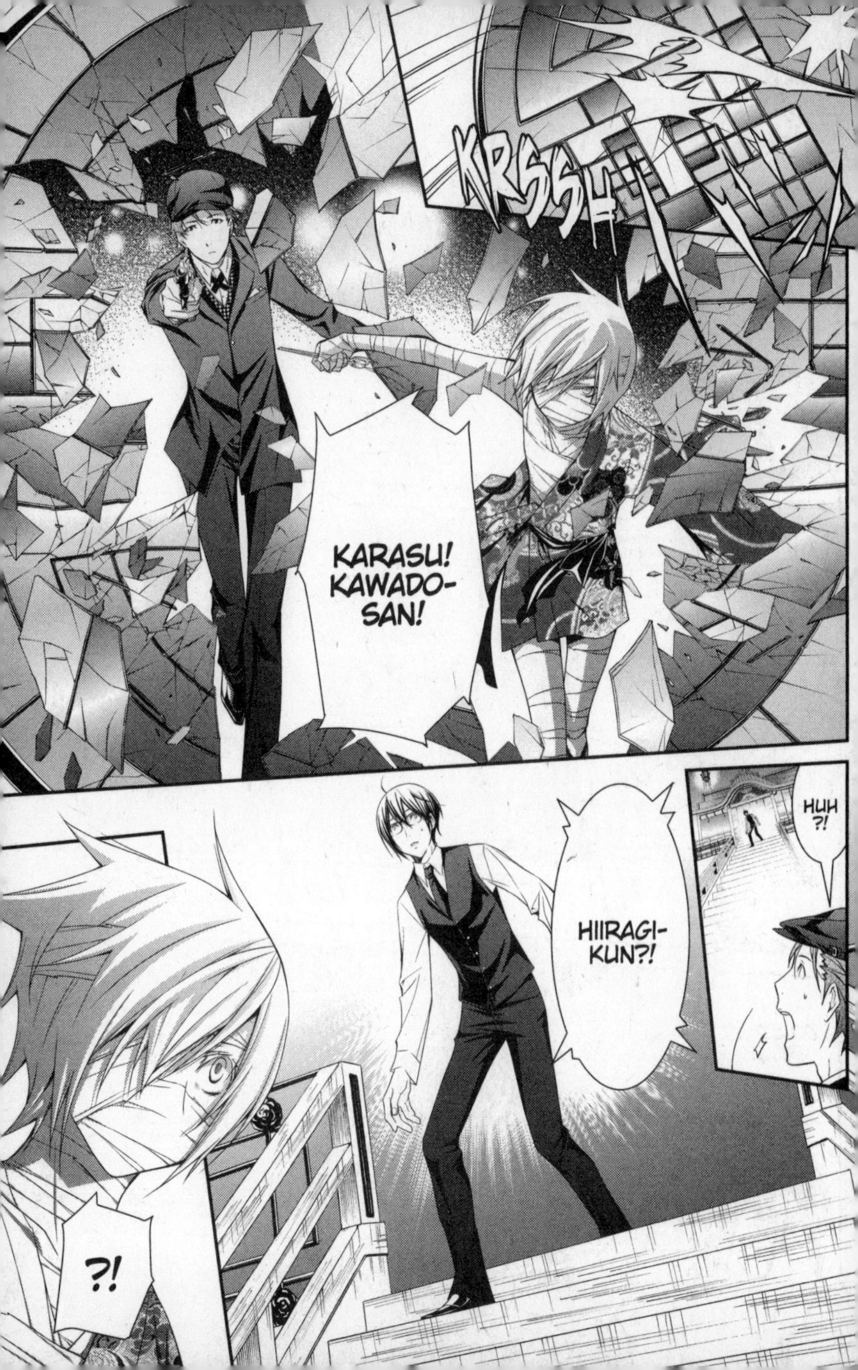
KRSSH
KARASU! KAWADO-SAN!
HUH?!
HIIRAGI-KUN?!
?!

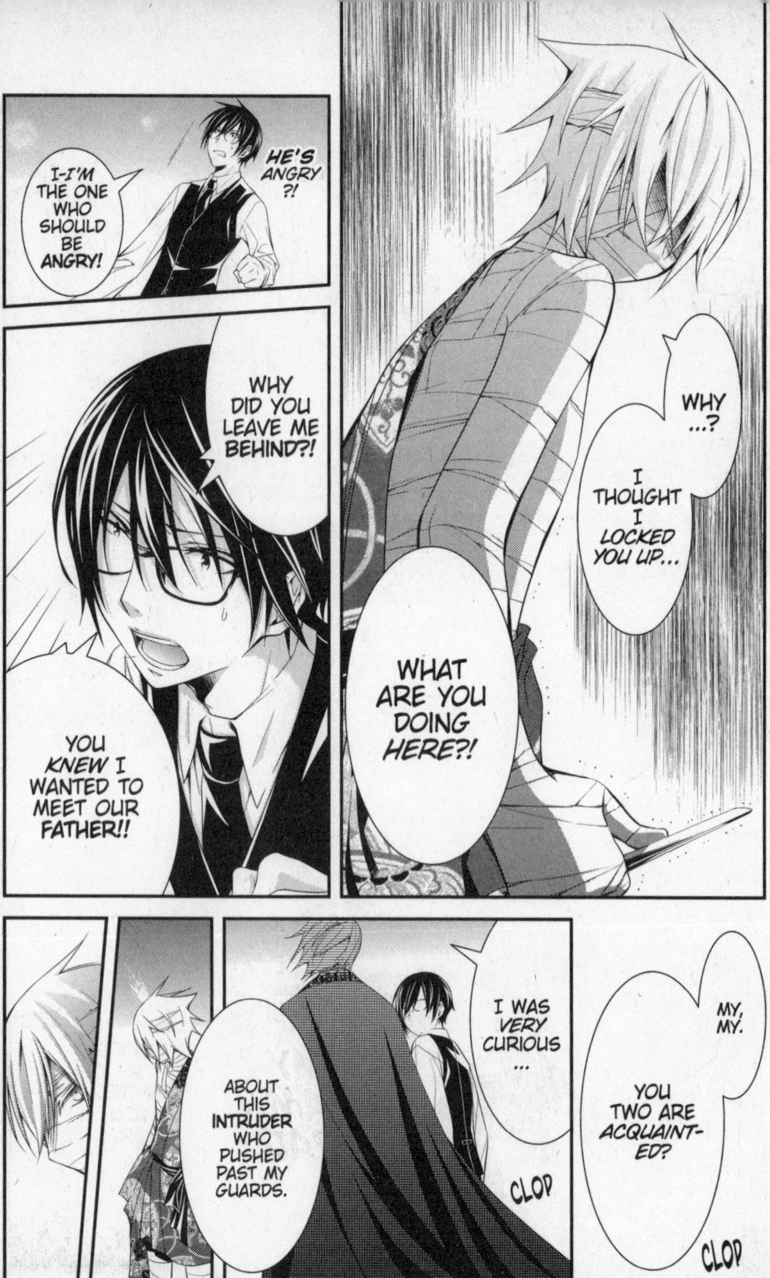
WHY ...?
I THOUGHT I LOCKED YOU UP...
WHAT ARE YOU DOING HERE?!
HE'S ANGRY?!
I-I'M THE ONE WHO SHOULD BE ANGRY!
WHY DID YOU LEAVE ME BEHIND?!
YOU KNEW I WANTED TO MEET OUR FATHER!!
MY, MY.
YOU TWO ARE ACQUAINT-ED?
CLOP
CLOP
I WAS VERY CURIOUS ...
ABOUT THIS INTRUDER WHO PUSHED PAST MY GUARDS.

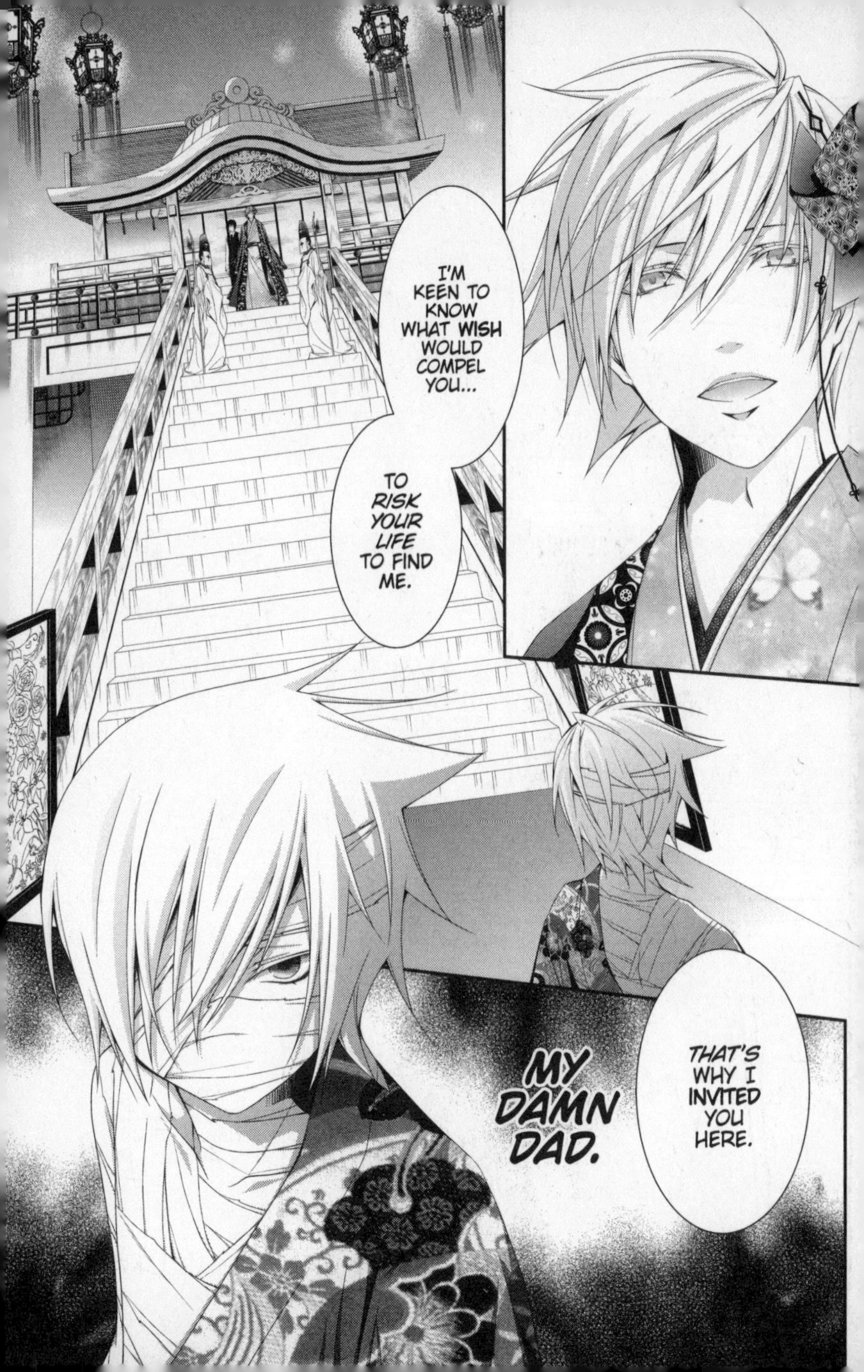
I'M KEEN TO KNOW WHAT WISH WOULD COMPEL YOU...
TO RISK YOUR LIFE TO FIND ME.
THAT'S WHY I INVITED YOU HERE.
MY DAMN DAD.

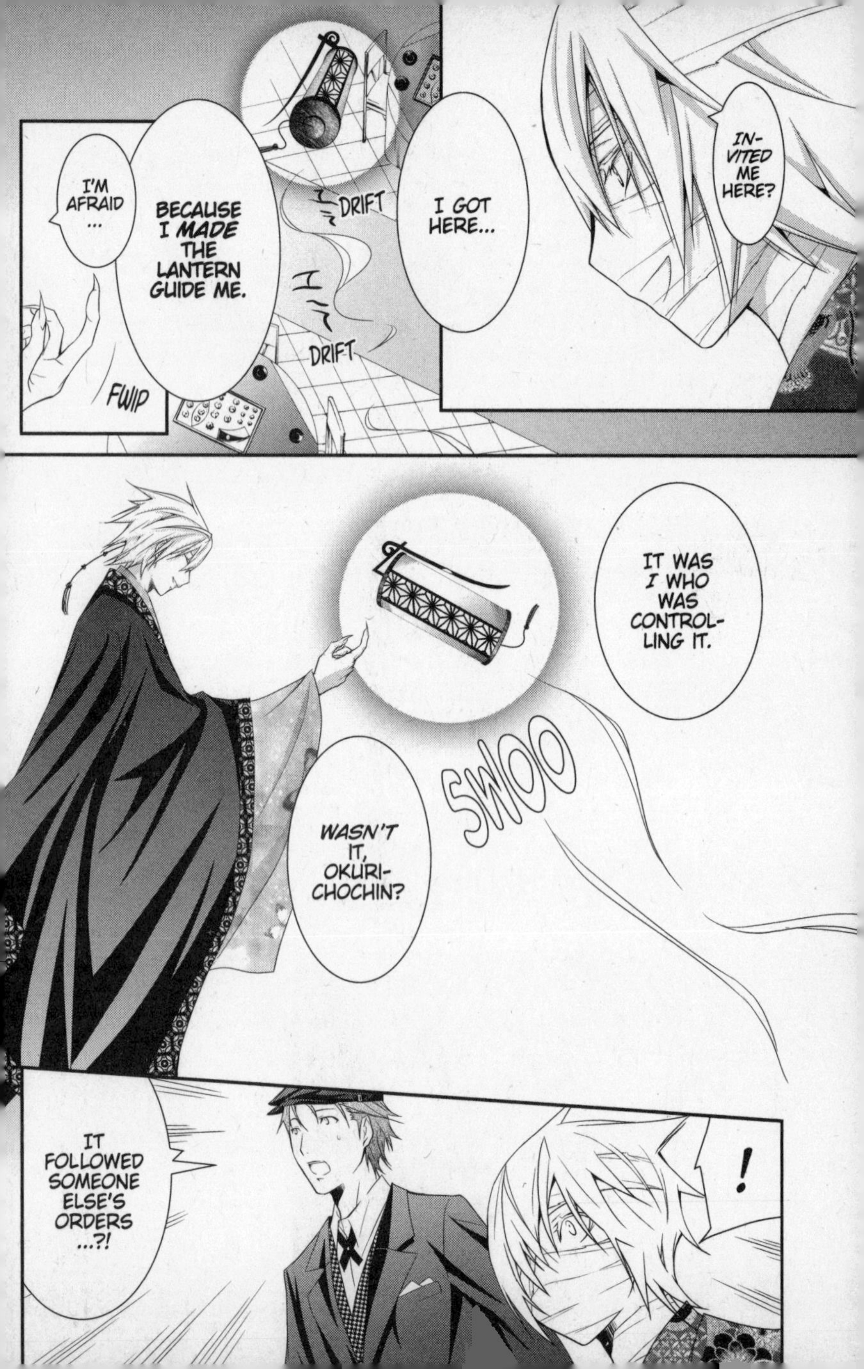
IN-VITED ME HERE?
I GOT HERE...
DRIFT
DRIFT
BECAUSE I *MADE* THE LANTERN GUIDE ME.
I'M AFRAID ...
FWIP
IT WAS *I* WHO WAS CONTROL-LING IT.
SWOO
WASN'T IT, OKURI-CHOCHIN?
!
IT FOLLOWED SOMEONE ELSE'S ORDERS ...?!

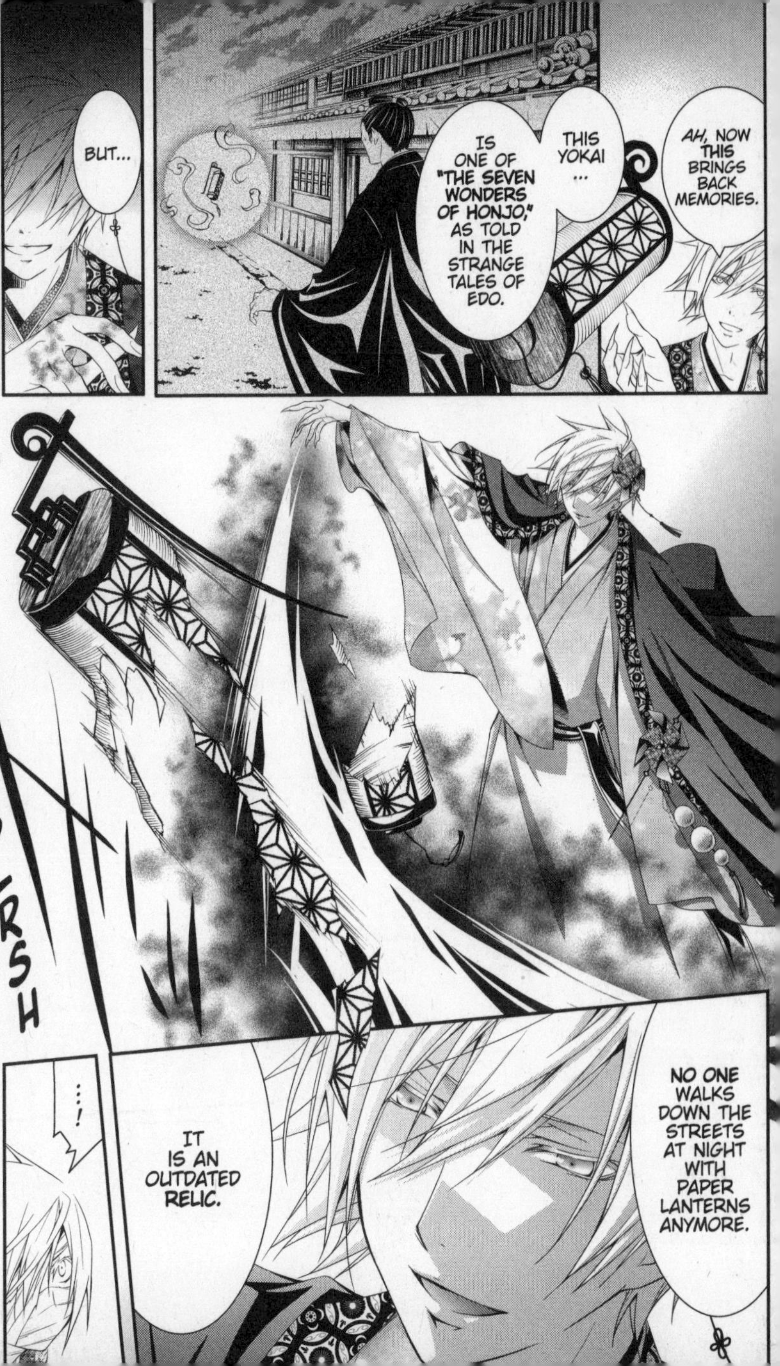
AH, NOW THIS BRINGS BACK MEMORIES.
THIS YOKAI ...
IS ONE OF "THE SEVEN WONDERS OF HONJO," AS TOLD IN THE STRANGE TALES OF EDO.
BUT...
SLRSH
NO ONE WALKS DOWN THE STREETS AT NIGHT WITH PAPER LANTERNS ANYMORE.
IT IS AN OUTDATED RELIC.
...!

*A SUPERNATURAL PHENOMENON RESEMBLING A PAPER LANTERN THAT WOULD MISLEAD THOSE WHO WALKED THE NIGHT STREETS WITHOUT A LIGHT.

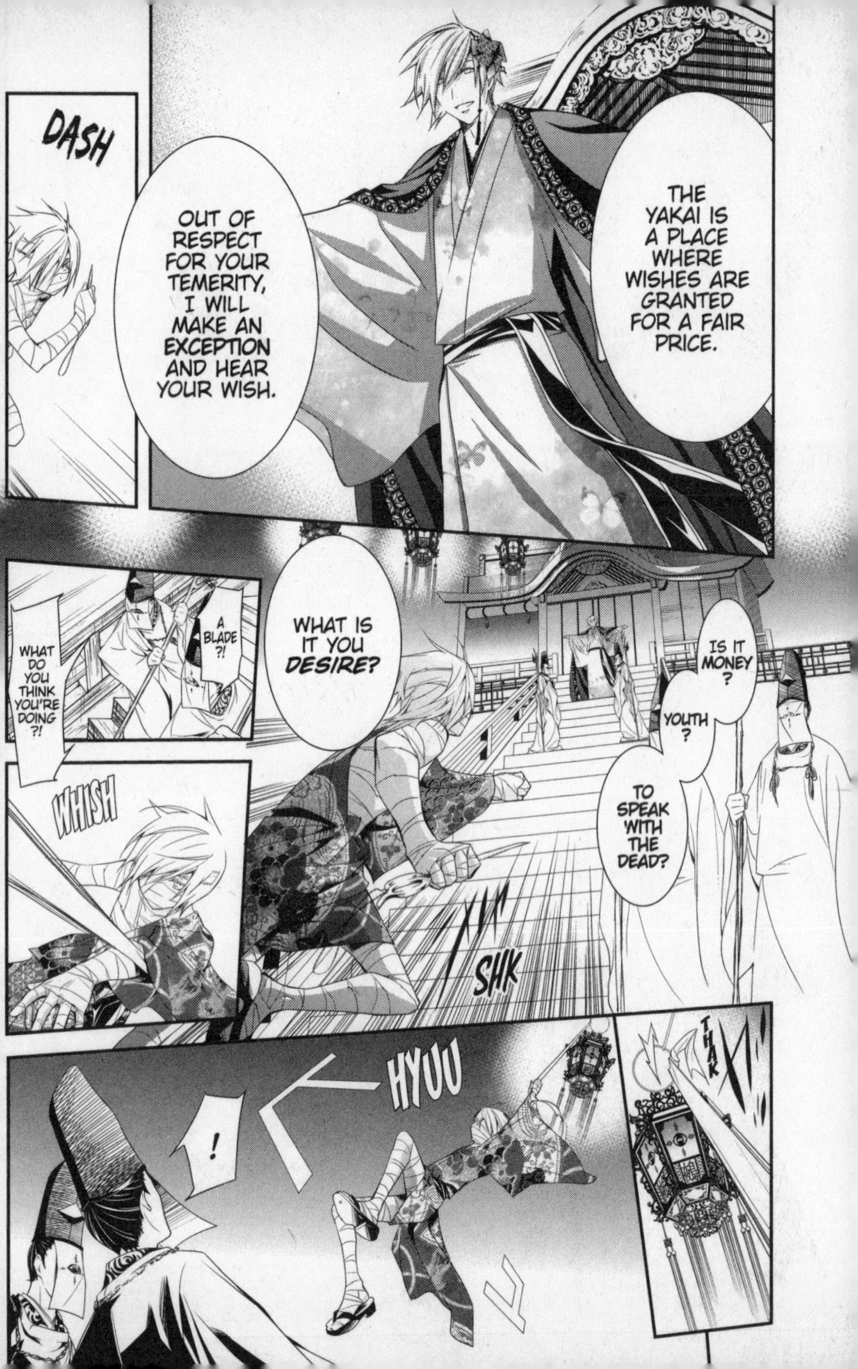
THE YAKAI IS A PLACE WHERE WISHES ARE GRANTED FOR A FAIR PRICE.
OUT OF RESPECT FOR YOUR TEMERITY, I WILL MAKE AN EXCEPTION AND HEAR YOUR WISH.
DASH
IS IT MONEY?
YOUTH?
TO SPEAK WITH THE DEAD?
WHAT IS IT YOU *DESIRE?*
SHK
A BLADE?!
WHAT DO YOU THINK YOU'RE DOING?!
WHISH
THAK
HYUU
!

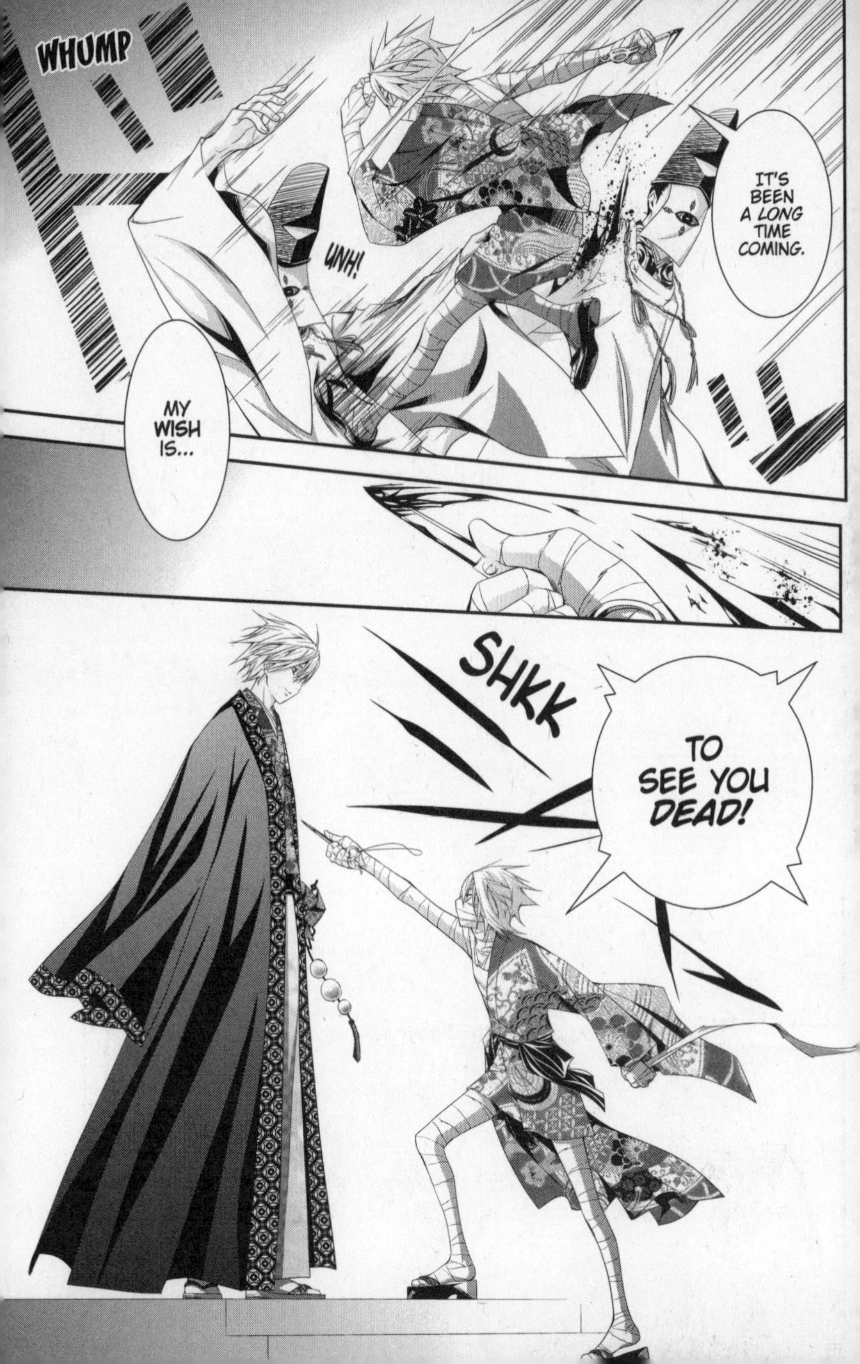
IT'S BEEN A LONG TIME COMING.
WHUMP
UNH!
MY WISH IS...
SHKK
TO SEE YOU DEAD!

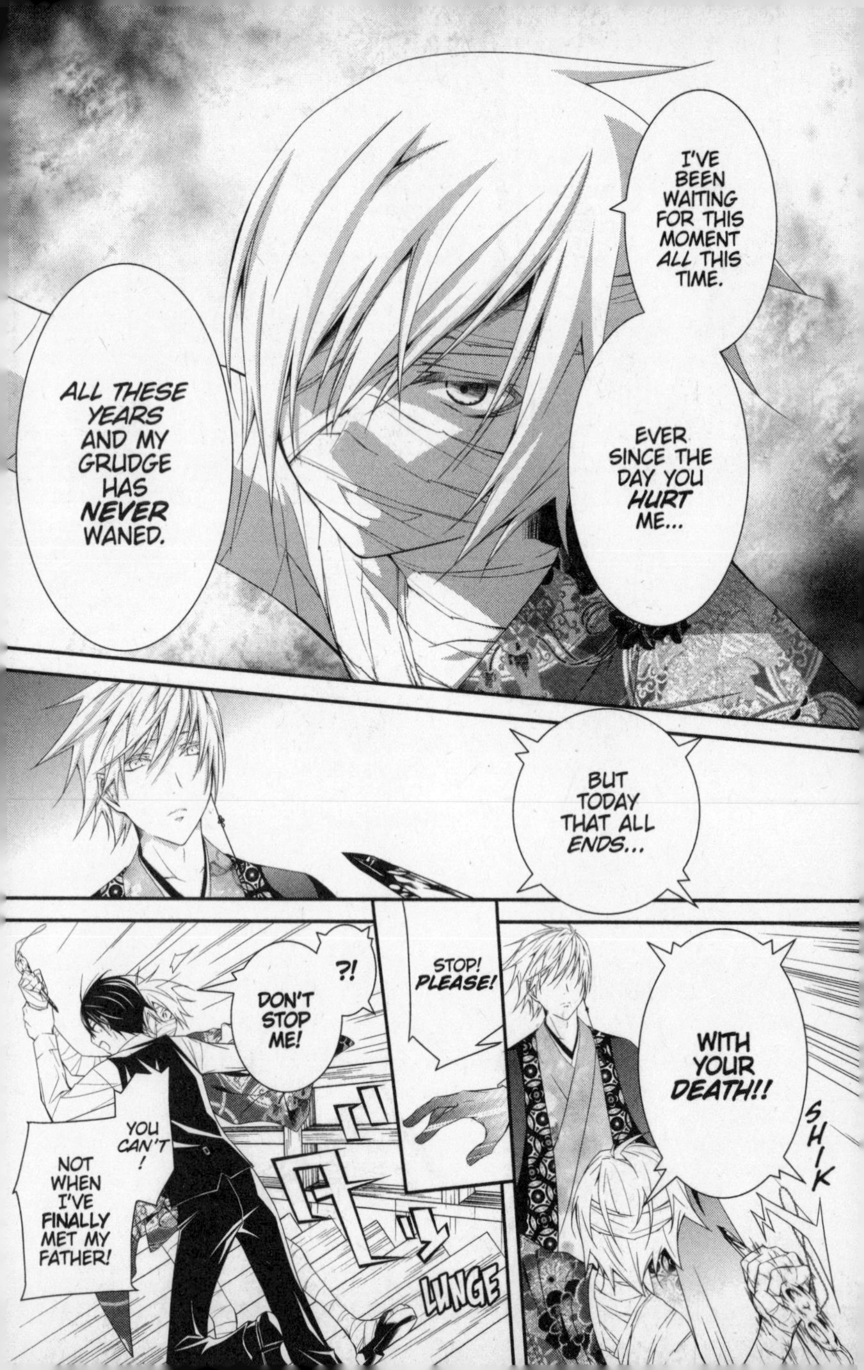
I'VE BEEN WAITING FOR THIS MOMENT *ALL* THIS TIME.
EVER SINCE THE DAY YOU ***HURT*** ME...
ALL THESE YEARS AND MY GRUDGE HAS ***NEVER*** WANED.
BUT TODAY THAT ALL *ENDS*...
WITH YOUR ***DEATH!!***
SHIK
STOP! ***PLEASE!***
?!
DON'T STOP ME!
YOU CAN'T!
NOT WHEN I'VE FINALLY MET MY FATHER!
LUNGE

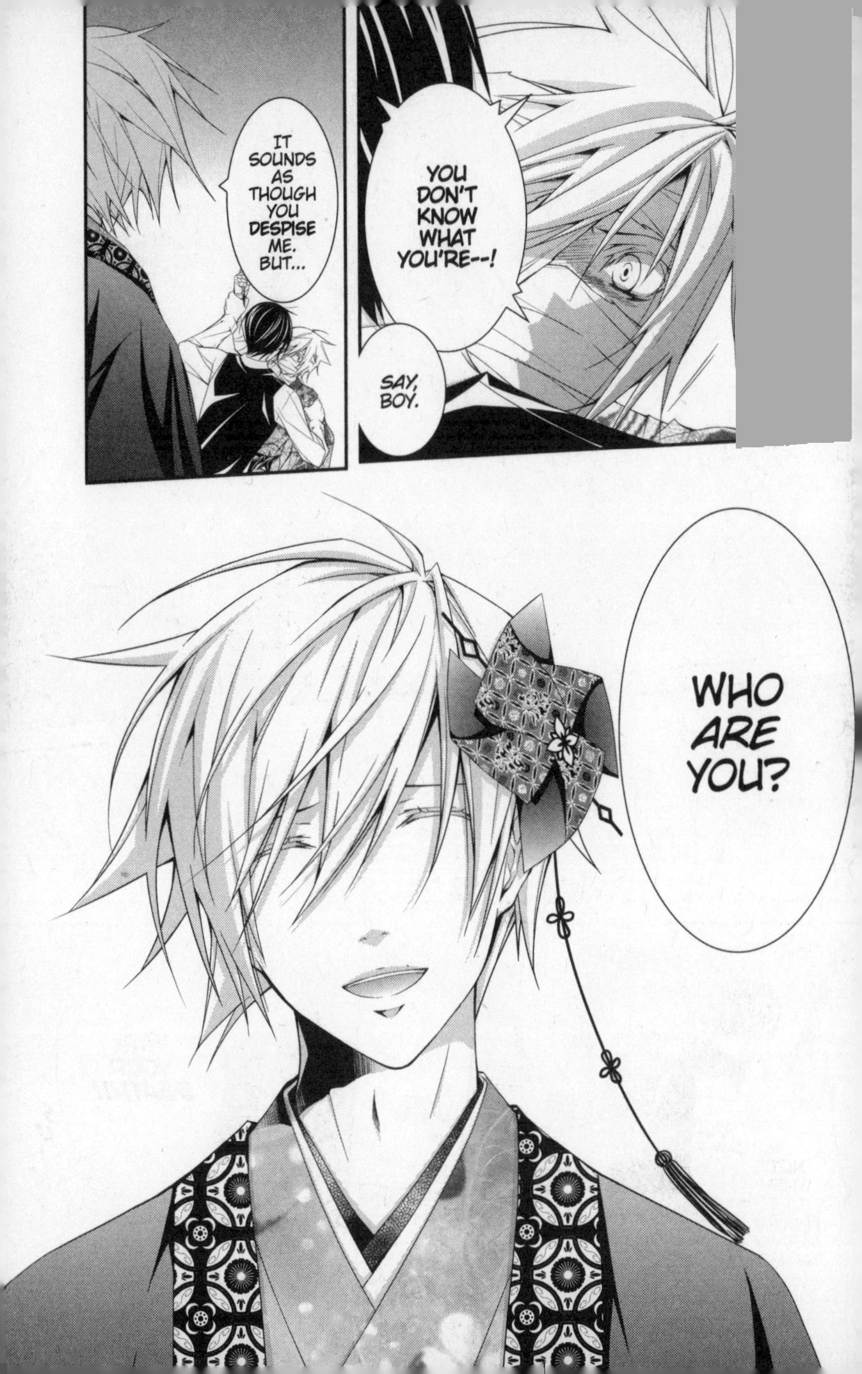
YOU DON'T KNOW WHAT YOU'RE--!
SAY, BOY.
IT SOUNDS AS THOUGH YOU DESPISE ME. BUT...
WHO ARE YOU?

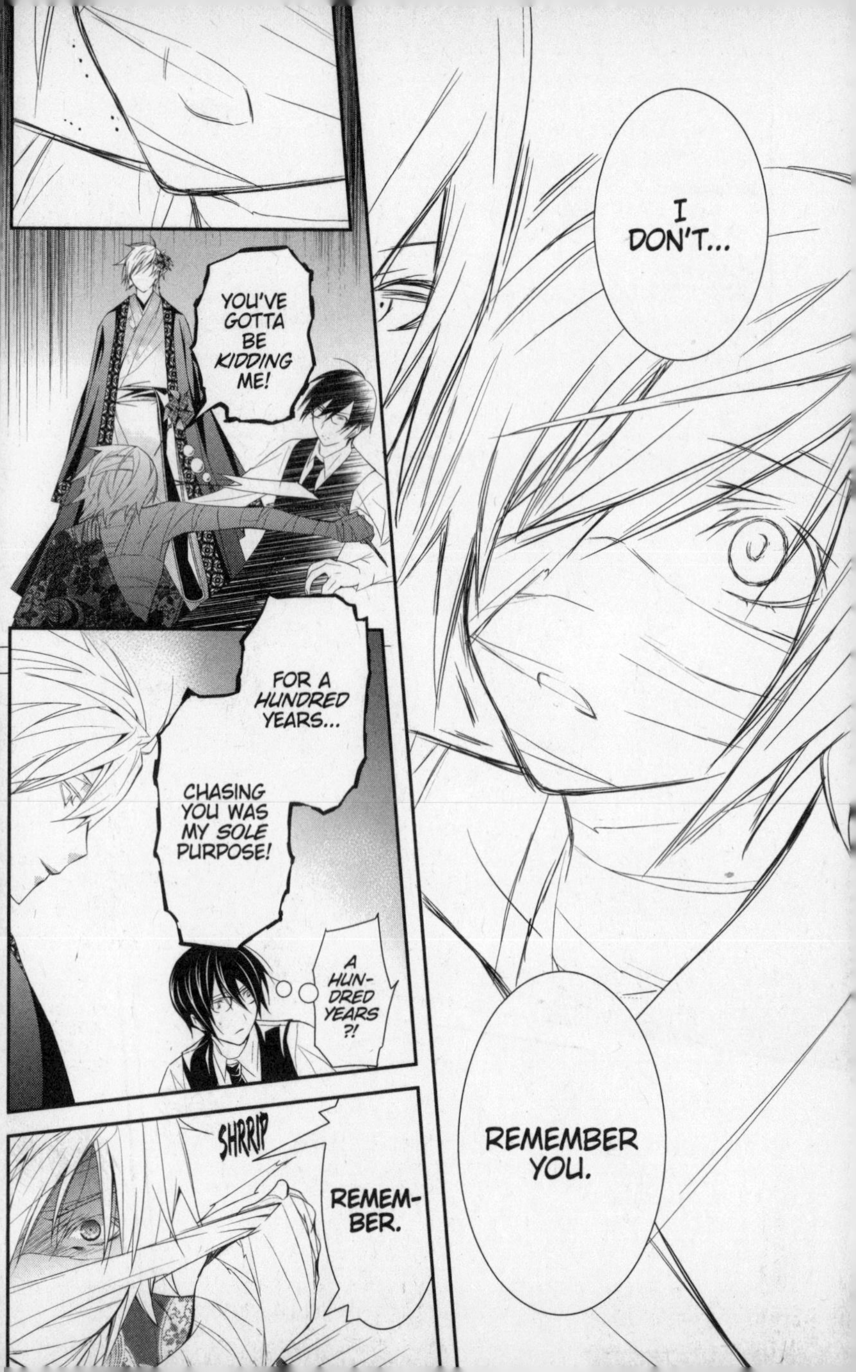
I DON'T...
REMEMBER YOU.
YOU'VE GOTTA BE *KIDDING* ME!
FOR A *HUNDRED* YEARS...
CHASING YOU WAS MY *SOLE* PURPOSE!
A HUN-DRED YEARS?!
SHRRIP
REMEM-BER.

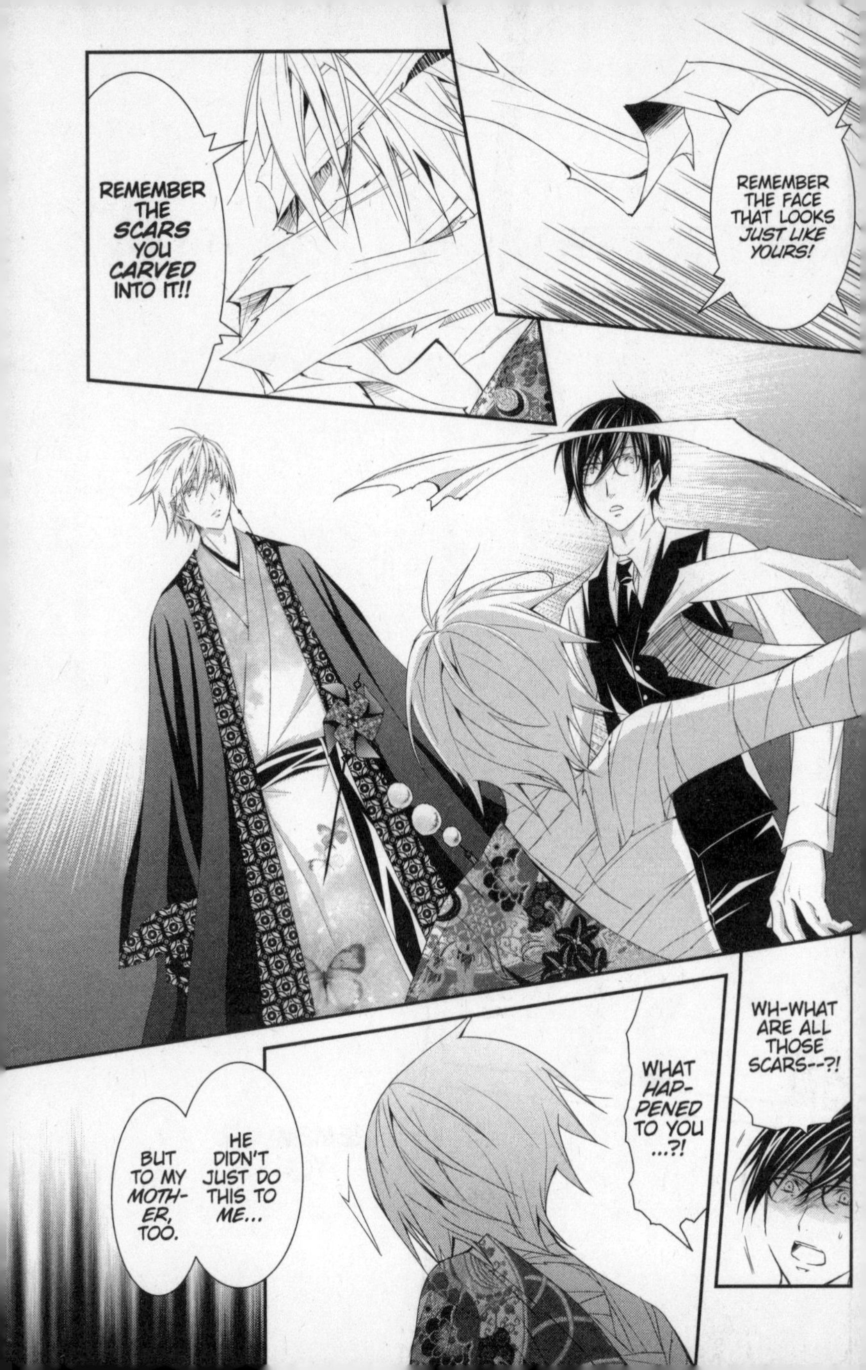
REMEMBER THE FACE THAT LOOKS *JUST LIKE YOURS!*
REMEMBER THE *SCARS* YOU *CARVED* INTO IT!!
WH-WHAT ARE ALL THOSE SCARS--?!
WHAT *HAP-PENED* TO YOU ...?!
HE DIDN'T JUST DO THIS TO *ME*...
BUT TO MY *MOTH-ER,* TOO.

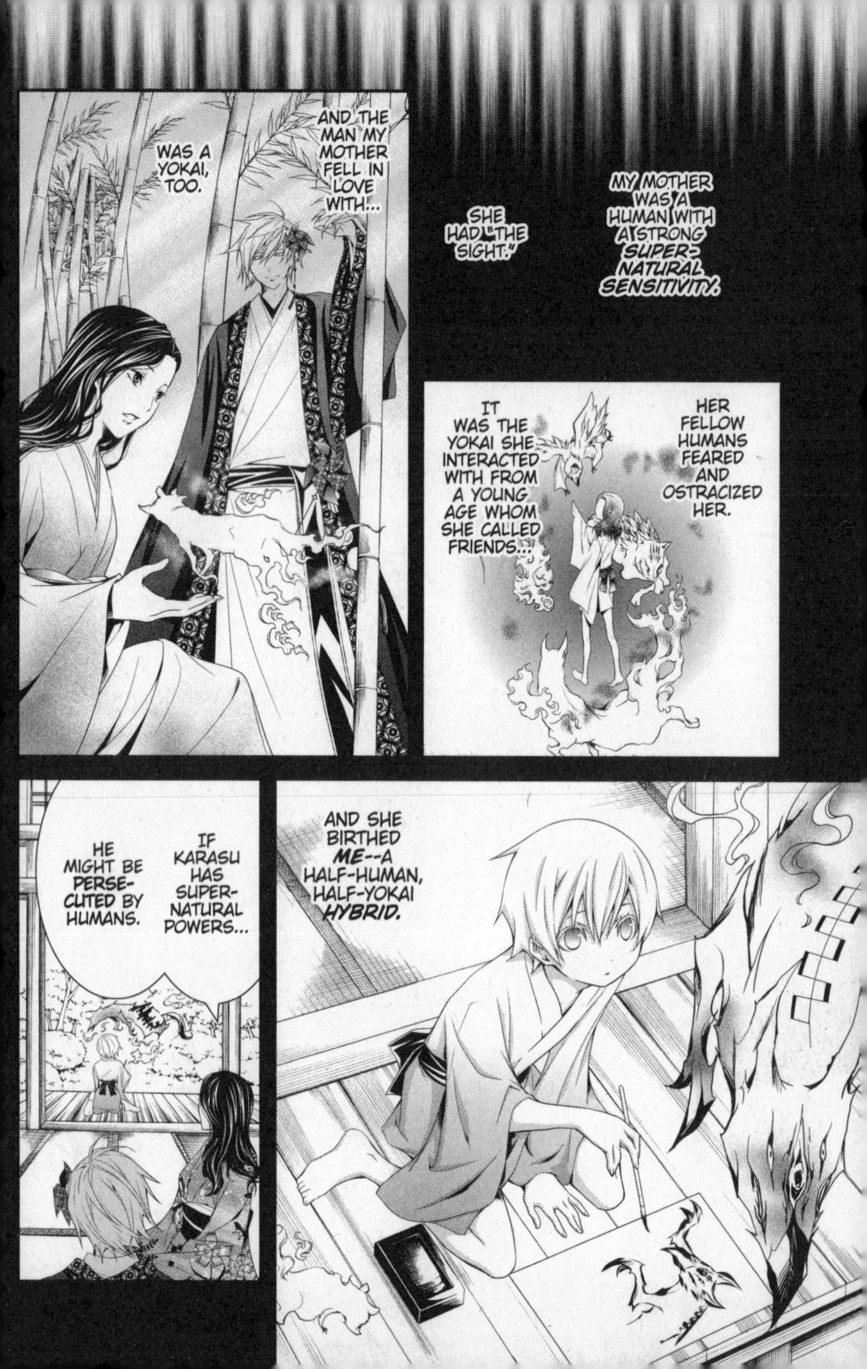
MY MOTHER WAS A HUMAN WITH A STRONG SUPER-NATURAL SENSITIVITY.
SHE HAD "THE SIGHT."
HER FELLOW HUMANS FEARED AND OSTRACIZED HER.
IT WAS THE YOKAI SHE INTERACTED WITH FROM A YOUNG AGE WHOM SHE CALLED FRIENDS...
AND THE MAN MY MOTHER FELL IN LOVE WITH...
WAS A YOKAI, TOO.
AND SHE BIRTHED ME--A HALF-HUMAN, HALF-YOKAI HYBRID.
IF KARASU HAS SUPER-NATURAL POWERS...
HE MIGHT BE PERSE-CUTED BY HUMANS.

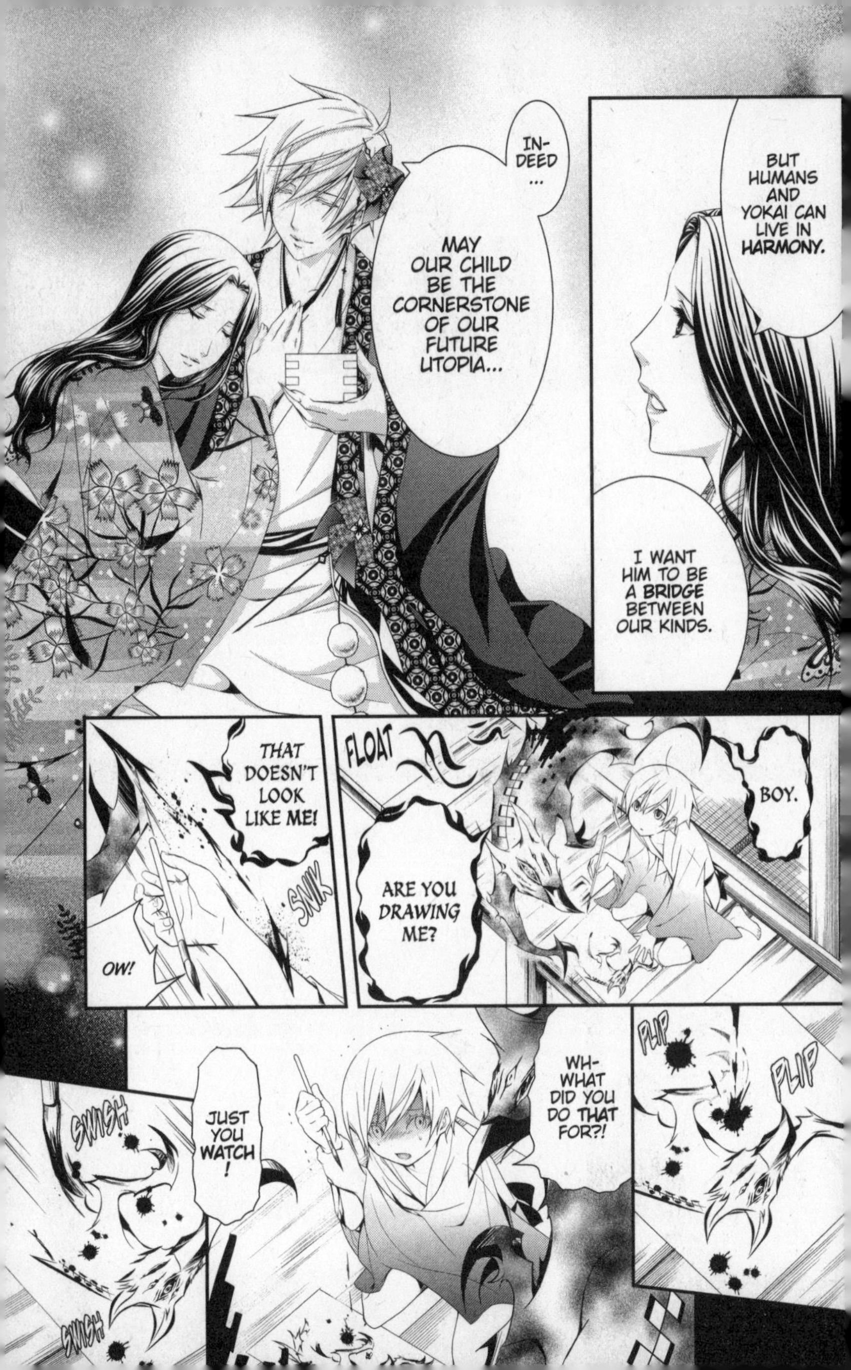
BUT HUMANS AND YOKAI CAN LIVE IN HARMONY.
I WANT HIM TO BE A BRIDGE BETWEEN OUR KINDS.
IN-DEED ...
MAY OUR CHILD BE THE CORNERSTONE OF OUR FUTURE UTOPIA...
BOY.
FLOAT
ARE YOU DRAWING ME?
THAT DOESN'T LOOK LIKE ME!
SNIK
OW!
PLIP
PLIP
WH-WHAT DID YOU DO THAT FOR?!
JUST YOU WATCH!
SWISH
SWISH

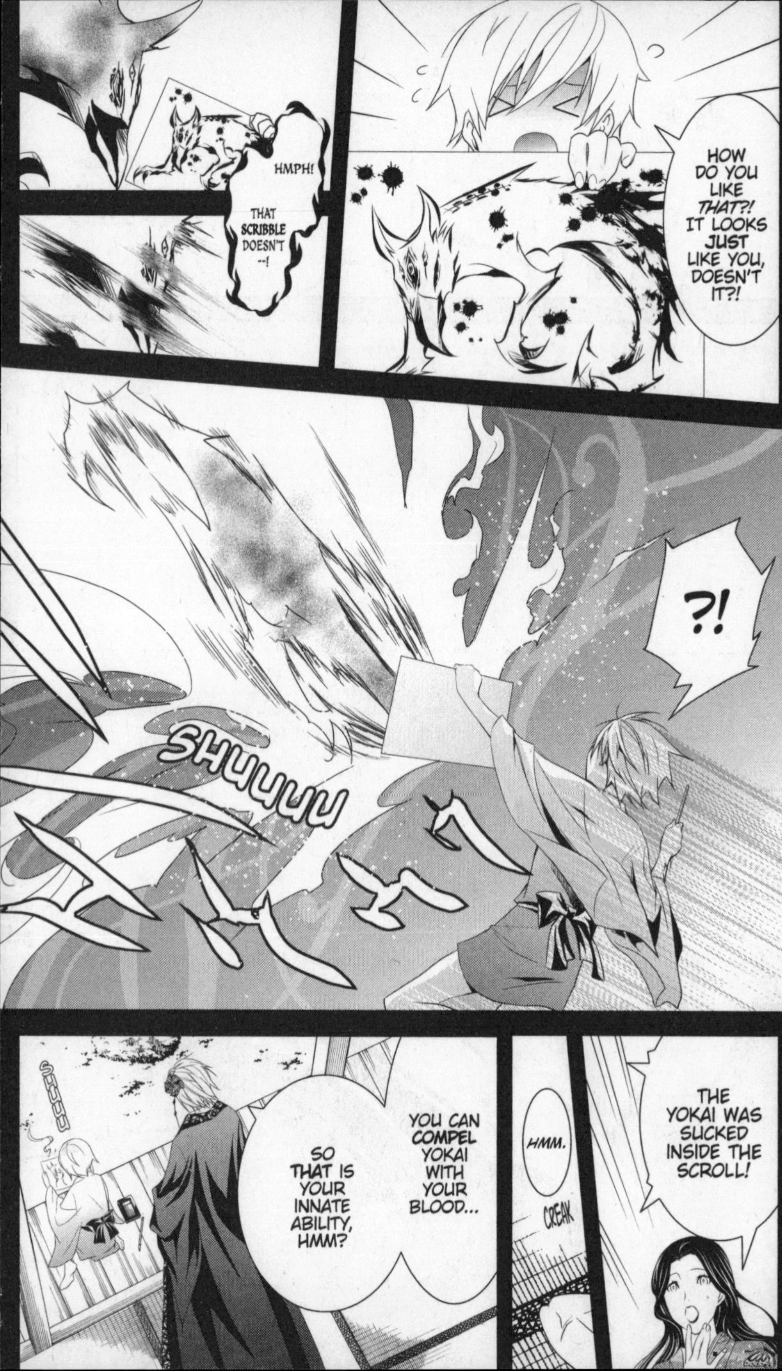
HOW DO YOU LIKE *THAT?!* IT LOOKS JUST LIKE YOU, DOESN'T IT?!
HMPH!
THAT SCRIBBLE DOESN'T --!
?!
SHUUUUU
THE YOKAI WAS SUCKED INSIDE THE SCROLL!
HMM.
CREAK
YOU CAN COMPEL YOKAI WITH YOUR BLOOD...
SO THAT IS YOUR INNATE ABILITY, HMM?
SHUUU

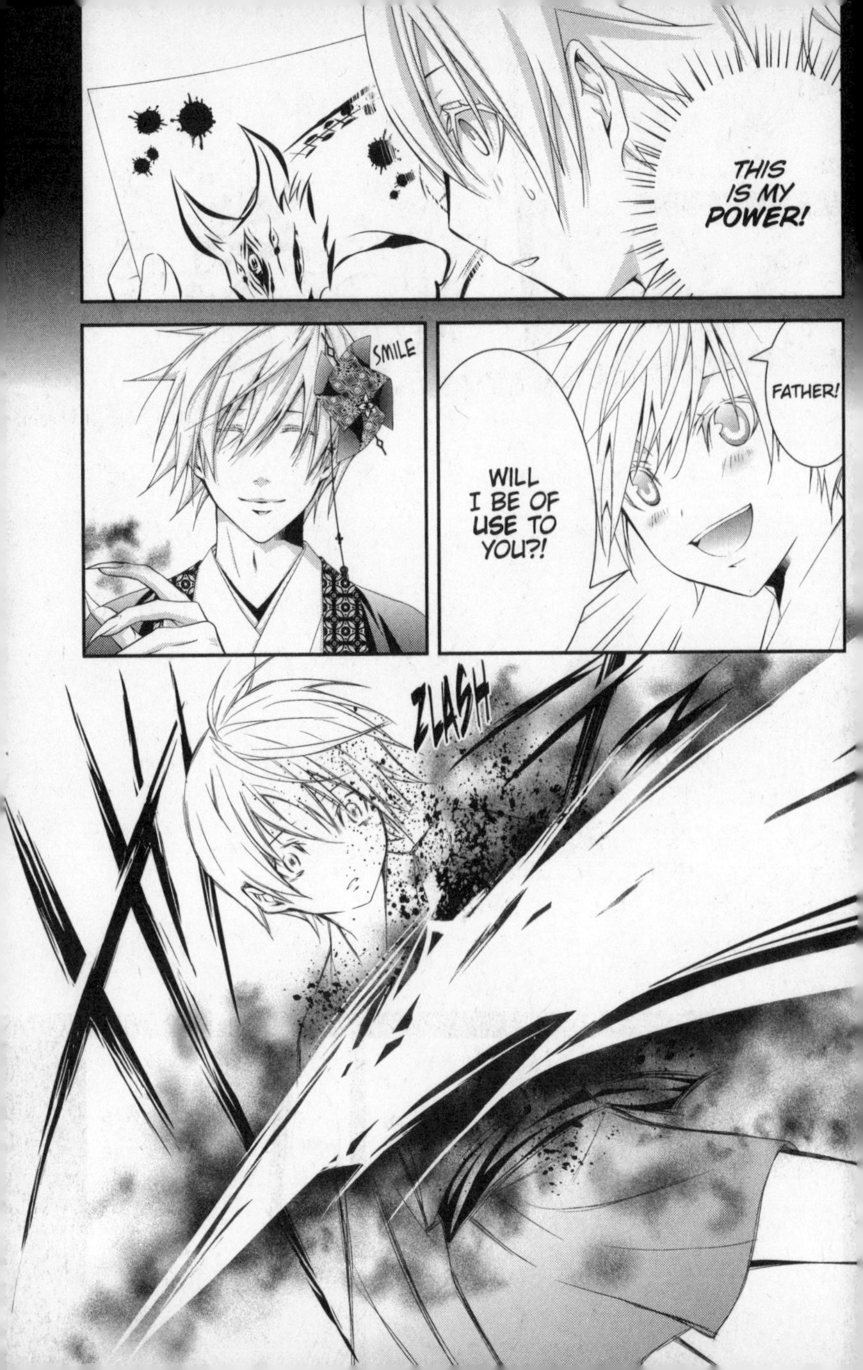
THIS IS MY POWER!
FATHER!
WILL I BE OF USE TO YOU?!
SMILE
ZLASH

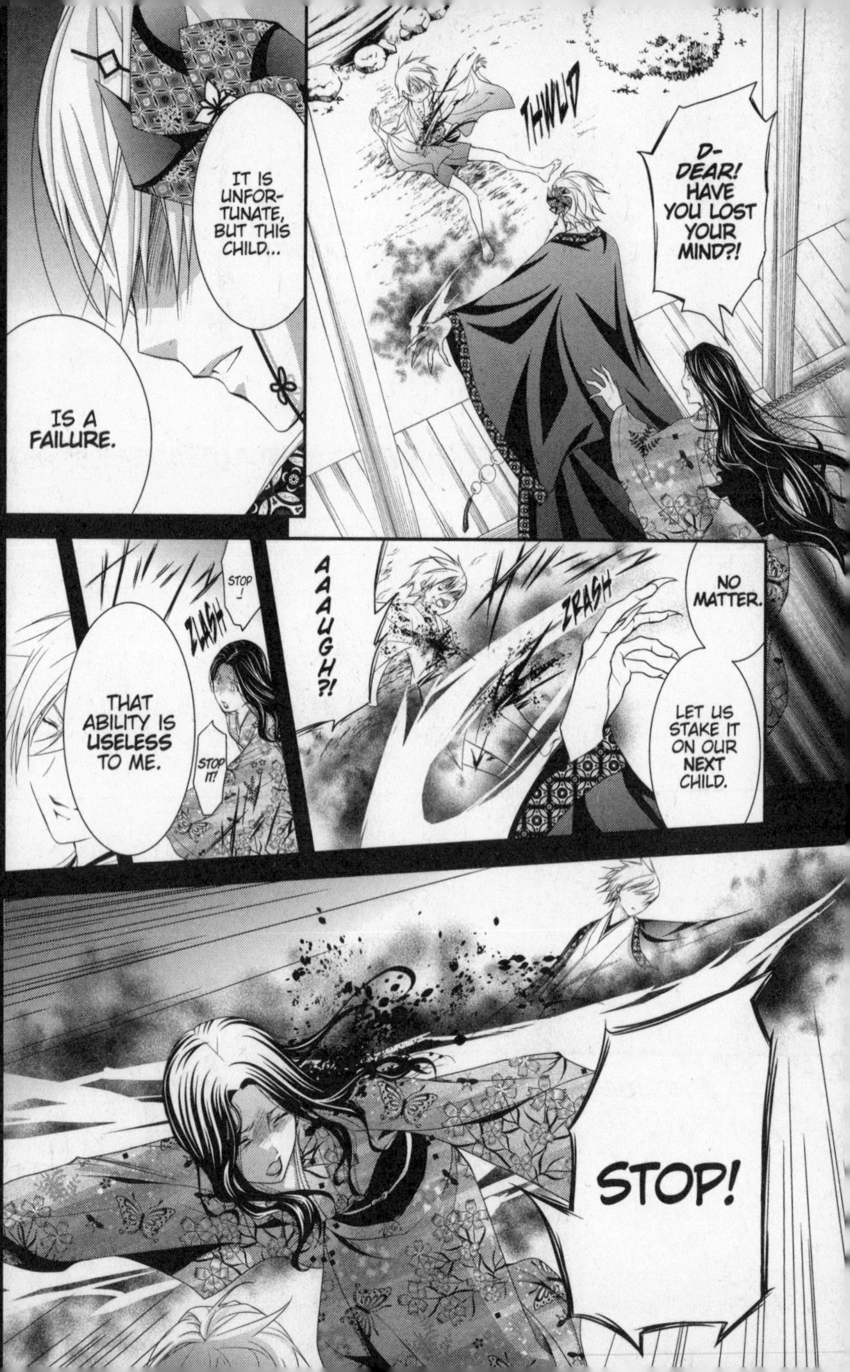
THWUD
D-DEAR! HAVE YOU LOST YOUR MIND?!
IT IS UNFORTUNATE, BUT THIS CHILD...
IS A FAILURE.
NO MATTER.
LET US STAKE IT ON OUR NEXT CHILD.
ZRASH
AAAAUGH?!
STOP-!
ZLASH
THAT ABILITY IS USELESS TO ME.
STOP IT!
STOP!

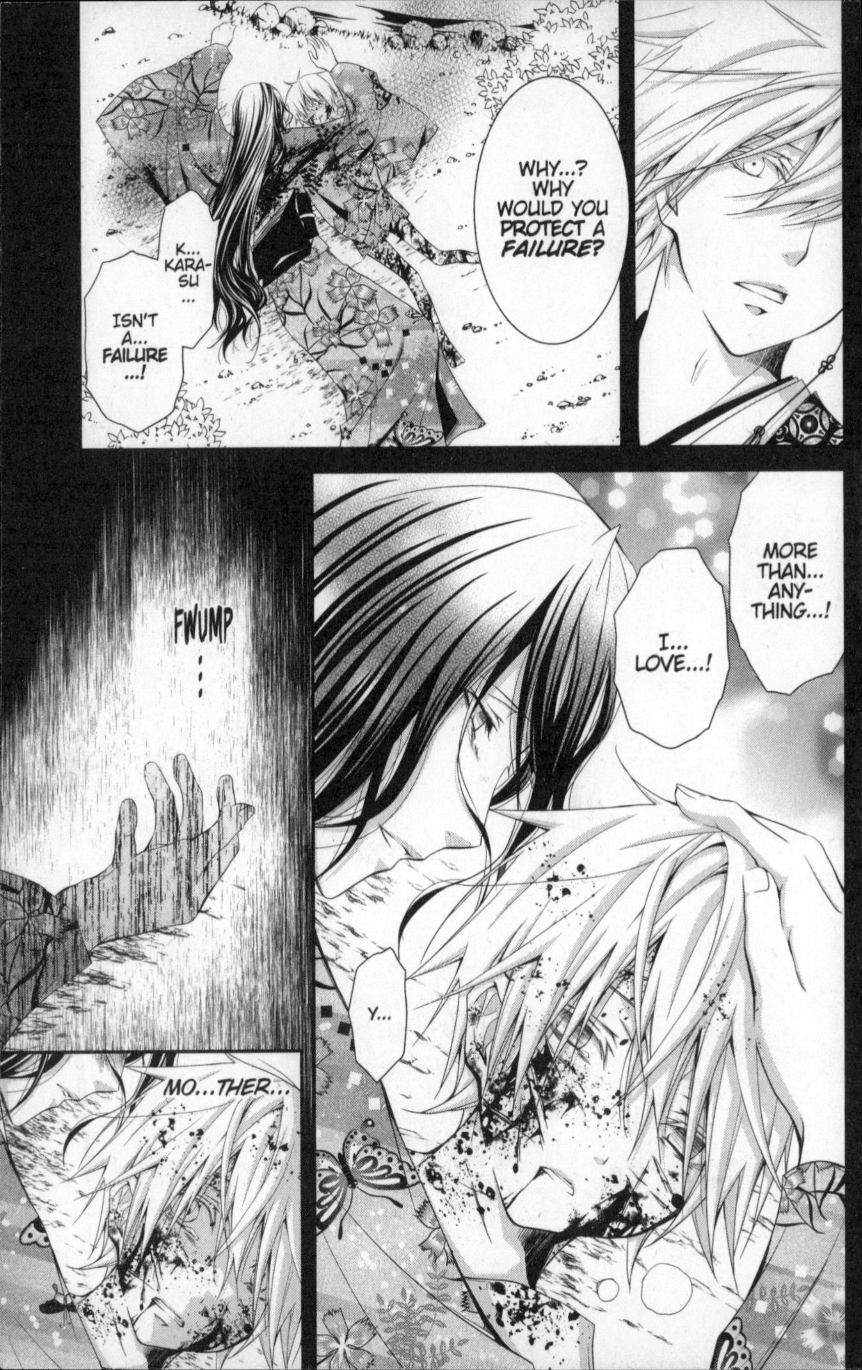
WHY...? WHY WOULD YOU PROTECT A *FAILURE?*
K... KARA-SU ...
ISN'T A... FAILURE ...!
MORE THAN... ANY-THING...!
I... LOVE...!
Y...
FWUMP
...
MO...THER...

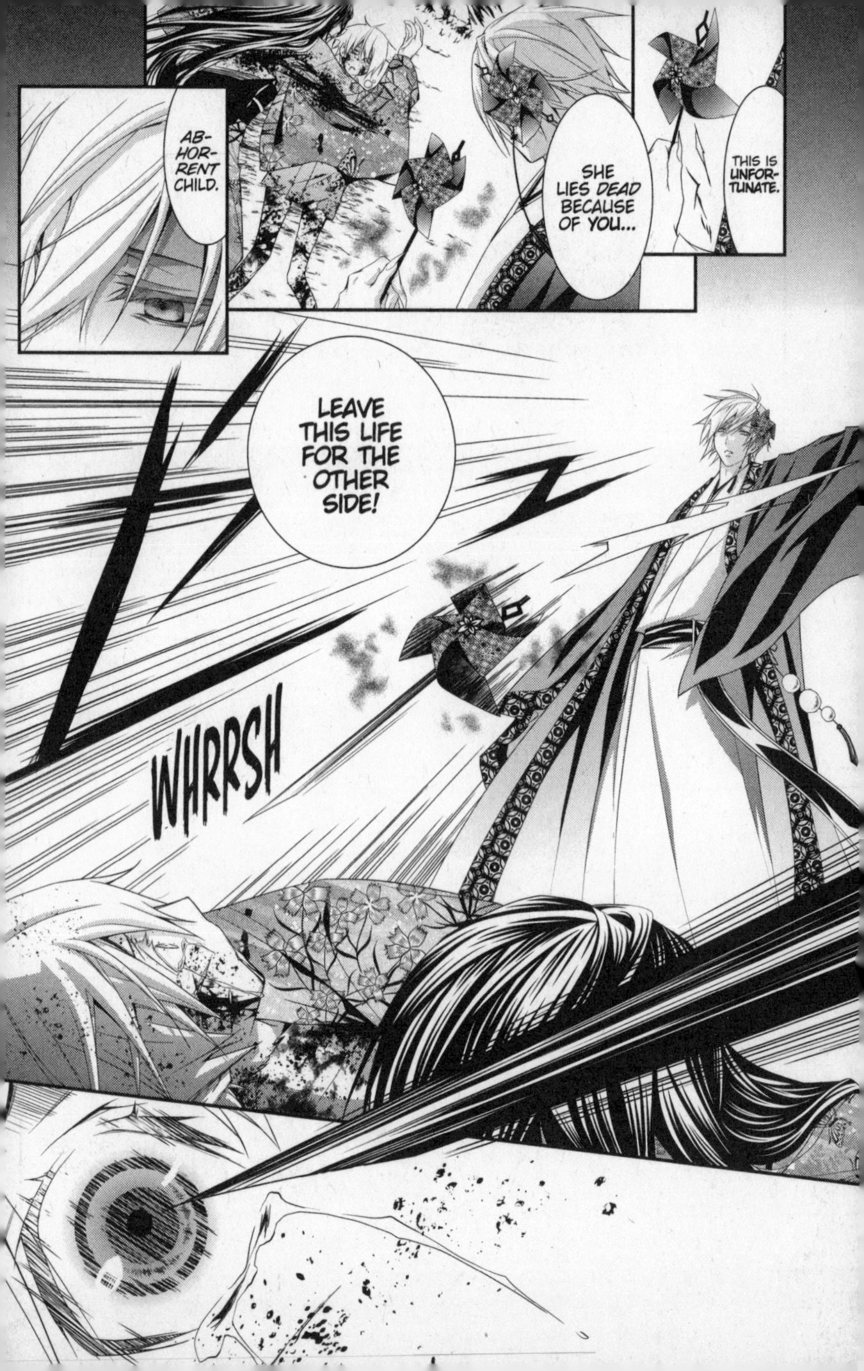
THIS IS UNFORTUNATE.
SHE LIES *DEAD* BECAUSE OF YOU...
ABHORRENT CHILD.
LEAVE THIS LIFE FOR THE OTHER SIDE!
WHRRSH

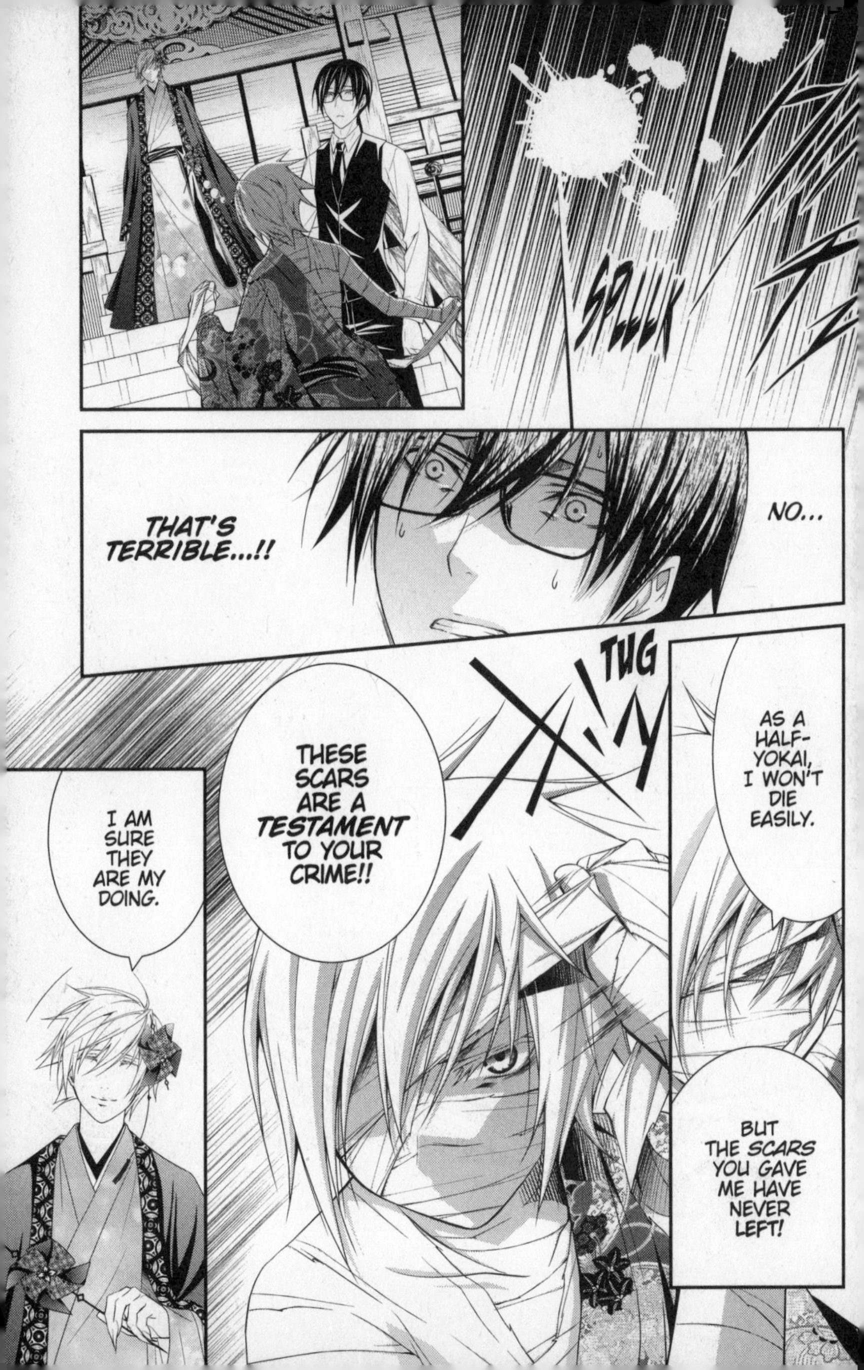
SPLLK
NO...
THAT'S TERRIBLE...!!
TUG
AS A HALF-YOKAI, I WON'T DIE EASILY.
BUT THE SCARS YOU GAVE ME HAVE NEVER LEFT!
THESE SCARS ARE A TESTAMENT TO YOUR CRIME!!
I AM SURE THEY ARE MY DOING.

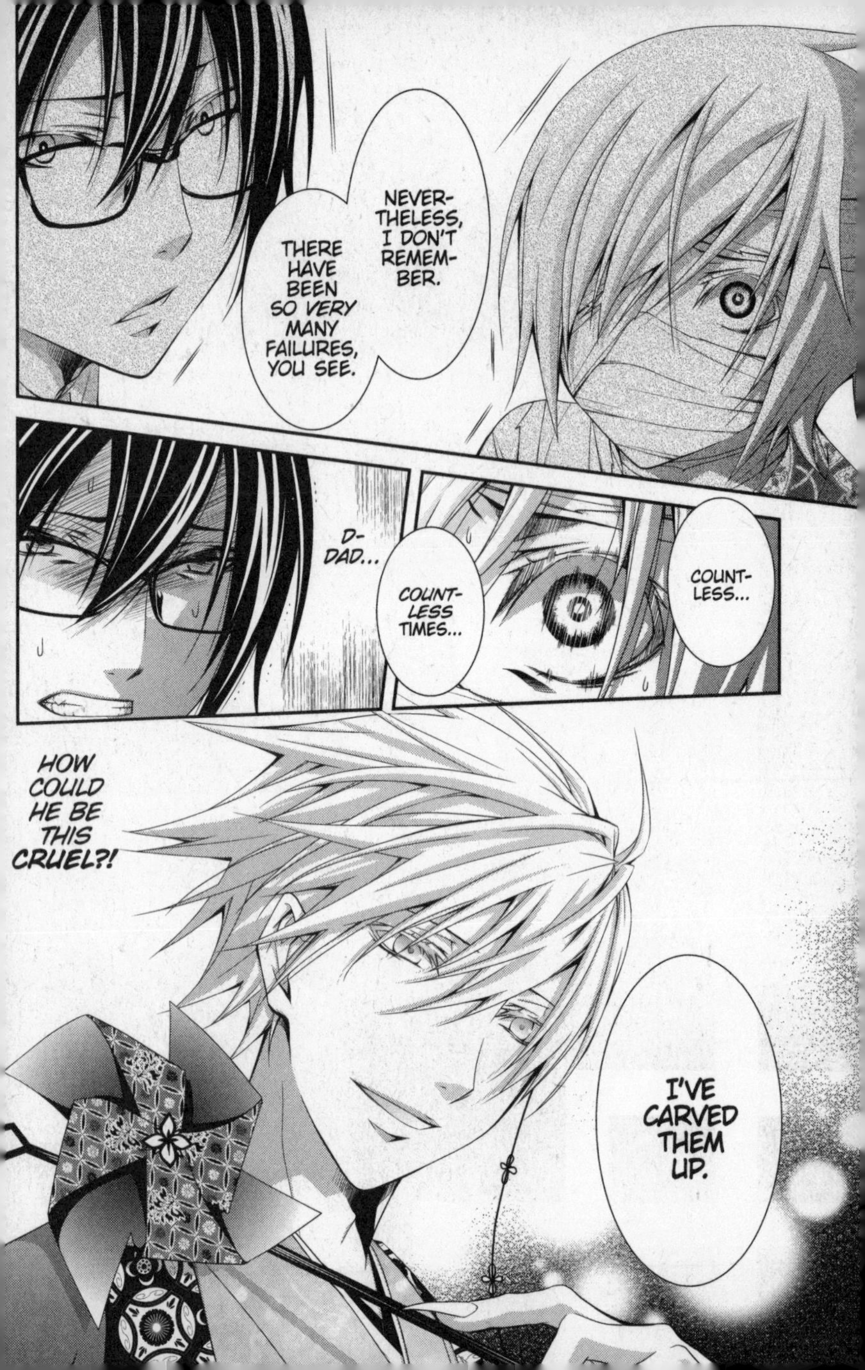
NEVER-THELESS, I DON'T REMEM-BER.
THERE HAVE BEEN SO VERY MANY FAILURES, YOU SEE.
COUNT-LESS...
COUNT-LESS TIMES...
D-DAD...
I'VE CARVED THEM UP.
HOW COULD HE BE THIS CRUEL?!

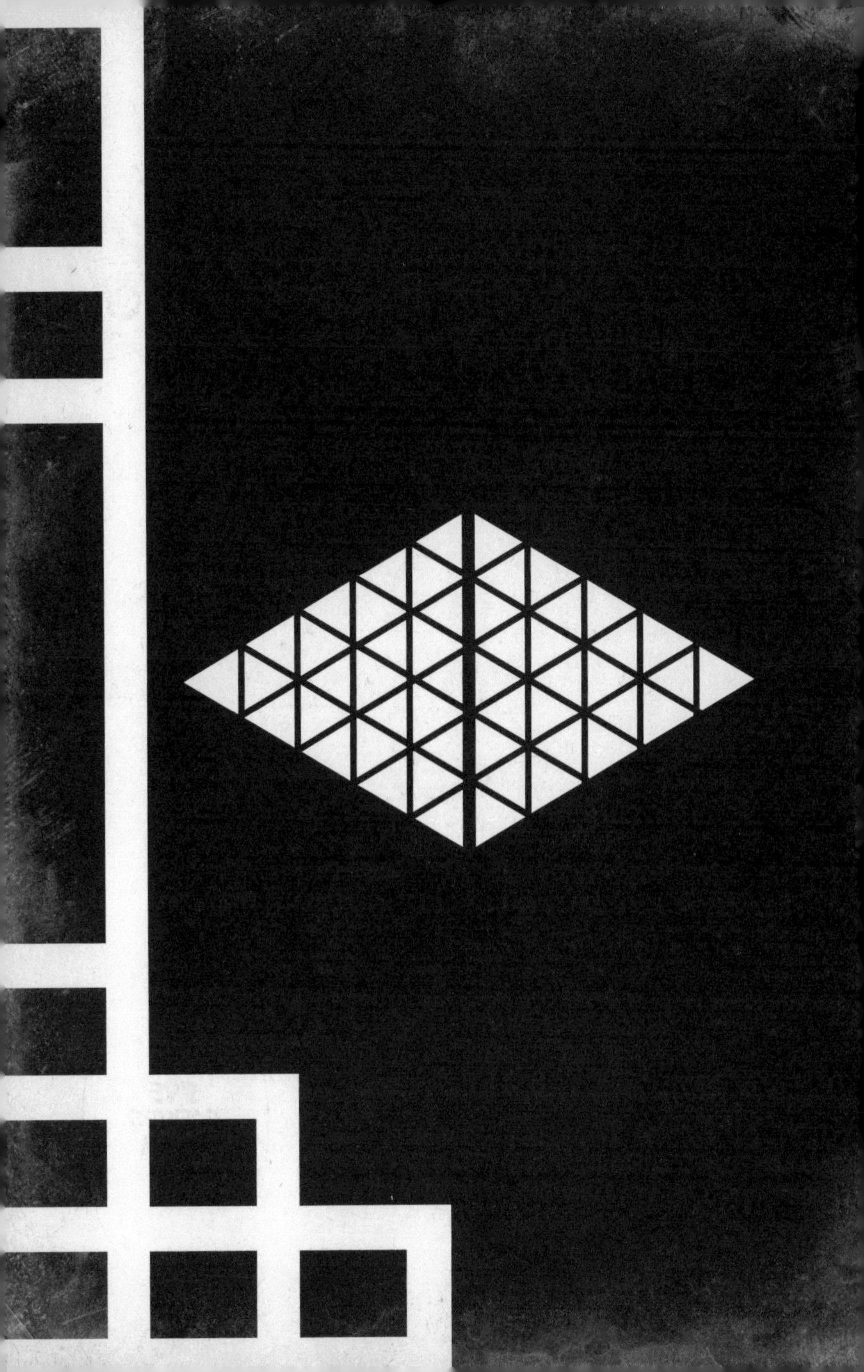

Yōkai Rental Shop

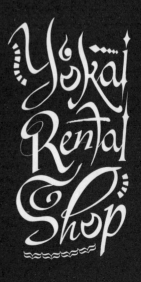

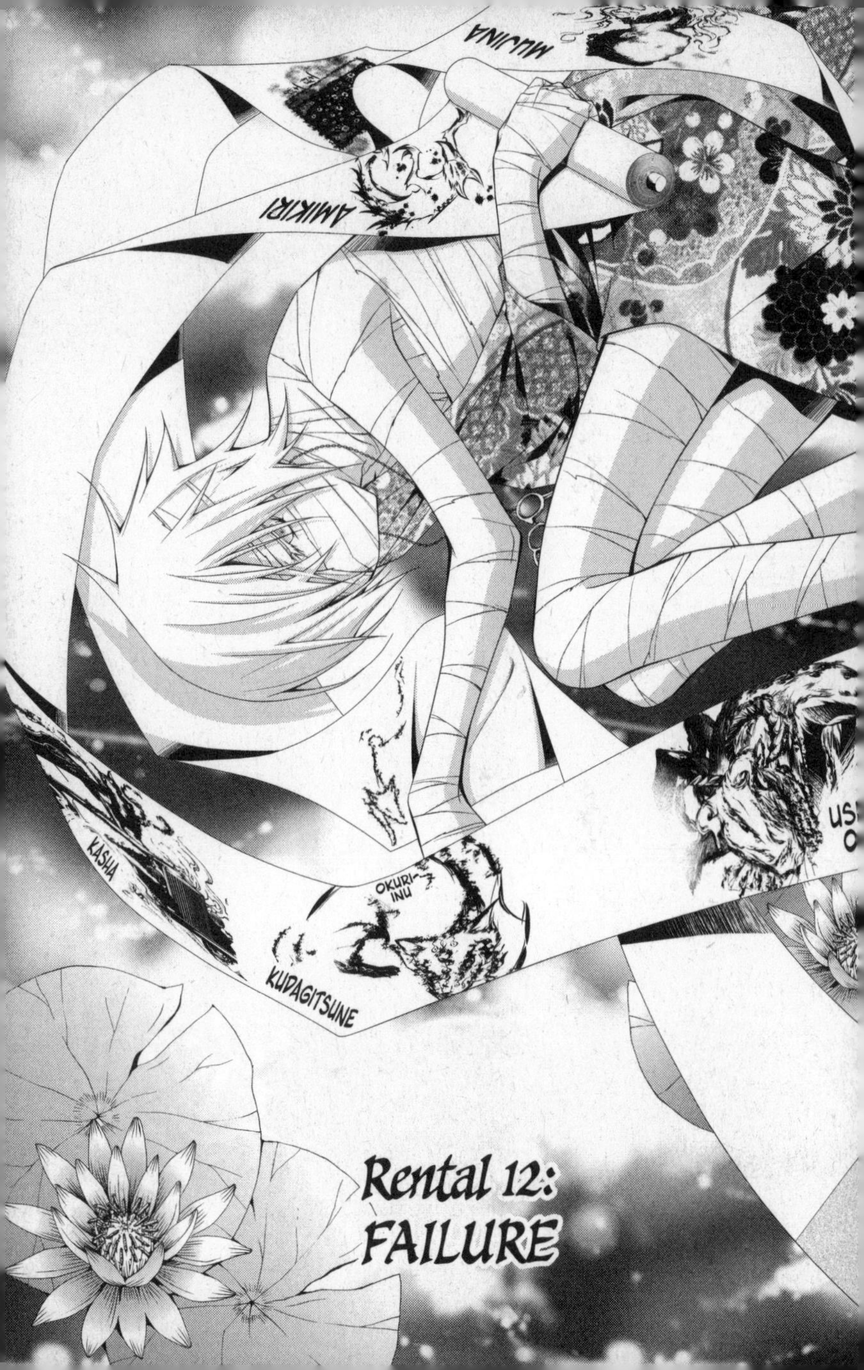
MUJINA
AMIKIRI
OKURI-INU
KUDAGITSUNE
KASHA
Rental 12:
FAILURE

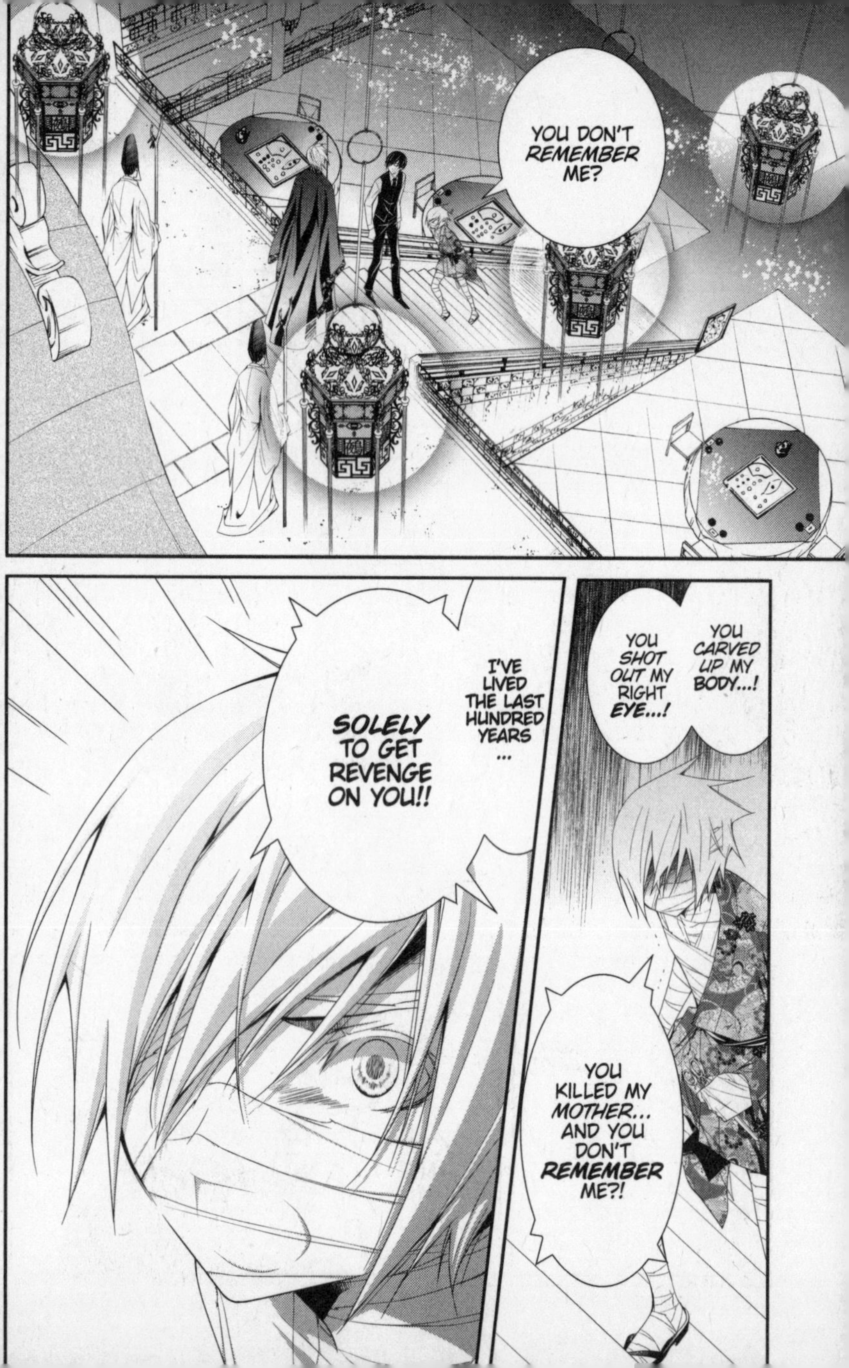
YOU DON'T REMEMBER ME?
YOU CARVED UP MY BODY...!
YOU SHOT OUT MY RIGHT EYE...!
YOU KILLED MY MOTHER... AND YOU DON'T REMEMBER ME?!
I'VE LIVED THE LAST HUNDRED YEARS ...
SOLELY TO GET REVENGE ON YOU!!

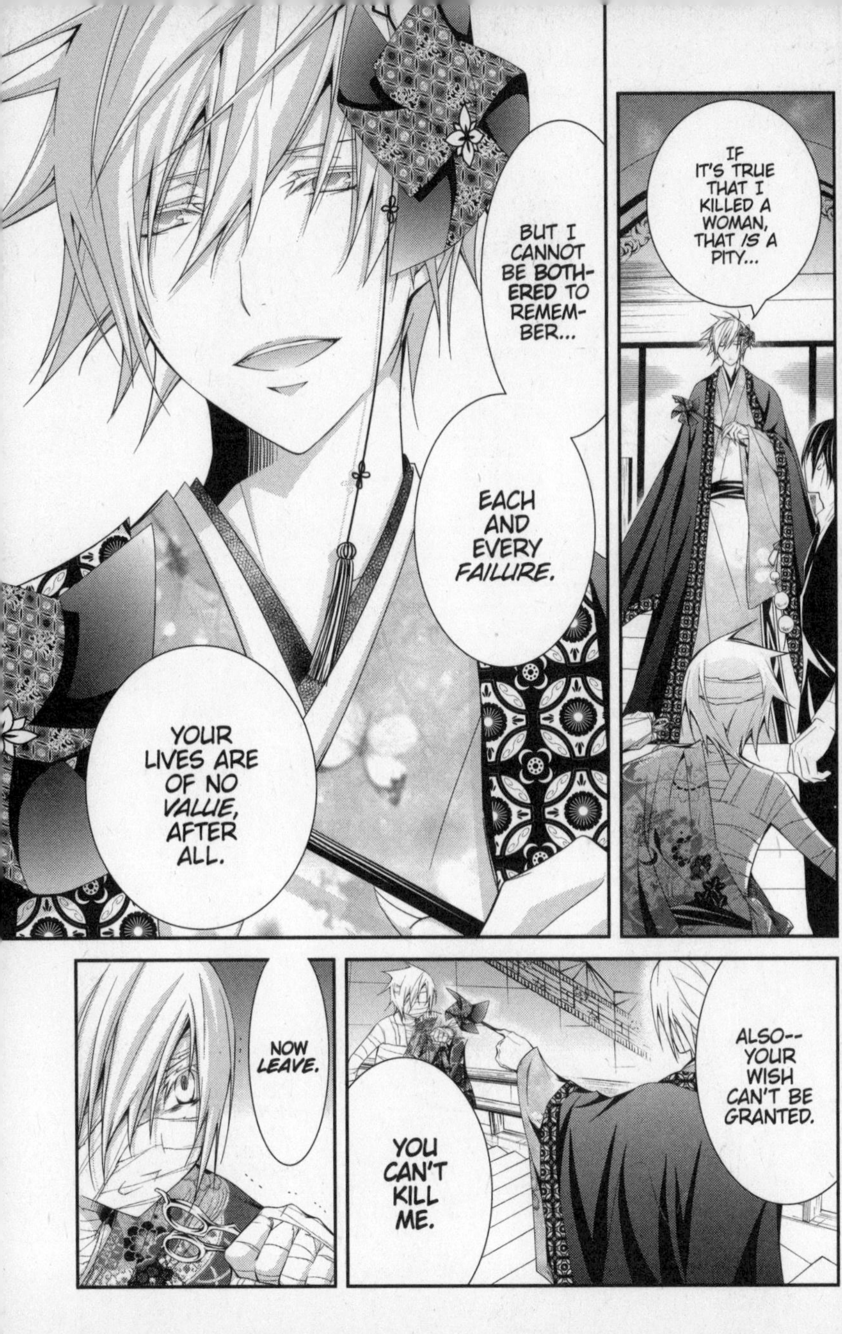
IF IT'S TRUE THAT I KILLED A WOMAN, THAT *IS* A PITY...
BUT I CANNOT BE BOTHERED TO REMEMBER...
EACH AND EVERY *FAILURE.*
YOUR LIVES ARE OF NO *VALUE,* AFTER ALL.
ALSO-- YOUR WISH CAN'T BE GRANTED.
YOU CAN'T KILL ME.
NOW *LEAVE.*
...
...

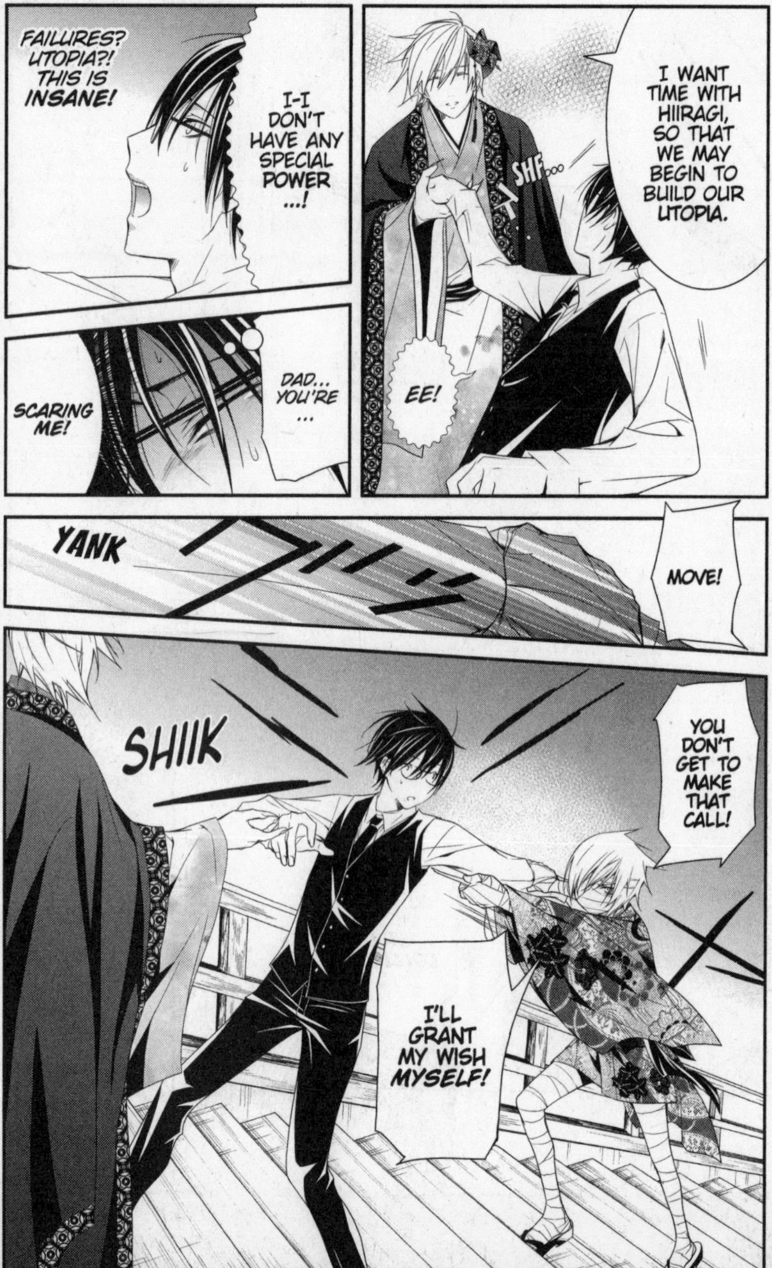
I WANT TIME WITH HIIRAGI, SO THAT WE MAY BEGIN TO BUILD OUR UTOPIA.
SHF...
EE!
I-I DON'T HAVE ANY SPECIAL POWER ...!
FAILURES? UTOPIA?! THIS IS INSANE!
DAD... YOU'RE ...
SCARING ME!
MOVE!
YANK
YOU DON'T GET TO MAKE THAT CALL!
SHIIK
I'LL GRANT MY WISH MYSELF!

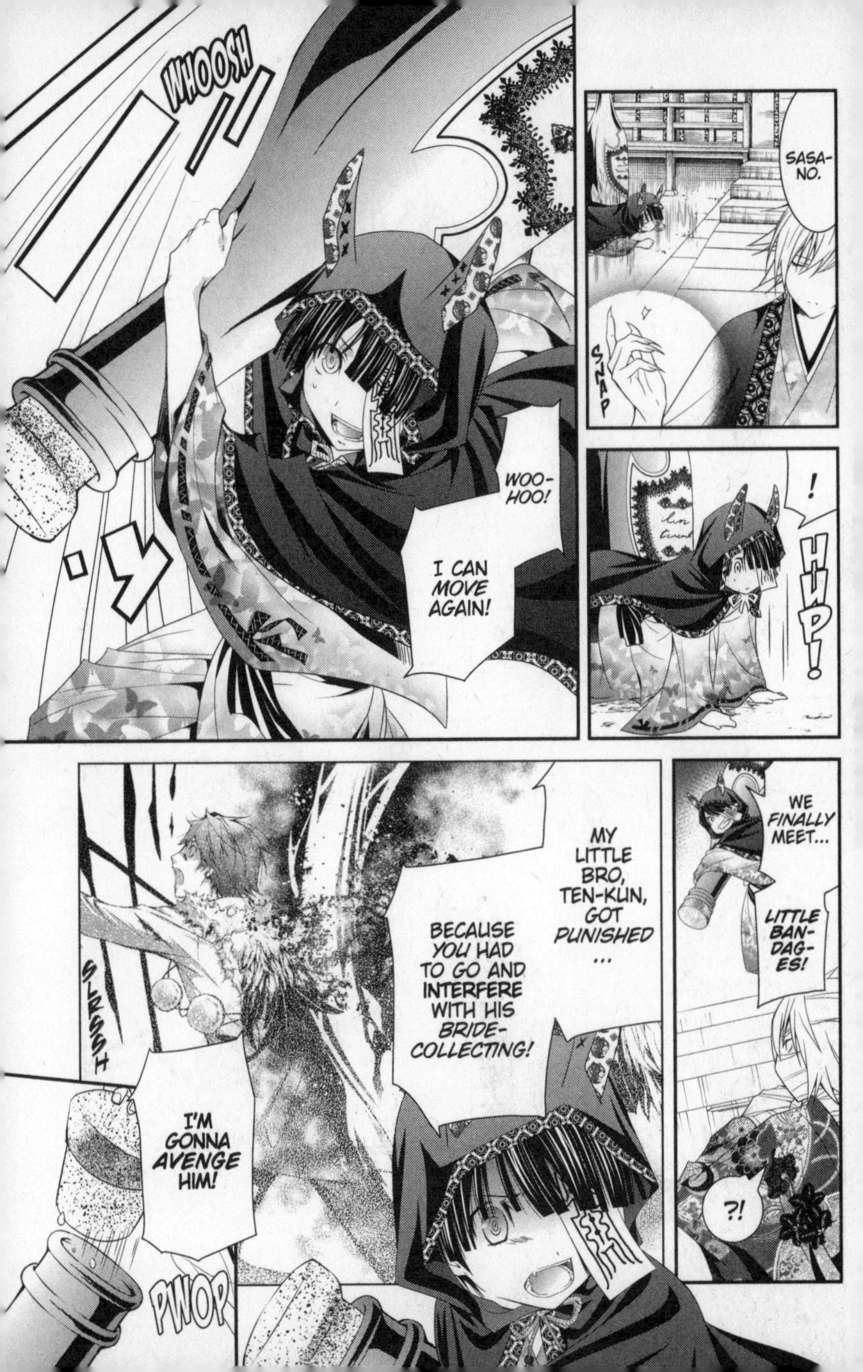
SASANO.
SNAP
!
HUP!
WHOOSH
WOO-HOO!
I CAN MOVE AGAIN!
WE FINALLY MEET...
LITTLE BANDAGES!
?!
MY LITTLE BRO, TEN-KUN, GOT PUNISHED...
BECAUSE YOU HAD TO GO AND INTERFERE WITH HIS BRIDE-COLLECTING!
SLRSSH
I'M GONNA AVENGE HIM!
PWOP

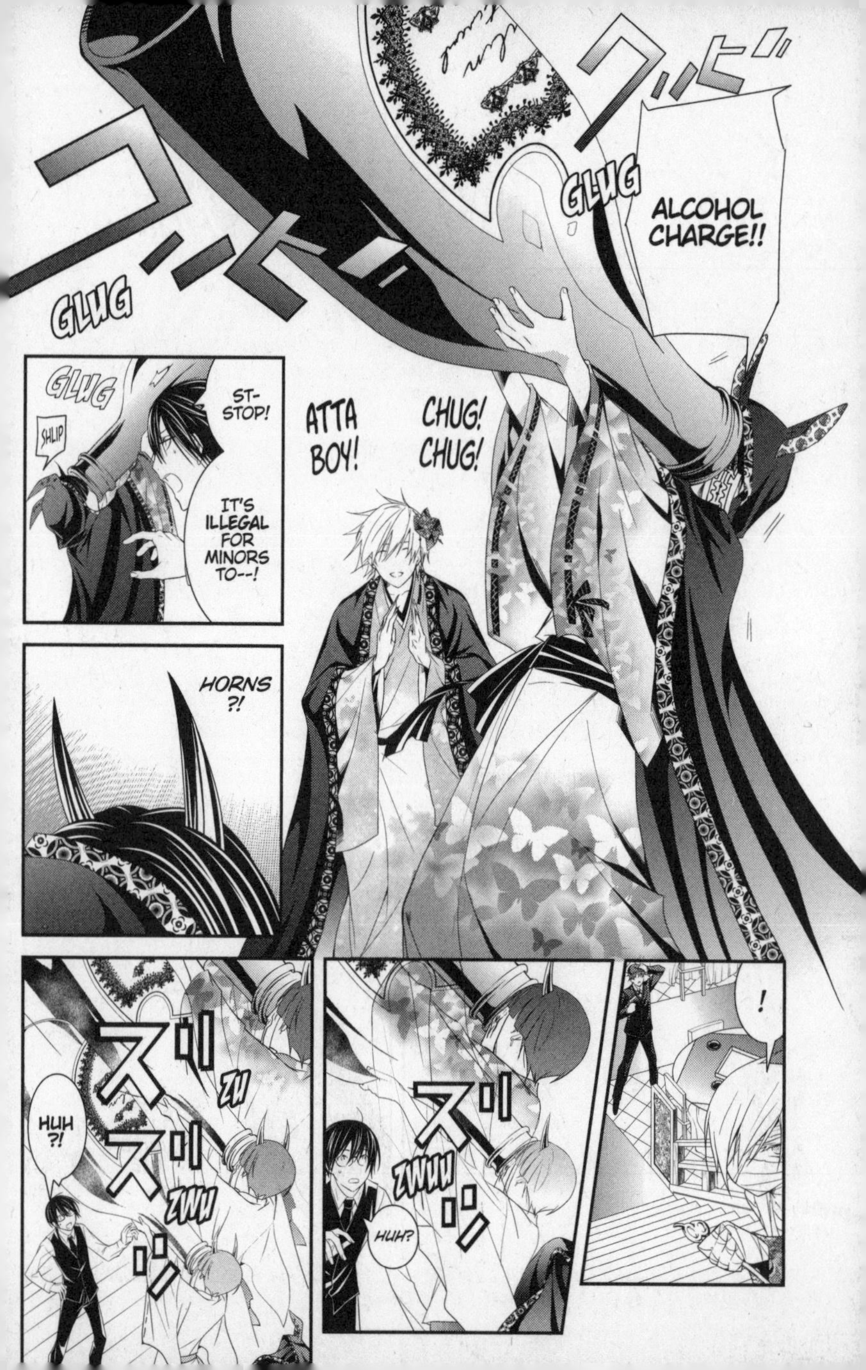

ALCOHOL CHARGE!!
GLUG
GLUG
CHUG! CHUG!
ATTA BOY!
GLUG
SHLIP
ST-STOP!
IT'S ILLEGAL FOR MINORS TO--!
HORNS ?!
!
ZWUU
HUH?
ZWU
HUH ?!
ZWUU

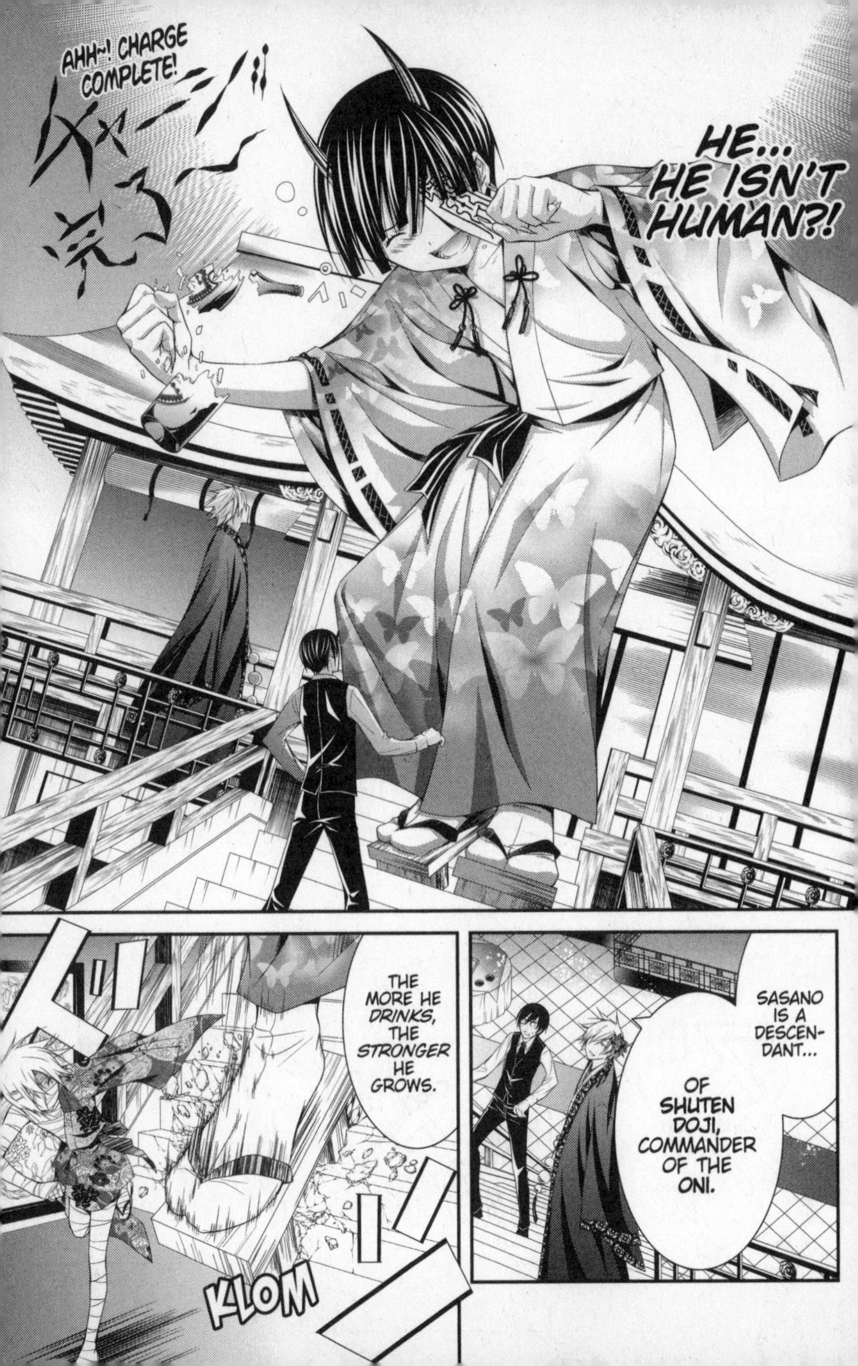
HE... HE ISN'T HUMAN?!
AHH~! CHARGE COMPLETE!
SASANO IS A DESCENDANT...
OF SHUTEN DOJI, COMMANDER OF THE ONI.
THE MORE HE DRINKS, THE STRONGER HE GROWS.
KLOM

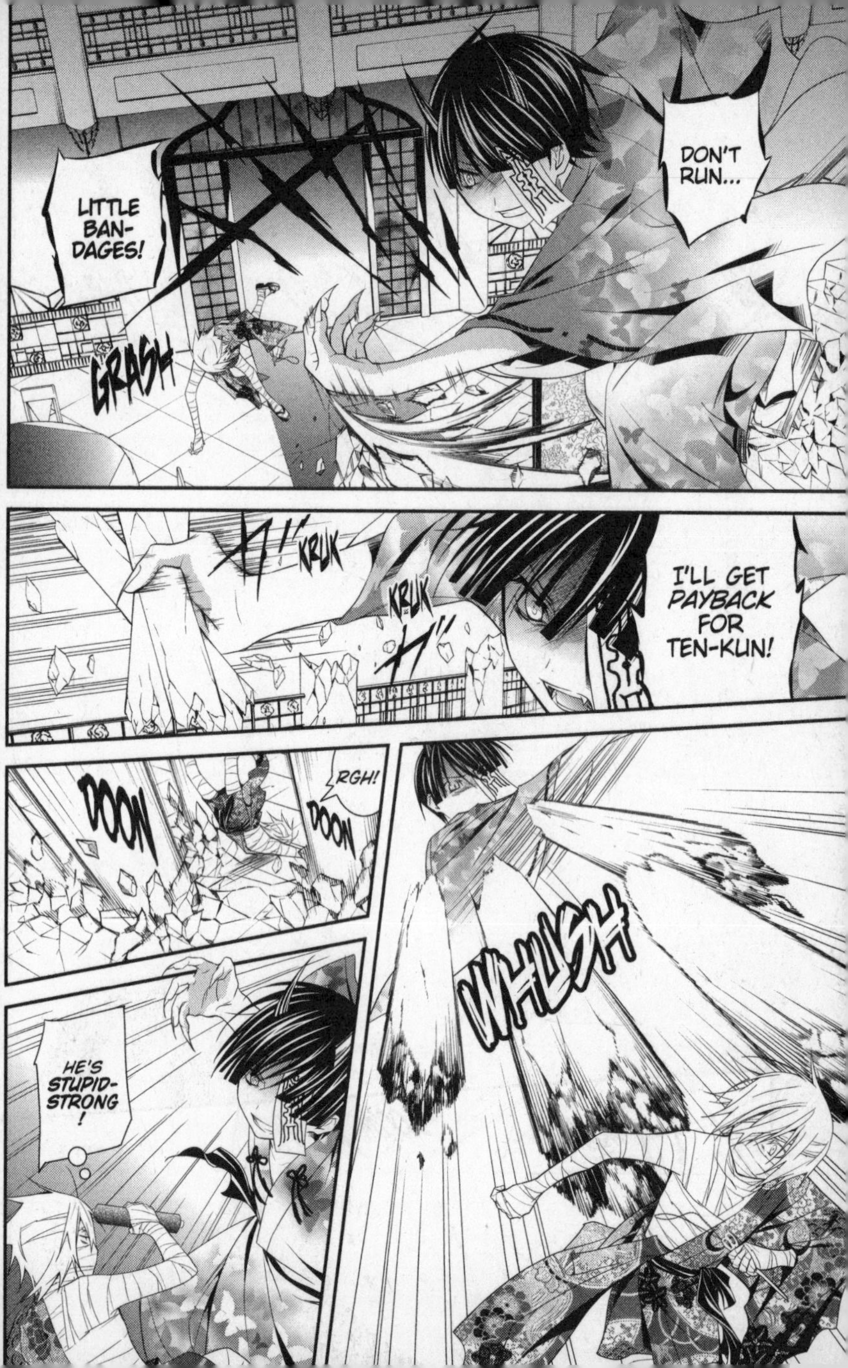
DON'T RUN...
LITTLE BAN-DAGES!
GRASH
I'LL GET PAYBACK FOR TEN-KUN!
KRUK
KRUK
WHUSH
DOON
RGH!
DOON
HE'S STUPID-STRONG!

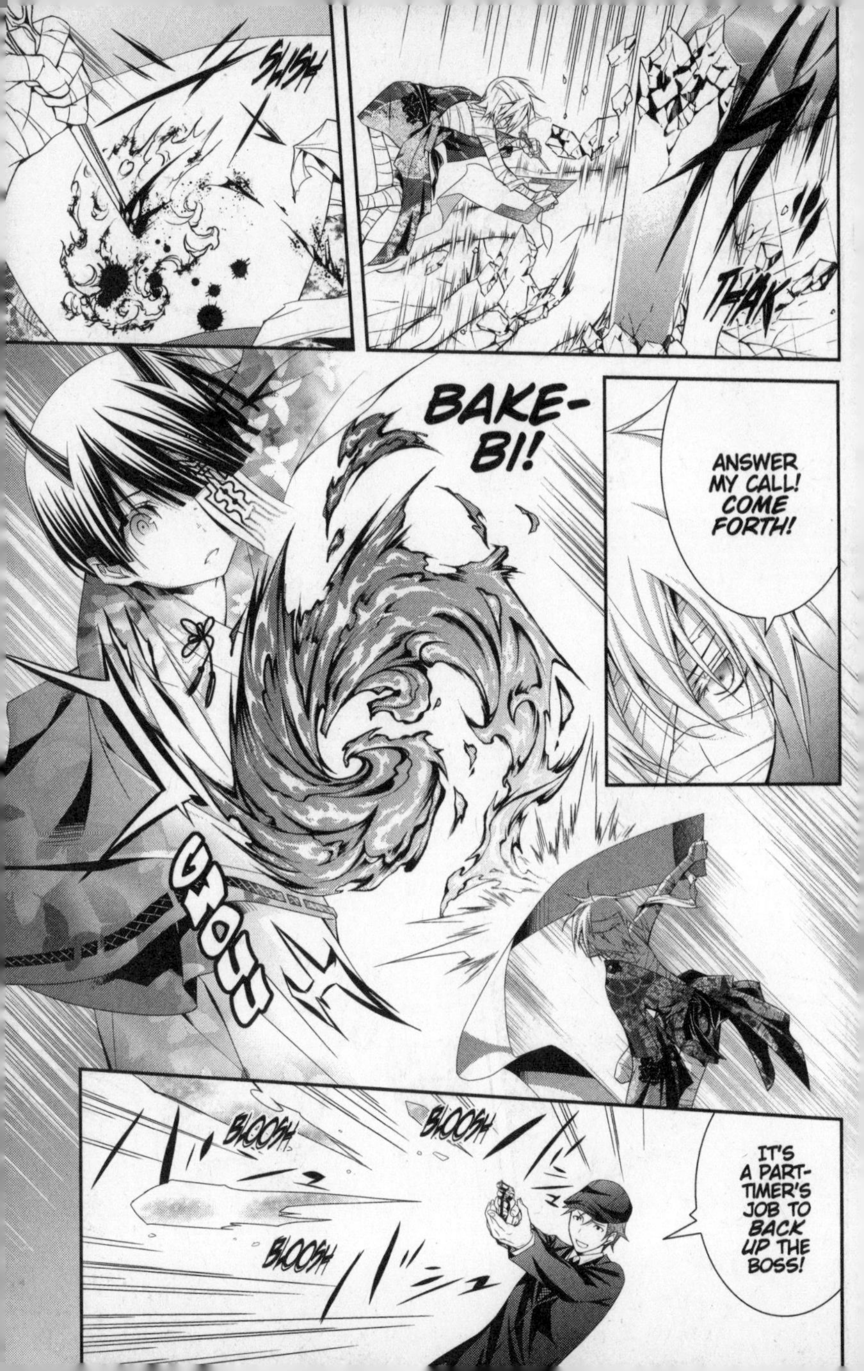
THAK
SLISH
ANSWER MY CALL! COME FORTH!
BAKE-BI!
GHOUU
IT'S A PART-TIMER'S JOB TO BACK UP THE BOSS!
BLOOSH
BLOOSH
BLOOSH

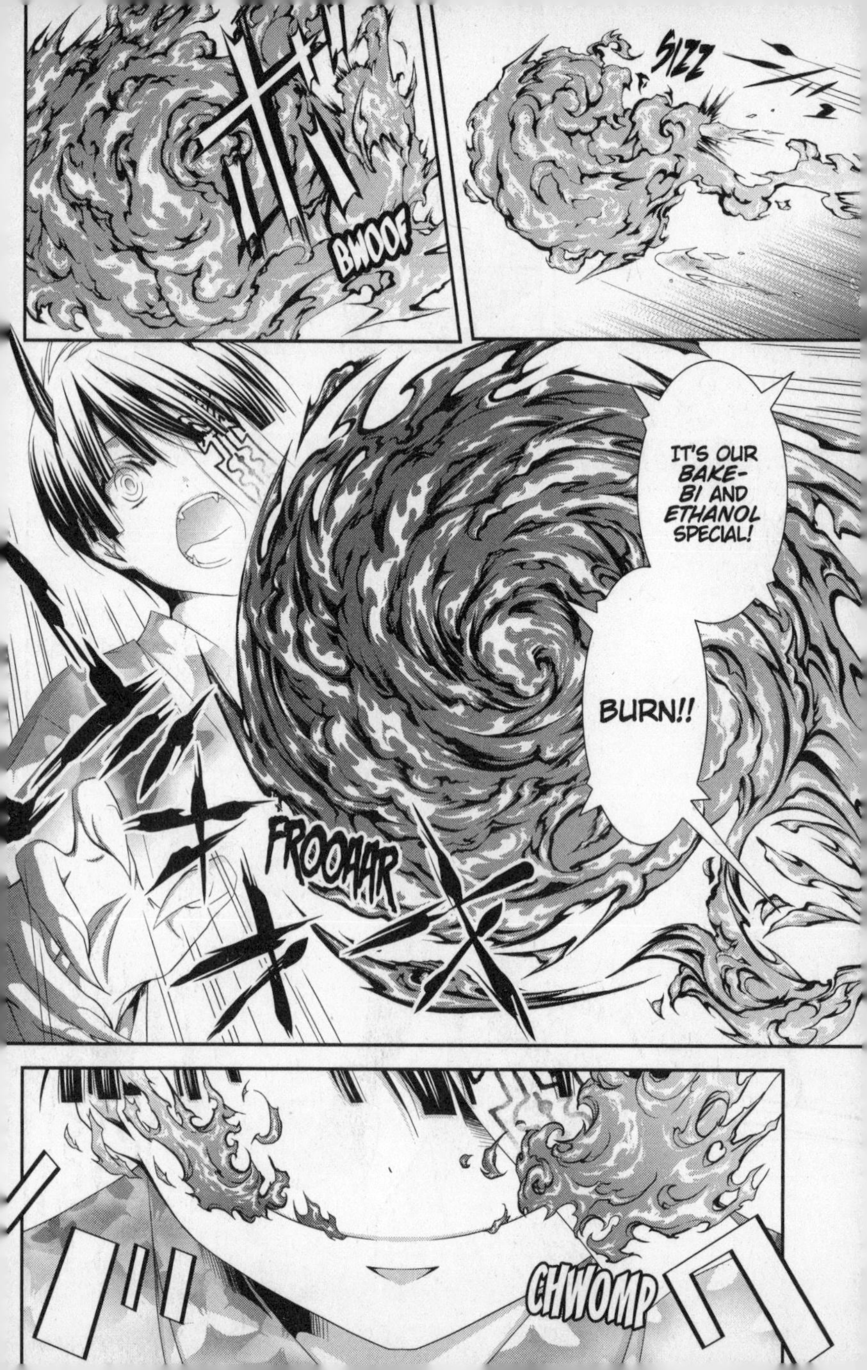
SIZZ
BWOOF
IT'S OUR BAKE-BI AND ETHANOL SPECIAL!
BURN!!
FROOAAR
CHWOMP

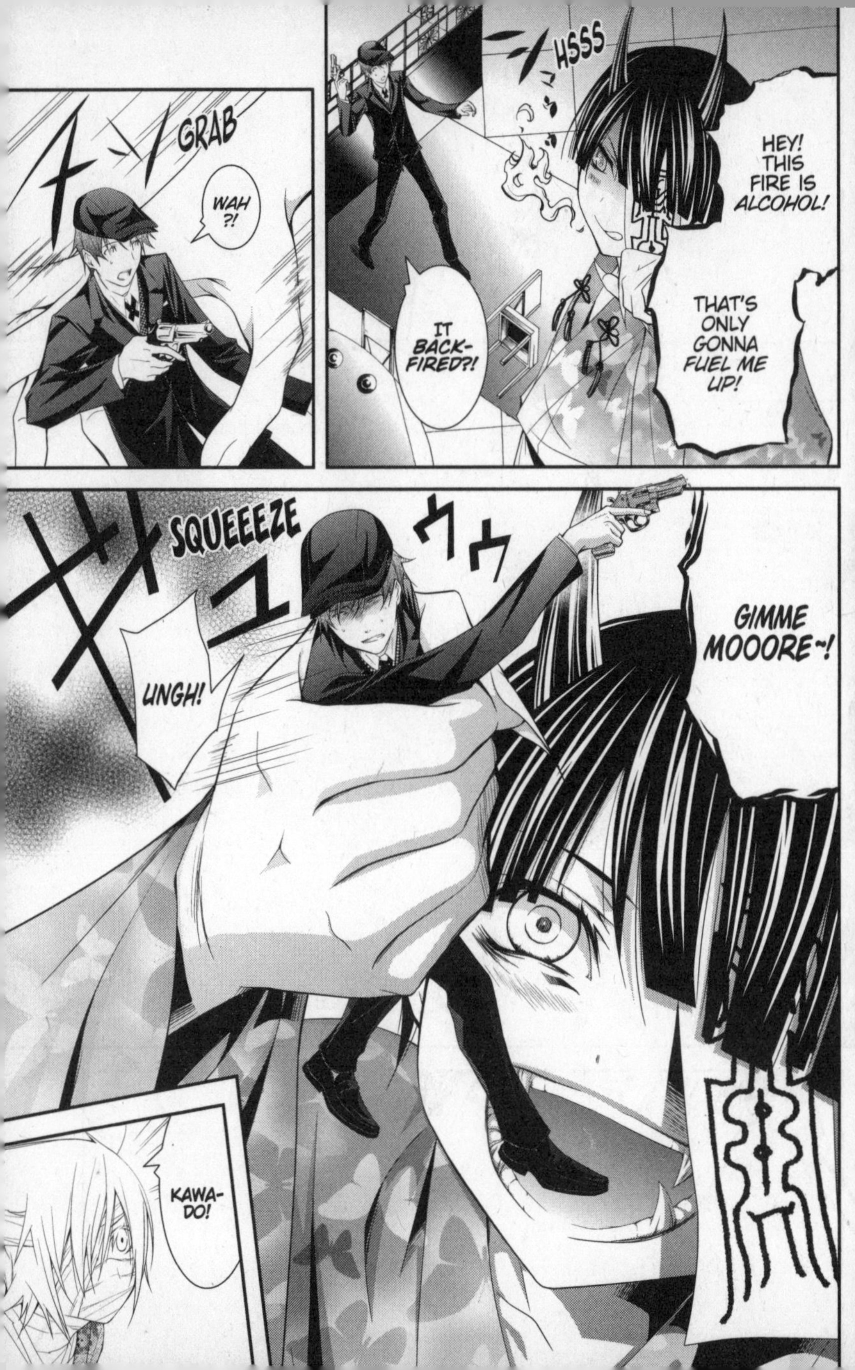
HSSS
HEY! THIS FIRE IS ALCOHOL!
THAT'S ONLY GONNA FUEL ME UP!
IT BACKFIRED?!
GRAB
WAH?!
GIMME MOOORE~!
SQUEEEZE
UNGH!
KAWA-DO!

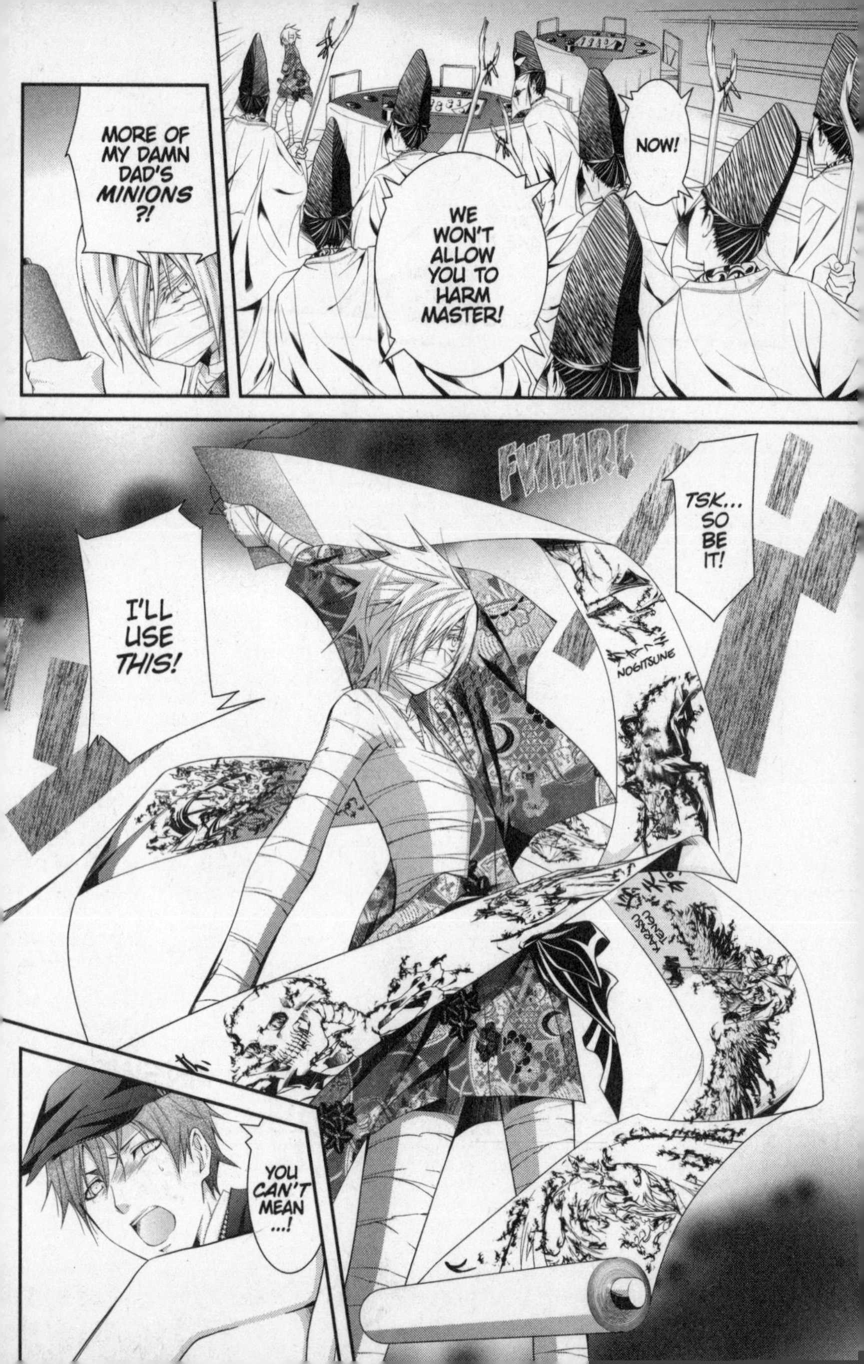
NOW!
WE WON'T ALLOW YOU TO HARM MASTER!
MORE OF MY DAMN DAD'S MINIONS ?!
FWHIRL
TSK... SO BE IT!
I'LL USE THIS!
NOGITSUNE
KARASU TENGU
YOU CAN'T MEAN ...!

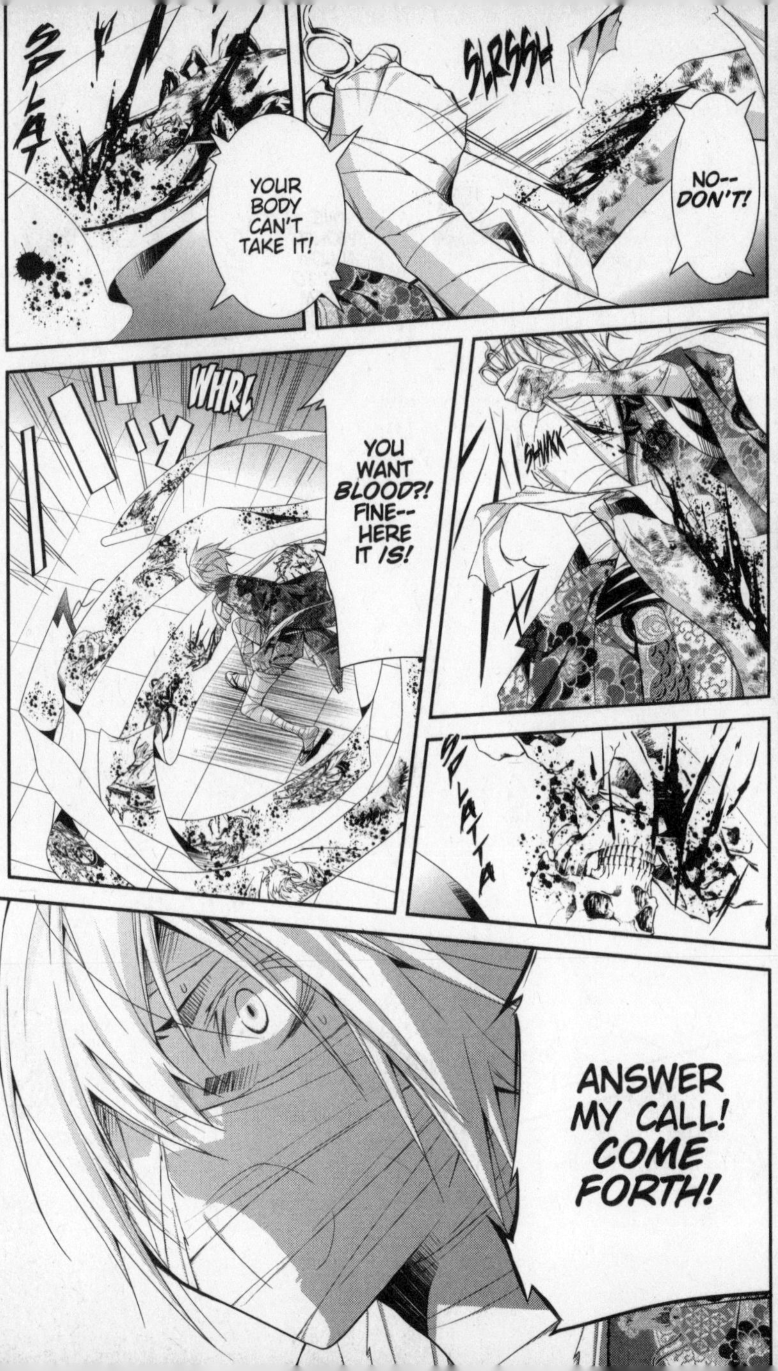
SLRSSH
NO-- DON'T!
SPLAT
YOUR BODY CAN'T TAKE IT!
SHUKK
SPLATTA
WHRL
YOU WANT *BLOOD?!* FINE-- HERE IT *IS!*
ANSWER MY CALL! COME FORTH!

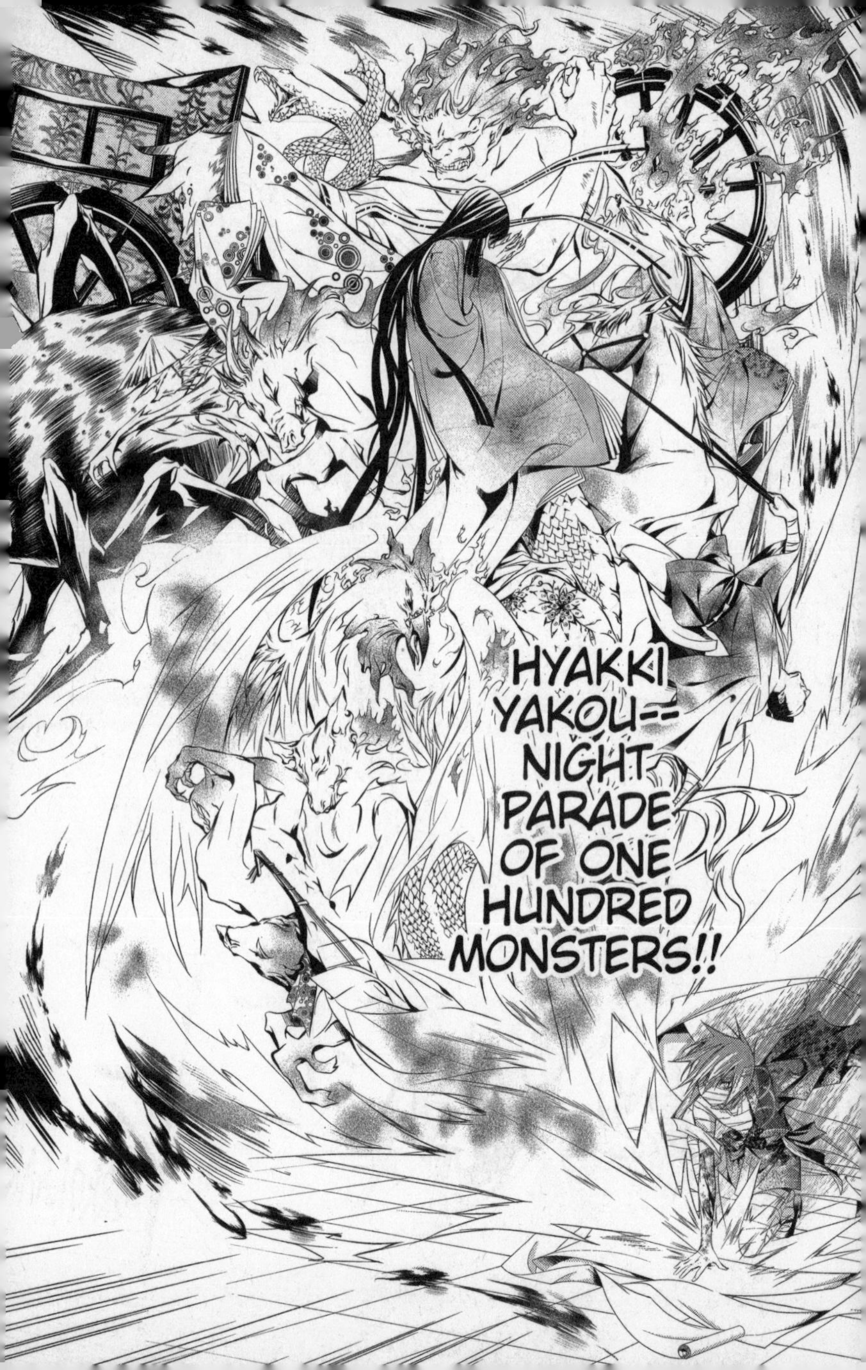
HYAKKI YAKOU-- NIGHT PARADE OF ONE HUNDRED MONSTERS!!

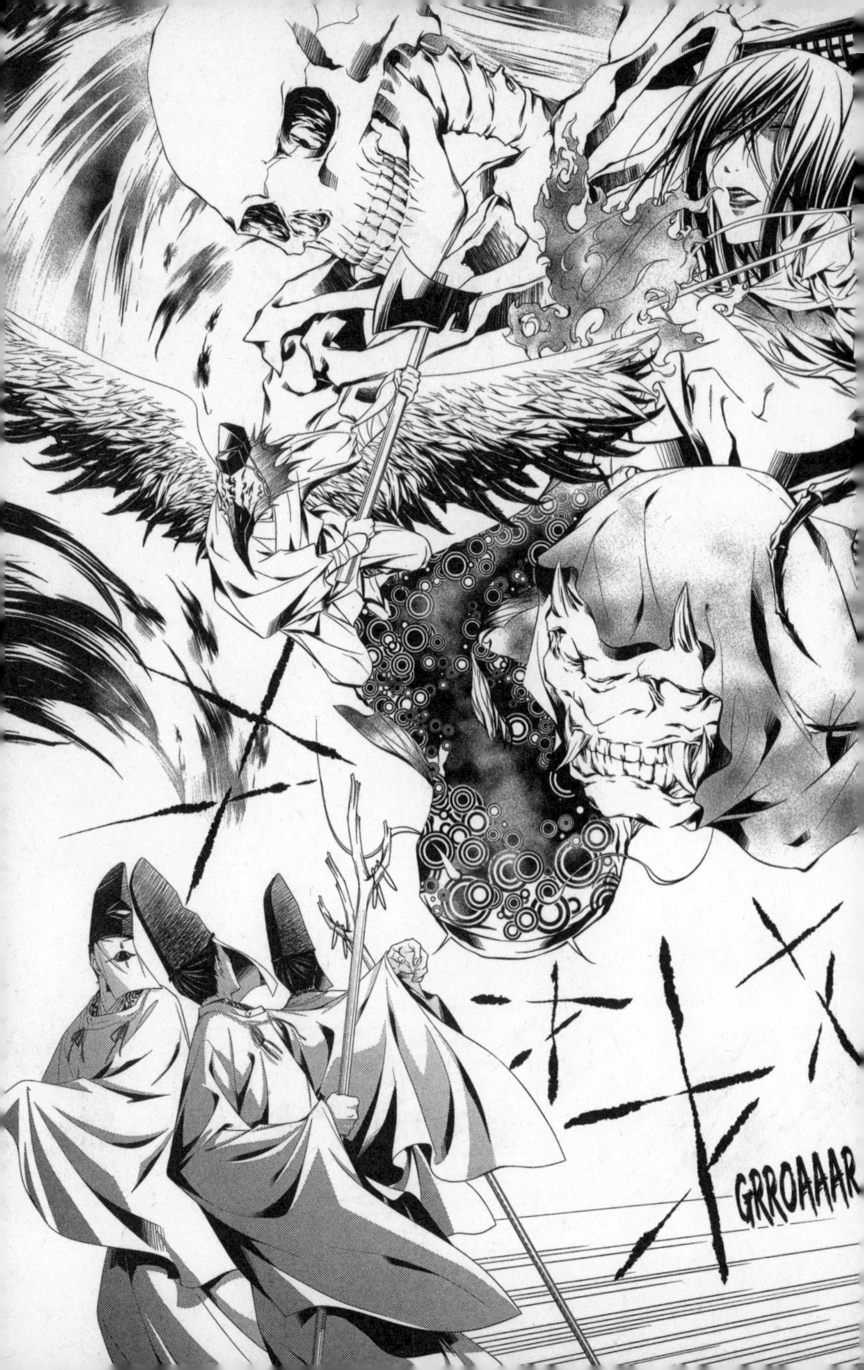
GRROAAAR

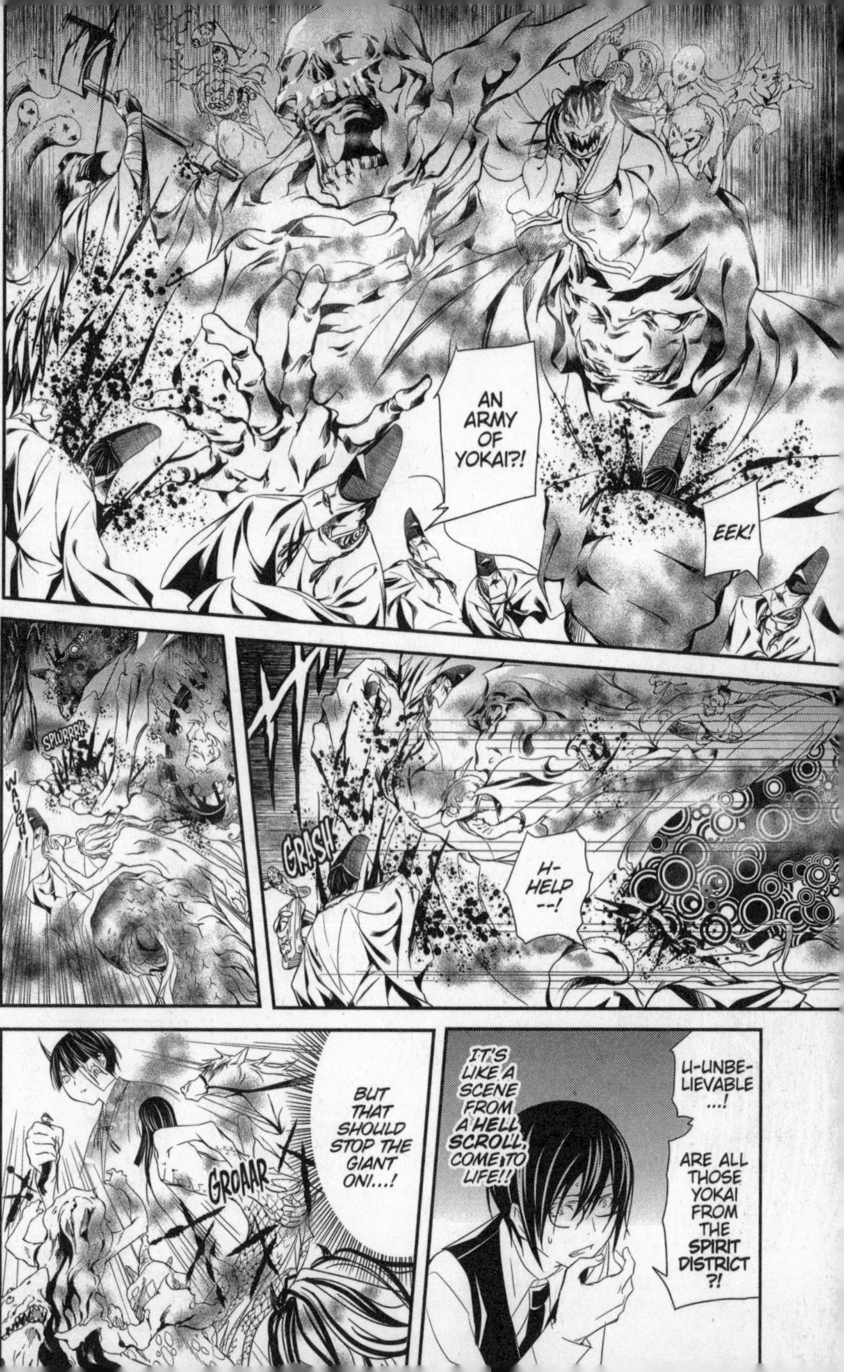
AN ARMY OF YOKAI?!
EEK!
H-HELP--!
GRASH
SPLURRRK
WAUGH!
U-UNBELIEVABLE...!
ARE ALL THOSE YOKAI FROM THE SPIRIT DISTRICT?!
IT'S LIKE A SCENE FROM A HELL SCROLL COME TO LIFE!!
BUT THAT SHOULD STOP THE GIANT ONI...!
GROAAR

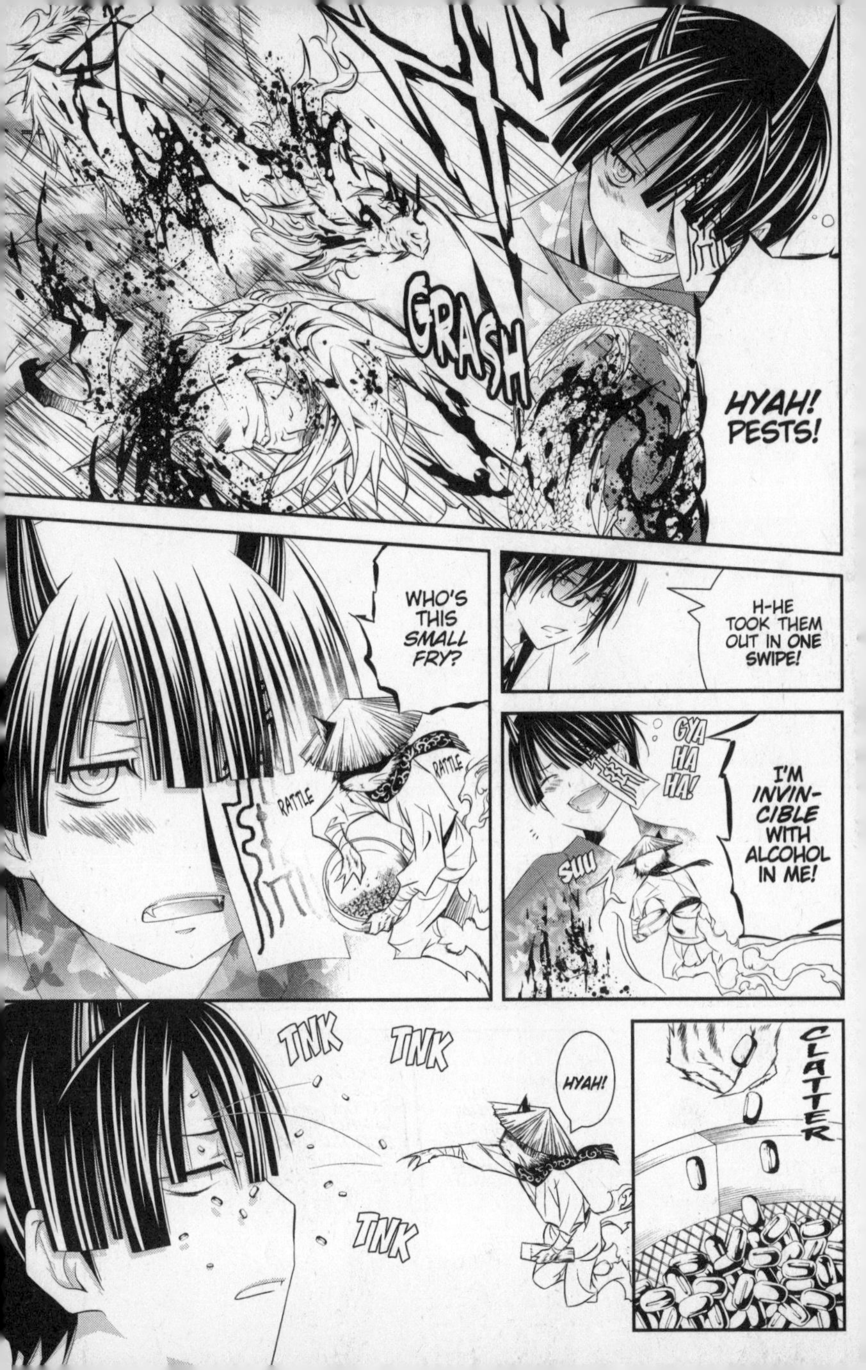
HYAH! PESTS!
CRASH
H-HE TOOK THEM OUT IN ONE SWIPE!
I'M INVINCIBLE WITH ALCOHOL IN ME!
GYA HA HA!
SUU
WHO'S THIS SMALL FRY?
RATTLE
RATTLE
CLATTER
HYAH!
TNK
TNK
TNK

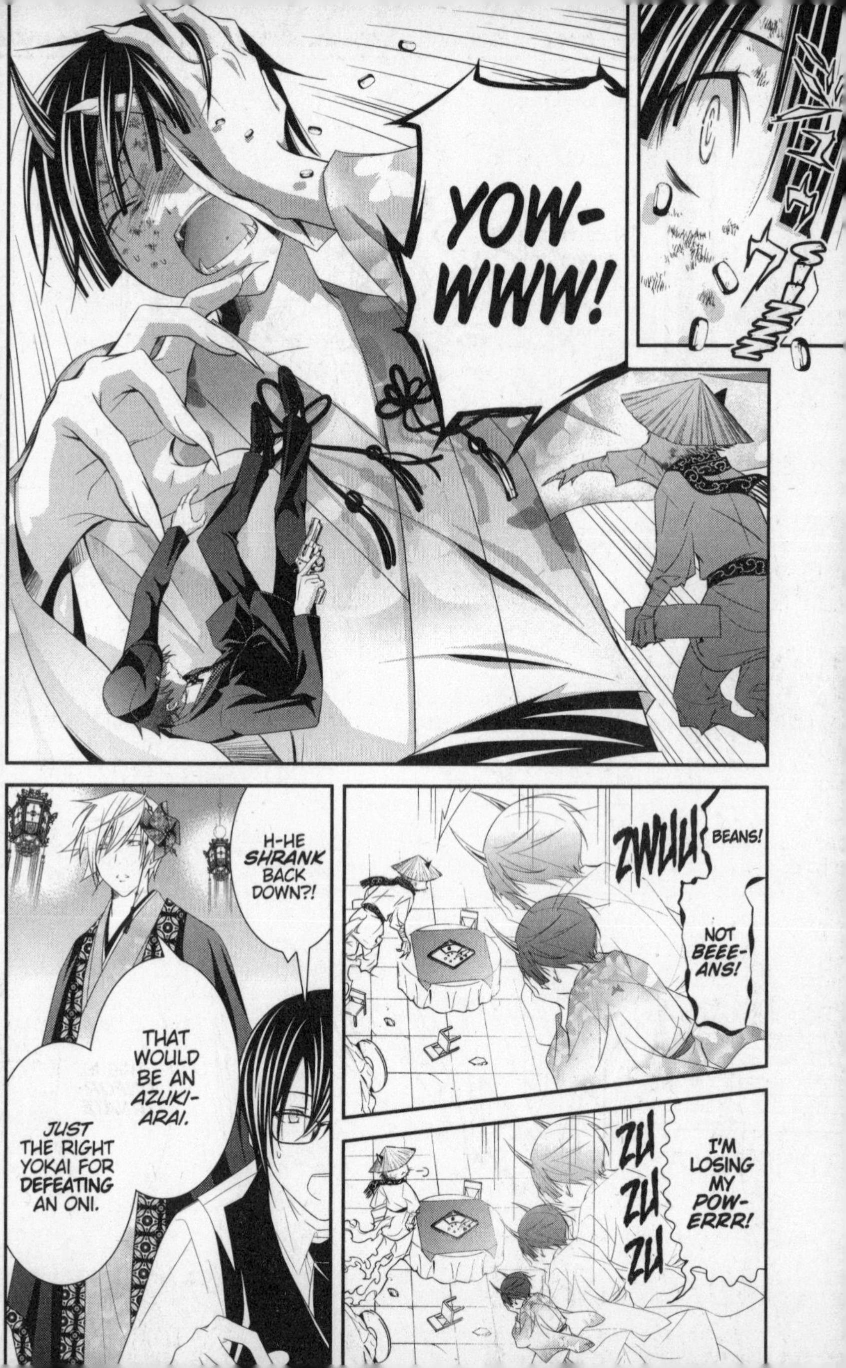
YOW-WWW!
ZWUU
BEANS!
NOT BEEE-ANS!
ZU ZU ZU ZU
I'M LOSING MY POW-ERRR!
H-HE *SHRANK* BACK DOWN?!
THAT WOULD BE AN *AZUKI-ARAI.*
JUST THE RIGHT YOKAI FOR DEFEATING AN ONI.

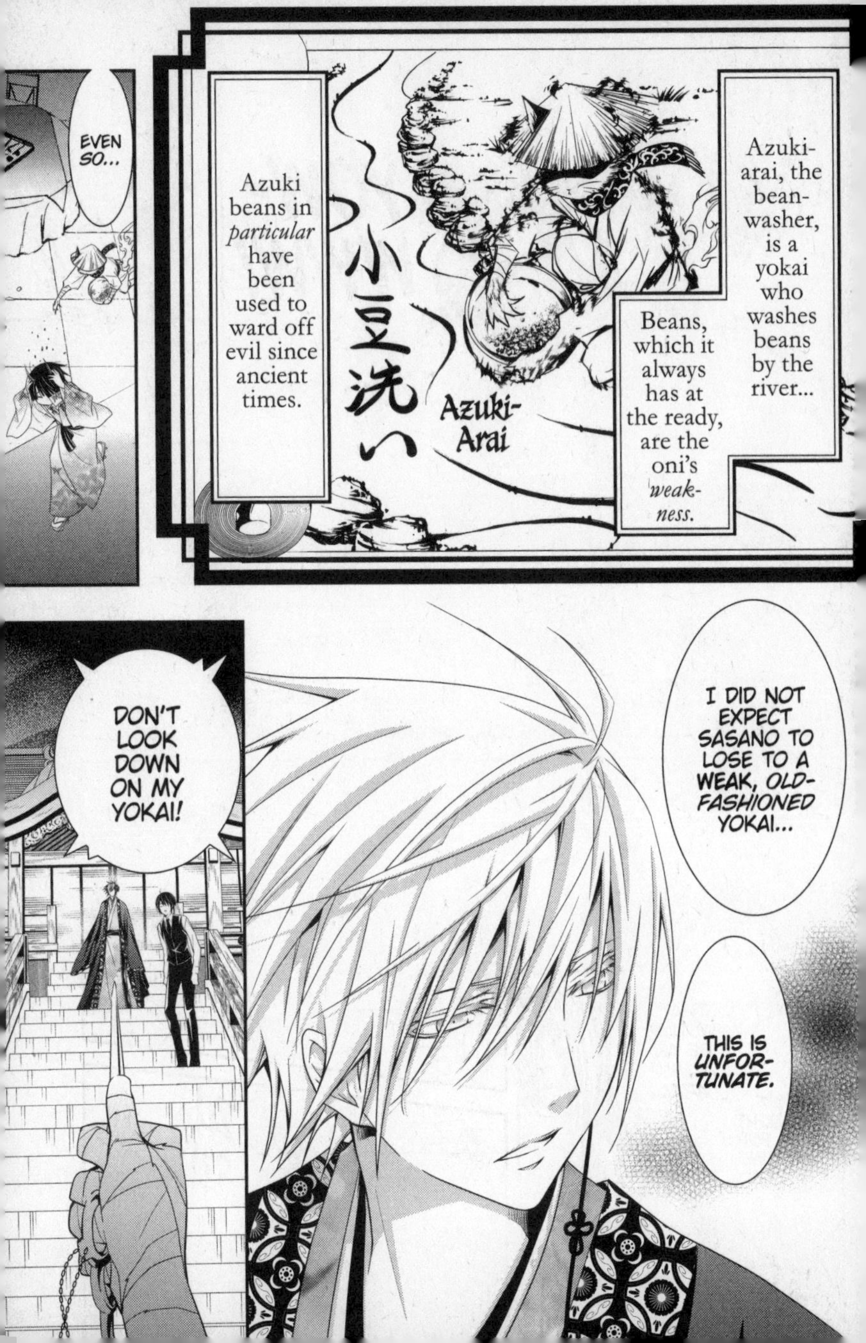
Azuki-arai, the bean-washer, is a yokai who washes beans by the river...
Beans, which it always has at the ready, are the oni's *weakness*.
小豆洗い
Azuki-Arai
Azuki beans in *particular* have been used to ward off evil since ancient times.
EVEN SO...
I DID NOT EXPECT SASANO TO LOSE TO A WEAK, *OLD-FASHIONED* YOKAI...
THIS IS *UNFORTUNATE.*
DON'T LOOK DOWN ON MY YOKAI!

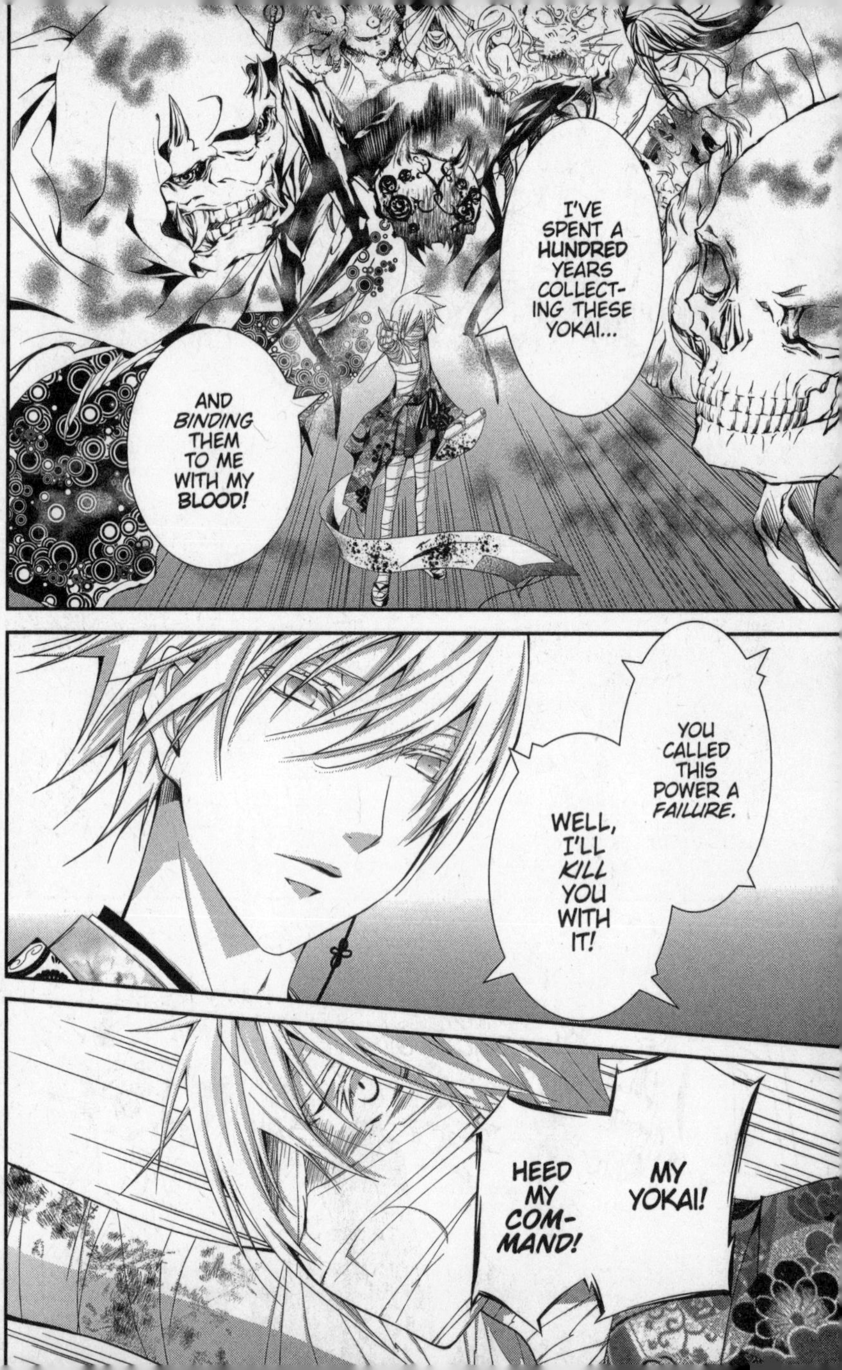
I'VE SPENT A HUNDRED YEARS COLLECTING THESE YOKAI...
AND BINDING THEM TO ME WITH MY BLOOD!
YOU CALLED THIS POWER A FAILURE.
WELL, I'LL KILL YOU WITH IT!
MY YOKAI!
HEED MY COMMAND!

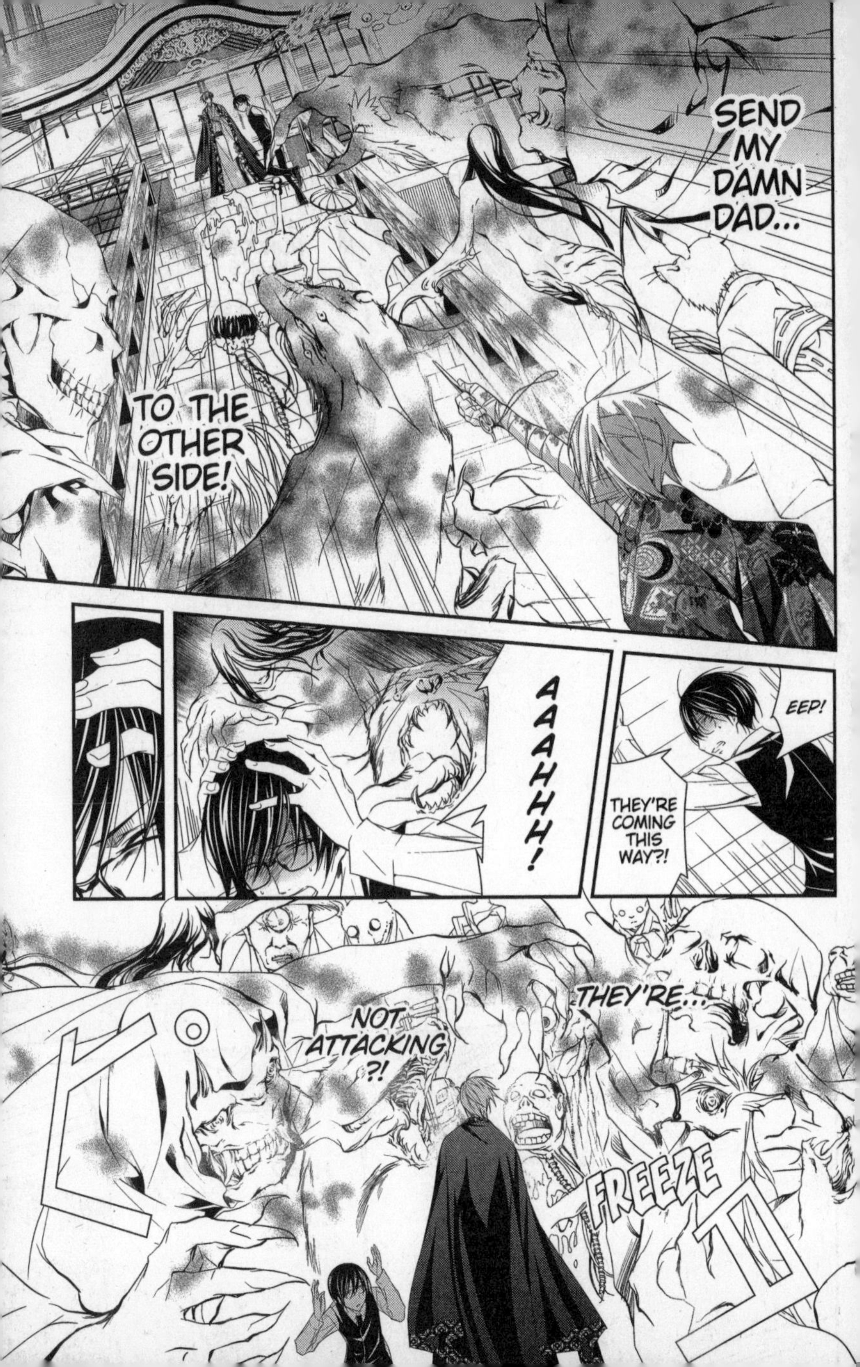
SEND MY DAMN DAD...
TO THE OTHER SIDE!
EEP!
THEY'RE COMING THIS WAY?!
AAAHHH!
THEY'RE...
NOT ATTACKING?!
FREEZE

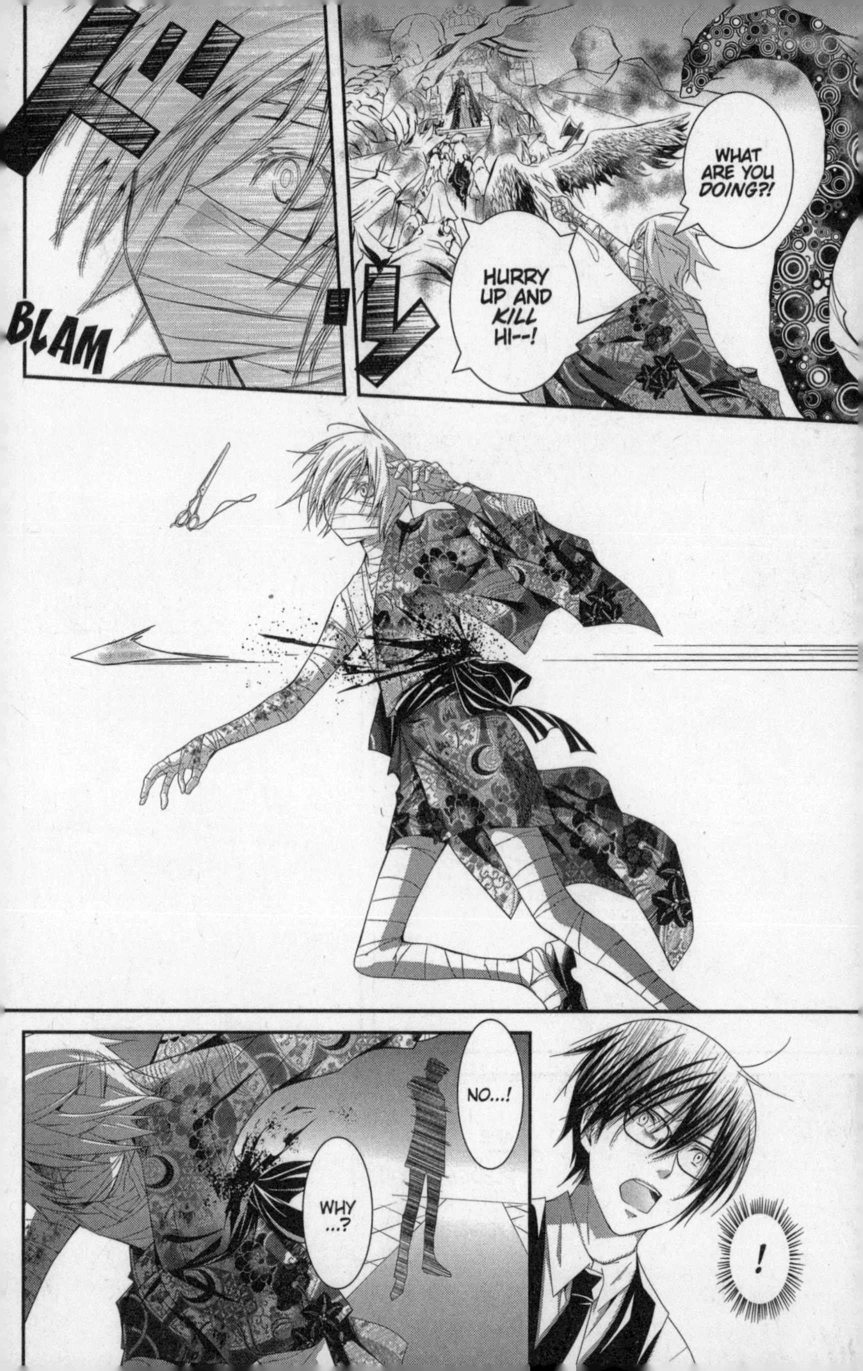
WHAT ARE YOU DOING?!
HURRY UP AND KILL HI--!
BLAM
!
NO...!
WHY ...?

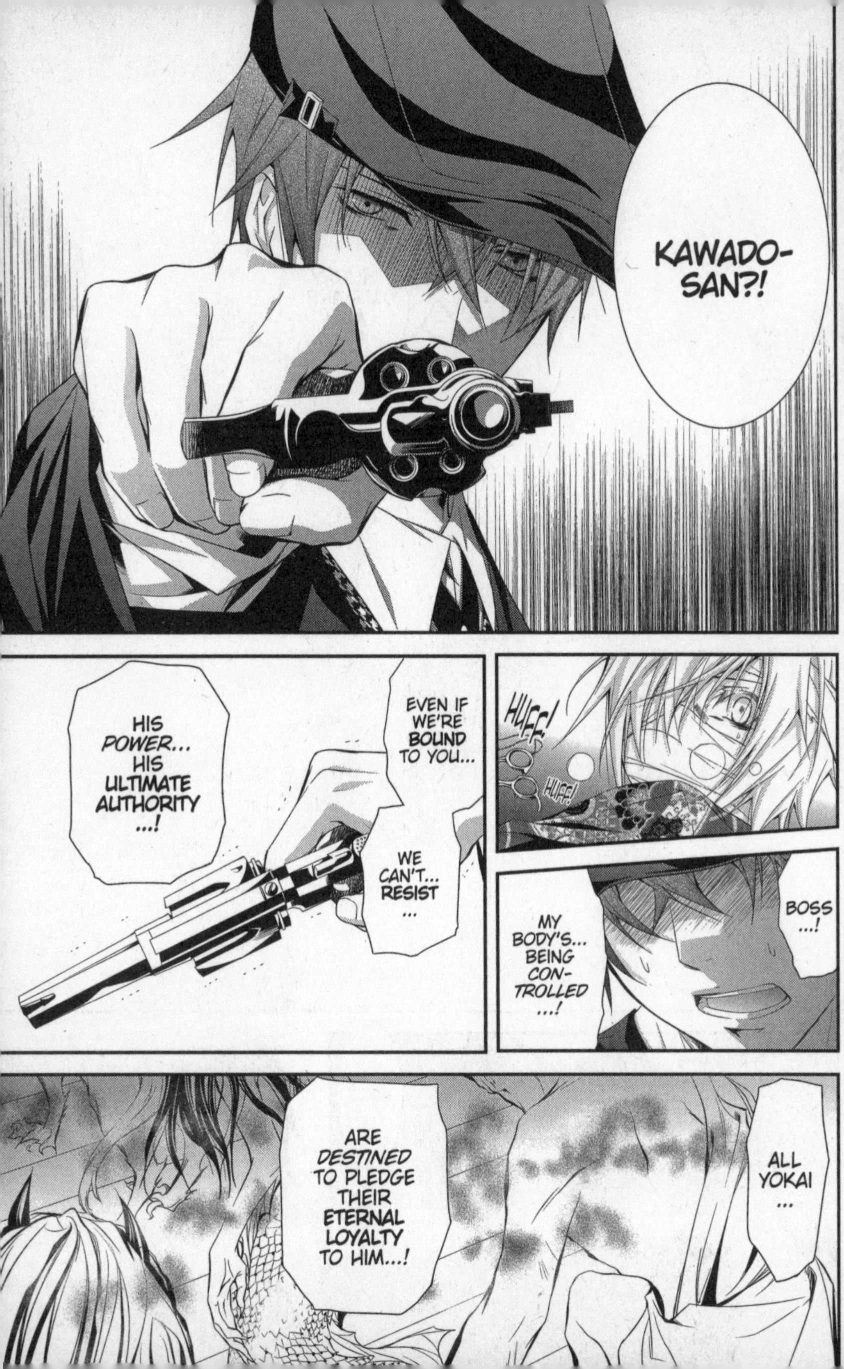
KAWADO-SAN?!
HUFF!
HUFF!
BOSS ...!
MY BODY'S... BEING CON-TROLLED ...!
EVEN IF WE'RE BOUND TO YOU...
WE CAN'T... RESIST ...
HIS POWER... HIS ULTIMATE AUTHORITY ...!
ALL YOKAI ...
ARE DESTINED TO PLEDGE THEIR ETERNAL LOYALTY TO HIM...!

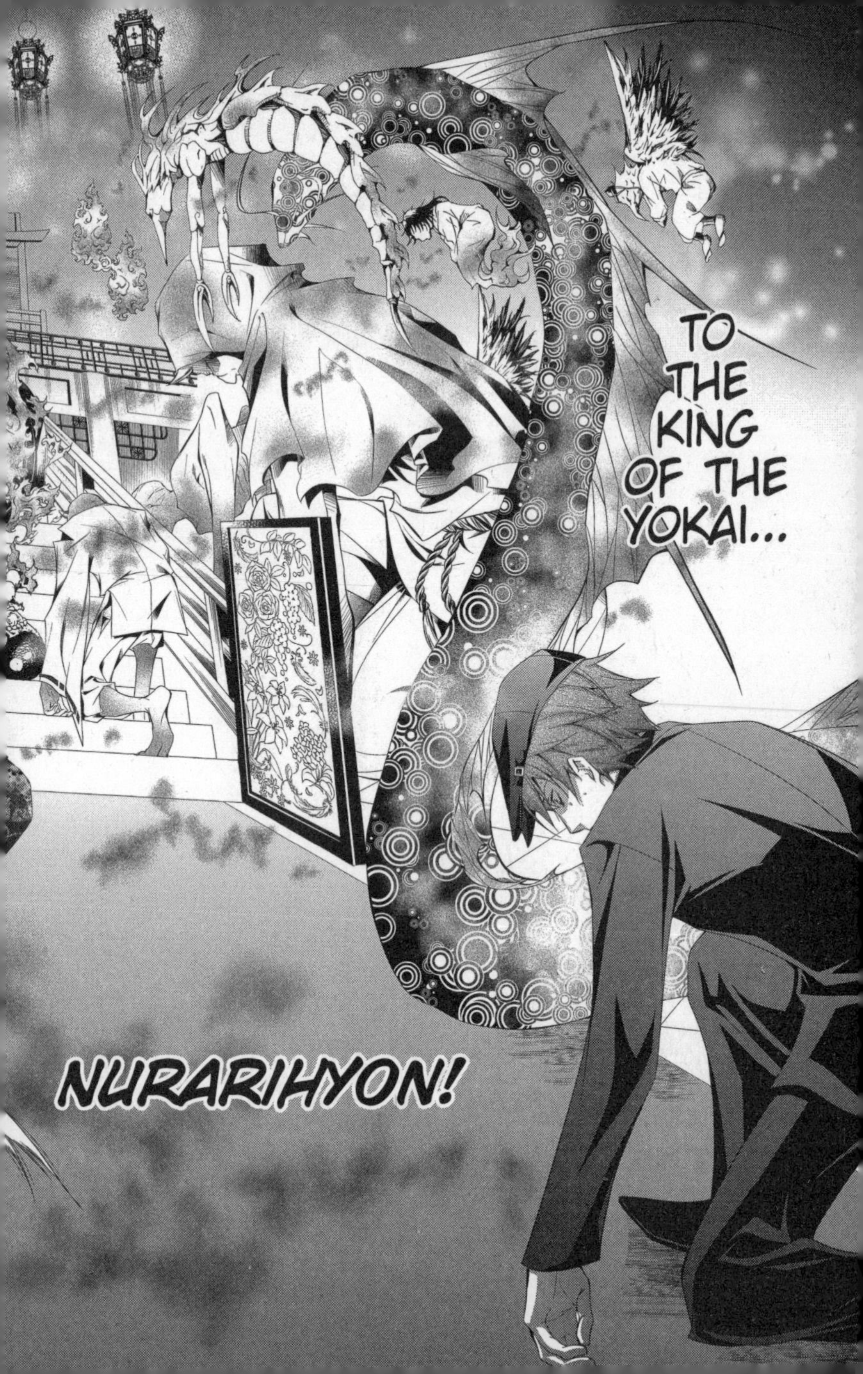
TO THE KING OF THE YOKAI...
NURARIHYON!

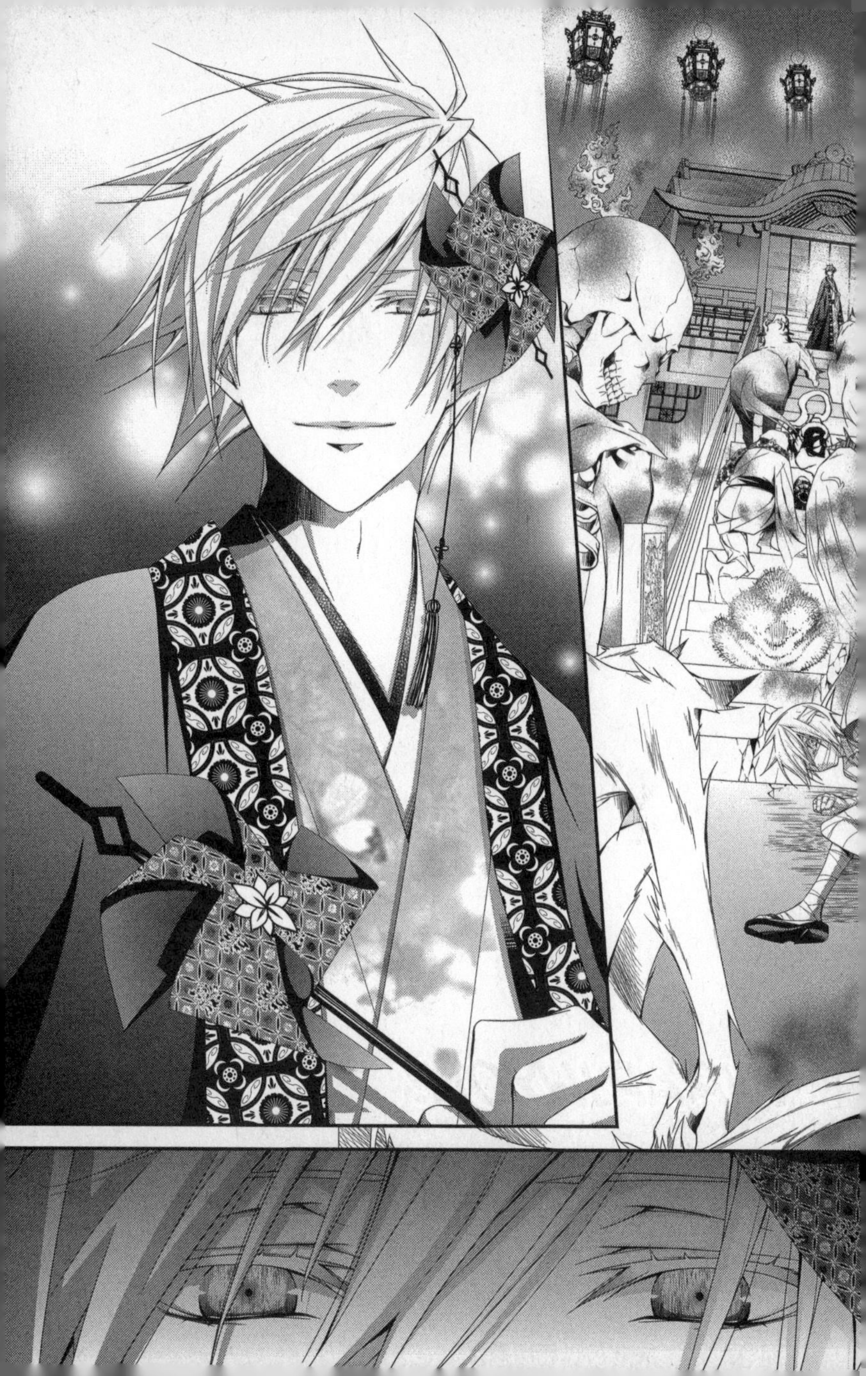

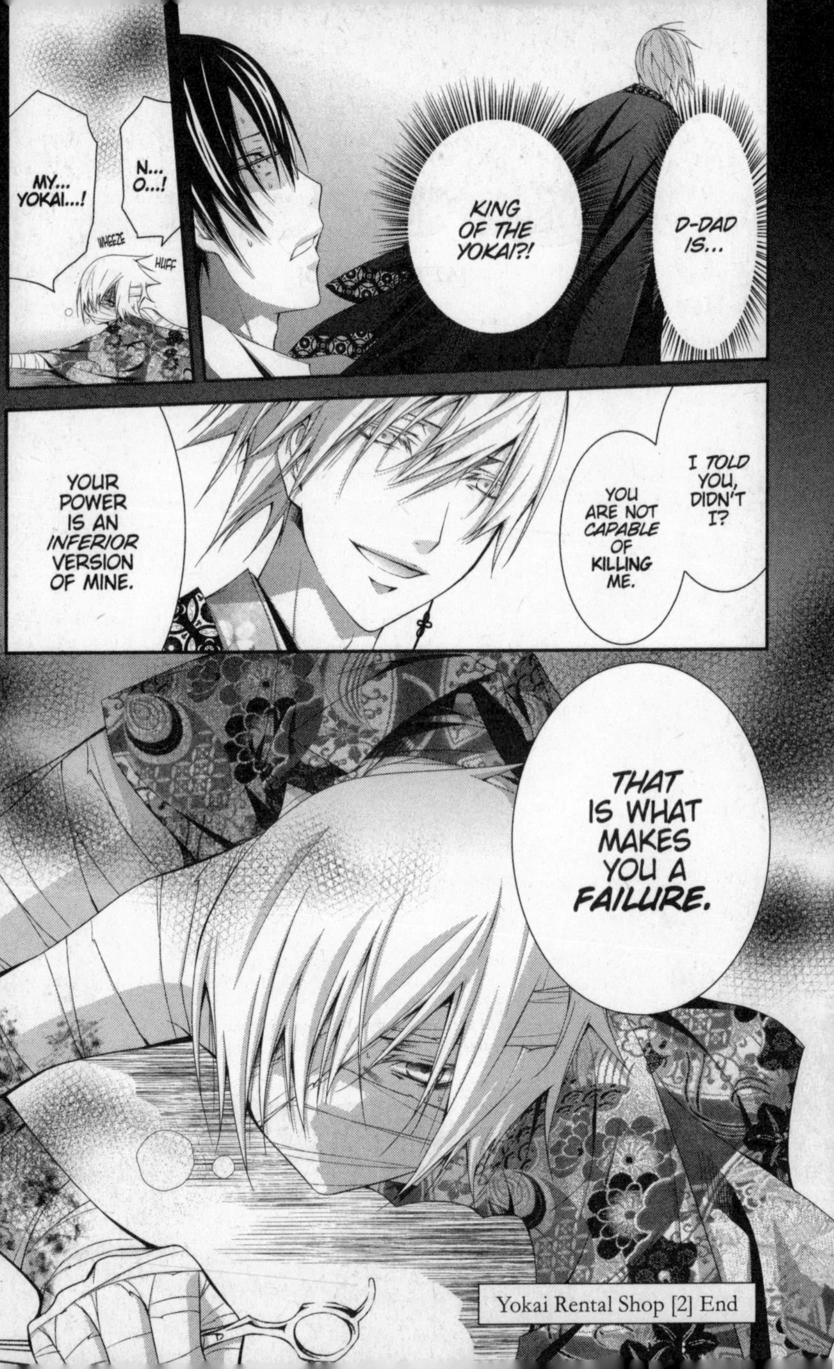
D-DAD IS...
KING OF THE YOKAI?!
N... O...!
MY... YOKAI...!
WHEEZE
HUFF
I TOLD YOU, DIDN'T I?
YOU ARE NOT CAPABLE OF KILLING ME.
YOUR POWER IS AN INFERIOR VERSION OF MINE.
THAT IS WHAT MAKES YOU A FAILURE.

Yokai Rental Shop [2] End

[AFTERWORD]

Hello. Shin Mashiba here. Thank you very much for picking up Volume 2. Karasu was feeble in Volume 1, but he's gotten a little stronger. I think it's because he's been cleaning his plate when his little brother cooks for him. I hope to see you again in the next volume...!

[Assistants]

◇ Wan Wan Shiroi-sama <black inks, screen tones>
◇ Riru Shirayukii-sama <shadow tones>
◇ MOAI-sama <information>
◇ Maru-sama <backgrounds>
◇ Mori-sama <backgrounds>
◇ Katou-sama <backgrounds>

You all work so fast that even though I'm frantic to prepare my pages, you get more done than planned. You're always a huge help..

[Square Enix]

◇ My editor, Kumaoka-sama
◇ The editor-in-chief
◇ Everyone who was involved

I'm always making trouble in various ways. I'm so grateful that you stick with me all the way through to detailed corrections.

[Main Reference Books]

Nihon youkai daijiten (Japanese Yokai Dictionary) /
Illustrations: Mizuki Shigeru /
Compilation: Murakami Kenji (Kadokawa Shoten)
Zusetsu Nihon youkai taizen (Illustrated Compendium of Japanese Yokai) /
Author: Mizuki Shigeru (Kodansha)
Youkai zukan (Yokai Picture Scroll) / Writing: Kyogoku Natsuhiko /
Editing & commentary: Tada Katsumi (Kokusho Kankokai)

次巻予告

NEXT VOLUME PREVIEW

The older brother abandoned by his father as a failure...

The tables are turned on Karasu when his father, Nurarihyon, takes control of Karasu's own yokai menagerie. Just when things look hopeless, Kawado risks his life to save his employer. The shadowy past behind their contract finally comes to light!

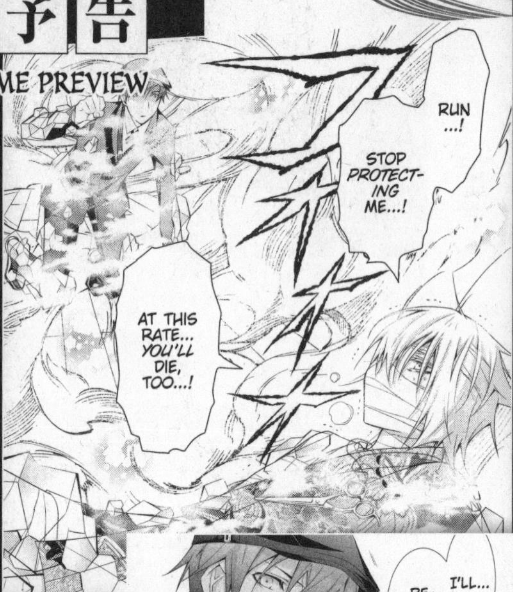
RUN ...!
STOP PROTECTING ME...!
AT THIS RATE... YOU'LL DIE, TOO...!

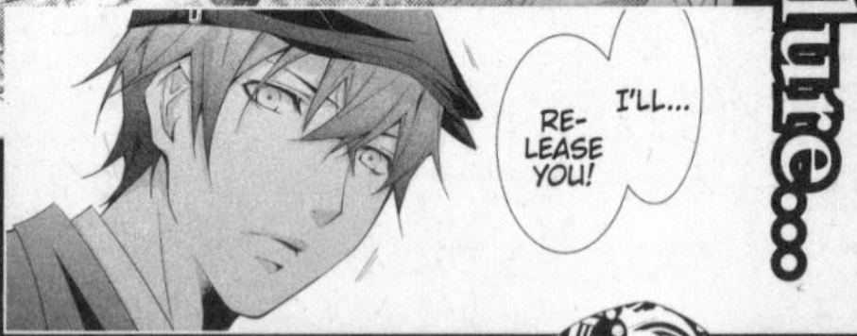
I'LL... RELEASE YOU!
"I'LL PROTECT YOU!
I REFUSE TO LET...
OUR ONE HUNDRED YEARS TOGETHER END LIKE THIS!"

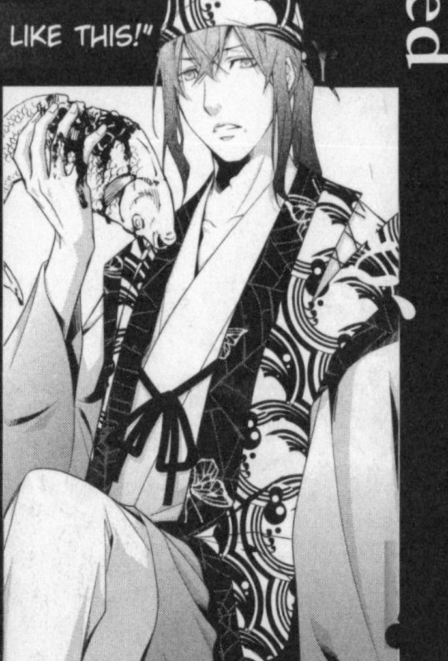

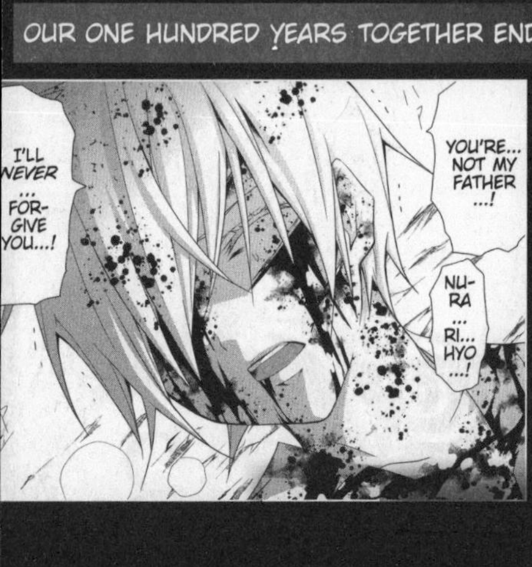
YOU'RE... NOT MY FATHER ...!
NURA ... RI... HYO ...!
I'LL NEVER ... FORGIVE YOU...!

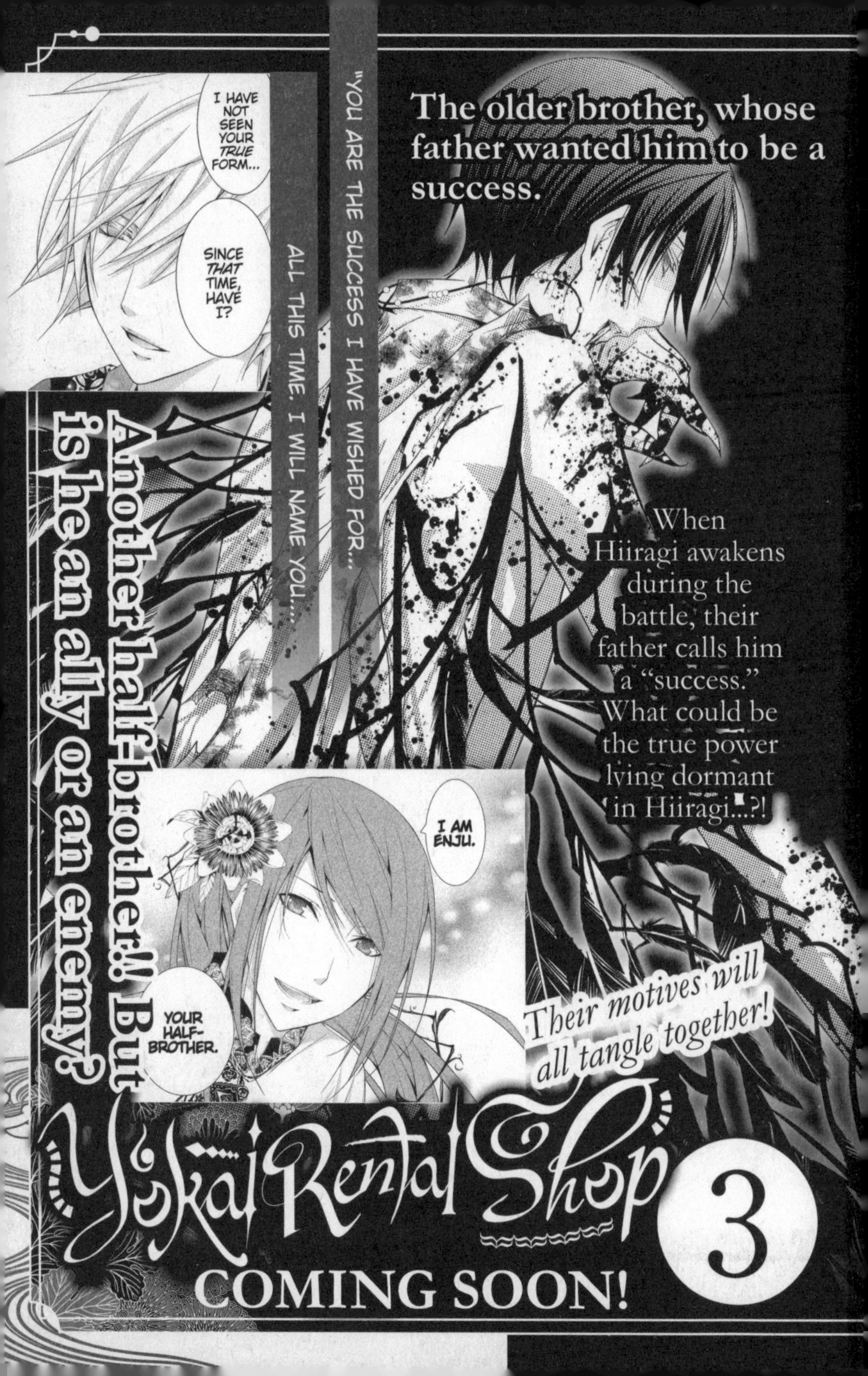
The older brother, whose father wanted him to be a success.
"YOU ARE THE SUCCESS I HAVE WISHED FOR...
ALL THIS TIME. I WILL NAME YOU...."
I HAVE NOT SEEN YOUR TRUE FORM...
SINCE THAT TIME, HAVE I?
When Hiiragi awakens during the battle, their father calls him a "success." What could be the true power lying dormant in Hiiragi...?!
Another half-brother!! But is he an ally or an enemy?
I AM ENJU.
YOUR HALF-BROTHER.
Their motives will all tangle together!
Yokai Rental Shop
3
COMING SOON!

SEVEN SEAS ENTERTAINMENT PRESENTS

Yokai Rental Shop

story and art by **SHIN MASHIBA**   **VOLUME 2**

TRANSLATION
Amanda Haley

ADAPTATION
Julia Kinsman

LETTERING AND LAYOUT
Rina Mapa

COVER DESIGN
Nicky Lim

PROOFREADER
Danielle King

ASSISTANT EDITOR
Jenn Grunigen

PRODUCTION ASSISTANT
CK Russell

PRODUCTION MANAGER
Lissa Pattillo

EDITOR-IN-CHIEF
Adam Arnold

PUBLISHER
Jason DeAngelis

YOKAI NIISAN VOL. 2
©2016 Shin Mashiba / SQUARE ENIX CO., LTD.
First published in Japan in 2016 by SQUARE ENIX CO., LTD.
English translation rights arranged with SQUARE ENIX CO., LTD. and
SEVEN SEAS ENTERTAINMENT, LLC. through Tuttle-Mori Agency, Inc.
Translation © 2017 by SQUARE ENIX CO., LTD.

Seven Seas books may be purchased in bulk for promotional, educational, or
business use. Please contact your local bookseller or the Macmillan Corporate
and Premium Sales Department at 1-800-221-7945, extension 5442, or by e-mail
at MacmillanSpecialMarkets@macmillan.com.

Seven Seas and the Seven Seas logo are trademarks of
Seven Seas Entertainment, LLC. All rights reserved.

ISBN: 978-1-626927-36-0

Printed in Canada

First Printing: January 2018

10 9 8 7 6 5 4 3 2 1

FOLLOW US ONLINE: *www.gomanga.com*

READING DIRECTIONS

This book reads from *right to left*, Japanese style.
If this is your first time reading manga, you start
reading from the top right panel on each page and
take it from there. If you get lost, just follow the
numbered diagram here. It may seem backwards at
first, but you'll get the hang of it! Have fun!!

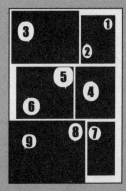